BORN OF WATER

AN ELEMENTAL ORIGINS NOVEL

A.L. KNORR

Edited by
CHRISTINE GORDON MANLEY

Edited by
S D PETERSEN

WWW.ALKNORRBOOKS.COM

ALSO BY A.L. KNORR

The Elemental Origins Series

Born of Water

Born of Fire

Born of Earth

Born of Aether

Born of Air

The Elementals

The Siren's Curse Trilogy

Salt & Stone

Salt & the Sovereign

Salt & the Sisters

Earth Magic Rises Trilogy

Bones of the Witch

Ashes of the Wise

Heart of the Fae

Mira's Return

Returning

Falling

Surfacing

Rings of the Inconquo Trilogy *(co-authored with Aaron D. Schneider)*

Born of Metal

Metal Guardian

Metal Angel

The Kacy Chronicles

Descendant

Ascendant

Combatant

Transcendent

Learn more at www.alknorrbooks.com

For those in peril in the sea.

BORN OF WATER

AN ELEMENTAL ORIGINS NOVEL

PROLOGUE

Poland. Modern day.

"THESE ARE the best in the world," Antoni said, handing a file folder filled with documents to Martinius. "Although, I'm still not sure why you want to look abroad. We have a perfectly good team available to us here in Gdańsk."

Martinius took the file folder in his age-spotted hand and pulled his chair up to his wooden desk. It was the same desk that had been used by his father and his grandfather before him. "It's very simple," he answered. "This is not just any job. We need the best there is, Polish or not."

"I can't think how your supporters will feel about us choosing a foreign team," Antoni speculated. "I don't have a problem with it, may the best company win and all. But we might hear grumblings in the village if you know what I mean."

"We have only a few supporters left now and most of them aren't even Polish. The world forgot about *The Sybellen* long ago. Who we choose is none of their affair." Martinius took a pair of wire specs from his front pocket and perched them on the end of his nose. His eyes were still good for a man well into his seventies, just a little help with the reading was all that was needed. "Thank you, Antoni," he said, by way of a dismissal.

Antoni nodded and left the room.

Martinius began to flip slowly through the pages in the folder. A hot cup of Darjeeling tea sat at his right hand. The early morning sunlight dappled through the trees and fell across the pages, lighting them for his consumption. As he lifted his steaming teacup to his lips, he flipped over one of the loose pages to expose an article with a photograph underneath. His eyes widened in shock and the cup halted halfway to his lips. His hand trembled and he set the teacup down, missing the saucer and leaving a water ring on the antique wood.

Martinius used both hands to pick up the page and hold it in a patch of un-dappled sunlight to ensure his eyes hadn't betrayed him. "It's not possible," he said, squinting at the photograph. "Is it?"

Mom?" I spluttered around my toothpaste foam as I stood in our living room in my pjs with my toothbrush in hand. The morning news was on and beside the anchors heavily make-upped face was a photograph of movie-star Rachel Montgomery partying on the deck of a yacht with her entourage.

I was getting ready for the last day of the school year when I heard the words "storm," "yacht," and "rescue," come from the television.

During the week, we always kept our small screen TV tuned to the news in the mornings. Most of the time I ignored it, but not when there was news like this.

"When we return," the anchor was saying, "more details on Miss Montgomery's hair-raising rescue from our own Devil's Eye Cove." Then it cut to commercial.

"What is it, Targa?" I heard Mom through the screen door as she replied from the driveway where she was loading up her work truck.

"There's been a wreck!" I managed to get out before toothpaste suds dribbled down my chin. I ran into the kitchen, spat in the sink, and grabbed a towel to clean my face. It took me no time at all to get from the living room to our kitchen because they were the same room, the only division was a small kitchen island.

We live in a renovated trailer. Since my dad passed away when I was eight – which was almost nine years ago now – our quality of life has backslid. Mom didn't work at that time so we could no longer afford to stay in the two-storey we had in the suburbs. We had down-sized to a doublewide located in the trailer park at the edge of Salt-ford, the small Canadian east coast town where we live.

The trailer park is pretty, as trailer parks go. The residents care for their properties and small gardens as though they were Italian villas. 'Trailers don't have to be trashy,' is the unofficial community motto. If I'm really honest, Mom and I are the worst residents in the park if property beauty is the measuring stick. Our place is nearly the very definition of a trashy trailer. We have no garden or even so much as a geranium in a flowerpot. We have gravel instead of a lawn and the concrete steps leading up to our front door have a menacing crack right down the middle.

Don't think that we're destitute though, my mom works her ass off to make sure that I have whatever I need. But the state of our home has never been a priority for her.

As the commercials played in the background, I rinsed our stovetop espresso maker out in the sink. I lifted the lid on the over-flowing compost bucket under the sink to dump the old grounds when the lid snapped off its hinges and the bucket shook. Slimy onion skin and rotting orange peel splatted onto the ground and on top of my bare foot. I sighed and held my breath as I picked up the stinking mess and took the bucket outside to dump it.

It's my job to make note of anything that requires maintenance. Mom spends too much time working to worry about the house. According to her, as long as we are warm in the winter and have elec-tricity and running water, we live like royalty.

My mom Mira MacAuley is the opposite of materialistic. She's so far in the other direction that she can't relate to people who spend their time investing in art for their houses, thousand-count cotton sheets, or a nice vehicle. She doesn't judge people for their choices, she's just bored out of her mind to find herself in conversations revolving around these things. Consequently, she has a tough time making and keeping friends. Not that she cares. Sometimes, I think I'm the only person in the whole world who matters to her at all. She cares about my friends, but only because I care about them. If someone is important to me then they're important to her, too.

I brought back the empty bucket, rinsed it out and put it back under the sink before continuing to make the espresso. I put fresh coffee grounds in the reservoir and twisted the top and bottom together. I lit our sixty year-old gas stove with a match and set the espresso maker over the blue flame.

I looked out the front window. Mom was just about finished loading her gear into her work truck. The boxes of diving equipment that she lugged around were just part of the many props she needed to keep the illusion for her job intact. They were also the bane of her life.

Every black box was stamped with the words BLUEJACKET UNDERWATER RECOVERY & SALVAGE. The same was written on the side of her truck that Simon, her boss, had given to her as part of her new contract. The vehicle was a perk that no other employee had and is a testament to her value. The ironic thing is that of all of the Bluejacket employees, my mom needs the truck the least.

I smiled as she threw the last box in the back and the whole truck shook. It must have contained the diving weights. She slammed the hatch and looked up with her crystal blue eyes to see me watching her. She gave me a sheepish grin. I shook my head at her.

The espresso was bubbling and as I went back to the stove to pour it, a wave of sadness washed over me. I know how much she hates the facade she has to present to the world, and I also know she does it because she loves me.

Sprinting up the drive and taking the porch steps in a single bound, she came into the house. She closed the door behind her with too much force and I winced as the trailer shook. My mother is stronger than anyone I know and she shows our property the same disdain she shows her useless diving equipment.

"Really, Mom?" I said as I held out her java. "Tens of thousands of dollars in company equipment that Simon has entrusted to your care and you treat it like it's a wrecking ball."

"Was there a question in there?" she said before shooting her espresso like it was whiskey. She handed back the empty cup. "Did you say there's been a wreck?" she asked, her eyes bright.

I jerked my chin towards the television as I took her cup back to the sink to rinse it. The news jingle announced that commercials were over and the report was about to continue. We both watched, me from the small kitchen island and Mom from our tiny entry way.

"A-list actress Rachel Montgomery and her entourage were sailing a sport yacht off the coast yesterday when they became caught in high winds and thirty foot waves," the news anchor was saying. "The yacht struck rocks and was wrecked on Devil's Eye, like so many boats before it." The anchor was supposed to be impartial, but he was also a local and clearly of the opinion that Rachel Montgomery and her friends had been galactically stupid.

Devil's Eye Cove is a big bay encircled by jagged rock formations. It's less than five miles from Saltford beach, the main beach that all the tourists flock to in the summertime. The Cove is infamous for its powerful currents, big waves, and sudden storms. The shape of the cove on a map looks like an angry eye, earning it its official name. As if Devil's Eye wasn't sinister enough, the combination of violent waves crashing on jagged rocks had also earned the cove the nick name The Boneyard. Of course, only the locals call it that.

Not a summer has gone by that I don't remember some unfortunate tourist getting into trouble there. They were drawn by the rugged beauty and the privacy it offered. Locals know better so they never go out to the Cove. But in spite of the warnings the city of Saltford has peppered their tourist information with, tourists still go.

"Idiots," Mom muttered under her breath. While she watched the report, she raked her long black hair back from her face and up into a mess of a ponytail. She grabbed a full bottle of water from the multipack on the floor near the door and chugged the whole thing in one go. My mother drinks more water than a racehorse.

"No one was seriously injured," the anchor concluded. "But the yacht was completely destroyed and everything on board was lost. Authorities continue to warn the public to stay away from Devil's Eye Cove..."

The reporter's voice was drowned out when Mom's cell phone rang. She snapped open her ancient flip phone with the same fluid grace she did everything. She wouldn't update her phone until the day it died. I was already impressed with how long it had lasted considering the abuse it endured.

"Mira here," she answered in her silvery voice.

I listened to the one-sided conversation as I finished bagging my lunch. It wasn't hard to fill in the gaps -- I knew it was Simon. He is the entrepreneur who started Bluejacket and my mom is his star diver. Just like the rest of the team, he has no clue what the real secret to their success is.

I went back to my bedroom to finish getting dressed and run a brush through my hair. I kept my ears tuned in to what she was saying. There was little to no privacy in our tiny trailer and the sound of her voice traveled easily through my open door.

"Yeah, I just saw it on TV," she was saying. "They've already called? That was fast. Must be valuable stuff. It's Devil's Eye... is Davis on it? You know he won't give it a pass," she scoffed. "Yeah, ok. I'll be there in 10."

I frowned as I pulled on my jeans. The Bluejacket office was down in the harbour, a 20-minute drive away. I had given up on trying to prevent my mother from speeding. She speeds every time she gets behind the wheel and she's been stopped dozens of times. Has she ever been slapped with a ticket? Nope. She turns on that siren voice and charms her way out of it every time.

My own phone chirped and I picked it out of the front pocket of my backpack. Saxony sent an audio text to our group of friends - Saxony Cagney, Georjayna Sutherland, and Akiko Susumu.

I pressed the play button on the message and Saxony's voice rang out from my phone, sounding exactly like the vivacious redhead she is. "Last daaaaaaay! Last day, last day, last day! No more pencils, no more books...," her message stopped there. As I was about to record the rest of the rhyme, my phone chirped again. Georjayna had beat me to it.

"No more teachers dirty looks," her voice concluded.

My phone dinged again and there was a text message from Akiko: *I think I'm having a panic attack.*

She was kidding, of course. Akiko adores school and mourns the end of it every year as though a beloved pet had died. She's also the last person of the four of us to ever have a panic attack. I don't think Akiko's heart rate ever changes, even between sleeping and sprinting, she's the proverbial cool cucumber.

Saxony wrote back as quick as a flash: *Really? I'm having a hot dog and it's delicious.*

Georjayna: *For breakfast? Gross.*

Out in the kitchen, I heard my mom zip her bag closed. "Gotta go, sunshine!" she called.

"Yeah, I heard." I came out of my room dressed in jeans and my favourite t-shirt, a black off-the-shoulder with the number 89 emblazoned on the front. I left my long brunette hair down in loose waves. "I guess you're going to go out to The Boneyard tonight after work?"

This was my mother's secret and the main reason she was so busy. During the day she played the professional salvage diver but at night was when she did all the real work, completely alone and in dark and sometimes dangerous waters.

Her eyes sparkled. "Yeah, do you mind?"

"No, Mom. What are you after this time?" I perched on the edge of our faded pistachio-coloured sofa and pulled on my socks.

"Heirloom jewelry. Rachel's manager has already called us to ask about salvage possibilities," she answered, kicking my running shoes over to me.

I yanked my shoes on without undoing the laces. "That was fast. But, did I overhear you say that Eric has declared Devil's Eye off-limits?"

Eric Davis is Bluejacket's team analyst. His job is to analyze the dive site and decide whether it's safe to take on the salvage contract or not. The sites he declares unsafe are the ones my mother does on her own time. Of course, any payment offered then goes to her alone. Sometimes the Bluejacket team finds out that she dove on her own, sometimes they don't. If they do find out, the whole team is furious with her, Eric more than any of the others. He takes it as a personal insult even though its got nothing to do with him.

"Since when has that ever stopped me?" she cocked an eyebrow. She wasn't breaking any company rules by diving on her own time, but every dive school in the world would condemn her for diving alone. She'd earned herself a reputation for being foolhardy, but only because no one knew her secret.

"Since never," I answered. "But every time you dive on a wreck he's declared off-limits, you make things harder for yourself. He already has a serious problem with you."

She was back at the front door, her slender hand on the knob. "I don't care how he feels about me as long as he stays out of my way. Besides, what he doesn't know won't hurt us."

I sighed, then gave her a kiss on the cheek. "Be careful, okay? I know this is your brand of fun but you know I worry about you when you go to The Boneyard. Especially at night," I shuddered. Just the idea gave me the willies.

"Hey, who is the parent here anyway?" she laughed as she grabbed another bottle of water. When I didn't reply she looked at me, her violently blue eyes scanned my face and she became serious. She reached up a pale hand and laid her palm on my cheek. "If you only knew what it was like. You'd have nothing to be afraid of."

I nodded. I'd heard it before but it was still hard to imagine, and it didn't really make me feel any better.

She gave me a quick hug and said, "have a great last day, sunshine." And she was gone.

As I gathered my things, turned off the lights and locked the door behind me, I fought the familiar twinge of guilt that came when I thought about how my mother was trapped in a life she hated because of me.

What if dad were still alive? Would she still be here?

My mother is a creature of the deep, a siren, a mermaid. And because her daughter is human, she can never really go home.

2

After the last bell, my friends and I met at the South entrance of the school and walked to Flagg's Cafe for a celebratory treat. The day was perfect. There wasn't a cloud in the sky and the air was still enough that we could put our sweaters into our backpacks and go bare-armed. On Canada's East coast sometimes even summer weather can be cool.

We chatted about how our last days went, dodging excited high school kids as we walked. The sidewalk was full of celebrating teenagers acting like they'd just gotten out of prison.

"Did you hear about Rachel Montgomery?" I asked Saxony. I knew she liked the actress.

She gasped. "Yes, isn't that crazy? She could have died. I love her but she was pretty daft to go out partying in The Boneyard, man what an idiot. Seriously."

"That's what my mom said too," I added, smiling.

"On the news it says she went home already," Saxony continued, "but I bet you she's still in the city. They always say stuff like that to throw you off the scent. Maybe we could find out where she's staying and stalk her." She waggled her eyebrows.

Akiko snorted. "Good luck with that."

I squirmed internally. Saxony would flip to know that Rachel was indeed still in town and my own mother would be making a personal delivery to the star. That thought sparked an idea and I made a mental note to ask my mom about it later that night.

"So, remind me when you both leave again?" Georjayna asked Akiko and Saxony. Both girls had plans to spend the summer abroad.

Saxony answered first, "My flight is in six days, and Akiko leaves the day after me. So we have to have one last get together the four of us before we go. Saturday night?"

"Works for me," said Akiko.

"Me too. You, Targa?" Georjayna said, looping an arm through mine. As always, I felt like a child next to her. Georjie was a good half-foot taller than me.

"Yup. I have nothing going on. I was thinking about getting a summer job and signing up for one of the summer school courses," I said. "Get a head start with my science credits for next year."

"That's a great idea, Targa," said Akiko in her soft voice.

"No, that's a terrible idea!" said Saxony, her long red curls bouncing in protest. "Why would you subject yourself to more school on purpose? Hang out at the beach. Get a boyfriend. Read one of the thousand books on your reading list if you must, but for Pete's sake, don't go back to school."

Akiko smiled at Saxony's rebuff. She was never offended when Saxony disagreed with her because that's just how they are. They have opposite points of view on most things. Sometimes I don't understand how those two had ever become best friends.

Georjayna, Saxony and I have known each other since preschool. We grew up together. We weren't always as close as we are now. Sometimes it takes kids a few years to sort out who they like and who they don't, but by the time we hit junior high the three of us were inseparable.

Akiko lives on the border of two school districts so she'd gone to a different elementary school and junior high than the rest of us. She and I had become friends years later during the second half of Grade 9 when we had a history and math class together. She'd been a loner but was also the smartest kid in math class, so I'd asked her for help since math was my weakest subject. She and I started meeting in the library and she'd tutored me for the rest of the year.

When Georjayna had a pool party at her house for her fourteenth birthday, I asked if I could bring a friend. When I walked in with Akiko, Saxony and Georjayna squashed the tiny girl with hugs. Unexpectedly, Akiko and Saxony had bonded.

We arrived at Flagg's and Akiko and Saxony grabbed one of the tables on the patio while Georjie and I went inside to order. The place was abuzz with activity, mostly students who'd had the same idea we'd had. We waited in line for a good ten minutes before our turn came.

"Two cappuccinos, a flat white, and an iced coffee please," Georjayna said to the redheaded boy behind the till. I recognized him as one of the kids from our school. He was a year behind us. He blinked at her like an owl and then stuttered our order back to her as he punched the buttons on the computer. Georjayna didn't seem to notice but I sure did, he was blushing to the roots of his hair.

Georjie is leggy, blonde, tanned and looks like a fashion model. On the outside, she's tall and intimidating. On the inside, she's a total geek. She's amazing with computers, cameras and all things digital. She has over five thousand followers on her blog and don't even get me started on her social media accounts. She gets a kick out of it and she even makes some money with it, although it's a complete mystery to me how. The idea of putting my life up online for anyone to look at gives me the creeps.

"You must have made quite the mad dash from school to get here in time for work?" Georjayna said to him.

"Who me?" he said, his voice cracking. His look of shock that this blonde goddess was conversing with him made me hide a smile behind my hand. One look at gorgeous Georjayna and most people assume she's a snob. People are always shocked to find out that she's nice, and interested in people no matter who they are. I have seen her stop and chat with a vagrant on the street more than once because she's curious. I'm not sure how she ended up this way because her mother certainly doesn't see the value in chatting with a homeless person. Georjie is the first to admit that her mother is a snob.

"Of course, you," she said, kindly. "Oh, almond milk for the iced one please. Sorry, I forgot." She put her palm to her forehead.

"That's ok," he said while fumbling with the milk container and splashing the front of his apron. She chatted with him while he fixed our drinks but he was so distracted that I doubted we'd end up with what we ordered.

"Thanks a lot," Georjayna said warmly when he'd finished, flashing him a smile full of dimples and perfect white teeth.

He dropped the foamy spoon he was holding in the sink with a loud clatter. "Welcome," he mumbled.

Akiko had chosen a table in the shade and was waiting patiently while Saxony was standing in the sunlight and chatting up a cute boy I didn't recognize. I didn't know what they were talking about but she was laughing and had her hand on his arm. She has no shortage of admirers with her curves and huge green eyes.

The boy looked over at us as we carried our drinks to the table and I watched him visibly wilt as Georjayna walked up and set the drinks down. He shifted his open backpack from one shoulder to the other and a textbook fell out. Saxony picked it up and handed it to him. He took it, said something to her and walked away, giving a last anxious but appreciative look over his shoulder.

Saxony came and sat down, shooting me with an exaggerated glare. "You couldn't have stayed inside just a few minutes longer? He was cute and you scared him away. Way to go."

"What are you looking at me for? Blame the six foot blonde, not the pasty brunette," I said, pointing at Georjayna.

"I'm not six feet!" Georjie said, affronted. She's been sensitive about her height for as long as I've known her.

"Close enough," said Akiko, pulling the flat white closer.

"It's not me, it's you," Georjayna said to me, and my jaw dropped.

"Did you not notice that every single flipping boy we passed on the way here stared at you like you're a sirloin? I mean, I know you're gorgeous, but gads. Could they be a little less obvious about it?" She rolled her eyes.

"You're so deluded," I said, shaking my head. "They have pills for that you know."

"Then you should get on that prescription too," said Saxony. "You've always been blind as a bat when it comes to men."

"What is this? Pick on Targa o'clock? I have perfect eyesight, thank you very much."

"Men," Akiko said sarcastically, but more to herself. She was looking down and stirring her drink. When she lifted the cup to take a sip she noticed the rest of us were looking at her. "What? These high school kids aren't men, they're boys," she said simply, gesturing to the world around us in general.

At barely 90 pounds, Akiko is very petite and her half-Japanese half-Caucasian heritage gives her a racially ambiguous look. To look at her gives the impression that she's tough. But really, Akiko is quiet, hard working, dutiful and humble even though she has a brain like a computer. She also gives the impression that she knows things no one else knows and she's patiently waiting or biding her time until... until what, I don't know. She doesn't talk about her past at all, and not even much about her future. Most times we don't know what she's thinking until she's made a plan and it was right about to happen.

This summer, Akiko is going to Japan because her grandfather made plans for her to spend time with relatives she's never met. He wants her to learn more about the Japanese side of her heritage. At least, that's what she told us, but it seems a bit strange to me that she should go spend two months with people she doesn't even know, relatives or not. It's hard to tell how she feels about it. When she told us about it a few months ago, she presented herself as neither happy nor unhappy, just resigned.

"You're so right," Georjayna sighed, bringing me back to the present. "They are just boys."

I took a sip of my cappuccino. "Are you looking forward to Japan, Akiko?" I asked.

She shrugged. "In some ways," she replied. Then she deflected, which is what she always does. "How about you Saxony? Are you looking forward to Italy?"

Saxony lit up. "Are you kidding me? It's Italy! I can't wait. The coffee, the cheese, the history, the art," she sighed, then added with emphasis, "the *Italians*. I'm so lucky." We all knew she meant the Italians of the male variety.

"Don't you mean the diapers, the sippy cups, and the strollers?" said Georjayna. We all laughed, and no one more than Saxony.

Saxony had applied for and been granted an au pair position for a family in Venice. The family had two boys and they'd wanted an English speaking, live-in au pair to take care of them for the summer. I had a hard time picturing Saxony as a nanny but she insisted that as long as she could give them back at the end of the day, she loves kids.

"Thank God they're not that young," she said, "I'd have turned them down flat if the kids were toddlers. Thankfully, at six and nine they're past the sticky stage. Besides," she reminded us, "I'll have full room and board and my own apartment." We all agreed, she'd lucked out.

"What about you, Georjie?" said Akiko. "Have you decided about Ireland?"

Georjayna's mom Liz was trying to convince her to go stay with her beatnik Aunt Faith in Ireland for the summer. We knew Liz was just trying to foist her off. Liz was very focused on her career. Georjayna used to go to Ireland when she was little, but when her mom made partner all that stopped and its been ages since she's been back.

"Oh, that's easy," she said. "As long as Targa is here for the summer then I'm staying too. We'll hang out at the beach, catch a few hot summer flicks and binge watch all the new TV series, right T-Nation?" she said, batting her brown eyes at me.

I smiled at the use of my old nickname. She'd given it to me years ago, shortly after my dad died. I'd emotionally retreated and always appeared to be in my own little world, my own little 'Nation of Targa'. So, she'd christened me and it had stuck. "Right," I said in agreement.

Georjayna's wheat blonde hair was in two loose braids and she grabbed one in each hand and pressed them together in prayer, making her look like a penitent milkmaid. "Aye," she said in a strong Irish accent, "cuz if yur leav'n too I promised me Mam I'd go, and last time I was there they talked all funny-like and I could'na understand a single word."

I laughed. Georjie had always been a talented mimic. "Well, that doesn't sound so bad," I replied. "I'd love to see Ireland, or anywhere in Europe really."

She continued with the accent, "That's because you've never been to Anacullough, the small town me aunt lives near. Blink and you'll miss it. I'd go crazy." Georjayna crossed her eyes and dropped her braids.

"You could always come visit me in Venice, Targa," Saxony said, then slurped up the last of her iced coffee. "As long as you don't snore you can share my bed, but if you do I'll push you into a canal."

"I appreciate the offer," I smiled. "I don't have the money for that but maybe one day."

We chatted for another half hour before we started looking at our watches and phones. We agreed to meet for lunch at the park the next day and also to get together on Saturday night at Georjayna's house for a farewell dinner.

Georjie texted her mom for a ride after Akiko and Saxony said goodbye and left to walk home together since they lived near each other. Georjayna and I took the empty cups inside.

"Your mom is able to pick you up today?" I asked as we dumped our garbage in the appropriate recycling bins. I was surprised because Liz basically lived at her office and left Georjie to her own devices.

"Yeah, but only because she had a hair appointment at Oasis and just finished. Lucky timing" she replied. Oasis is a high-end salon only two blocks from the cafe. "Mira picking you up?" Georjie asked.

"Nah. I like walking," I replied, covering for my mom. She might even be out at The Boneyard by now.

A look of disapproval crossed Georjayna's face. The trailer park was at least an hours walk from the café. I know what Georjie thinks. We've talked about it before. She likes my mom for her devil-may-care attitude but she also thinks she's irresponsible when it comes to me. Mira is the kid, and I'm the adult. She's not totally wrong about that.

3

G eorjie grabbed my hand as her mom pulled up in front of the cafe in her white S.U.V. "Come on. We'll give you a ride."

Liz is a high-powered lawyer. Both of us have moms who work too much and we both sometimes wrestle with feelings of abandonment, but in terms of wealth, Georjayna is my polar opposite. She's got everything that money can buy short of a private helicopter, and I'm sure they could afford that too. They have the mansion with the indoor pool and gym, the designer clothes, the gadgets and technology. But Liz never stops working and barely notices her daughter. Trying to oust Georjayna for the summer is such a Liz move.

"Hey Targa. How are you?" Liz asked, giving me a plastic smile from between the front seats as I got into the back seat; her bluetooth earpiece perpetually stuck in her ear. Her blonde hair looked fantastic. Liz sounded more British than Irish. Georjayna had told me that she'd taken accent correction classes to try and make herself sound more English after she'd moved to London to study.

"I'm fine, Liz. Thanks. You look nice. How are you?"

Liz didn't answer. She went back to a conversation with someone in her ear about the 'Michaels file'.

Georjayna looked at me from between the front seats, rolled her eyes and mouthed 'sorry'. I shook my head and smiled. I knew Liz. I didn't expect anything different.

"Is your mom still at work?" Georjie asked. "Why don't you come home with us for dinner?"

I was about to accept when I noticed Liz give Georjayna a hard look, even as she was speaking to the person on the other end of the call. I never really knew if Liz wasn't all that fond of me because I was 'trailer trash' or if she didn't like any of Georjayna's friends. Georjie has explained that it's nothing personal. Her mom is just stressed and busy so she can come across as cold, but Georjayna rarely says anything bad about anyone so I took it with a grain of salt. I suspected Georjie was harboring some bitterness against her mom but worked hard not to show it.

"No, that's ok. Thanks," I answered. "I've got dinner waiting for me." It was partially true. There was food in our fridge.

They dropped me off at home and I entered an empty trailer. I hit automatic dial on my cell for Mom's office.

"Bluejacket Recovery," answered an energetic male voice.

"Hey Micah, it's Targa."

"Targa! How are you?" Micah was always enthusiastic when he talked to me. That was because, like most men, he had a thing for my mother.

"I'm great thanks, Micah. Is my mom still there?"

"No, she's left for the day. I'm surprised she's not home already. Did you need me to track her down on the radio?"

"No thanks, I've got her cell. I just thought I'd try the office first." And then I slipped in the real reason I called. "So, is there going to be a trip out to Devil's Eye for Rachel Montgomery?"

"Man, gossip travels fast," he marvelled.

"Well, it was all over the news this morning."

"Yeah, I guess that's what celebrity will do for you. Splash your 'bidness all over the place." He chuckled.

I waited. There was a brief silence on the other end of the phone, and then, "No, we turned it down. Eric pulled rank. No surprises there. I don't think we'll ever take a job there."

"Probably for the best though right? Safety first."

"Yeah. But we got a call from a rich guy in Poland today, so you never know. Maybe that one will pan out."

"Oh wow, Poland. That would be cool." That was news. I made a mental note to ask mom about it when she got back. "Ok, gotta jet. Thanks, Micah."

"No problem. Take care eh, Targa?" he said, warmly. The guys had issues with my mother, but most of them were pretty nice to me.

"Thanks." I hung up and wondered why some loaded Polish dude would call a Canadian dive team.

I guessed that Mom was already in the water and wouldn't be back until late, so I turned on the TV for background noise and searched the web for summer jobs until my stomach started to growl. I made myself a dinner of rice noodles with pesto, broccoli, and some leftover chicken. I made an extra dish for Mom and put it in the fridge. She was always starving when she came home from a swim. I cleaned the kitchen, then aimlessly flipped through the only three channels we got and found nothing interesting, so I read until I fell into a fitful sleep on the couch.

I was dreaming about a cold sea snake swimming past my face when I came to. Mom was trailing a strand of wet hair across my cheek. "You're back!" I sat up and rubbed my eyes. I glanced at the clock on the kitchen wall. 2:05am. "Did you find it? That was fast."

"Of course I found it. It's a junkyard spread across the ocean floor for half a mile. What a mess. Those kids really were lucky to escape with their lives. By now, The Boneyard looks like a hurricane swept through a lumber yard with all the wrecks down there. The hard part is in distinguishing the new mess from the old."

"What did you find?"

She held out two white fists, clenched shut. "What do you want to see first?"

I tapped on her right knuckles and she revealed three rings, each set with precious jewels - rubies, emeralds, and diamonds. I gasped. They were beautiful. I tried them on.

"How much do you think they're worth?" I asked.

"I don't know, but her manager offered me five grand for their return, plus anonymity of course. So I guess we did alright for your college fund tonight." She kissed me on the top of my head. I didn't need to point out that she'd make more money if she hawked them herself; that wasn't her style.

Mom's work pays well but work is on a contract-by-contract basis. Good salvage jobs are hard to come by and the Bluejackets have to bid for them against other companies. As a result, we live a sort of feast/famine life. Private, reward-based jobs like the one for Rachel Montgomery are even fewer and further between. Mom takes advantage of them when they come up and always socks away the reward for my future. Sometimes she even finds treasure randomly and sells it to a local collector.

"What's in the other hand?"

She flipped it open to reveal a bracelet and necklace. These two pieces matched the diamond ring.

"How on earth did you find them? It must have been tricky to spot them amongst all that rock and coral."

She shrugged. "No, it was easy. Things like this are almost always in a safe. So I just look for a metal box. It wasn't hard to find."

I froze. "They were in a safe?"

"Yeah."

"Mom, how are you going to explain that they're not in a safe anymore to Rachel Montgomery's manager?" My mother has an insatiable curiosity about almost everything. I swear she's half cat instead of half fish. She's not so interested in people, but she loves to explore when she's out in the water. A closed metal box would have begged to be opened. I visualized her cracking a safe with her bare hands and the precious jewellery spilling out. "What if there had been paper money?"

She shrugged. "There wasn't, and that safe wasn't waterproof anyway. I'm returning her heirlooms and she'll be happy to have them back. Who cares about what happened to the safe? It could have been smashed on the rocks, right?"

"I guess. But you've always said that anything that might make someone more suspicious is not a good idea." Sometimes it seemed like we'd had a role reversal at some point. The cautious mother of my youth had evolved into a risk-taker and I'd become the proverbial crossing guard of our lives. Maybe she'd just grown tired of having to be so careful all the time.

"Heeeeeeyyyyyy..." she said, dragging out the word with her musical voice. "I would never do anything to endanger us, you know that." She tugged gently on a strand of my hair.

"Yeah, well our opinions on what might endanger *you* seem to differ." I tried not to think about what might happen to her if she was ever discovered. But I forgave her, like I always do.

I heated up her noodle dish and asked her to describe her late night salvage adventure. She described the underwater world with vivid description and relish, and I listened even as I brushed my teeth and got ready for bed. I was crawling under the covers as she was finishing her story. She bent and kissed me goodnight. Just before she closed my door I remembered something. "Mom?"

The door opened slightly, "Yes, sunshine?"

"Micah said something about a Polish guy who called the office today. Did Simon tell you anything about that?"

"Hmm. No. They might have gotten the call after I left. I'm sure I'll hear about it tomorrow."

"Ok. Let me know."

"Sleep now."

I did. I always slept well when she was in the house.

4

"I'm really interested in seeing the glass-blowers..." Saxony was saying when we heard the sound of tires squealing on pavement. I recognized the sound of Mom's diesel before we saw her truck come screeching around the corner. "On Murano," Saxony finished, but we were no longer thinking about her Venice to-do list. We watched the Bluewater truck come to a sudden halt, its nose dipping at the rapid stop.

We'd met at a park overlooking the beach for a picnic lunch. I brought the lemonade, Georjayna made the egg salad sandwiches, and Saxony had brought home-made brownies. Akiko was supposed to bring veggies and dip but she'd texted last-minute that she had to run an errand for her grandfather and wouldn't be able to make it.

"Dude, your mom should take it easy on those brakes," Saxony remarked. Saxony has two car-crazy brothers and a sensitivity to vehicles had rubbed off on her.

Mom left the diesel running and the door open but had started across the lawn towards us, her black hair billowing back from her shoulders with the speed of her stride. I grabbed our lunch garbage and stuffed it into the cooler that Georjayna had brought. Whatever was on my mom's mind, it looked like it was going to be something that my friends shouldn't overhear. "Looks like I gotta go, guys. Sorry. Text you later," I said, getting up and grabbing the thermos I'd brought.

"Sure, Targa. No problem," said Georjayna. "I hope everything's ok."

Saxony just nodded, but both of them were staring at my mom. "She's such a rocket," Saxony said under her breath. She always made some comment about what a fox my mom was. If she thought it, she said it.

"You're worse than the guys," I cuffed her affectionately on the shoulder and went to meet my mom. She stopped and waited for me to join her, she waved to the girls and they waved back. "Is everything ok?" I asked. Mom didn't look upset or concerned so my heart began to slow its clatter.

She threw an arm over my shoulder as we walked back to the truck. "It's great. I have a proposition for you."

"Oh yeah? Can't wait to hear it." I went around to the passenger side and got in. Mom pulled away from the curb before anything more was said. As I waved goodbye to the girls I had a sudden remembrance of the Rachel Montgomery thing.

"Before you lay it on me," I said, "Did you return Rachel's heirlooms yet?" I'd intended to ask her if I could come and bring Saxony too. I'd been so distracted that I'd forgotten all about it. I was hoping it wasn't too late.

"Yes, first thing this morning," she replied.

"Damn it!" I said, feeling like a crappy friend. At least what Saxony didn't know wouldn't make her mad at me.

"Why, what's wrong?"

"I just didn't think you'd get it done so quickly," I sighed. "Was she happy? What was she like?" I asked, curious about what the reigning teen-queen of Hollywood was like in person.

"What do you mean 'what was she like'?" Mom looked puzzled. "She was a walking, talking human with a real live heartbeat and everything, and of course she was happy to get her stuff back."

"Did you at least get a picture with her? Tell me you got a picture." I already knew what the answer was.

"Why would I do that?" She looked at me like it was the most idiotic idea she'd ever heard.

I sighed. "No worries, my mistake."

"What? Why?" She was blinking at me in complete and utter confusion.

"Saxony is a fan, and I meant to ask you... never mind, forget it. Go on with your story." I tried not to be frustrated with her. It would never occur to her to ask a celebrity for a photo or an autograph.

When I told my mother to 'never mind' something, she took me at my word and instantly the subject of Rachel was forgotten. "Remember you'd asked about the Polish guy that called the office?" she said, switching subjects as easily as she switched the trucks gears.

"Yeah, what was that all about? Do you have a job in Poland?" I felt the cold fingers of dread creeping in. I didn't want her to leave me alone for the summer. She'd already taken too many trips away every winter. Somehow, I got the sense that that wasn't it though because she wasn't as glum as she usually is when the Bluejackets take on a foreign contract.

"The guy who'd called is named Antoni Baranek," she began, "He's personal assistant to the wealthy Polish guy, Martinius Joseph Novak. Isn't that a mouthful. And get this, he own a 150-ish year old ship-building company in Gdańsk."

"Gdańsk?" I said, feeling the strange word bounce off the back of my throat like a rubber ball.

"It's a city in Poland, on the Baltic Sea."

"I figured as much." I tried not to sound sarcastic; it was lost on her anyway.

"His company has been searching for a ship from their fleet that was wrecked a long time ago and thanks to a tip from the British Navy, they've finally found it."

"And they want the Bluejackets to salvage it," I said. "Why do they want to bring in a team from so far away? Don't they have their own salvage divers in Poland?"

She nodded, "Novak Shipping actually does have a small salvage team, but they're busy with other projects and they don't specialize in historical wrecks. Martinius came across our website and saw our track record. Simon told him it would be expensive to have us come all the way over there, how we'd have to rent equipment and pay for accommodations and everything but the old guy is insistent."

"Wow. How flattering." Good for them, crap for me.

"Antoni sent the wreck analytics to Eric who has already declared no restrictions to the dive site, so the project is a go. I've actually never seen Eric so enthusiastic about any site. The guys are salivating to take this job; all the metrics check out perfectly."

"What do you think?" I asked. She hadn't gotten to the heart of it yet. Something was up or she wouldn't have come to get me in the first place.

"He's offering a huge amount of money. He also said we can use all of his floating and flying assets, whatever we need. And he's putting us up for the duration of the project."

"Sounds like a dream job."

"It is. There is a catch though. Martinius read about me in the press, and he's offering the job only on the condition that I'm part of the team." Mom steered the truck onto our street.

I could see the article Martinius would have read in my mind's eye. *Mira MacAuley, the remarkable master diver who has led to much of the Bluejacket's success and fame in the diving world, can perform like no other diver before or since.*

"Simon fell all over himself to agree," she was saying. "Without speaking to me about it first." She gave me a look that said she wasn't impressed. "I told him he needs to ask me about foreign jobs and not just assume that I'll always be on board."

My heart sank. "Does that mean you're leaving for the summer?" My phone chirped and I looked down. Georjayna had texted: *Everything ok? Come over early tomorrow and catch me up?*

"I gave a condition of my own." She pulled the truck into the driveway and put it in park. Then she turned and looked at me.

"What was the condition?" I put my phone away.

"That I could bring my daughter," she said, smiling.

I gasped and my heart jump-started. "What did Simon say?"

"He tried to talk me out of it, but I know when I've got him by the short ones, which lets face it, is most of the time," she said. I laughed. "So he called Antoni back and relayed the condition. He explained that summer break was starting and that I didn't want to leave my daughter home alone."

"What did Antoni say?" I grabbed her by the arm in my excitement.

Clearly perplexed, she said, "You wouldn't believe it, Targa. You should have seen Simon's face. Martinius said that he wouldn't have it any other way, in fact when he found out I have a daughter, he insisted that I bring you. I'm not sure why, but there you have it." She looked at me expectantly. "So, want to come to Gdańsk with me for the summer?"

My face must have appeared clownish with the amount of enthusiasm pouring out of me because she quickly tempered the offer with, "I'm not sure how long we'll be there, it depends on what we find onsite and how long the manifest is. But it'll probably be six weeks or more of work. Either way we'll have you back before your Grade 12 year starts. What do you say?"

I leaned across the console and into her arms. "Yes! Yes! Yes! I don't even know where the hell Gdańsk is, but I am so ready to go. I can't believe it!"

She squeezed me and then pulled back, concern in her bright azure eyes. "You know I'll be busy though, right? It's an important job and I'll be double-timing it the way I usually do. I've asked for weekends off, and that's fine by Simon even though the rest of the team has to work Saturdays. So we'll have a bit of time together on weekends. Is that ok by you?"

I have wanted to go to Europe for as long as I knew it existed, we just never had the extra money to go. Poland isn't at the top of my list and I don't know a thing about it, but it's Europe and it's a free ticket. "Hell yeah, Mom!" I said, squeezing her tight again. "Are you kidding? Lets go to Poland!"

5

"You're going where?" Georjie wailed over the popcorn maker blowing hot air and kernels everywhere but into the bowl. She flicked off the machine and stared at me.

I had come over to Georjayna's place a couple of hours before Saxony and Akiko. It was something Georjie and I did often. We needed time, just the two of us.

"Please tell me I did not hear you right," she was saying. "You did not just tell me that you're going to Poland for the summer. At least tell me that you made a mistake and you're actually going to Costa Rica or somewhere cool if you're going to be abandoning me." She bent her long frame in half, picked up a stray kernel off the hardwood floor and threw it into the sink. She stood and gave me a look. "And it is abandonment, make no mistake about it."

I felt a stab of guilt but I also knew she was happy for me because I knew her tell. Georjie can't smile without dimpling first. Two craters appear in both of her cheeks right before she grins. While she wasn't smiling yet, she was dimpling. I breathed an internal sigh of relief. "I know, I'm sorry but I had no idea this was going to happen," I explained handing her the pot of melted butter and watching as she drizzled it over the popcorn kernels. "When someone comes along offering you a free ride to Europe, you don't say no. This kind of opportunity doesn't come along everyday. Especially for me."

She nodded. "I know." She picked up a spoon and tossed the popcorn. "Ok, explain to me again the bit about the old Polish guy? I didn't think you were going to drop such a bombshell so I wasn't really listening."

"Oh, thanks." I flicked a kernel at her.

She dodged it, laughing. She ground sea salt over the popcorn, tossed it and then put the spoon in the state-of-the-art dishwasher. I followed her and the popcorn to the sliding door that led into her back yard, which she opened with her long toes. We made our way to the chairs sitting in front of the fire pit in their backyard. The sky was a lovely shade of peach.

Five hand-made wooden chairs sat around a fire pit built of stone. Each chair had a soft blanket folded and hanging over the back of it. A pitcher of iced tea and a stack of plastic glasses had already been set on the small table. Every once in a while, when I saw things like this, it struck me how different Georjie's life was to mine.

Georjayna's house was in the richest neighbourhood in Saltford. It's called Bella Vista and for good reason. Every house in her suburb is huge and has a view of the Atlantic.

We settled ourselves and munched away on the popcorn as I told her what my mom had said about the Novak Shipping job.

"What are you going to do there while your mom is working?"

"I've already made a list." I turned on my phone and showed her some photos that I'd found online of Gdańsk. I told her about some of the historical attractions I wanted to see.

"Wow!" she said, genuinely impressed as she scrolled through the images of colourful old buildings lined up side by side along an inner city canal. "Holy crap, this place looks gorgeous. Why have I never heard of it?"

I shrugged. "It's not the sexiest destination out there I guess, maybe it's a best kept secret. Hopefully, that means it won't be swarming with tourists. I don't think Saxony is aware of how busy Venice is going to be in July and August," I shuddered. I hate crowds.

"No, I don't think she's thought about it," said Georjayna. "And to be honest, she's not as turned off by crowds as you are, especially crowds of Italian men."

I laughed. "To each their own."

I told her that Poland had some nice beaches. They weren't like the white sandy beaches of the Caribbean, but being Atlantic Canadians we were used to that. "I have a big reading list to get through too," I said, relishing the thought of laying on the beach with a good book.

"I bet you do. But I also bet you'll be so busy exploring that you won't have time to read," she sighed. "It sounds amazing. Now you're all going somewhere cool this summer, what am I going to do?"

"You wouldn't reconsider Ireland?" I still didn't fully understand her reticence. "I remember when you came back from the last visit. You seemed so much happier. I thought Ireland had been good for you."

She nodded, "Yeah, but that was a long time ago. I was just a kid who'd lost her dad. Things are different now. I'm not that kid anymore. I already told Liz that the reason I was staying was because you'd be here. Now that you're going, I don't have a reason anymore." She shrugged, "So, I guess I'm going to the emerald isle after all."

"You'll love it," I encouraged her. "I would have chosen Ireland over Poland, but I'm not about to complain."

"Yeah, it's pretty. So green and lush," she said. "Its been a long time since I've been there. The last time I was there was before your dad passed away."

"Almost three years before, Georjie. You were only five." Georjie and I had been friends a long time, but the year I lost my father was the first year I really knew what friendship meant. Georjie and I were young but even then she'd been a comfort to me. She'd had such maturity for being just a kid, far more than I had.

"Speaking of dads," I said, "I don't suppose you've heard from yours?" I eyed Georjie as I picked the last few kernels from the bottom of the buttery bowl. I liked the hard crunchy ones that hadn't fully popped, even better if they were a bit burnt.

She shook her head, "No, last we'd heard he was still living in Edmonton with his new wife. I think the father ship has long since sailed for me." She dusted the salt off her hands. "Even the mother ship has sprung a few leaks. Thirsty?"

I nodded and she poured me some iced tea. I studied her face as she poured, the corners of her mouth turned down. Both of us were fatherless only mine didn't leave by choice. She blamed herself and probably always would. It was hard not to feel angry with the man I could barely remember. Liz and Brent had divorced when Georjayna was only five and that was one of the reasons she'd taken Georjie to Ireland the following summer. Things had been such a mess at home.

Her father had hung around for a while trying to do the joint custody thing but soon he'd started missing their play dates, then he'd disappear for a month and not tell anyone where he was. Eventually, he vanished completely leaving only an email address and a cell number where Liz could reach him. He'd scrawled the words 'for emergency' beside the number, which made things pretty clear. As if Liz or Georjie would want to call him after finding a note like that, emergency or not.

"So, when do you think you'll leave for Ireland?" I asked.

"I don't know, I guess soon, since you're leaving..."

"In a week." I got a little jolt of adrenalin every time I thought about getting on the plane.

She nodded. "I'll ask Liz's secretary to see what flights are available around that time then." Georjayna referred to her mother as Liz most of the time, and any logistical stuff for Georjayna's life like flights and dental appointments went through Liz's office. I couldn't imagine calling my mom 'Mira' or having my mom's secretary look after my personal needs.

"I know you don't know yet, but keep me posted about your return date and I'll try to come back around the same time. Maybe we'll even have a few weeks of summer left to hang out."

I agreed. "I want you to have a good time though, Georjie. It's Ireland, not Winnipeg."

She laughed. "I know. And I like my Aunt Faith, she's kind of a cool hippy chick, y'know. I have a cousin I haven't met yet either." Georjayna pulled the throw from the back of her chair and spread it over her legs.

"I thought your aunt was single and had no kids?" My memory of Georjayna's family in Ireland was blurry at best. A breeze raised goosebumps on my skin and I covered myself with a throw too.

"She is single," Georjayna explained. "And my cousin is actually older than me by two years or so, I think. My aunt adopted him after the last time I was there so he's not a blood relative and I haven't had the chance to meet him yet. Liz hasn't told me anything, like why Aunt Faith adopted him and stuff. I'm sure I'll find out when I get there. His name is Jasher. Isn't that a cool name?" Her feet were peeking out from under the blanket and she sat up and pulled it down in an effort to cover them. I guess it wasn't always easy to be so leggy.

"Super cool. Is he cute?" Not that I cared much, but a nice smile and a set of broad shoulders would go a long way towards a good summer for Georjayna.

"No idea but I'll sneak a pic and send it to you and you can decide," she promised. She brightened as a thought occurred and added, "Maybe you'll meet a cute Polish boy to hang out with."

"Maybe." I conceded.

She looked at me with a sidelong glance. "Why so doubtful?"

She was digging a bit now. It had been a while since we'd talked about guys in a serious way. I usually tried to avoid it as I was never sure what to say. Whenever the four of us were together and the topic of guys came up, Saxony and Georjayna had plenty of opinions. But Akiko and I never had much to add. The difference between Akiko and I was that she had sentiments she could make clear in a few short words, but I didn't have opinions at all.

"I'm just..." I began, and Georjayna waited patiently. "Not that attracted to guys," I finished.

"Are you attracted to girls?" she asked plainly, without so much as a raised eyebrow. It was a logical next question, and Georjie was great at making me feel safe. She's the least judgmental person I know. That question would have sounded laced with potential judgement coming from Saxony.

"Big fat no there too," I said. "I mean, I am fully capable of recognizing an attractive person when presented with one, it's not like I don't appreciate them. I've just never had those butterflies that you and Saxony always talk about."

"But you've been on dates before," Georjayna recalled. "With Peter in Grade 9, wasn't it?"

"There was also the basketball player, Scott."

"Right, he was nice. But Peter was way too short, even for you."

I laughed. "Only you would say that." Peter had been at least two inches taller than me.

She snorted. "True."

"They weren't really crushes. I was sort of humouring them to be honest. They asked, so I went. That's what girls our age are supposed to do, right? Go on dates? Make out?"

"Yeah, but ideally with someone you actually *want* to go out with. You and Scott kissed, right? I remember needling you for details afterwards. I thought you'd liked it, didn't you tell me that you liked it? So, how was it, really?"

I made a show of patting my hand over my mouth and yawning.

Georjayna winced. "That bad?"

"Poor guy. It wasn't his fault. Is it possible to be born without a sex drive?" I said. At the end of the night, I'd recalled just wanting to get away from him. I was happier in my pyjamas with a good book.

"Maybe, I don't know. I doubt it though because if that's the case then wouldn't there be some other symptoms, too? Wouldn't it mean your hormones are out of whack? Something would have shown up in puberty wouldn't it? I mean, your puberty was so..." she searched for the right word, "...peaceful. You didn't get acne or cramps or anything. I could have killed you. There I was vomiting into the toilet at least once a month from the pain and my mother going on about birth control pills. My face was a mess in Grade 9, remember?"

I blinked. I couldn't remember Georjie as having anything other than a perfect California girl complexion, even in winter.

She rolled her eyes at my vacant expression. "Dude, I almost went on that nasty drug for acne, what's it called? The one that gives you brittle bones when you get old?"

"No idea." Why did I not remember these details, was I more like Mom than I thought I was?

"Well anyway, with the silly boys in this town its no wonder you haven't fallen in love or felt that spark yet. If you met the right person, I'm sure you'd feel differently," Georjayna said confidently. "It'll happen. You'll see."

I wasn't so sure but I didn't protest. I didn't know what to say about it anyway so there was no point in arguing.

"Make sure you get an international texting plan before you leave," she said, randomly.

I laughed. "Sure thing, Georjie."

As I listened to her wonder out loud about things she might do in Ireland, I was comforted to hear that she was warming to the idea. We chatted away until Saxony and Akiko arrived.

The sky was finally growing dim and the stars came out. We built a fire in the backyard, roasted marshmallows and talked about our plans. I caught Saxony and Akiko up about Poland.

"That's amazing, Targa," Akiko smiled at me and held my gaze. Sometimes, when she looked at me it almost felt as though I couldn't look away.

Saxony bounced in her chair, her marshmallow jouncing over the flame. "Except for Akiko, we'll all be in Europe. We have to promise to stay in touch, ok? I know we'll be busy but lets touch base when we can."

Georjayna and I agreed, but Akiko looked doubtful. "I'll try," she said, "I'm just not sure how good the signal will be. From what I know the family is kind of remote and I'm not sure how fond they are of technology."

"Who doesn't have wifi these days?" asked Georjayna, horrified. "Seriously, where is your grandfather sending you, to a mountain cave?"

Akiko gave her half-smile, the one where just one corner of her mouth turned up. "Who knows. His descriptive skills are scanty at best."

Akiko is an orphan who'd been raised by her grandfather. She says that she can't remember her folks at all. They'd died from a contagious illness that had spread through several villages, taking hundreds of lives. Her father had been an American expat. She says her Japanese grandfather on her mothers' side had brought her to Canada to raise her because his life had been so devastated by it.

"How come your grandfather isn't going with you?" I asked. "Doesn't he want to go back home for a visit, too?"

"He's too old for that kind of traveling now," she answered. She didn't say anything more and I watched her face as she stared into the fire. Her expression was so hard to read. Was it just my imagination or was she pleased that her grandfather wouldn't be going with her? Did she want to get away from him? How would she feel when he passed away? From the sounds of it, he didn't have too many years left and he was all she had here in Canada. Would she go back to Japan if she liked the family? They were all questions I knew she'd deflect.

I caught Georjie's eye and we shared a look of understanding. We both felt that there was always more going on under the surface with Akiko than any of us knew. I stole a glance at Saxony but she was taking a sip of her iced tea and gazing into the fire. She was Akiko's closest friend, but sometimes it seemed like she was oblivious to her. Another strange thought struck me in that moment, too. Maybe Akiko liked Saxony precisely because she didn't dig too hard for information.

I'd only met Akiko's grandfather once. It was at an outdoor market in Saltford, and he and Akiko were buying vegetables. She'd been loaded down with bags of produce and he was shuffling along with a cane, bent over and wizened. He was a tiny man with fine bones and paper-thin skin but he also had a look of vitality and iron-strength. He had a scraggly white beard and a strange hat pulled down to his ears even though the weather had been warm. He'd been wearing a brown felt jacket held closed by small wooden toggles all the way up to the mandarin collar.

Akiko had introduced us awkwardly, like she'd rather be anywhere else. She didn't tell me his name, she'd just introduced him as, "My grandfather." I'd held out my hand but he didn't take it. He'd looked me straight in the eyes and said nothing. I don't think I'll ever forget that moment because I had such a chill at what I saw. It was as though he'd lived more than one life and none of them had been good.

I remembered asking Saxony and Georjayna if they'd ever met him and they said they hadn't. I was especially surprised that Saxony hadn't met him. Saxony explained that she'd stopped asking Akiko if she could meet him because she'd made it clear that she didn't want to mix her home life with her friends. We were her real family, or so she said, but she is still a mystery in a lot of ways even to us. We've known her only two years so I guess that is to be expected.

We had fallen into a companionable silence, listening to the fire crackle and the crickets chirp. It was moments like these when I appreciated my friends the most. No one felt the need to fill the air with conversation.

Saxony finally broke the quiet, "Lets promise to have a sleep over when everyone gets back."

We agreed. It's strange, but in some ways, Saxony is the glue that holds our group together. If we fall out of contact for too long, she's the first to pull us all back together. Georjayna and I will never lose touch, but it's harder for a foursome to get together regularly. More often than not, it's Saxony who makes it happen.

Of the four of us, Saxony is the only one who has a 'normal' family life. She has happily married parents and two brothers whom she adores. Being the only girl means she enjoys a spoiled existence at home. Saxony is the funniest, the most confident, the biggest flirt, the most opinionated, and she's very popular at school. Because of this she also polarizes people, they seem to either love her or hate her.

This was to be the first summer that I'd spend without my friends. Saying goodbye was both sad and exciting. I felt like this was my chance to get to know myself without the influence of my circle. Maybe I had been defining myself by our little group for too long. As we enjoyed the fire and our last moments together dwindled away, I found myself wondering if they each felt the same way.

6

I was only three when I saw my mother as a mermaid for the first time. On a hot summer night she'd taken me down the beach under cover of darkness. I watched in wonder as my mother's pale legs glittered in the moonlight and then bonded to form an iridescent tail. For a child who never knew any different, her fins and gills were just another wonderful feature my mother had. They were no different than her vibrant blue eyes or her inky black hair. Our night swims were my favourite thing.

She'd amaze me with her acrobatic ability in the water, at least, as well as could be seen in the dark. But in the dark or not, it was hard to top swimming with a mermaid as your companion. She used to disappear under the surface, leaving me scanning the for ripples and guessing where she would pop up next. She'd explode out of the water and spin rapidly in the air, calling "what am I?" Then she'd disappear again with hardly a splash. Then she'd appear right next to me and I'd gasp, startled.

'Spinner dolphin," I'd say, breathless.

"Very good!" she'd say, kissing my cheek.

"Do a whale, mommy!" I'd request, patting her cheeks with my chubby little hands.

She'd disappear again and I'd watch the water and hold my breath. She'd show only her hip and move very slowly to mimic the shape of a whale's back gliding just above the surface and then submerging again.

"Eel!" I'd yell. She'd skim the surface revealing enough to appear long and sinuous. She'd swim in a serpentine fashion, creating the 'S' shape with far more accuracy with her flexible body than any human would be able to.

I would stroke her scaly tail, admiring the emerald colours in the moonlight. It was firm and smooth if I brushed it one way, but rough if I brushed it the other way. She could even lift her scales away from her body and make a wave across her tail that caught the moonlight. Her skin was pale and smooth as porcelain and took on a pearly sheen when she was in her mermaid form. She could spiral her long black hair in the water and come up to show me that it had wrapped itself around her like a ribbon round a maypole. She was utterly enchanting; no wonder I grew up feeling that she was person I wanted to spend the most time with.

"It has to be our little secret," she'd impressed upon me more than once, and I'd always nod solemnly.

"Daddy?" I had asked.

"Even daddy can't know," she'd say, and her voice would take on a hypnotic musical quality.

"Why?" I'd asked. Surely daddy loved her as much as I did and deserved to see her in her full glory.

"The world doesn't believe in mermaids, sweetheart," she explained. "It would be dangerous for me if people knew, and it might be dangerous for you and your father too. The fewer people that know a secret, the safer that secret is. Do you see?" she'd asked, the violins in her voice soothing my concerns.

I would nod and look up at her with adoring eyes.

She used to ask me to concentrate, to see if I felt any different in the salt water, to will myself to transform. But as much as I wanted to, there was nothing I could do. I would lay submerged in the saltwater, closing my eyes and picturing my legs fusing and scales sweeping across my skin. But my body simply refused to change.

And so, I grew as a normal child. Well, as normal as one can be who cries almost every night for several years because she's not a mermaid. My father was completely baffled by this phase in my life. Poor guy.

Sometime around my sixth birthday, I sensed a change in my mother. She grew distant from dad and I. I didn't know at the time that she was wrestling with a powerful biological need to go back to the ocean. Now that I understand it, I'm amazed that she didn't disappear. It must have taken some kind of crazy strong will not to leave. I would observe her lost in thought for long stretches of time. She spent more and more time out of the house without having told us where she'd gone. She and my father started to argue about it. Of course, he could never understand what the real problem was and had no way of helping her. I knew that it had to do with our secret, but also had no idea how to help.

After Georjayna's parents got a divorce and her father disappeared, an awful new possibility began to haunt me. If her father could just up and leave his family like that, what was stopping my mom from leaving too? I would ask her outright if she was thinking about running away, and she'd kiss me on the top of my head.

Of course not, baby. I love you.

But I knew that she was. She had become unhappy on land. I imagined her happy and free in the water, and miserable on land with me and my dad. The contrast I imagined she suffered terrified me.

I had nightmares that I'd wake up and run into my parents room to find my father dead of a broken heart and my mother gone. Then I'd wake up for real in a cold sweat and be so relieved that it was a dream, but my fear was stirred up again. It was never allowed to die.

I began to get up quietly every night and peek into their room after they'd gone to sleep just to make sure I could count two bodies in the darkness. Sometimes one of them wouldn't be there, and I would know that she had gone out for a swim. I would go back to my room, my heart pounding and my mouth dry. I'd sit on the floor inside my door until I heard the front door open and close, so quietly that I had to strain to hear it. Then I'd watch for her through the crack. Only when I saw her come back did I go to bed, but I never knew for sure if she was going to come back at all. And just when I was sure we were going to wake up and find her gone and never to return, my father died for real and everything changed.

We never even knew that he'd had a heart condition. He was a young, strong man. He liked to play hockey in a beer league every winter. He'd always come home happy after his games. I would struggle to stay awake because I knew he'd be home before midnight. He'd sneak into my room and kiss me good night. He'd have cold cheeks and the sweet smell of beer on his breath. Sometimes I'd throw my arms around his neck, trying to pull him down. He'd laugh and rub my face with his beard scruff.

But during one of these games he simply collapsed. The doctor told us that he'd likely been dead before he hit the ice and that he'd felt no pain. He was just gone. We'd grieved for a long time, my mom and I. It was hard on both of us but it was especially hard on her. Because then, not only had she lost her love but she had a daughter who'd failed to turn and yet couldn't be left alone. She couldn't even escape the grief by drowning her memory in saltwater. She either had to live through it or abandon her little girl, so she stayed. How she fought the call of the ocean and grieved her loss at the same time, I'll never know. Years later, she'd joked that she was the only mermaid alive who knew what the five stages of grief were, let alone to have gone through them.

We received some insurance money but it wasn't enough to last and so she was forced to find employment. She used to serve at a local restaurant called the Sea Dog before I was born, but it wasn't enough to raise a child on. So, what does a siren do for a living? My mom never even finished high school, she went into the ocean after her mom passed away from cancer. She was only eleven. I guess even mermaids aren't immune to the big C-word. Mom was living in the ocean at a time when most women are focused on getting an education. The testament to her brilliance is that she built herself a career as a human salvage diver, from scratch. You know what they say about the truth being hidden in plain sight? The irony of it still takes my breath away.

She got the idea when she saw an ad in the paper offering a reward to anyone who could return some valuable items which had been lost at sea. The items had been lost where else but Devil's Eye Cove. There had been talk around town that they'd never be found and anyone who attempted would die trying. Naturally, she recovered them easily and she made sure the media knew it was she who had done it. At the time, I think she was hoping for others who had lost items at sea to approach her so we could live off reward money. But it didn't take long for the story to reach Simon at Bluejacket and soon she had a job offer.

There was some scrambling in the beginning to make sure she'd covered all her bases. She had to learn how to use diving equipment and handle herself on salvage dives. She joined the all-male team and they didn't make it easy on her. The first few years were pretty bumpy, but she hung in there. My mother is so tough she's almost callous, and I doubt there are many human women who would have stuck with the job the way she has. I know I wouldn't have.

The truth is, I really don't know how she does it. Whenever the Bluejackets have a salvage job, she dons the diving gear along with the rest of them and plays the part. It just about drives her insane. I have tried to imagine what it's like for a mermaid to enter the deep encumbered by human legs and diving gear instead of her own gills and fins.

But the secret of the team's success lays in what she does on her own time. She dives under cover of darkness and sets the dive sites up for maximum success. She unearths the valuables and places them strategically throughout the site for the team to find with efficiency but without raising suspicion that the site has been tampered with.

It's so easy for her to do that I had asked her once why she didn't start her own company. She'd said that the business side of it would probably kill her. She had no interest in being an entrepreneur. She just wanted to make enough money to keep us reasonably well looked after, and she wanted to spend as much time in the ocean as possible.

She used to try and hold back and let the men stumble across as many pieces she had strategically placed throughout the wrecks as possible, without 'finding' them herself. But with all the Bluejackets' success it had only been getting harder and harder for her to spend time in the diving gear. So, she gave up the pretence and now works as though she knows the sites like the back of her hand, which of course she does.

Her performance underwater soon made her a legend. She doesn't even need GPS to find a wreck site a second time, once she knows where it is she can find it again like it has a built in homing beacon. The men can't account for her clairvoyant-like skill, and it has sparked jealousy and sour feelings towards her.

Every dive she does in gear wears her patience thinner. She can't call in sick and skip the dives because her pay is contingent upon her being present. She used to have a bit of a reprieve every winter because the Bluejacket team could only take foreign jobs once the snow and ice had blown in. Cold water is no problem for a mermaid so winter quickly became her favourite season. But as the Bluejackets' success has grown, Simon wins more foreign jobs and the team has to make trips to the Caribbean or wherever the work is. Unlike the rest of the gainfully employed, my mother is never more miserable than when she has to make a work trip to somewhere tropical. It means she has to spend a lot of time in the hated diving equipment and away from me. It also means she has to tolerate the guys on her team and their jealousy.

She couldn't care less about the way her team feels about her. When I urged her to be more considerate toward them she'd say that she didn't work there to make friends. Her lone wolf attitude mixed with her siren's allure makes for a lot of confused emotion in the office. For her exemplary performance, Simon has given my mother lots of bonuses. He puts her on a pedestal and encourages the team to emulate her. But the guys don't have a hope of competing with her.

Simon went through a phase where he tried to get my mom to break down her 'techniques' and give the guys workshops so they could all learn how she did it. That was a disaster. Mom couldn't teach them what she couldn't explain and she hated being the centre of attention.

To make things worse, the men don't understand why she's so damn attractive to them. They resent her, but they all want to be with her at the same time. I used to drop by the office just to watch the subtext play out. I have come to recognize two emotions very keenly, desire and resentment, the latter of which is just a hairsbreadth from hatred.

At my urging, she finally asked Simon to stop recognizing her in front of the team. She'd also asked him to minimize the amount of press she got. She doesn't want the public accolades. Supposedly he tried, but the media is often insistent. Salvage diving has its own following, and the press always wants to talk to the rock star of the deep. That's what they call her, even though most of their dives aren't even close to being 'deep'. A few years back there was a television producer who wanted to make a reality series centred around her, and Simon saw dollar signs. Mom threatened to leave if he didn't shut up about it.

She's now a legend in the diving community and the press loves her because she's gorgeous, rough around the edges, and makes for a great interview. She makes people laugh just by being her blunt self and giving one-word answers. They can't tell if she really is that rude, or if she's just playing a part.

We don't talk about my father or her work struggles much anymore. I know that the pull of the ocean is very strong on her but between the diving time and constant busyness, somehow she copes. These are my mom's demons and I know she wrestles with them daily.

As for mine? I could never bring myself to tell her I'd be ok if she left. It's my biggest fear that she'll leave and never come back. I don't want her to go, even when I am all grown up. I can't picture a day when I won't need her.

As a siren, the entire ocean should be her playground but for my sake she's restricted to staying close enough to Saltford to be back in time for supper. It's the equivalent of keeping a tiger on a three-foot chain.

It pains me to know how much she denies her true nature. I blame myself. If I had only been able to change, things would be so different. I carry the guilt with me always because I know that I have failed her.

So, she has her demons and I have mine. Sometimes it feels like life is just a test to see who will crack first.

7

Before I knew it, it was the night before we were to leave and we had boxes and bags of gear and luggage crammed into the truck. We had to be at the airfield at 4:30 am. Martinius had arranged for his own pilot to pick us up in his private jet.

There was no way I was going to sleep tonight; I was way too excited. Mom made me go to bed early anyway, which was weird because she never enforced bedtime. She went to bed early too, drawn and anxious looking. This was out of character for her but for a good reason. My mother hated flying, it made her feel sick. She was meant to be swimming in the depths of the sea, not hurtling through the sky in a metal cigar-tube at 30,000 feet. I hated to watch her stress levels mount before a flight. At least I would be with her the whole time.

I did fall asleep after a while and by the time my alarm went off at 3:30 I woke up and bounced out of bed, wide awake. I hadn't been on a plane since I was just a kid. I was eager for the experience of a private jet.

Mom on the other hand, had shadows under her eyes. I watched her as we ate breakfast in sleepy silence. She was staring out the window watching the sky turn from black to black that was thinking about turning pink.

"Did you sleep ok?" I asked as I watched her eat her oatmeal slowly, her eyes at half-mast.

She gave me a wan smile. "I slept a bit. You know that I've never been a big fan of flying. It's the only thing that really saps my energy."

"I'll be with you, Mom," I said, giving her a hug.

"Thank God for that." She squeezed me back. "Don't worry. I'll be fine, lovey. I'm old hat at this now. Just don't be worried if I sleep the whole time."

"That sounds like the perfect solution."

We arrived at the airfield a half hour before take off. Today's Blue-jacket Team was eleven men strong, including Simon. My mom, the only woman, brought the crew to a dozen.

I shook a lot of hands. There were many team members I didn't know but I was too excited to remember all their names. Mom explained to me that some of the men were strangers to her, too – they were contractors that Simon found just for this job. She called them the 'cowboys'.

The small jet had the words NOVAK STOCZNIOWCÓW BRACIZ stencilled on the side. As part of the logo there was a styl-ized image of an old-fashioned sailing vessel with three masts painted on the aircraft's body in navy and white. I assumed the image of the ship was to add character, because from what I'd heard, the Novak corporation's empire was the most cutting edge shipping company in Europe. I didn't know anything about the industry, but I was pretty sure their vessels didn't look like the ship out of Peter Pan.

We entered the plane through a small door beside the wing. The interior was nicely finished in navy leather with cream coloured piping. The pilot was a smart looking man with a lot of laugh-lines. He introduced himself as Ivan. His warm eyes lingered on my mother as she boarded the plane and turned to go down the narrow aisle.

My phone chirped as I was stuffing my carry-on into the overhead bin and I reached into my purse, wondering who was texting me so early in the morning. I looked at the screen to see that it was Georjayna.

Have a good flight, T-Nation. Let me know when you arrive! Muah!

Me: *I will. You're up early. Everything ok?*

Georjayna: *Yeah. Couldn't sleep. Bit of anxiety.*

Me: *You made the right decision.*

Georjayna: *Thanks. Guess I needed a reminder.*

Me: *Text me when you get to Ireland too, k?*

Georjayna: *Fer sher.*

I powered down my phone and returned it to my backpack. I took off my sweater and shoved it up into the overhead bin with the rest of my stuff. I scanned the guys as they settled in. Of the Bluejacket team, I knew Micah, Jeff, Simon, Tyler, and Eric. I liked Micah so I had directed Mom to a seat that was near him.

"How delightful to have both of the ladies on the plane within flirting distance," Micah teased.

Mom rolled her eyes, and I bit my cheeks to hide a smile. I made her sit near the window so she could sleep. I sat beside her and Micah sat across the aisle from me. The window seat next to him remained empty.

During takeoff I noticed my mom gripping the armrests of her seat until her knuckles turned white. I put a hand over hers. Not only was I worried about her anxiety, a state I rarely saw her in, it would be really bad if she accidentally broke the seat. She shot me a stressed smile.

"Breathe," I mouthed to her.

She nodded back on a stiff neck.

Occasionally, Ivan would speak to us over the intercom and let us know where we were. He gave us interesting tidbits about what was below us, whether we could see it or not. He had an accent I couldn't place; Mom told me he was from Belarus. Ivan explained that we'd be given two snacks and a meal during the flight, and that the in-flight entertainment system would be available for use as long as the plane was above 10,000 feet.

I had thought we'd be able to see the Atlantic underneath us, but the clouds were so thick that all I could see was a sheet of lumpy cotton. Up where we were, the sky was piercingly blue and clear and the flying was smooth. Mom fell asleep once we got above the clouds so I pulled down the window shade and put a blanket over her.

I pulled a book out of my backpack and cracked it open. I had barely started reading when I felt Micah looking over at me. I looked up and smiled at him.

At 27, Micah was the youngest member of the team and was just starting out in his salvage career. He was the kind of guy Saxony would fall for. He had curly, strawberry blonde hair and always wore a ball cap. His hair curled out from under his hat, making him look boyish. He was a broad fellow and looked uncomfortable crammed into the small seat.

A random thought about what he might be like to kiss came unbidden to my mind and I had the tiniest involuntary cringe. Nope. No desire to do that whatsoever, even though he was attractive. Well, at least I was consistent.

"Do you want to see some pictures of the wreck?" he asked, holding up a file folder with the words SYBELLEN, GDAŃSK written on the label. His knee was jiggling madly and he had an over-caffeinated look in his eye. It was going to be a long trip if he was going to be like this the whole way.

"Sure," I replied, putting my book in the seat pocket. He handed me the folder. I opened it to find pages full of graphs and readings.

"Fascinating," I droned.

"The photos are in the back," he laughed.

I flipped through until I found printouts of a murky underwater shape. Some of them looked like sonar imagery, which were really just outlines and blobs of ink. In most images it was hard to tell that it was even a ship, but there were a handful of clearer shots.

"Those were taken by an underwater robot. No one has actually been down there in person yet," he explained, leaning over the aisle to look at the pictures. "Pretty cool, huh?"

I agreed, mostly to be polite, but I wasn't all that impressed because the images were blurry. I kept flipping until I came across one that was taken from the side and I was able to make out the shape of the masts. "How did it land perfectly upright like that? Aren't most shipwrecks a yard sale across the ocean floor?" I asked. Mom described most wrecks as dump sites.

"Amazing, right?" replied Micah. "She's called *The Sybellen* and she's the most gorgeous thing I've ever seen. I haven't been at this business long but even the veterans on the team say they've never seen anything so beautifully preserved. It'll be like going back in time, to see her in person."

Two masts were visible in the image, but the length of the ship suggested room for three. I noted the crisp edges and lack of obvious decay. "Are they sure this is the one they've been looking for all those years? It doesn't look that old."

"It was lost in 1869 so it's pretty darn old. But the fact that it's in the Baltic and not some other ocean is its saving grace."

"Why is that?" Mom never talked about these kinds of details with me. I liked to hear about her diving adventures when she went out on her own, but I never really dug for information about dives that she did with the Bluejackets. Micah was painting things in a whole different way. My mom was bored to death during the team dives, but Micah was clearly in his element. He spoke about it with the passion of an artist.

He pulled out his phone and scanned through some images until he landed on a shot of another shipwreck. He handed his phone to me saying, "This is an old British vessel found in the Caribbean. It's twenty-three years younger than *The Sybellen*. Notice a difference?"

I looked at the image and it was obvious what he meant. The British vessel was much more decayed, really just a shell. Large curved ribs gave the impression of a wreck but there were no masts, and the entire rear of the ship had completely collapsed.

"Why is this one in such bad shape? Was it how it went down?" I asked.

"That can be a factor," he answered. "There are lots of factors involved in how fast a wreck decays but the biggest thing is the water. See, the Baltic is brackish. It has hardly any salt and no shipworm. So even though *The Sybellen* is older, the one in the Caribbean broke down at a much faster pace. That's the power of salt water."

Micah explained how because of the inflow and outflow of fresh and salt water, the salt in the Baltic sits in layers. The water on the top is often so fresh that its nearly drinkable. The deeper you go, the saltier the water becomes. Most of the salt sits below a depth of 130 feet. The wreck is in the perfect position because it came to rest at a depth of only 90 feet.

Micah let me look through pictures of the other wrecks on his phone for a while until the early morning caught up to me and my eyelids began to droop. I thanked him, handed back his phone, pulled a blanket over myself and curled up against my mom, who was still out cold.

I don't know how many hours later it was when I awoke to a dark cabin full of sleeping men. The shutters had been drawn and snores drifted up from a few seats. I got up and went to the bathroom and on my way I could see that Eric and Jeff were still awake and talking quietly a couple of seats ahead of us.

I stretched my legs and back, and then went back to my seat and curled up for some more sleep. But as I lay there with my eyes closed, I couldn't help but catch snatches of Jeff and Eric's conversation.

"...can't do that, Eric."

"...got heat on me..."

"...For $335 a pound..."

"...US dollars?" Then more mumbled words I couldn't make out.

Then, "Don't be a pansy, Jeff."

Whatever they were talking about, it sounded like Eric was in some financial trouble and he was trying to get Jeff to help dig him out of it. I strained my ears to pick up more.

"...breathing down my neck."

"...50/50 split..."

A new voice made me jump. "What are you boys scheming about?" I sat up and snuck a peek over the seat in front of me. The voice belonged to Simon. He'd stopped in the aisle. "Up to no good, I'm sure."

Eric forced a laughed. "Not much boss. Just going over these schematics for *The Sybellen*. Looking forward to seeing this beauty up close and personal."

Probably because he was so excited to see the ship himself, Simon was fooled. His round face lit up and he began to chat with them about the wreck. Mom had told me that this job was a dream come true for him.

After that, there was no more talk for me to eavesdrop on. My thoughts turned to Gdańsk and all the wonderful things I planned to see and do there. I forgot about their conversation and drifted off to sleep again, dreaming of cobblestone streets and picturesque canals.

8

Martinius' young assistant met us at the Gdańsk Lech Walesa airport. It was 16:45, local time. We stepped off the plane and took deep breaths of the ocean air. I swear that I could watch the colour return to my mom's cheeks with every inhalation. "Feeling better?" I asked her as she stretched her legs.

"You have no idea," she said, smiling.

Our Novak escort introduced himself as Antoni Baranek and said that he'd been Martinius' personal assistant for nearly three years. He was tall and broad shouldered with shortly clipped dirty blonde hair and a toothy grin. He pumped the hands of everyone who stepped off the plane, including me. He had a deep voice and a strong Polish accent, which doubled his charm. His eyes were hazel with long dark eyelashes, and his lips were full and naturally carmine. His shoulders were so wide and his waist so narrow that he looked almost ridiculous. He was so full of colour and health that he reminded me of a cartoon character, as though he were some animated hero in a comic book. His cheeks were ruddy and he had a day's worth of beard growth. He was also so tall that I had to crane my neck to look up at him.

I was aware that I was looking at a man that my friends would consider extremely sexy. I was even more aware that neither my heart nor my stomach reacted in the ways that Georjayna and Saxony described in detail. To me, he was pretty to look at in the same way as a sunset or a work of art.

It crossed my mind to sneak a photo of him some time and text it to my friends. The comments that came back would be worth the risk. I immediately paired him up with Georjayna in my mind. I couldn't help but do that with tall guys. The two of them would make a bizarrely beautiful couple with their absurdly long limbs and larger-than-life appeal.

Antoni had a team of men who helped transfer all our gear into a caravan of black vehicles. I felt like I was in a spy movie when I got into our SUV and watched the world go by through tinted windows.

Antoni had made sure that Mom and I were riding in the same vehicle as he, along with Simon and Tyler. "I look forward to practicing my English with mother tongues," he said, as we settled into the vehicle. He also requested that we correct him whenever he made a mistake. "Please," he said, holding his hands together in a gesture of prayer. Then he moved a broad hand to cover his heart, "Do me the honour of correction and save me future humiliation." We all laughed. It wasn't what he said that was funny so much as how he sounded when he said it. I doubted he needed any corrections, so far his English was perfect.

Like all men, his gaze lingered on my mother. I could tell he was trying not to be rude because he'd blink and look away before he made her uncomfortable. I appreciated the effort. Most men didn't even try to hide their stares. The poor guys never knew they were in the presence of a siren, a being that was perfectly equipped with everything she needed to lure any man she wanted (and unfortunately, also those she didn't).

My mother isn't just beautiful, she's bewitching whether she tries to be or not. I wondered what she was like when she actually wanted to attract someone. I shuddered and thought for the thousandth time that my father never had a chance. I also wondered who was really the lucky one in that relationship. It couldn't be easy being married to a mermaid. I wondered if it would have been easier for him if he knew what she was, or if it would have broken him somehow.

The Novak estate was a 40-minute journey through and past Gdańsk. It was just as beautiful as the pictures online had shown. The city was filled with waterways and colourful buildings crammed side by side with not so much as an inch between them. There were churches, quaint parks, and canals everywhere. My face was glued to the window. I couldn't wait to go exploring.

As we left the city we passed charming seaside villages, one after the other. I caught glimpses of golden sand beaches and sparkling blue water with whitecaps. The trees were lush and green. I cracked my window just a little and smelled the air. It had the fresh salty tang of the ocean, which made me feel immediately at home.

Antoni threw an arm over the seat and looked back at us. "So, this is the famous master diver that makes the news all the time." He shot us a boyish grin and it struck me that he must have started working for Martinius right out of university.

My mother's mouth twitched, but I couldn't tell if she was annoyed or entertained. She'd not been asked a question, so she didn't respond. This was a siren trait; she didn't care to make polite conversation or build rapport with a colleague just to make a professional relationship more enjoyable.

After a moment of awkward silence, Antoni cleared his throat and moved on. "Martinius gave me instructions to arrange for a welcome dinner tonight. After you rest of course. He's looking forward to meeting the team, but you most of all, Mira."

I caught Tyler rolling his eyes in my periphery. Tyler is a master diver too, and has been diving for longer than I've been alive. I'm sure that it galls him that my mom outshines him, even though she's been diving professionally for less than a decade.

I really wished Antoni would stop laying it on so thick. He couldn't know that Mom already had it tough with her colleagues.

Antoni pointed out some features while we travelled until we pulled up to two huge gates. The black iron had been wrought in twists and curls of intricate shapes suggestive of churning water and bubbles. Where the gates met in the middle were two mirror image mermaid figures covered with gold leaf. Their curling tails met in the centre and rolled away from each other in elegant curves. Mom and I shared a look and she winked. I smiled. My mother was a living legend in more ways than one.

We entered the estate and I abandoned politeness and gawked. Conversation in the car ceased as we entered the beautifully kept grounds. A red brick mansion loomed at the end of a long drive lined with trees and flowering shrubs. Stone walls lined either side of the massive yard, covered in wisteria not yet in bloom. The manor itself was a palace, its red stone crawling with ivy.

Our convoy pulled up into the semi-circular drive and doors opened, feet hit gravel and necks craned at the beauty around us. While the guys unloaded, I took photos of the grounds. My friends were going to flip when they saw this place. My eyes burned with exhaustion but inside a perpetual quiver of excitement clutched at my stomach.

Three men and two women dressed in navy uniforms came down the wide stone staircase. They began taking the luggage to an entrance along the side of the manor. "Take these ones up to the Muszla Suite," Antoni said to one of the staff, pointing to my mom's luggage and mine. We followed Antoni up the stairs and in through one of the many open double doors of the main entrance.

A massive marble foyer with a huge sweeping staircase was the first thing we saw. It ascended to a landing and then broke off in two, disappearing off to the right and left. An elaborate railing could be seen lining the hallways of the upper levels and I caught a glimpse of a profusion of artwork and tapestries on the walls – mostly seascapes.

I scanned the grand foyer, looking up at the massive chandelier over my head. A painting hanging over the main doors caught my eye. It was a huge panorama of the ocean with a tall ship in the distance. A rock jutted out of the sea in the foreground, water hitting it violently and sending spray in all directions. Sitting on the rock and looking out at the ship was a mermaid with yellow hair. Her shoulders sloped sadly downward. I elbowed my mom and pointed it out to her.

"Huh," was all she said.

More staff appeared and Antoni spoke to them in Polish. They greeted us foreigners and began to show us to our rooms. Most of the team were taken around the outside of the manor to another entrance.

"I'll show you to your suite," Antoni said to us. "It's on the third floor." As we approached the landing at the top of the staircase, there was an ornate red marble table on top of which perched a mermaid sculpture. It had been carved out of wood and looked very old. Antoni stopped so we could admire it.

"Interesting taste in art," I commented. "I'm sensing a theme."

"Martinius comes from a long line of collectors," Antoni explained. "The syrena is on their family crest so the Novaks have always had a thing for mermaid artwork."

"Don't we all," replied Mom.

"There is a legend that stroking her breasts brings good luck," he explained as we examined her. The siren's bare breasts were worn smooth and shiny from hands running across them year in and year out. Antoni kept his eyes politely on the sculpture after this statement.

I grinned at Mom and she swatted my butt. "Grow up," she said with mock seriousness.

"Do you live here too?" I asked as we made our way up to the third floor.

"I have a suite here," he said. "My home is in Gdańsk but I often stay here depending on work. I'll be staying here for the duration of the salvage project."

As we passed under the copper label over our door engraved with the words *Muszla Suite*, he explained that muszla translated as seashell. The furnishings, like most things we'd seen so far, had a nautical theme. The decorations were dated but rich looking. Our suite had five rooms including two bedrooms, each with a king-sized bed. Each bedroom had its own ensuite bathroom and we also had a parlour with a view of the front grounds. If it hadn't been for all of the trees we would have had a view of the ocean in the distance.

"I've been in a fight with Martinius about cutting a few trees down to allow for a better view," Antoni explained. "But I suppose, seeing as those oaks have been there since his great grandfather's time, it's understandable he'd be sad to see them go."

There was a knock on the door and Antoni went to answer it. A fellow in uniform delivered our luggage and Antoni spoke with him in Polish and helped him bring the bags into the suite. They laughed at something and I suspected they were probably friends on their own time.

"I'll leave you to rest," Antoni said, once our luggage was inside. "Meet me in the foyer at half seven and I'll show you to the dining room." He dismissed himself and closed the door.

As soon as he left we sprawled on one of the beds. I looked over at my mom and frowned when I noticed the dark smudges under her eyes. "Tired?"

"Very. Being high up in the air for hours on end is a special kind of hell. It always takes a little while to recover."

We got up and moved my luggage to one bedroom and took hers to the other. I changed into pyjamas and drew the curtains. Mom closed herself into the other bedroom.

I tried to sleep, but I was overtired. My eyes wouldn't relax no matter how much I tried. I tossed and turned. And then I noticed that the lamp on the bedside table had a mermaid base and there were sirens among the sea creatures that were swimming along the wallpaper border.

I wondered for probably the millionth time in my life how things would be if I had been born with the mermaid gene. I wondered how long it would be before my mother left me for good, and felt the familiar hollow feeling seep into my belly like a mist drifting in from the sea.

Mermaid genes are passed down from mother to daughter only. When a siren gives birth to a female child it is the epitome of happiness for her. It means she can take her daughter back to the ocean with her when the girl is ready. If she gives birth to a male child, it means the child will only ever be human. The birth of a son is a bittersweet event for a mermaid. No matter how much she may love her child, the call of the ocean will eventually become too powerful to deny and will cause her to abandon him and his father. It's pretty much a hero or zero situation for the kid. Except for me. For me, it was zeroes all around. My mother had never heard of a siren's daughter not making the change, the genes were supposed to be 100% in a female child. So I was some kind of unfortunate anomaly.

We had done everything we could think of to try to get the gene to express itself, but it wasn't like we'd had people to ask or scientific books to read on the biology of the mermaid. I'd even tried filling the bathtub with sea salt once and sitting in it until my skin puckered and stung, thinking I just needed more salt than the ocean could provide. That failed too, just like everything else.

"Did you never think to try for another child?" I'd asked my mom years after my father had passed away, and we'd long since given up hope for me.

"We couldn't," she'd answered. "A siren has a cycle. She leaves the sea to have a child, but in order to have another baby she has to go back to the ocean and spend some time in salt water to trigger the cycle again." There was no set amount of time needed, every siren has her own cycle and only she would know when she was ready to come out of the sea to try again. The only way a mermaid could have two children in one phase on land was if she had twins. My mom had never gone back to the ocean after me, so her natural cycle had stalled.

Mom spent hours patiently answering my questions over the years, so even though I don't have the gene, I have a pretty good understanding of the way things are for mermaids. And let me tell you, the myths have it mostly wrong.

The siren cycle plays out something like this: When the time is right, usually shortly after puberty, a mermaid will leave the ocean in search of a mate. The urge to procreate becomes more powerful than the desire to stay in the ocean, so she leaves her watery home until she falls in love, and eventually produces a child. She adopts the human form and lifestyle in order to do so. Like many sea-dwelling creatures, sirens have long lifespans. They are picky about their mates so even if it takes years to find one, they'll stay on land until it happens.

Since mermaids are always born on land, they are able to get a birth certificate, social insurance number, bank account, and any other official documents they need to function as a human. It's the years spent in the ocean that can throw a siren's records into a mess if she isn't careful. Leaving land needs to be planned for, not done on a whim; otherwise, she'll come back to the identity of a missing person, or worse, a dead woman. Usually, she explains to people she knows that she's moving somewhere far away. She can submit to the government that she has emigrated and give a foreign address so that she doesn't have a tax nightmare to come back to. More often than not, she'll never see the people that were in her life ever again. For a mermaid, relationships with humans are always finite.

Mom says she's one of the lucky ones. She'd left the ocean and used her stash of money and identification, which her own mother showed her how to prepare, to get herself a job at a pub down at the Saltford harbour called The Sea Dog. The Sea Dog is still there today. Within a couple of weeks, Nathan (my dad) went to the pub with his hockey buddies for a drink after a game. She says that the moment she heard his voice she knew he was the one. And once she'd decided she wanted him she could not be denied. It was a little hairy for a while because Nathan was dating a girl who had befriended Mom and gotten her the serving job. I even had a few vague memories of Crystal, the blonde lady who used to babysit me sometimes. When Crystal moved away from Saltford, she and Mom lost touch and Mom never made another friend like her.

Once on land, sirens are able to flush themselves with fresh water to suppress the instinct that is enhanced by salt in order to stay on land as long as is needed. They can swim in salt water during this phase as long as they keep themselves hydrated with fresh water. In a way, the fresh water makes them forget their siren selves. In the moment, some of them feel almost fully human and barely feel the need to swim at all.

When a mermaid falls in love, she fully intends to stay with her mate forever and live the rest of her life on land. If the man is old fashioned, as my father was, they marry. To a mermaid, the idea of marriage is foreign. After all, she's a sea creature and not attached to human customs, but she usually goes along with the ceremony to make her lover happy. Soon, she becomes pregnant and goes through all of the same nesting phases that a human woman would.

But after the birth of a child, things slowly begin to change. If the child is a daughter, her mother will take her to the ocean under cover of darkness. The exposure to sea water triggers the mermaid gene and the girl's legs morph into their true form, a powerful tail. In a sense, it is a second birth. When mermaids talk about their birth, they always mean their salt-birth – the moment they first took their siren shape.

Mother and daughter might live on land with this secret for a while to allow the child to grow sufficiently strong to survive in the ocean. Even then, the mermaid will have lapses where she desires to stay on land with her family. This transition phase is very difficult emotionally. The siren bond to her mate is strong, but the call of the ocean will always win in the end.

If the child is a boy it is much more painful. She'll generally last long enough to wean her son, but it's guaranteed she'll eventually disappear. Mom says it's *a mathematical certainty*.

The father would never know what really happened, and if she's done a good job keeping her identity secret, he would never know that he had married a siren.

In cases where the mermaid leaves without preparing for it, there is a missing person's report and a protracted search, which always fails. She'll have vanished without a trace.

I went through a phase when I was twelve or thirteen where I researched missing women reports, reading the details and looking for clues that she might have been a siren. The cases where a mother and female child disappeared were the ones I obsessed over, printing off and collecting any articles I could find. I never did anything with them, but I guess I wanted to get a sense of how many sirens were really out there. Based on what I found, there aren't many.

Mom explained that mermaid memory and consciousness is highly affected by their exposure to salt or fresh water. Fresh water makes them function more like a human while salt enhances the siren instinct. It was entirely possible for a siren to have a son, leave him on land to go back to the ocean, and then spend so many years in salt water that she eventually forgets her former family, all trace of her memory erased by the salt. She might come back to land to find another mate years later, without recalling that she'd already done so in previous years.

I also went through a phase where I was obsessed by the possibility that I might have brothers or sisters somewhere out in the world, but Mom reassured me over and over again that I was her only child.

It was a strange thing, the effect of salt, and both a blessing and a curse. If she had to abandon a lover and a son, the salt would lessen the pain. But when she came back to land and flushed her system with fresh water years later, her memories may or may not come flooding back to her. Every siren was different. It seemed cruel to me, but then, nature is heartless from a human perspective.

I wondered how long my mother could hold out. She'd had the daughter that all mermaids wanted, and I had no doubt of her love for me, but I'd also turned out to be a dud. I was fully human and eventually, human children moved on and started their own lives. So, when I finally did leave home it only made sense for her to go back to the ocean. And once she went would she ever come back? Would my children ever know their grandmother?

An image came unbidden to my mind of bumping into my mother on some beach when I was old and grey. She walked out of the ocean just as young and beautiful as she was right now and I went running up to her with my arms out only to have her step back and say, "I don't know you." My eyes prickled and I shook off the horrible vision.

Maybe she wouldn't forget me and maybe she would, but either way she would leave me. It was only a matter of time. A mathematical certainty, like she'd always said.

9

I had just convinced my eyelids to relax when I felt the bed
depress beside me. I rolled over. Mom didn't look much better
than before we'd gone to bed. "Did you sleep?" I asked.

"A little. You?"

I nodded even though I hadn't. I didn't want her to worry. "Are
you going to the site tonight to check things out?"

"No. The schedule calls for us to spend all of this week and part of
next week going over objectives and familiarizing ourselves with the
equipment. Looks like I'm also going to be getting some Polish
lessons, so I'll be able to read the signs on all the gear." She mimicked
shooting herself in the head. To the rest of the crew, all this prep work
was critical to their success. To my mother, it was a waste of time.

It made me feel better that she wouldn't have to dive for a while.
Mom needed less sleep than a human did, but she still needed to
catch up whenever she was double-timing it. If she was working both
days and nights her cycles seemed to go in multiples of days rather
than one day. She'd dive during the day and at night when there was
a need for it, but every four days or so she'd sleep for well over 15
hours. No one else on the team would get away with such an odd

schedule, but because she was Simon's prize diver, she did whatever she wanted, within reason.

When we were at home, things worked well for her. There was a lot of time spent at the office in between jobs doing equipment maintenance, ongoing courses, as well as research and prep for upcoming work. She had a small home office and Simon allowed her to work from home on days when they weren't diving. Unbeknownst to him, she often used that time to sleep.

"That flight really did a number on you, huh?" I said, sitting up against the headboard.

She smiled. "I'll be all right. Don't worry, sunshine." She brushed my hair back from my face. "Getting hungry? We should get ready for dinner. It's quarter to seven already."

I threw the covers off. "Yeah, I'll grab a quick shower. Meet you in the parlour in half an hour?"

Together, we made our way down to the main floor. I had freshly blow-dried hair, but Mom's was still damp and she'd pulled it up into a bun on the top of her head. She looked fantastic anyway.

Mom left the clothes selection to me since her idea of great fashion was bare breasts and a scaly tail. We both wore dark denim, dress sandals, and summery blouses. I wore a cardigan too since I was chilly. Mom never had that problem, her body seemed to regulate no matter her environment.

Antoni was waiting in the foyer along with most of the crew and a few new faces. I assumed these were members of the Novak team. Every single one of them was a man. As we came down the stairs, the conversation ceased. Every head turned, and every eye was on my mother.

I noticed with curiosity that Antoni was the only one who wasn't looking at my mom, he was looking at me. His expression made me wonder if I had caught a fraction of mermaid gene after all, even if I wasn't a siren.

I also noted that while nearly every eye expressed admiration, there was one pair that was hard and full of malice. Eric wasn't appreciative of the attention Mom was receiving and he elbowed Jeff, who was standing beside him. That seemed to break the spell and the men started to chat amongst themselves again.

"Did you get some rest?" Antoni asked as we followed him down a long, wide hallway lined with windows. Shafts of evening sun, broken and dappled by trees, streamed in and gave the impression that the hallway was half outdoors.

"Some," Mom answered.

"Thanks for asking," I added awkwardly, always trying to soften the effect of my mother.

"I'll show you to the dining room, " continued Antoni, "but I won't be joining you for dinner."

"Why not?" I asked as we walked by window after window.

"I have some things to catch up on. It's really a welcome dinner for you to meet Martinius, and I imagine he'll regale you with the tale of *The Sybellen*."

"I guess you've heard that before."

"A few times," he laughed.

I was distracted by all the artwork on the right side of the hallway. I counted two more mermaid paintings among those that decorated the walls. I pointed them out to Mom.

"They really take their mascot seriously here, don't they," she whispered.

We turned towards a set of double doors and Antoni opened them into a large dining room. Two alcoves of bay windows graced one side. One alcove had a little chess table set up, and two chairs waiting to be filled with players. The other had a tiny odd-looking piano, which Antoni explained was an antique spinet.

The windows looked down into a courtyard. A fireplace was the focal point at one end of the room, and artwork filled the wall opposite the windows. These paintings were all portraits of Novak family members, the same distinct nose on almost every subject. There were no portraits of women, only men. Perhaps they didn't paint the ladies of the house? Or maybe they were in another room.

"I wonder if one of these is Martinius." I mused. Mom shrugged. I looked for Antoni so I could ask him but he was chatting with Simon and Tyler at the dining room doors.

A long table set with crystal glasses, china plates, and silverware ran the length of the room. Two elaborate floral arrangements sat in the center. A glass chandelier hung down from the high ceiling, lit with real candles.

A server in white tie held a silver platter with slender flutes filled with a pale, bubbly liquid. Another server held a platter with glass mugs of beer. Most of the team chose beer over champagne.

"Look, Mom." I pointed to the place cards at each setting. The names were handwritten in a delicate script and there was an imprint of a three-masted ship in the top right corner of each card. "Do you think that's *The Sybellen*?"

"Could be," she said. "You can ask Martinius, if he ever decides to show up."

"What do you think he'll be like?"

"He'll be like an old Polish guy," she deadpanned.

I gave her a look.

"What?" she said innocently.

After a few minutes of allowing us to mill about, Antoni gestured graciously toward the table. "Please, ladies and gentlemen take a seat. Martinius will be with us shortly."

"Awfully formal around here," Mom whispered as she scanned the names on the place cards. She was seated to the right of Martinius, who was at the head of the table. I was seated next to her. Simon sat down across from my mom, and Tyler beside him. On my other side, happily, was Micah.

Before I sat down I noticed a small pedestal in the corner of the room. On top of it was a crystal sculpture of a mermaid. A sunbeam came in from the window and lit it up, sending a spray of rainbow colours onto the wall and drapes.

I stepped closer to examine it. The siren was leaping out of a wave with her arms stretched towards the sun. Her long hair was flying back, her breasts were bare and there was an expression of ecstasy on her face. The details of her features were obscured as she was made of crystal, but the bone structure of her face was familiar.

I looked up at my mom as she chatted with Antoni and my eyes traced the curve of her cheekbones, her straight little nose, and her full soft lips. Looking back at the sculpture I wondered if all mermaids looked alike and if the artist had perhaps met one at one time. A little brass plaque inscribed with a Polish title had been screwed to the base. A translation in English was provided below - 'Breaking Free'. The year was 1903. The artist's name had so many consonants I couldn't dream of pronouncing it.

I looked up at the sound of the double doors opening. A man that could only have been Martinius Joseph Novak entered the room.

10

I guessed that he was close to eighty but he looked fit and strong. He had a white moustache and a ring of closely cropped white hair around his head. He was deeply tanned as though he'd spent most of his life outside in the sun. He stood up straight, with broad shoulders and an even broader smile. Even though he wasn't overly tall, he cut an imposing figure.

"May I introduce your host, Martinius Joseph Novak," said Antoni to the room. Martinius bowed formally and there was a hilarious moment when the men didn't know what to do. Some of them bowed awkwardly and others shifted from one foot to the other. Jeff gave a deep formal bow and Eric whacked him on the arm.

"Welcome to my home," Martinius said in a deep voice. "I apologize for keeping you waiting. I come from a press conference in Gdańsk and we hit construction on the way back." He began to work his way along the table, shaking hands and asking names. His accent was similar to Antoni's, only stronger, but his English was close to perfect. I supposed a businessman as successful as he had to have excellent English in today's marketplace. I wondered how much he still worked.

He shook each hand and repeated every name. His smile wide and genuine, his brown eyes crinkling at the corners like tissue paper.

"He seems likable," I whispered to Mom. She shrugged, reserving judgment as she always did.

Finally, he came to my mother. He took her outstretched hand and studied her face. It was quiet for just a little bit too long. She wouldn't speak until spoken to, it was one of her siren traits.

"You must be Mira?" He continued to hold her hand and covered it with his other hand warmly. "The press really likes to splash your image around, don't they?"

"Unfortunately. They do, sir," she replied.

"Please, call me Martinius. I'm grateful that you've come such a long way to help me." He let go of her hand and moved to his place at the head of the table, which was when he spotted me. He reached out to me. My slight hand felt dwarfed in his. He held mine the same way he'd held my mother's, in a two-handed grasp. "And you are clearly Mira's daughter. I'm Martinius." He waited expectantly.

It took me a second to realize that I was supposed to say my name. All this formality was foreign to me, and I certainly couldn't expect Mom to teach me the necessary social graces. "Targa, sir," I finally responded.

He actually kissed the back of my hand. "A pleasure. You must call me Martinius. A hearty welcome to you. I've already directed Antoni to make sure you have everything you need, including an escort into Gdańsk should you wish to explore our little city. But please don't hesitate to ask him for any other thing your heart desires."

I was astonished by his thoughtfulness. "Thank you." He patted my hand and then released it.

He pulled his chair out and took his seat, which seemed to be a signal to the rest of the room to take a seat too.

I looked around and noticed that Antoni was no longer there. He must have slipped away while Martinius was shaking hands.

The wait staff was already entering the room with individual white soup bowls covered with porcelain lids. They set them before us in one synchronized movement. It seemed extravagant that there was a waiter for each guest. The servers reached out and each put a hand on a lid. As they pulled the lids away, the steaming soup was revealed and a delightful smell filled the air. My stomach growled and I realized I hadn't eaten anything since the plane.

One of the staff announced the food. "For the first course. Barszcz." His accent was the strongest yet. "It is a vegetarian soup made with mushroom and sauerkraut dumplings. Smacznego."

Martinius leaned over and whispered to me, "That means, have a nice meal."

"Smacznego," I said back to him, picking up my soup spoon.

He raised his bushy white eyebrows and tipped his wine glass in my direction.

As the soup bowls were drained, new dishes were brought. Platters and plates heaped with things I didn't recognize, steaming bowls, pitchers, and platters. Each dish was announced in Polish and then described in English, but there was so much that I forgot half of what was there. Vegetable dishes and seafood, as well as sausages, pork, and venison. There were potato dishes, vegetable mashes, fried onion dishes, gravies, and platters of cheese.

As we ate, Martinius began telling the story of *The Sybellen* to Simon. Mom and I were within earshot so we listened in. But before long the whole room tuned in. He spoke slowly and seemed to relish telling the tale as much as I enjoyed hearing it. I had a sudden desire to be sitting on the beach in front of a bonfire toasting marshmallows.

"I can't tell you the story of *The Sybellen* without telling you the story of the Novak shipping empire. It began with my great-great-grandfather, Mattis Novak. Before Mattis, the Novaks were tradesmen and laborers, not businessmen. But on top of being hardworking, Mattis had an entrepreneurial streak, and before the age of 20 had already started a small newspaper delivery service. Once he had a taste of being his own boss, he couldn't dream big enough."

"He sounds like a man after my own heart," said Simon, taking a sip of wine.

Martinius nodded. "Yes, I can imagine all of you

entrepreneurial types have a singular kind of drive. With the help of his father Emun, they scraped together enough money to acquire a loan and build a small vessel to be used for shipping commissions. People in Gdańsk knew Mattis was trustworthy from his newspaper venture so the community was in full support. Without the community of Gdańsk, it's fair to assume that Novak Stoczniowców Braciz may never have gotten out of port." He switched easily from English to Polish, both languages rolling easily off his tongue.

"In the early years, he was chartered by the postal service to carry letters and packages across the Baltic and the North Sea. Within a few years, he was able to pay back the loan and was soon turning down private commissions. He'd signed a government contract that was to last for two further years. It frustrated him to turn down these higher paying jobs and he became impatient while waiting for this contract to expire."

"So, he worked even harder. He sacrificed a social life and leisure time until he'd saved enough to build a second ship. He did this in less than a year."

"Impressive," muttered Simon, and there were nods of admiration around the table. I had no idea whether it was impressive or not, but I assumed these men knew something about what it took to build a ship in those days.

"The ship he built was a three-masted barque," Martinius went on. "Before the ship was finished, Mattis fell in love and was married. He christened the ship *The Sybellen*, after his wife. The ship was fast and sleek and catapulted his business into a new age."

I was so engaged in his story that I was surprised to look down and see that my dinner plate had been cleared and dessert was now sitting in front of me - a crepe topped with raspberries and icing sugar. I bit into it and discovered it was filled with a tart and creamy substance. Martinius noticed my wonder and interrupted his own story to say, "It's called Nalesniki, and it's filled with quark. It's my favorite," before continuing with his tale.

"*The Sybellen* remained the pride of Novak, even after he added many more ships to his fleet. You'll notice an illustration of her is still part of our logo.

"Meanwhile, Sybellen gave birth to twin boys. Michal and Emun Junior. Mattis wasn't present for the birth of the twins as he was more away than home. The company was growing by leaps and bounds.

"Lady Sybellen soon became tired of missing her husband, and of her boys being without their father. So, she made an agreement with Mattis to join him on one journey a year. Since these commissions often took months, the boys were to come with them until they were old enough to stay behind with a tutor. Lady Sybellen loved adventure and Mattis did whatever he could to make her happy, so he agreed."

"I thought it was considered bad luck to have a woman on board?" interjected Eric from the other end of the table.

Mom shot Eric a steely look at his not-so-subtle jab at her presence on the team. He looked back at her without shame, a smirk on his lips.

"In many places that's true," admitted Martinius, "but the Baltic peoples don't hold with this superstition. In fact, they thought it lucky that the woman who had given her name to their ship had joined them for their journey. Unfortunately, for one particular commission, the luck didn't hold.

"In 1869, Mattis and Sybellen set out on their yearly journey. The twins were eight. They'd taken Emun Jr with them but Michal suffered terribly from seasickness so he stayed home with his grandparents. That seasickness saved his young life, the future of the Novak name." He paused to take a sip of water, his voice more hoarse than when he'd started.

He patted his lips with his napkin and went on. "The Baltic is known for its sudden storms and *The Sybellen*, with a full cargo, was caught in one of these fast moving gales. The ship was never seen or heard from again." He allowed these words to sink in before continuing. Even the clink of silverware against china had ceased as the table sat in silence.

"The Novak family was thrown into turmoil. The young Michal

found himself without mother, father, or brother. And, further to the tragedy, the company was at great risk. Mattis' father Emun Sr had long been retired and was advanced in years. Two sisters of Emun's and their husbands, who were also elderly, stepped in. They abandoned their own lives to keep the shipping company from going under. The family shared the responsibility of running the company until Michal was old enough to finally take the wheel. Four heads in charge and none of them schooled in business, it was a very volatile time, and until Michal was in his twenties and able to run things, the company was always on the brink of collapse."

"I can imagine," said Micah. "My father can't make toast without my mother telling him he's doing it wrong, running a company with family must be a nightmare." Everyone laughed.

"Exactly, when everyone is in charge, no one is in charge," Martinius nodded. "The experience of the disaster pushed my ancestors to set an agreement. From then on, as soon as children were old enough to walk they were being groomed to take over. Executives were brought in to share the burden and learn the company's ways so that should someone ever find themselves in Michal's shoes, they would have the support they needed until they were ready to lead. They vowed never to be caught unprepared for the loss of their President again. There was too much at stake."

"By the time Michal was married and his wife Saffi had given birth to my grandfather Jan, the company exceeded its prior growth. It has since been recognized by many of the Scandinavian and European governments for its contributions over the last 168 years. Its story is one of the phoenix rising from the ashes.

"Not a single Novak ancestor has forgotten about the loss of *The Sybellen*. Since then, the company has set a budget aside every year to be spent on her search. With our success, the budget has grown too. We notified all of the port countries and their naval forces, in case anything was ever found by a third party."

"Why was it so important to find her?" I asked. Normally I wouldn't have said anything in a room full of my mother's colleagues, but curiosity got the best of me.

"Well, aside from having a cargo full of valuable and imperishable goods which would only be more valuable today, the ship has become a sort of holy grail for the Novaks. Finding her became an obsession, starting with Michal and passed down. In a way, I think finding her would mean putting the ghosts of Mattis, Sybellen, and Emun Jr to rest, along with all the sailors who were lost. It is a relief that the search ends with me," Martinius added, emotion wavered in his voice.

"Why is that?" Simon asked.

Martinius paused, as though he wasn't sure if he wanted to answer. Then he took a breath and said, "Because I no longer have an heir to carry on the search."

Looks were shared around the table. I glanced at my mom and even she had a look of surprise on her face. So, Martinius had had an heir at one point. I wondered what had happened to him or her.

"Novak has always been a family business," he continued. "My own father, Ludwik, passed when I was only fifteen. I've been controlling the company for most of my life. Thankfully, I had a wonderful relationship with my grandfather. Jan loved to regale me with stories of the early days when the company was young and always seemed to be on the edge of oblivion. But he also taught me everything I know about the shipping business.

"In the middle of the twentieth century, the search for *The Sybellen* captured the public's imagination. Her story was published in every newspaper and nautical journal that covered the Baltic and the North Sea. Donations poured in from our contemporaries. Everyone wanted to see her found and got caught up in the mania."

"Like The Titanic," added Tyler.

Martinius nodded, "Yes precisely, and just as happened with The Titanic, time passed and the attention faded away. *The Sybellen* was forgotten. We remained faithful, whether the public cared or not. And every year we've exhausted the budget without success. Until last year.

"We received a tip from the British Navy who, while searching for a wreck of their own, stumbled across a mysterious vessel sitting upright on the ocean floor. It was a three-masted barkentine of the same era as *The Sybellen*. The most incredible thing was that it's less than 30 miles off-shore.

"We spent the remainder of our budget scouting the wreck, taking as many sonar readings and photographs with underwater robots as we could. I wanted to be sure it really was our Sybellen before we poured money into salvage activities."

"How did you conclude that it really was her?" asked Simon. "Identification can be a tough thing, even in less salty waters. Did you find the bell?" Heads around the table turned with interest.

"We haven't found the bell, but everything else about the ship lines up with *The Sybellen*. It's the right size, it had three masts, and it's the right age. I had the team take images of the ship's wheel, as I knew it to have a unique design unlike others of the same era. It was a match."

"Remarkable," murmured Micah. "Remember that job in the BVI's?" he asked, looking at Simon and Tyler.

"Yeah, I was just thinking the same thing," said Simon. "We had to identify a wreck by the wheel once too. It's not common, but it can be done."

"What age was this wreck?" asked Martinius, curious.

Tyler squinted, remembering. "She was what... 1890?" he said, looking at Micah for confirmation.

Micah nodded, "1896."

"Oh, well done," said Simon. "We've done so many now I can't keep all of the dates straight."

"Were the spindles of the wheel by any chance-" started Martinius.

"Designed to look like Celtic knots?" finished Micah.

Martinius' eyebrows shot up. "How interesting, are you able to share the documents for that wreck?

Simon nodded, "Yes, that one is public domain."

"I would love to see them." Martinius continued. "So, I took the decision to bring in a professional dive team, the best I could find. We have many accomplished teams in Poland, of course, but Antoni and

I spent many hours personally researching the performance of salvage teams from all over the world. Your team is small, but it's appeared in nautical news continuously for your remarkable work. And that's what led us to call you." He gestured to Simon with this last statement.

The table was quiet for a time. My mother finally broke the silence with a question that had probably occurred to everyone at the table, but no one was bold enough to ask. "Who will succeed you then?"

I could have kicked her. Simon closed his eyes in embarrassment and Micah dropped his gaze to his dessert plate. Tyler buried his face in his wineglass.

Martinius blinked at her question but recovered quickly. "With the passing of my only son..." he began, quietly. "Well, let's just say my legal team and I meet regularly to discuss this issue, and as of yet, it remains unresolved. I have a selection of Novak executives in place should something unexpected happen to me." Martinius steepled his fingers and appeared dissatisfied. That was fair; for the first time ever, the company would pass to those outside of the Novak family.

My darling mother, not gifted with any social graces whatsoever, took the opportunity to make things even more awkward. "What happened to your boy?" She at least asked this with a modicum of sympathy in her voice.

"A degenerative blood condition that we'd known about since his birth finally got the better of him, I'm afraid. We did everything we could to increase his chances for a long life, but it seemed God had other ideas. My wife is also no longer with us. The loss of our child proved too much for her to bear." This speech was delivered plainly, although the topic must have been extremely painful for Martinius.

Another hush descended, which was again broken by my mother. "What about Antoni?"

I shot my mother a look of horror. I wanted to slap my palm to my forehead but I held back.

"Mira," Simon said under his breath.

I was relieved when Martinius laughed. "It's quite all right, Simon. I'll be sure to take him into consideration."

The tension was broken with his chuckle and some of the men took the opportunity to ask Martinius more details about the wreck. Before long, the men moved into an adjoining room to talk. Mom gave me a kiss on the forehead and went with them.

I was happy to head back to the suite as I felt very full and wanted to relax. I made my way back through the windowed hallway which was now barely lit with the glow of sundown when I saw Antoni's broad-shouldered shape coming down the main staircase.

"How was dinner?" he asked, as we met in the foyer. He had a stack of file folders in his arms.

"It was great. Martinius seems... great," I said, feeling lame.

"He is. Did he tell you about *The Sybellen*? How long we've been looking for it?" He had such an open expression. It was difficult not to like him.

"Yeah, it's a pretty amazing story."

"We're very excited that you guys are here. So, Martinius told me to show you around, did you want me to take you out to Gdańsk sometime? Or perhaps, show you some of the best beaches?" He held my gaze very directly, an anticipatory smile on his face.

"Yeah, that would be nice. Thank you, Antoni." I wasn't entirely sure how I felt about being assigned a chaperone but he seemed like he'd make good company. I agreed to meet him the next day after breakfast.

I mused to myself as I made my way back to our suite. I was going to be spending some time with a very handsome twenty-something. True to form, I was more excited about seeing my friends' reactions to a photo of him than actually spending time with him.

11

M uch to my surprise, Antoni and I ended up spending time together every day that week. I barely saw Mom since she was stuck in meetings with the team every day. She fell into bed complaining that men talk too much. I don't know if it was because she was bored with the tedium of analytics or if spending her time in a room full of guys who both desired and detested her sapped her energy.

Although the temperatures were warm, we had cloudy skies and sprinklings of rain all week so we spent a lot of time in Gdańsk. It was weather for museums and cafes. Antoni knew a lot about the city and it was obvious from the way his face lit up when talking about the architecture that he loved history. On Monday and Tuesday we visited three different museums, and on Wednesday he showed me the shopping district and we walked along the canals. On Thursday, we visited Malbork Castle, a UNESCO World Heritage Site and a gorgeous Gothic construct. It was the largest medieval castle in Europe and easily the site that thrilled me the most.

We took the night tour, one that Antoni had taken at least three times already and said he'd never be sick of. It had been built by

Teutonic Knights and crusaders and was filled with art, armour, and courtyards with shadowy corners.

We strolled the grounds after our tour, not wanting to leave. Antoni stopped to admire a sculpture of a knight and stepped into a circle of light. Under the guise of photographing something beyond him, I zoomed in and snapped a picture. I sent it off to the girls with the caption: *Strolling Malbork Castle with my own personal tour guide.*

Right after I hit send, Antoni looked over at me, his expression thoughtful. A dimple appeared in his cheek. Our eyes met and he held my gaze for longer than was polite, but then broke the tension with a grin. I couldn't help but smile back.

He took me to a place called Kubicki for dinner, and translated everything on the menu. I wasn't picky so I asked him to choose a local dish for me. What arrived was an artfully arranged plate of perogies stuffed with duck. Antoni had wild boar in gingerbread sauce and insisted I try it. The flavour combination was something completely new to me, as was the feeling of being on a date with someone who wasn't a high school buddy. *It's not a date*, I reminded myself, but it sure was hard to tell the difference.

"I'm the oldest of three," Antoni was saying. "I have a brother Otto and a half-sister Lydia. I adore both of them but I'm closer with my brother. My mom remarried and had Lydia, who is still in high school, I'm pretty uncool to her right now," he chuckled. "How about you? Any siblings?" He popped a piece of boar into his mouth.

I shook my head. "Only child. Although I have three girlfriends who pretty much feel like sisters."

"And your dad? The man who got your mom must be quite a guy," he grinned. "Wish I could meet him."

"Sorry to say that's not possible," I said. "My dad passed away when I was seven."

Antoni's wine glass paused halfway to his lips. "I'm sorry." He took a sip and then put his wineglass down. "My dad passed away, too. I was five. Lung cancer. Vicious smoker."

"That sucks," I said, making a face. "I'm sorry, dude."

He looked at me thoughtfully. "Turns out we've both done most of our growing up without fathers."

I nodded, and my heart gave an old familiar ache. Grief was a deep-sea monster lurking far below, occasionally wrapping a cold tentacle around an ankle to pull me under. The monster used to have me completely tangled up, suffocating me, but as the years went by its grip loosened. It still liked to remind me that it hadn't gone away completely. I changed the subject. "How did you end up working for Martinius?"

I scraped my plate clean with a piece of bread from the basket and a waiter appeared at my elbow to remove it.

Antoni spoke to the waiter in Polish before he asked me, "Do you like strawberries? It's what they have for dessert tonight."

"Of course!"

The waiter nodded and left.

"I graduated with a degree in Business Admin and was lucky to win a four month internship at Novak as part of my final year. I must have done something right because Lambert Pykelk, the Director of Business Development, offered me a permanent position as his assistant. Before long, he started inviting me to strategic sessions which was how I was able to work more closely with Martinius."

The waiter returned, cleared away Antoni's empty plate and set a bowl of lumpy pink soup with a dollop of something white and creamy on top. I thanked him in Polish and both men smiled. I had probably butchered the words.

Antoni watched me inspect the dessert. "It's strawberry soup with white chocolate mousse."

I took a spoonful of the soup and closed my eyes as the tart sweetness filled my mouth. I swallowed and smacked my lips. "Wow. Can I have a vat of this?" Antoni laughed, which made me laugh. The sound was goofy and contagious.

Antoni took a bite and went on. "Martinius asked me if I'd like to take on the role of his P.A. and I jumped at it. I manage his personal schedule and attend meetings with him, but I really took it because I want to learn as much as I can. He's a brilliant businessman."

"So, what's the long term goal then?" I asked as we finished off the sweet soup.

"Well, I'd be lying if I didn't say that I hoped to be a contender for Director of Business Development. Novak has a great reputation and low turnover. We tend to promote from within. But I'm young and there are a lot of smart people who have been in the company for a long time. I'll have to put in my time and really prove myself if I want to be taken seriously."

"Man, you sound so driven," I said, licking the last of the dessert from my spoon and looking sadly into my empty bowl. I looked up at him. "I still have no idea what I want to do with my life."

"You'll figure it out," he said, smiling. "One day at a time."

"What are you doing chaperoning a teenager around instead of climbing the company ladder? You must resent me a little bit." I was joking but I must have hit the nail on the head because he paused, his mouth half open.

"You're far too astute for someone so young," he said, finally.

"Am I right, then?" My cheeks coloured with embarrassment. I didn't want to spend time with someone who saw me as a waste of time.

"Let me just say that firstly, when Martinius asks a favour of me, I find it easy to put aside my personal feelings. Serving him is a pleasure. And secondly, even if I had concerns about spending my time this way before I met you, I am happy to admit that I was sorely mistaken. This is just where I need to be right now."

My mind skipped over his sweet sentiment, caught by something else he said. "Martinius asked you to host me as a favour? Why would he do that?"

He shrugged, "Something to do with wanting to keep your mom focused on the salvage, I suspect. She'll do her best work if she knows you're well taken care of. Martinius doesn't do anything without a good reason."

The waiter came to clean away our dessert. He put two, steaming mugs of in front of us, saying something to Antoni.

"How kind," Antoni said, peering at the brown liquid. "It's a complimentary digestive tea."

I sniffed it. It smelled like dirt. I blew on it and took a tentative sip. It tasted better than it smelled, sort of like liquorice.

"Tell me more about your dad," Antoni said. "What was his name?"

"Nathan. He used to play guitar and sing to me every night before bed. He'd sing me made up songs and tell funny stories. A lot of times they featured my mom as a princess. He was pretty nuts about her."

There was a pause and he held my gaze, his eyes lingering on my face. For a moment I forgot what I was saying.

"I'm sure he was," he said, softly.

I cleared my throat. "He was a hardworking guy, my dad. A contractor. He never had to advertise a day in his life because everyone knew that he'd get the job done right. He was also a great hockey player and played in a beer league over the winter."

"Ah yes," laughed Antoni. "The famous Canadian hockey game. You know we Poles aren't so shabby at hockey ourselves."

"I have heard that. In fact, I'm pretty sure my father played with a few Polish guys."

"Is that a fact?"

"Well, no," I laughed. "I was only eight when he passed away so I can't say for sure."

"What happened?" His brows pushed downward, his pupils roved over my face. I couldn't decide whether his attentiveness meant he was attracted to me or just that he was an active listener. It was impossible to guess what he was thinking. He would make a very good politician.

"He died on the ice. Heart failure. It was a real shock because he was still so young. We never even knew he had heart issues."

He shook his head and made a single 'tsk' sound with his tongue. "What a shame. And your mom never remarried?"

I tried not to laugh. "Mom is more focused on dodging men than dating them. Her passion is diving. Who knows, maybe one day she'll fall in love again. But I haven't seen her take an interest in anyone since my dad died."

"I'm sure she has her hands full if she wants to stay single. You don't see women like your mother every day." His eyes lingered on mine.

"Are you crushing on her too?" I took a sip of my water, keeping my eyes on him.

He laughed. "She's pretty amazing, but no. Your mom..." he paused and leaned in to whisper, "...she scares me."

I laughed. "Dude, you have no idea."

As we pulled up to the garage and left Antoni's Jeep for the valet to park, I was surprised by how much I had enjoyed the night. I found myself sneaking glances at him when he didn't know I was looking, trying to search within myself for how I felt.

Before we went into the manor we stood in the yard to admire the stars. We walked out into the darkness, the soft grass cushioning our footfalls. His hand went to the small of my back, a caring gesture as we couldn't see where we were stepping. The clouds had finally broken and the black sky was filled with fairy lights. He dropped his hand from my back when we stopped walking and looked up.

"Gorgeous," I said. This sky looked very different than the one I had seen from Georjie's back yard less than two weeks ago.

"Yep. We might actually get a nice day tomorrow. If it's warm enough would you like to go to the beach?" He turned his face towards me in the dark.

"Yes, please. I love the ocean." How could I not, with a siren for a mother?

Our serenity was interrupted by boisterous male voices. Two people entered through the gate at the end of the driveway. I recognized their voices: Eric and Jeff. It was obvious they'd had a few drinks. They weren't aware of our presence.

"Idiot Pollacks," spat Eric. "If they wanted the job they shouldn't be such shit divers. Old man Novak ain't stupid. He knows pros when he sees 'em. That's the last time I'll spend my money in that pub."

"Ha!" Jeff responded. "Your money? Does your bookie know you're drinking his earnings away in Poland?"

There was the sound of a fist making contact with a body and air leaving a chest by force. "Shut up, jackass. You're gonna help me make it right."

They disappeared around the side of the manor. We heard a door open and close.

"I'm sorry," I said. I was embarrassed and horrified that Eric had used a racist slur. Simon would have been mortified.

"It's not your fault," Antoni answered. "I know men and I know drink. I also recognize men with gambling problems, and I think that guy Eric is in a bit of trouble."

"How do you know?" I asked as we climbed the steps to the main entrance.

"I've overheard them in the evenings a couple of times now. They like to play poker and he gets a little too involved, let's say. They invited me a few times, which I appreciate but I don't know how to play poker. Besides, they play for real money and I'm not interested in losing mine that way."

He sounded more straight-laced and responsible than any other guy I'd known. Surprisingly, I found it more attractive than I'd ever found the guys with a reputation for being 'exciting' to be. The dangerous guys were more to Saxony's taste.

We went through the foyer, the lights had been dimmed for the night and the space was full of shadows. We went up to the first landing, where Antoni and I needed to go our separate ways. Suddenly, I felt awkward, like it was the end of a date. "Thanks for another great day, I had a lot of fun," I said, clasping my hands in front of me and feeling like an idiot.

"Thank you too. It's not every day that I get to spend time in such lovely company and be paid for it," he responded.

And there it was. He was being paid to take care of me. In the game of he likes me, he likes me not, I just swung back in the direction of *not* for the tenth time that day. I was getting a little seasick. I gave him a boyish shove on the shoulder with my fist. "Night, Antoni."

"´Spij dobrze," he responded, and turned away.

My phone vibrated when I was just outside my suite.

Georjayna: *Who's the cute marine?*

She was referring to his short hairstyle and his Novak Shipping jacket, which looked like a navy uniform.

Me: *That's Antoni. I've been assigned a babysitter.*

Saxony piped in too. *Hello. He can babysit me anytime. Is he funny?*

Me: *He's Polish. Everything he says is funny. We're just frnds.*

Saxony: *WHAT. R U Unwell? WkeUp, T-Nation.*

Georjayna: *He's rather pretty, isn't he. Nice guy?*

Me: *Very.*

Georjayna: *Lucky you.*

Georjayna sent through a photograph of a young man walking in front of a vine-covered building that looked like it might be a garage. He was carrying several broken old windows. I clicked on the photo and zoomed in on him. He was muscular and darkly tanned. Dark hair curled out from under a baseball cap, and he had dramatically dark eyebrows and eyelashes.

Me: *Looks like you lucked out too. Tall?*

Georjayna: *He's a giraffe. Even next to me.*

Saxony: *What the... Is that your COUSIN?!*

Georjayna: *Not by blood. Adopted, remember?*

Saxony: *Merciful heavens.*

Me: *What's he like?*

Georjayna: *Friendly as a nest of vipers. Nothing lucky about it.*

Saxony: *Would you like me to have him killed? I've been here two weeks and I've already made friends in the mafia.*

Poor Georjayna. It didn't sound like her summer in Ireland was off to a good start if her cousin was going to be a miserable sod.

I closed my phone case and let myself into our suite, thinking back to the boys I'd dated. They'd all seemed so young, so immature. So, in Antoni, I had found an older guy – a very attractive older guy. He was smart, sincere, driven, funny, and gentlemanly. All things being equal, I should finally be feeling the heart palpitations and the butterflies, shouldn't I?

12

The next day was overcast but we deemed it worthy enough to be a beach day. I was excited to do something different. I loved the history and architecture, frequenting the cute cafes and strolling by the canals. But I was dying to let my hair loose and go for a swim.

Antoni had the staff put together a picnic lunch and we walked from the manor to the ocean through sandy bluffs and scrubby trees. The wind tugged at my hair, and even though it wasn't bright enough for sunglasses I put them on to keep sand from blowing in my eyes.

The beach was a half hour walk from the Novak estate and as we crested the hill, I saw it up close for the first time. It was a golden yellow colour. The water was a dark, murky blue, not dissimilar to the beaches of home. Hardy grasses poked up from the sand, waving in the wind like wheat, and at the edge of the bluff was a cluster of large stones. We crossed the scrubby section and hit the sand. The grains were large and coarse and squished up through my toes. I only wished it was a bit warmer. A lot of people must have agreed with me as there weren't many out on the beach.

"Did you know that the Baltic has much less salt than other

oceans?" Antoni asked me as we scouted for a good place to put down a blanket.

"I did actually. I mean, I didn't until the flight over here. Micah told me. He said it's one of the reasons that *The Sybellen* is in such good shape."

Antoni nodded. "That's right. We also experience big fluctuations in how much sea life we get from year to year. The currents that bring the salt down from the North Sea are always different. Sometimes, there are large areas of the Baltic that have virtually no sea life except for bacteria," he continued, sounding teacherly. "We also sometimes have algae problems over the summer because of fertilizer runoff."

"Really, how interesting, professor," I said, unfurling our beach blanket on a clear patch of sand.

He looked at me like he couldn't tell if I was being sarcastic. "Enough with the biology lesson? Time for a sun tan?"

"No," I said, stripping down to my bikini. "Time for a swim." I tossed my sunhat and sunglasses down on the blanket, which was already starting to blow away.

"You said beach. I brought you to the beach. You didn't say swim," he deadpanned, setting the sun chairs on the corners of the blanket to hold it down. He sat down in one and made a show of getting comfortable.

"You have to. It's your job, remember?" I teased.

He balled up his towel and threw it at me, but he stood up and took off his shirt and ball cap. He wore navy swim shorts with the mermaid icon embroidered on them.

"Nice shorts, princess."

He looked down. "Embroidery is very masculine I'll have you know," he said. "I have quite the reputation in town due to her." He rubbed his thumb over the mermaid. "No one messes with me."

"I'm sure they don't. You're downright intimidating."

Through shedding his layers he revealed not only that he was fit, but also that he spent more time in clothes than out of them. He was almost as pale as me, only his hide included freckles across his shoulders. Otherwise, his body was a perfect landscape of blank white skin. He was a tattoo artist's dream. He was broad and long, with a deep chest and back. But he had no ink that I could see and I wondered if he'd ever been tempted. Probably not. He was too square for that.

I laughed at his grimace when we waded into the cool sea. Cold water had never bothered me and I dove in and swam out far enough to lose the bottom. I stuck my tongue out to taste the Baltic. Nothing.

Antoni didn't give me the satisfaction of splashing him before he'd had a chance to adjust to the temperature. He braced himself and dove in, popping up moments later and bellowing something in Polish. I laughed but didn't ask him to interpret.

We chatted while we swam out to sea and then parallel along the beach for a while, and then back. Antoni's teeth started to chatter.

"Ok, I'm a popsicle. Can I go now? You're a freaking polar bear." He put his feet down on the sand and stood. His nipples were completely erect and gooseflesh covered his lean body.

"Go on, then." I splashed his back as he ran away.

He made a caricature of himself as he ran out of the water, exaggerating being stiff and frozen. It worked – I laughed. I found myself feeling wistful as I watched him dry off. He was perfect and by far the most interesting, attractive guy I'd ever spent time with. Yet, somehow, I was still void of desire. I wanted the warm feeling Saxony always talked about.

Before long he was back in his clothes with his towel around him. He sat down in the sun chair and pulled a book out of the beach bag.

I swam for long enough to tire myself out then headed back to shore. It wasn't that much fun swimming on my own. The wind picked up and goosebumps swept across my skin as I left the water and ran back to our blanket. I pulled a giant towel out of our bag and wrapped it around myself.

Antoni said, "I know it's early, but swimming always makes me hungry. Do you want to eat something?" he asked as he stuck his nose into the bag. "We've got fish sandwiches, apples, and cheese. Oh, and..." he pulled out a bottle full of brown liquid and squinted at the label doubtfully. "Iced tea?"

My stomach growled. "Absolutely, I'm actually starving."

The sound of the waves breaking on the shore had intensified. My wet hair whipped into my face, stinging my eyes. "The wind is picking up," I said. "I'm not so sure we picked the perfect day to spend at the beach." I sat down on the blanket, towelling my hair.

Antoni pulled out one of the sandwiches and handed it to me. He looked thoughtful. "You're right. You know what we should do instead? I can't believe I'm only thinking of it now. The wind is perfect for it."

"What's that?" I unwrapped the herring sandwich and took a big bite. It was saltier than I'd expected but delicious. The bread was fresh.

"Take out the laser." He unwrapped his own sandwich.

I swallowed my bite. "What's a laser?"

"It's a two-person boat. It's fun and it's fast. You want to?" His eyebrows shot up and he gave me the enthusiastic look I had come to like.

"I'm game."

"Do you get seasick?" he asked as we were eating our apples and cheese.

I shook my head. "I never have so far, but I don't spend a lot of time on boats. Is it pretty..." I mimicked the movements of an unstable vessel with my hand.

He laughed. "Yes, it's as tippy as a surfboard. That's part of the fun."

"Good thing we just ate."

He looked concerned. "Should we wait until after we've digested?"

"No, I'm only kidding. I think that's an old wives tale anyway."

Fifteen minutes later we headed back to the estate. I changed into shorts and a sun shirt, and Antoni said he'd find me a pair of water shoes.

We took the staff at the boathouse by surprise and they scrambled to get the laser down and ready to go. Although they weren't speaking in English, I could sort of tell what was being said. Antoni kept apologizing and telling them not to worry, that it was a last minute decision. He was kind, but they still looked embarrassed that they hadn't been able to read the mind of Martinius' PA.

The laser turned out to be even smaller than I imagined. There were two diminutive sails and the boom was so low that you had to almost lay flat in the boat to duck under it as it swung back and forth. The vessel was so shallow that it was more like a raft.

Antoni held the boat still in the shallows while I got in. Just as we were pushing the boat out into deeper water one of the boathouse staff called something to Antoni from the dock. Antoni told me he'd asked us to wait a moment.

The man dashed back into the boathouse and emerged with a two-way radio, which he tossed to Antoni. He caught it and snapped it onto his belt. He took hold of the rudder and turned the raft so the sail caught the wind. The laser immediately lurched forward. The shore fell away behind us.

Antoni taught me how to steer with the rudder, and lean out over the water when the boat seemed like it was going to tip. The faster we went, the steeper the boat angled.

"Want to go for another swim?" he asked. Before I could answer we were tilting so sharp and going so fast it took my breath away. I laughed, half joyful and half freaking that we were going to tip. We both leaned out over the water together for counterbalance. The waves zoomed by underneath us. The feeling of being on the edge made my heart leap into my throat.

The wind pushed us along at an increasing speed and the beach curved alongside, moving away and then moving closer as we traveled. We sailed for close to an hour, and I was amazed at how much ground we'd covered in that time. I could see the Gdańsk port off in the distance.

A small ray jumped out of the water less than five feet from us. It flashed his belly at us and I got a clear view of his straight mouth and tiny eyes.

"He's checking us out. Those devil rays are super curious," Antoni said.

A few minutes later, Antoni called over the wind and waves, "We should turn around. Going back is going to take longer because we'll have to tack against the wind."

"Just a little further. Please?" I begged. I loved it. "I might have to put 'laser' on my Christmas list."

He grinned. "Like it?"

"I haven't had this much fun in... Ever."

"Hang on to your sunglasses!" We caught another gust of wind. We picked up speed again, and as we leaned out over the water together the boat went up on its side. I felt like my face was going to crack from grinning.

We hit choppier water and skipped like a pebble. The scenery of the beach had changed, now there were more rocks and artificial breakers. There were a few people on the beach, picking their way along the rocks - small figures in the distance. A few of them waved.

After another fifteen minutes, Antoni slowed the laser. "Let's turn around. The wind is picking up and those look mildly unfriendly." He pointed and I turned and looked back in the direction we'd come. Mildly unfriendly was an understatement for the thunderheads darkening over the water. I swallowed down my anxiety. If Antoni was calm, then I would be too.

Calmly, Antoni steered the boat in a circle, giving me directions. "Pull the tiller towards you and lean back to push the bow out of the water. Yep. Just like that."

We had to sail in a zigzag fashion when going against the wind. The thunderheads looked heavy and full of rain, but I thought we had a good chance of making it back to the boathouse before the showers came. The ride turned rough, my neck jarred a few times as the boat dropped into hollows between waves. I kept my mouth shut so I didn't bite my tongue.

Once Antoni had shown me how to tack, he stopped talking. He was at the rudder and I was in front. It wasn't until I looked back at his face after he'd been quiet for a while that I noticed that his mouth was tight. There was a deep line between his eyes that hadn't been there before.

"Anything wrong?" I asked. "The look on your face is making me nervous."

"We're ok. Just wish we'd headed back sooner. These waves are a little too choppy for my liking."

We settled back to the business of sailing, but soon I felt like Antoni was having difficulty keeping us on course. The wind was much stronger now, ripping at the sails and ropes. Fear began to curdle in my belly when I realized that the boathouse was no closer than it had been ten minutes earlier.

A huge gust caught our sail and before I could react, the laser was wrenched over and I was dumped back into the cold embrace of the Baltic.

13

I flailed under the water, twisting to right myself. When I finally popped up I saw that the laser was on its side and Antoni had crawled up on top of it and was clinging to it like a monkey. I paddled towards him but the wind shoved the boat away from me much faster than I was able to swim.

Antoni looked around, his face serious. He spotted me and called over the growing expanse of ocean between us, "Targa, are you hurt?"

"No, I'm ok!" I replied, and received a mouthful of water for my efforts. I coughed and spat and then called, "The wind is pushing you away from me. I can't keep up!" I was swimming as fast as I could but the waves had more control over where I went than I did, and the life-jacket made my movements sluggish.

I watched as Antoni tried to yank the laser upright. I was surprised by how rapidly he was moving away from me. His face was growing smaller, harder to read. I never would have thought the wind could push a tipped boat so fast through the waves.

The laser wasn't very big but it had two sails which were both now under the water. It was completely on its side with Antoni perched awkwardly on top. It wasn't going to sink because it was made of fiberglass, but the only chance Antoni had of rescuing me was to get it sitting upright again.

He yanked and pulled on the mast with all his might, using his considerable weight. The sails lifted out of the water a few inches but wouldn't go any higher. Lasers were made to flip upright easily, but this one was designed for two people.

"The radio," I called, and got slapped in the face with another wave. I gasped and coughed.

He already had the radio up to his mouth. I couldn't hear him over the wind. In one angry motion, he threw the radio violently into the water. Why had he done that? Cold dread expanded in my stomach.

He called something over the water to me but he was so far away now that I couldn't make out a word. I was beginning to tire. If he didn't right the boat now, we each had an impossible decision to make. Antoni could abandon the laser and we could try to swim to land together, or he could continue to try to right the laser. The longer he tried, the more exhausted he would become and the further from me the wind would push him. At what point would we not be able to find each other anymore?

I on the other hand, could flail after him uselessly with my life vest holding me back or just stop swimming and bob in the wind and the waves and wait for him, hoping. A third option presented itself. I could take off the lifejacket and hold it out in front of me like a water-board and use my legs to swim, either after the laser or towards the shore. I knew that I could swim a lot faster than I was swimming now. With every stroke I could feel the water swirl between my back and the life vest, creating drag.

Antoni and the laser were now so far away that I couldn't make out his face anymore. The boat was still on its side and I could see him pulling on it for all he was worth. He was yanking on it so violently, I wondered if he might accidentally snap the mast off.

I lay back in my life vest and floated, mulling the situation over. I closed my eyes and took deep breaths to squash the voice screaming *panic* in my head.

The cold was finally seeping into my bones. I shivered and my jaw clacked. I did not relish the thought of waiting and getting colder. I always felt better when I took action. This must have been something that my mother passed on to me. Never was she one to sit around and react to what life dealt her, she always took matters into her own hands.

I opened my eyes and my heart fell into a pit. The sky was getting darker by the second. A huge wave smashed me in the face, leaving me spitting and panting. That was it. I had to try.

I unsnapped my life vest, twisted the loose ends of the belt around my wrists and pushed it out in front of me. Up and down in the swells I went. I strained to look over the waves to see what had happened to Antoni and he was now a distant figure, barely visible. He disappeared behind a wall of water, and then appeared again, still struggling.

He was too far now for me to reach, so I pointed myself towards shore, which was alarmingly far away. I flattened out on the surface and began to kick my legs, but my kicks seemed useless to propel me. Was it possible that, despite my efforts, I was getting further from land? It felt like I was just getting dragged out to sea. I had never felt so powerless. My chin wobbled, and I fought back the urge to cry. How had things turned so bad so quickly?

A huge wave engulfed me and I was pulled under. My right hand let go of the lifejacket and that was all it took. The vest yanked out of my left hand like it was the ripcord of a lawn mower. The rope burn was hot and sudden. What a stupid mistake I had made. If I had had time for emotions other than fear and panic I might have felt humiliated, angry, and stupid.

Immediately I sank. All energy redirected to locating the surface. My lungs burned for air. I finally emerged and gulped oxygen greedily, looking around for the lifejacket.

The yellow vest was already several meters away. I splashed toward it but my exhausted limbs flailed uselessly. I had no control anymore and without something to hang onto I sank low in the water, feeling the enemy of my own weight in this saltless sea.

Another wave buried me, pulled me under, pushed me down and turned me over.

Panic set in full blast as I tumbled like a sock in a washing machine. *Survive*, my mind screamed. *Oxygen*, my lungs wailed. *Surface*, my limbs cried. *Which direction is up?*

I opened my eyes. There was a source of light and a blob of dark in my muddled vision, but I was churning around so fast that they kept changing places.

Stop spinning and swim away from the dark, Targa! My chest burned. I rallied my fatigued limbs and made a push towards what I thought was the surface, but given my disorientation, I could have been sending myself deeper.

Where are you, Mother?

Another voice, one unattached to the outcome, laughed at the irony of the daughter of a mermaid, dead by drowning. Was this really how it was going to end?

As I made one more desperate push toward what I thought was the surface, something hard hit me brutally on the very top of my head.

In shock and pain, I gasped for air, but there was none to be had. Water flooded my mouth and filled my lungs. Liquid went where it was not wanted and filled every branch in my lungs that was screaming for sweet, life-filled oxygen. The pain was excruciating, but worse than that was a feeling of betrayal. My own body had failed me. My body spasmed in an effort to expel the sea water but it lasted only a moment, for everything then went black and I knew no more.

14

Pain.

I was alive. I had to be, because I was in agony. There wasn't supposed to be pain in heaven, right? Or maybe I'd gone to hell. I didn't think hell would be quite so prescriptive with its discomforts though. My eyes hurt and my neck burned. My head ached with a dull throb. I felt weightless, temperature-less. I felt myself turning, drifting, being cradled. I was suspended in fluid, but this fluid was richer than water. There was so much more... information, in this fluid. Had I died and been re-born? Was I drifting in amniotic fluid, about to be born anew as some other person?

A crack of light entered my pupils and pain sliced through my head - a searing line of fire. I squeezed my eyes shut. Hands covered my face. My hands. I forced my eyes open. Why did they hurt so much? I felt confused, disoriented. My memory was fuzzy, as though I was trapped between deep sleep and consciousness.

Fluid. Not amniotic fluid. Water. Traces of salt. I could taste the salt, what little there was, through my skin. The salt pulled me, tugged me gently back to consciousness.

Why was I in the sea? I tried to take a deep breath to clear my head. Oxygen flooded my brain but no air filled my lungs. With the oxygen my vision cleared, and cleared, and cleared, now so sharp it was painful. Everything became acute lines, striking contrasts and jagged edges against softness.

I looked toward the source of light above me. *Baltic*. I was twenty or so feet below the surface. Water moved ferociously above me yet down here it was so peaceful. I looked down. Another thirty feet stretched between the ocean floor and myself. A small blue item rolled across the sand, caught by my razor-sharp vision. A water shoe. Mine?

I could easily see a long way in every direction. Underwater terrain and ocean scape stretched out beneath and around me. Sand drifted back and forth across the marine floor. Seaweed fronds waved with green tendrils, welcoming me to their environment. They were mesmerizing, as was the play of light and shadow across the rocks.

Red rock formations rose up from the sandy floor. One so high that it nearly reached the surface. A fuzzy memory of sudden pain on the top of my head surfaced to consciousness and I wondered if that was what I had crashed into. I touched my skull and winced. A goose-egg had formed, tall and proud like a horn.

A tickling sensation floated past my belly and I looked down, my shorts were shredded and caught around my waist. Below that I no longer had legs, but a silvery white tail. It gleamed in the light. The metallic, pearly sheen of it was all colours and no colours, like a sardine flashing in the sun. The light glinted harshly off it and into my eyes and I blinked at the strange sensation. My eyes had developed a new way of seeing, and what entered my vision and then into my brain was like sitting down to a feast of overly rich foods. I didn't have the ability to digest what was in front of me. It was all too much colour, too much texture, too much depth, too many dimensions.

My brain tried to move the legs that I no longer had. The metallic tail moved instead, propelling me abruptly and awkwardly towards the surface. I floundered and tried to stop; the sensation of movement threw every sense into turmoil. My arms shot out, my hands open and flat, trying to stabilize. Water caught between my fingers. Being still was all I could handle for the moment. I felt awkward in this foreign body, almost afraid of it. Underneath the information my senses were taking in, there was a throb of power, as though I had gone to sleep as weak an infant and woken up fully grown and strong.

Underneath the processing of my new reality was an awareness that this change, my new self, was something I had wanted for my entire life. There was someone that I loved deeply who needed to know what was happening to me, someone who would be incredulous. Joyful.

All concept of time vanished as I drifted, too overwhelmed to move. My brain adjusted slowly to my hyper-powerful eyes, and to the new sensations and information that my skin and scales were taking in. The painful edges of details jarring my heightened senses began to soften. The overwhelm slowly dimmed.

I curled my tail back and forth, using my arms and hands to stabilize and direct myself. I drifted forward, giving myself time to become accustomed to how to move my body.

I was not drawn to the choppy surface. Instinctively, I knew that down here was where the peace was. I changed direction and familiarized myself with my new musculature. My heart was pounding hard, but the speed of it was slow, much slower than my heart had ever beaten before. It was a heavy, powerful thud in my chest, but not more than once every two seconds. Though I was in shock I did not panic. I felt a calm amidst my confusion.

I looked down, inspecting myself closely for the first time. My tail was very long and covered in layered scales. Long delicate and transparent fins trailed from the end, which I could spread or close in a similar way to fingers. I ran my hands down my tail and discovered with surprise that it was much more sensitive to the touch than my skin was. I could feel the currents of water sweeping around me, and that the water below me was moving in a different direction than the water above me. I could read that the temperature closer to the surface was different than the temperature below me, but I felt neither cold nor hot myself.

A flash of annoyance at the fabric that was encasing me, irritating me, and I ripped my sun shirt off. I held it for a moment, looking at it with disdain. Why did I need such a hindrance? Not willing to discard it to float in the ocean like so much garbage, I knotted the long sleeves around my waist.

I began to swim with more purpose this time, and as my speed increased rapidly, I couldn't help but smile for the first time since my re-birth. I was flying! I lost all care for the pains throughout my body. The sensation of propelling myself through water intoxicated me. I laughed spontaneously and then laughed again at the queer sound of my own voice, how loud it was. Then I became aware of the sounds all around me.

Distant fish gliding through the water, snapping and crackling sounds, even the sound of a whale many miles away. In the back of my brain, very far away, someone had told me that there wasn't much sea life in the Baltic. I knew differently now because there was a symphony of sounds all around me proving there was plenty of life down here.

Water caught again at my hands and I looked to see transparent webbing between my fingers, and my skin was stark and white with a faint green tinge. Was that my colour or was it just the light that made me look green?

As I slowed, I registered that my neck felt stiff and wrenched out of place, like someone had tried to hang me. I also noted a burning sensation on either side of my neck. I moved my hands to touch, my fingertips searching for the source of my pain. There. Underneath and a little behind my ears. Four small gills on either side, opening and closing. Pulling in water, extracting the oxygen and feeding it into my blood.

I rubbed the muscles in my neck and the ache slowly subsided. I marvelled at the feel of water sweeping over my gills. They worked automatically, but I could also pull the water in and push it out at will. Sort of like hyperventilating with human lungs.

Oxygen and salt, no matter how trace it was, were working together to clear the death from my body. They were erasing it, diluting it, nullifying it. My memory began to return with more clarity. I began to register rational thought as well as emotions, as what had happened began to come clear. The shock of drowning was wearing off and the realization of what I had become was setting in.

I had died. Drowned in the Baltic. I now remembered the fire in my lungs as they had filled with water, the panic of suffocation, the awful feeling of betrayal. I had died. I knew it as surely as I knew that there was a sea turtle gliding low over the stones below me, its shell a symphony of greens and its movements as graceful as a dancer.

I had died.

And now, I was a mermaid. I had finally become my mother's daughter.

15

In a burst of excitement, I exploded through the water like a torpedo. I spiralled through the sea, shot toward the surface and broke through, my new body clearing the waves easily. Above the waves, air filled my human lungs before I sliced back into the water and my gills took over again.

With the air in my lungs, a quiet voice spoke.

Antoni.

I landed in the water and took oxygen in through my gills. I ignored the voice. I was having too much fun swimming and spinning, diving and ascending, observing this vast new world. I had explorations to make, which were far more important than the voice whispering in the back of my brain.

I spied something on the ocean floor that wiped the smile from my face. It was a crab walking across the sand but it moved slowly, awkwardly, painfully. I focused in on him, my eyes pulling him forward and sharpening his edges. He'd become tangled in a piece of fishing line.

I swam towards him and shocked myself again at the speed with which I could move. I had been far away but I was on him in half a breath. He put up his little claws in a defensive stance. I stopped before him, and his pincers slowly lowered halfway. Through the water, I picked up tiny waves of fear, but the emotion was dull, instinctual. He was a simple creature. He was frightened, but he had already accepted his new reality, that he couldn't move properly anymore. There was no self-pity or uncertainty, only wariness and a determination to live.

I had never seen much beauty in crabs before; I had always found them to be creepy. Their pincers were uninviting, and the way they scuttled around on too many legs was too much like a spider for my liking. But through my new eyes, he was as beautiful as a creature could get. His body was flat on top and the colour of rust. His pincers were cream coloured with little scarlet tips. He looked at me with his tiny black eyes and I saw emotion where I'd never been able to see it with my human eyes.

"You're ok. I'm not going to hurt you," I said, and was startled to discover my new voice. It didn't burble and gurgle the way a humans does when they try to speak underwater. No bubbles came out of my mouth because I wasn't dispelling air; I was just emitting sound. My voice had a multi-layered, musical quality. It sounded like three violins, each playing a single note harmonized with the others, each word blended into the next.

He lowered his claws all the way and was still. I reached my hand towards him very slowly. I untangled the filament from his body and tied it around my shredded shorts. The idea of leaving it to float in the water was abhorrent to me.

The little crab opened and closed his pincers and then shuffled off across the sand, moving much more naturally than before.

Antoni, said the quiet voice, a little more insistent this time. It was like I had two minds, one in the back that was trying to tell me that something urgently needed my attention and that I should surface, and one in the front telling me to explore this new world and my new body.

I swam up to where the water was churning from the storm. My head broke the surface. The wind hit me in the face and I took a huge breath into my lungs. Like a duster through thick cobwebs, my thoughts cleared.

Where is Antoni? I have to find him! How long have I been swimming about? What is wrong with me?

Holy shit. I'm a mermaid.

I scanned the surface of the sea, my anxiety mounting. The waves were higher and more powerful than before but instead of being alarmed by them, I relished the churning water. The storm was making the ocean alive, filling it with oxygen and distributing minerals and nutrients throughout.

I have to find my mother, tell her... tell her...

The clouds overhead were black and thunderous and I could feel a light spitting of rain in my face. There was going to be a downpour.

I have to find Antoni. Now. Now. Now.

Holy shit. I'm not human anymore.

A tiny, white dot far out to sea caught my eye. It had to be the laser. I dove and flipped my tail and took off towards it. The ocean floor flew by. Stones and rock formations zoomed by underneath me. I passed a small piece of broken ship and felt a strong urge to stop and investigate.

As my gills took over the job of breathing, the urgency of finding Antoni faded away. Something in me registered that it was important to stay close to the surface. So I rose again and began to swim like a dolphin, leaping out of the water, inhaling gulps of air, and then diving back under the surface. My thoughts cleared again and I focused on finding Antoni.

I approached the laser, still on its side and buffeted by the sea. Antoni was nowhere to be seen. A heavier panic set into my human brain. I scanned the waves wildly, desperate for anything that looked like a human form. I knew I'd be able to find him better under the water so I submerged and looked around.

There! A flash of yellow lifejacket. He had drifted a long way from the laser. I could read in the way his form moved that he was drifting lifelessly at the mercy of the ocean.

"No. No, no, no," I said out loud as I reached him. The violins in my throat were still there, melancholic and leaden with fear for my friend.

Antoni was face down in the water. "Antoni!" I rolled him over and lifted his face to the sky. I called his name, slapped his cheek. His hazel eyes were open and lifeless. Living eyes did not look like that. I put my sensitive fingers to his throat. No heartbeat. He was dead.

16

I buoyed him up easily. Placing an arm under his back, I lifted him up on top of the water and held us there with my powerful tail.

I fastened my mouth over his slack one and filled his lungs with air. Water burbled in his chest. I changed tactics. Instead of blowing into his lungs, I sucked, pulling very gently. I drew the sea water towards me, slowly, slowly, up from his lungs and into his mouth. I pulled steadily until I tasted the sea water in my own mouth and expelled it through my gills. It trickled down my neck. I kept pulling in one smooth motion until no more water came out. There wasn't a lot. It was remarkable how little water a human could drown on.

Then, without breaking the seal of my mouth over his, I changed gears again and pulled oxygen in through my nose and pushed it into his lungs. His chest inflated under my hands. When his lungs were full, I opened his mouth with one hand and pressed on his chest to expel the air.

Keeping one hand under his back to support him, I placed my other palm on his chest and pressed on his sternum, willing his heart to pump. I now had immense power in my limbs, but I wasn't conscious enough of it and I heard a crack. "Sorry," I said, grimacing.

Somewhere, I'd heard that you aren't doing CPR properly if you don't break a few ribs. I comforted myself with that thought and kept going.

I repeated this strange CPR without ceasing for what felt like a very long time until - *Thud.* His heart spoke to me, quietly. *Thud.* It was working. I stopped pressing on his chest and listened. His heart was finally beating on its own. Relief flooded through me. I kept breathing for him, but it didn't take long before he sucked in his own breath. My heart leaped. He was going to live. I turned my attention to getting him back to shore and finding help.

Cradling him in front of me, I tucked my forearms under his armpits and rested his head and neck on my shoulder. I aimed my back towards the shore and began to undulate my tail. Immediately, we moved rapidly towards land. Antoni's legs and arms trailed in the water leaving a small wake as the water hit my back and then splashed around us. The waves that had been my ruin only a short time ago were no barrier to me now. I sliced through them without effort.

Antoni coughed and gasped as rain began to fall in earnest. It came down straight, hard, and in sheets. So this was the kind of sudden, violent storm that Martinius had been talking about at dinner.

We were close to land now. I steered us towards the boathouse and found the dock.

I heard a cough and looked down at Antoni's face, so close beside mine. He was trying to open his eyes. It was hard to do in the pouring rain and with his face upturned to the sky.

The rain didn't impede my vision or bother me at all. The water hit me in the eyes but I didn't blink or react in a human way. I'd have to ask my mom about that.

Mother!

My heart did a skip as I thought of her again. She was going to be overjoyed. I couldn't wait to find her and tell her. Everything we had so wanted had come true. My mouth twisted in a wry smile. I only had to die to make it happen. I wondered if it had ever occurred to her to try drowning me when I was little, then I discarded the thought. There was no way she would have taken the risk.

We arrived at the boathouse. The door was closed but a light shone through the window. The fellows from earlier must still be inside, waiting for the storm to pass.

I lifted Antoni onto the dock like he was an infant. So this was how my mother felt; lifting 200 pounds up out of the water was no problem. Before I let him go, I felt his muscles tense and he groaned. He turned his face towards me, struggling to open his eyes in the pounding rain.

"Targa?" he croaked and started coughing.

Not good. Overwhelmed by a panicked urge to hide, I disappeared under the water, leaving him up on the dock. I grabbed a stone from the sea floor and resurfaced only long enough to hurl it at the boathouse window. It smashed through the glass and I heard someone yell. I disappeared under the surface again and swam away from the dock as fast as I could. Antoni would survive; what mattered now was not being discovered.

I followed the shoreline until I found a hidden piece of beach in between two rocky outcroppings.

Just the thought of walking was enough to transform me. My scales softened into human skin and my musculature reformed into legs in the blink of an eye. It was a nice feeling. In a moment I was walking through the shallows on bare feet.

My shorts were a shredded mess but there was enough fabric left to cover me, like wearing a tea towel that a couple of Rottweilers had used for a game of tug-o-war. I untied my sun shirt from my waist, thankful for it now, and pulled it on.

My head was pounding but I was thinking clearly. I had to get back to the manor. Antoni would either be rallying people to look for me, or he'd be raving about a mermaid like a madman.

With the wind and rain buffeting me, I ran back to the manor on tender feet. I noted my increased speed and stamina with pleasure, but by the time I got back to the property I was limping from cuts on both soles.

The gates were closed. I ran up to the intercom and pushed the buzzer.

"Tak?" said a rough male voice.

"It's Targa," I said into the intercom, not even sure that they would know who I was. "Antoni and I, we tipped the laser and then got caught in the storm. He's down at the boathouse and needs help."

The gate opened and two men came out. They took one look at me and one went back inside and reappeared with a blanket. He threw it around me. They obviously didn't speak much English, but they understood that the situation was urgent.

"Antoni," I repeated, pointing towards the ocean. "He's at the boathouse." They spoke to each other in rapid Polish. One of them wrapped an arm around my shoulders and steered me towards the manor, the other pulled a radio from his belt and spoke into it. The one with me noticed that I was limping and looked down at my feet. I didn't protest when he swept me up into his arms and carried me to the manor. My feet were stinging and bleeding. The wind and rain whipped at us as he almost ran with me down the drive.

As he was climbing the front steps with me, a Jeep pulled out of the multiple-doored garage at the far side of the property. It sped down the drive and out through the open gate.

Once in the foyer, the man set me down and yelled a stream of words. Three staff members came running. He turned to me and said, "You, ok?"

I nodded and said, "Dziękuję Ci." Or I tried anyway, my attempt at thank you was rough. He nodded but didn't smile. Worry creased his brow.

I was given a pair of disposable slippers by one of the maids and then ushered up the stairs. The man who had carried me watched me go, a deep wrinkle between his eyebrows. One of the staff, an older lady with a stern face and a severe bun in her hair, said something to the maid who then nodded and headed back down the stairs.

"Doctor," she said to me in her thick accent.

I balked. "No, please. That's not necessary. I'm fine. I'm just cold. Don't call a doctor."

"Already done," she said.

My mother never went to the doctor. She hadn't even gave birth to me in the hospital, she'd hired a midwife. I think she was worried that a doctor might notice that there was something different about her. "Do you know where my mother is?"

"At meeting. She comes," she answered.

We arrived at my suite where I heard bathwater running. These people didn't waste time. My teeth had begun to chatter. She took me into the bathroom in my suite. We passed another maid on her way out who shot me a condescending look. I didn't care. This was another change. A look like that before my change would have hurt my feelings or made me feel defensive, but now... I couldn't have cared less what she thought. If she had an issue with my getting into trouble, that was her problem, not mine.

"Edith," said the stern looking woman, pointing to her chest by way of introduction. "In tub," she pointed. She didn't seem like she was going to wait until I got undressed, and I no longer had shame about nakedness. I truly didn't care what she saw. I stripped off and got in.

The water was very hot and I gasped. My feet stung, my head throbbed and I felt the burn around my left wrist where the belt from the life vest had bruised it. I put a hand up and felt the bump on the top of my head. It was tender too, but it already seemed better than before. Mom had always told me that the mermaid gene meant faster healing. Between that and spending time in salt water, she had an unparalleled rate of recovery. I guess that was true for me now, too.

Edith noticed me touching my head and pulled my hand away to look. She clucked her tongue like a mother hen. She bent and picked up the rags of my wet clothing. She noticed the fishing line that I'd tied to my ripped shorts and gave it a puzzled look. Then she said, "Doctor comes. One hour. Mother before. I get ice."

I nodded and she disappeared, leaving the door open. I sank into the water and prayed for Mom to arrive before the doctor did.

17

I heard her before I saw her. Less than ten minutes after I'd sank into the tub, she exchanged words with Edith outside in the hall. Then she appeared in the doorway, worry etched across her face.

"Mom!" I cried out, all excitement and urgency.

"Targa!" She had her arms around me in a moment, holding me tight, my wet body soaking her Bluejacket button-down shirt.

"You hate this shirt," I sniffed. Now that I was a mermaid, I understood her revulsion for restrictive clothing better than ever.

She laughed, took my face in her hands and looked at me. She was all concern, but as she read my face she cocked her head with curiosity. "What happened?"

Emotion welled up inside me. Tears burned behind my eyelids, threatening to spill over, more from shock and happiness than the trauma of what had happened. "Let me get out and I'll tell you everything." I was pink and warm and while I was eager to tell my mother everything, I also felt an exhaustion settling into my bones. She held up a towel and I got out and wrapped it around me.

"Mom, they called a doctor," I whispered, urgently.

"Yes, of course they did."

"Can you... I don't think that's a good idea." I was still whispering. I didn't know how far away Edith was or who else was hovering nearby.

"What is it, Targa? We're alone. Come see." She opened the door and went out into the suite. I trailed after her. Our rooms were empty. We went into my bedroom and she closed the door behind us.

"I'm..." Where did I start? I just blurted it out. "I died today, Mom. I drowned and then I changed. I came back to life. Now, I'm..." I couldn't bring myself to say the name, just in case this was a dream and it fractured if I spoke the word. "...I'm like you."

Several emotions crossed her face. Shock, understanding, then disbelief. "How can that be?" she said. "That's impossible." Then she put a hand to her heart in a rare gesture of dismay. "What do you mean, you *died*?"

"I drowned! It has to be possible, because it just happened. I guess, I..." I searched for the words but she got there first.

"Had to die to change." We looked at each other in wonder and amazement. "You had to pull the sea into your lungs. You have had the gene all along, it just never expressed until it had the right conditions." My mother usually said everything quickly, but this she said slowly. It was too big. "Your body wanted to survive, so it found a way." She put a hand over her mouth, looking almost like she was stifling a laugh or a cry, or both.

I nodded. I started to laugh, and felt on the edge of tears too.

She put her arms around me again as I stood there in my damp towel and sore feet. "Shhhh. It's all right. You're ok. I'm so sorry I wasn't there."

"Don't be sorry, Mom. If you'd been there, this wouldn't have happened. You would have saved me."

"Can you tell me what happened? Do you remember everything?"

I gave her the short version as we sat on the edge of my bed. She digested every word and asked questions about how I felt, how I managed to use my new body, and about Antoni.

I told her what I remembered but I didn't get into all the emotional details, I knew that the doctor was coming so we didn't have the luxury of time.

Mom looked at the bedside clock. "Get into your pj's. I'll see what I can do about the doctor. We'll talk more later." She made for the door.

"Mom," I stopped her. "Antoni. Can you find out where he is? I had to leave him down at the boathouse. I saved his life." I hiccoughed.

"Of course you did. It's what we do. Into bed with you, please." She vanished.

I pulled my pyjamas from the dresser and put them on. As I squeezed the water out of my hair, relief and laughter swirled around each other like otters at play. I really needed to rest; I'd been running on adrenalin at full dose for several hours. I also needed to know that Antoni was ok. I needed to know how much he remembered and what he thought.

I had barely pulled the covers over me when my mother, Edith, and the doctor came in. He spoke no English, which was why Edith was there. I gave Mom several anxious looks throughout the exam until she finally mouthed, 'It's ok.' I tried to relax.

He took my pulse and listened to my heart, his fuzzy white eyebrows shooting up in surprise at how slow it was. I now had the heartbeat of an extreme athlete. He examined my head, and listened to my lungs. He looked at my feet, cleaned and bandaged my cuts. He said a few things to Edith throughout this but all she conveyed to me was, "All ok". So much for translation. The doctor gave me an ice pack for the lump on my head and spoke to Edith some more. The two of them conversed, taking turns shooting me looks I couldn't define - concern, disbelief, awe?

"Are you hungry?" asked Edith. I shook my head. Perhaps I should have been, but I was so distracted and in shock that food was the last thing on my mind. She patted my hand and said, "Just rest, now." She and the doctor left.

I waited until the door was closed to speak. "Did you find out about Antoni?"

Mom nodded. "Yes, he's here. He's resting in his suite. The doctor has already seen him. He has a hairline fracture in two of his ribs. He's in the early stages of hypothermia, but he'll be ok."

I breathed a sigh of relief.

"What's concerning everyone, though," she continued, "is that he seems really confused. When people ask him what happened, he just keeps saying he doesn't know. He remembers the laser tipping over and being blown away from you. He tried to call for help with his radio but the batteries were dead. The young men who work at the boathouse are beside themselves. They said that they didn't have any time to prepare for you properly. They even tried to radio you after you left when they saw how fast the weather was changing."

I nodded, "Yes, it was a last minute decision. Poor guys, they shouldn't blame themselves."

"Antoni doesn't remember anything more until he woke up in the boathouse," she finished.

"That's because he died too," I said. "We both died today. The only thing that saved us was the fact that I changed and somehow, I knew what to do for him. I actually heard the water in his lungs. Can you believe that?"

"Yes, I can. I know exactly what that sounds like." She combed my damp hair back from my face. "Why don't you get some rest and we'll talk about this tomorrow?"

"But... it's still early." It was all too exciting.

"You need to rest, darling," she insisted. "You'll need more hours than usual after what you've been through." She pulled the drapes to shut out the pounding rain, kissed my forehead and then closed the door behind her, leaving me in darkness.

I was afraid to fall asleep. What if I didn't wake up? What if it wasn't real? What if I was still dead and this was some kind of limbo? Irrational thoughts elbowed each other in my brain.

I grabbed a pillow and hugged it to my chest, curling my body around it. I took deep breaths and tried to remember what it was like to be in the ocean with the gentle tug of the currents swirling around me. It occurred to me that my eyes had stopped hurting sometime after leaving the water, and that was my last conscious thought.

18

My waking thought was a question. Had it all been real? I touched the top of my head and was answered by the tender spot under my fingers. Yes, it had been real.

I checked the clock. 5:15 am. Most of the house would be asleep. My stomach growled ravenously. I pulled on a pair of jeans and a cotton sweater. I looked out the window at a grey morning, still more dark than light. It was no longer raining and the wind had died down, but everything looked very wet and ruffled up.

I went into our sitting area and opened our mini-fridge. It was filled with drinks but no food. My stomach groaned again. Mom's door was closed so I ventured out of our suite and went down to see if there might be something happening in the kitchen, if I could even find the kitchen.

The house was an abandoned maze of hallways and closed doors. Occasionally, a door would be open but there would be no light or sign of life. I came to a hallway lined with windows on one side. The windows showed the courtyard in the centre of the house.

Through a window across the square, I spotted a girl in a white jacket disappear through a swinging door. I followed the hallway around the courtyard and followed her through the door. The smell of freshly baked bread just about floored me. Two girls in white aprons kneaded dough on a long wooden island. They looked up at me with surprise. One of them said something to me in Polish.

"It smells good," I said, putting a hand over my stomach.

"Hungry?" one of the girls asked, and I nodded. She beckoned me in. I followed her to a baker's rack and she pulled out a sheet of freshly baked biscuits.

"Oh my God, you're amazing," I said, taking one. She grabbed a paper towel and wrapped up three more biscuits, putting the warm package in my hands. I thanked her repeatedly and she dimpled at me and ushered me towards the door. I went through, taking a bite of my prize and ran smack into Antoni.

"Targa!" he said, grabbing my shoulders. Then he pulled me into a fierce hug. "My God. You can't imagine... Ow." He pulled back and put a hand on his chest just below his sternum.

I caught myself before I apologized. He didn't know that I was responsible for his cracked ribs. "Are you ok?" I asked, around my bite of biscuit. "You should be in bed, what are you doing up?" I said, vaguely aware that I was talking with my mouth full, but also that I didn't care.

"Pacing," he said, fiercely. "I've been doing laps, waiting until a decent hour to knock on your door."

He scanned my face with a look of agony. He was pale and drawn and there were dark circles under his eyes. "And, no I'm not ok. I've been going out of my mind!" He hugged me again in spite of his rib. I was pretty sure the doc would have disapproved.

I swallowed my bite of biscuit and inhaled deeply. The heady smell of him suddenly registered. I could smell his soap, but I could also smell him; his skin, his scent – the smell that was Antoni alone. My head spun. He was a tower of warmth surrounding me, his arms felt like hot iron, his chest like a solid wall of heat and muscle. My senses were full of him. Vertigo swept over me and I clung to him for balance.

He took my hand and pulled me away from the kitchens. "Come on. We need to talk."

Oh boy. "Can I eat something first? I'm famished." I was hungry, but I was also stalling for time because I was distracted by how attracted to him I felt. Where had that come from? My mind scrambled numbly to make sense of these new feelings.

He noticed the baking in my hands. "That smells amazing. Yes, yes. Come on, we can eat in my suite. I have breakfast coming. 5:30 is the earliest I can have it delivered, and that's," he looked down at his watch. "Now."

Half of me wanted to say, "Shouldn't you be resting? Surely you don't have to work today?" But the other half was bowled over by the intense impact he was having on me. So I followed him in silence, muted by my own confusion.

His suite was up one floor and to the rear of the manor, away from the courtyard. When we entered the tidy room it was obvious that he was not like most young men I knew. The place was virtually spotless. The furnishings were navy with white piping - Novak colours. There was white wainscoting on the walls. It was all very nautical. Even the carpet was a plush navy, reminiscent of deep water. He had a bookshelf loaded with Polish titles and a few English ones. Everything looked like it was either business related or historical.

The smell of him was everywhere. I realized as soon as I inhaled that coming into his suite was a mistake. I had stalled for time so I could try to think properly, and now I could barely think at all. Was this part of the deal? A heightened sense of smell? The baking had smelled great but I didn't think it smelled any differently than it had to my human nose. But Antoni was a different story.

In his living room, there was a couch and a chair. He sat on the chair and gestured that I should take the couch. I sat, obediently. I tried not to stare at him but even my eyes felt hungry for him, he was by far the most interesting thing in the room. I mutely offered him a biscuit. He took it, probably more as a reaction than because he was hungry. I bit into one and that helped refocus me. I stifled a groan at the pleasure of how it melted in my mouth.

Almost immediately, there was a knock at the door. Antoni went to open it and accepted the trolley. He thanked whoever had delivered it, and wheeled his breakfast in.

Now that I'd started eating, the floodgates of my hunger had opened. My eyes followed the food as it rolled in. Whatever it was, it smelled incredible. My mouth watered.

"Help yourself. I think you need it more than me," he said, eyeing the way I was now wolfing down a second biscuit.

I took the cover off the plate and was rewarded with a serving of scrambled eggs, toast, sausage, sautéed whitefish, and broiled tomatoes. It would be polite to ask him if he was sure he wanted to share his breakfast, but instinct told me just to eat. So I did.

Antoni sat across from me and watched. I was being rude, but I couldn't bring myself to care. Was this how my mom felt? She had always put away a lot of food, and quickly. I was so used to it I barely noticed anymore.

"Did they not feed you last night?" He cocked an eyebrow.

"I fell asleep right away," I said around a mouthful of toast.

"Ah."

When I had finished everything on the trolley including the fruit salad, the pat of butter, and the little cup of jam, my manners returned. I thanked him. I also apologized, sheepishly. He brushed it off.

"Targa." He leaned forward.

"Are you ok?" I gestured to the way his hand cradled his chest. He dropped it like he hadn't realized he'd been holding his rib.

"I'm fine. Doc says I have a couple hairline fractures. He taped me up. That's not what I wanted to... it's not important." He stopped and took a breath.

He opened his mouth again, but nothing came out. He clasped his hands together, interlacing his fingers very slowly and deliberately. I had never noticed his hands before; they were beautiful. Square and strong, his fingernails neatly trimmed.

"I am so sorry," he said, finally. "It's completely my fault. I was so eager to show you the laser that I didn't take proper precautions. I didn't check the weather. I didn't... plan. I.... We could have died. I could have killed you!" He stood up and said the last bit very loudly. He ran his fingers through his short hair, distressed.

So, he didn't know that he had actually died. That was good. "It's ok, Antoni. Everything turned out ok," I said. It was hard to see him looking so upset.

"No." He shook his head. "You don't understand. I don't do things like that. I'm not irresponsible, especially with your... someone else's life. I don't know what I was thinking. My God this is a nightmare." He covered his face with his hands.

I stood up and took his hands. "Please don't beat yourself up. Can't you see? I'm ok. I'm more than ok. I just ate enough food to feed two men, I feel great. You're fine. Other than being out a laser, everything turned out fine."

"Well, actually..." He squeezed my hands. "We got the laser back. Erik and Maarten were able to find it early this morning with The Zodiac once the storm had cleared. But that's not the point. I just..."

He startled me by putting his warm palm against my cheek. He'd never been so familiar with me before, the intimate touch jump-started a hunger of another kind. His scent broke over me again like waves smashing against rocks. My hearing fuzzed out.

Sounding far away he said, "I couldn't live with myself if something had happened to you. I will never forgive myself for taking you out yesterday. It was foolish. I was so foolish."

He was saying nice things. I needed to respond, to comfort him. To kiss him. I shook my head but I couldn't tell if I was disagreeing with the confession that he was foolish, or disagreeing with my own desire to kiss him.

I opened my mouth to comfort him but no words came. He dropped his hand from my face. He sat on the couch and put his elbows on his knees and his face in his hands. He let out a breath that sounded like he was in pain, which he probably was.

He spoke through his fingers, "And the worst part is that I can't remember anything. It's so frustrating. I don't know how we got out of that mess. I remember losing control of the laser and trying to flip it upright. I tried calling for help on that useless two-way. I was so angry when it didn't work that I threw it into the sea, another dick move. All I remember after throwing the radio is blackness, and then your face, but I think it was just a dream because we couldn't have been together. I must have hallucinated it." This came out in a stream of consciousness, his accent thicker than usual. It sounded musical to my ears. Everything about him had suddenly become so wonderful and beautiful. So sexy.

I sat down beside him and put a hand on his back. Another mistake as I was distracted by the feeling of his flesh under my palm. And that scent. What was I going to say? Shit. No, not shit. Something comforting. *Focus.* Tell him something that will make sense to him, something that will explain all the confusion away.

All I was coming up with were more questions. Would he believe me if I told him that I was able to swim to him and pull him to shore? It was beyond a superhuman feat. Should I try to pass it off as a miracle? Maybe say that I couldn't remember anything either?

He turned to me, his hazel eyes searching my face. "What happened to you? What happened to me? How did I wake up in the boathouse?"

I opened my mouth to respond but I still had no explanation. The beauty of his face filled my eyes. His lips were so soft looking, so inviting. And that shadow of a beard that I wanted to feel scraping against my palm, against my face. My mind stretched in two directions, wanting him and struggling for something to say. He was waiting. Time was ticking by.

His eyes dropped from my eyes to my mouth and that was all the invitation I needed. I leaned forward and kissed him.

Immediately, he responded. We stood up together and he crushed me to him with one arm, the other hand curled around the back of my neck. His fingers wove into the hair at the base of my skull. I heard a soft moan with my fuzzy hearing; sounding so far away. Was that me in pleasure, or him in pain?

He kissed me like it was more important than breathing, like a starving man, and I gave back as good as I got. A startling thread of electricity zinged through my body. Warmth flushed through me from deep in my belly. It swept outward through my limbs and up the back of my neck.

I had kissed and been kissed before but it had never felt like this. The kisses of my past had all felt foreign, alien. They'd happened because I had allowed myself to be kissed, not because I'd sought the kiss out or wanted it. At the time, I thought that's what girls my age were supposed to want so I let myself be kissed. Only deep down, I hadn't been that interested. Until now.

Antoni's kiss intoxicated me fully. I drowned in the smell of him. I put my hands on his face, his stubble a thrill to my palms. I reached up and wrapped my arms around his neck, pulling him closer, standing up on my tiptoes to reach him. I wanted to occupy the same space as him, be fused to him. I pressed my body against his from chest to knees.

Suddenly, he broke the kiss and pulled away, out of breath. I was panting too.

"Targa, we can't. This is crazy. You're so young... Too young." He unlocked my arms from his neck and took a deliberate step back. It was a clear sign of rejection.

I wasn't hurt. I didn't feel rejected. I didn't feel anything except for the desire to be with him. I had supreme confidence that I could have him. My siren self knew that if I went after him, he would give in. He would be helpless. He would be mine.

My skin began to tingle. There was a new scent in the air. It was musky, soft, and feminine. It was mine. "I want you," I heard myself say. Since when had I ever been so bold?

My hands reached for him of their own accord. I flattened my palms against his chest. He groaned and the muscles in his jaw popped as he clenched his teeth. I could hear them grinding in his skull. His nostrils flared.

My voice had changed when I'd said the words, just a fraction. There had been a lone violin - my siren sound. I reached into myself and called more strings forward, all it would take was a few more words. It would be so easy.

I opened my mouth to speak when he said, "I could lose my job, Targa." His voice was ragged.

I froze. With supreme effort, I swallowed the violins and stepped back. It took everything I had to drop my hands from his chest. My skin stopped tingling. Instinct was urging me to seduce him, but my rational side was screaming to stop. How did my mother cope with this battle of wills? She'd never told me how difficult it was.

I swallowed hard again, snuffing for good the voice I'd been ready to use on him. My throat felt dry, like it was coated with sawdust. I needed a glass of water. Forget a glass, I needed a bucket. I also had the urge to take a shower.

"I have to go," I said. In a few short strides I was at the door.

"No, Targa wait... " he said, his voice thick with regret. But I was out the door and running down the hall before he could say anything else.

19

After I'd showered and guzzled a litre of water, I waited in the sitting area for Mom to wake up. I was tempted to wake her to talk about what had happened, but she'd been working hard and needed sleep. I checked the clock. It was almost seven. I started pacing. Then I decided to go for a walk around the manor to kill some time. I climbed the stairwell to the next storey and wandered along, taking in paintings, sculptures, and antique furniture that dotted the hallways and little sitting areas. The place still seemed deserted.

I meandered aimlessly, replaying the events that had just happened in Antoni's suite. I got vertigo when I thought about it. For years I'd worried that something was wrong with me. Clearly, now there wasn't. Had the desire been lying dormant just like the mermaid gene? Were the two linked somehow? My feelings towards Antoni had changed so suddenly and so drastically that it was the only explanation. Just the thought of him sent dragonflies whirring through my stomach, their hearty wings battering my ribcage mercilessly. My hands were trembling as though I'd just run a mile. Was this better than not feeling anything? Now I felt weak for want of him, almost like it owned me instead of me owning it.

I didn't know where I was anymore. I was in a hallway that was completely lined with wood. The floors were hardwood and the walls were panelled. It looked nothing like the rest of the manor. I spotted an alcove that had a fireplace and a small teak door beside it. Curious, I cracked it open to see a set of stairs. I climbed the stairs and exited the stairwell through a similar tiny door to find another hallway lined with doors. This one was different. It hadn't been updated the way the rest of the mansion had been. It looked the same way I suspected it had looked when the manor had been built. I wandered down the hall, noting as I walked by a window that I was on the top floor.

Halfway down the hall I saw a set of double doors propped open. The crackling sound of a fire could be heard coming from the room. I suddenly needed to know who was in the room and what it looked like. I guessed this was the curiosity my mother was famous for.

I was a mere few steps from the door when I heard my mothers' voice. I stopped in surprise. So, she hadn't been sleeping in her room after all.

"It shouldn't be a difficult dive. The wreck is well situated. I don't anticipate any problems," she was saying.

"From what I hear," Martinius answered in his warm baritone, "there isn't much that seems to be a problem for you, Mira. Your record speaks volumes."

In true Mira style, my mother didn't answer.

Martinius spoke again after a moment of silence. "You're welcome to borrow any of those books while you're here if you like. I have quite a few English nautical history books if they interest you."

"Thank you," my mother said, and I fought the urge to applaud sarcastically at her manners.

"Simon has agreed that the first dive will be Tuesday?" Martinius asked.

"So I'm told. We've spent the week doing nothing but prep, if we're not ready now, we never will be."

"Wonderful!" said Martinius with real enthusiasm. "I am jealous that I shall not be the first to examine her. I wish I could go, but I have long since hung up my diving gear. Be sure to take the time to observe both the crowsnest design and the figurehead. Both of them were hand carved by a famous Polish craftsman."

"I will," said Mom.

"And, you have everything that you need? There is nothing else that you can think of that might make the dive go more smoothly for you?"

"Yes, we are well very equipped," she replied. "It's quite a fleet of floating assets you have. I think Simon just about had kittens when he saw your outfit."

There was a pause and then, "Kittens?"

"An expression for when someone is excited," Mom explained.

Martinius gave a delighted laugh and there was another long silence. It was quiet for so long that I wondered what was going on. There was no sound except for the crackling fire. I took a step closer and then heard my mother speak again. Her voice closer to the door now. "Well, I think I'll go check on my daughter," she said. Something about the way she said *daughter* told me that she knew I was outside the door.

"Certainly," answered Martinius. "I'm so glad everything turned out well. Give her my regards. Perhaps I'll be so lucky as to hear the story in her words. Antoni seems to be struggling with the memory of what happened, poor chap."

"Yes." Mom was just about at the door. "Good day to you Martinius."

"Good day, Mira," he said.

She came out the door and threw an arm around my shoulders, turning me around. She kissed my forehead, but she didn't say anything until we got back to our suite and she closed the door behind her. She found her way as though she'd grown up in this mansion.

"Odd," she said, leaning her back against the door.

"What?"

"He had one of his staff ask me late last night to come see him first thing in the morning. He'd arrived late from a meeting in Gdańsk and

heard that you'd been in an accident. He wanted to know that everything was ok."

"What's odd about that?"

"It's not that part that's odd. I realized something just now when
he mentioned the figurehead and the crowsnest."

"Figurehead..." I jogged my memory. "That's the thing at the front
of the ship, right? A seahorse, or a dragon, or a girl with big boobs?"

"Right. But until he mentioned it just now, no one has said a word
about it in any of the briefings. I saw a shot of the crowsnest in one of
the images, but the figurehead wasn't in any of the photographs. It's
not even on the list of assets that we're charged with finding. By the
way, where have you been?" She switched topics smoothly and we
moved into the sitting area. She cracked open a bottle of water and
handed it to me, then opened one for herself.

"Oh, you know. Eating Martinius out of house and home. Seducing
his staff. Having fights with myself. The usual." I chugged the water.

Mom just about spat her water out, laughing in mid-gulp. She
swallowed and wiped the water off her mouth with her sleeve. "Let
me guess, you found Antoni and you got a nice big whiff with your
new mermaid nose."

"Something like that."

"You're purebred siren now, sweetheart." She gave me a sharp
look. "You didn't," she gave me an emphatic look. "Did you?"

The old Targa would have squirmed if her mother asked her
point blank whether she'd just had sex or not. I was a virgin, but I saw
it differently now. All my teenage embarrassment was gone. It was
just a normal urge now, like eating or sleeping.

I shook my head. "No, but I could have. I wanted to. It was really,
really hard not to. Did I mention how hard it was not to? I only
stopped myself because he said he could lose his job."

"He could," she nodded. "Sleeping with a contractor's daughter,
especially one as young as you. It would be a scandal. Although, I
overheard one of the guys saying that the age of consent in Poland is
actually 15." She shuddered, "A woman knows when she's ready,

mermaid or human, but somehow he sounded super creepy when he said it." She sighed, "I guess I should explain a few things to you."

"Yeah, like how all of a sudden I want to eat everything in sight, including Antoni? How I can push pheromones out of my skin and make my voice sound like an orchestra? And you never told me how confusing it is. How there's an inner battle going on all the time. How do you cope?"

"It gets easier, I promise."

I gave her a cynical look and she laughed. "Look. I'm overjoyed that you're a mermaid. I don't know why you had to die to get there, but you did. Your blessing and curse is that you now have powers and sharper senses. You're a primal creature. You are able to function as a human well enough to fool them but as soon as you're in salt water you're a siren. You operate almost entirely on instinct, and a big part of that instinct is to mate."

She pulled me down on the couch beside her. "You know why I drink so much water?"

"It helps you cope?" I understood that better than ever now.

"Yes. I need fresh water in my body to keep the siren instinct under control. As long as you have lots of clean water in your system, you'll be able to think like a human. Even while you're in salt water."

"What happens when the fresh water leaves your system?"

"Salt is fuel to your siren instinct, so if you're saturated with it, it takes over. Salt is why we always end up going back to the ocean. It calls to us until one day our relationships don't seem to matter enough anymore to stay on land." She put a hand on my face. "Except for this one. This relationship will always matter." Then a puzzled look crossed her face.

"What? What are you thinking?" I asked.

"Well, it is unusual that you're already getting the urge to find a mate. Typically, a mermaid needs to spend some time living at sea in the salt before the cycle begins. It appears you're breaking all the rules," she said, cocking an eyebrow.

"That's not really comforting," I said. How could Mom prepare me for life as a siren if I kept breaking rules? And what rule would I break next?

"So typically," I continued, wrapping my head around what she was saying, "you only ever leave the ocean when your instinct tells you to find a mate, right?"

"That's right. It's the only need that is powerful enough to drive us out of the ocean. Falling in love is a consuming experience for a mermaid. All the other stuff that matters to a human doesn't matter to us. Jobs, education, material possessions. None of it means anything. Only he matters. You've got a lot of gifts at your disposal. If there is a man alive who can resist the call of a siren when she's got her sights on him, I haven't met him. Even when you're not interested, they're still going to be drawn to you. It gets very annoying when you're not in the game for a mate anymore."

"Are all mermaids heterosexual then?" I asked, curious. My generation had been raised to accept that not everyone was drawn to the opposite sex. I wondered if it was the same for sirens.

"As far as I know," she said. "There are so few of us and our drive to procreate is so strong."

"Did you use your siren abilities to entice dad into a relationship with you?"

A wistful expression crossed her face and a secret smile touched her lips. "Actually no, I made a resolution not to use my abilities. When I found your father, I wanted our love to be as genuine as possible."

"That's what I want, too."

"There is a biological reason for that," she said, giving me a sidelong glance. "There might be more to it than just wanting an authentic love."

"What's that?"

"My mother once told me that the strongest siren offspring are made from relationships where no siren wiles are used. Possibly even to the point of producing an elemental."

"What's an elemental?"

"According to her, its a mermaid who has power over the ocean.

She can bend water to her will, and sometimes she even has the power to heal. I wanted to give my child those gifts if I could. So I wanted your dad and I to fall in love naturally, to the extent that we could. I think, with a siren, there will always be some level of supernatural appeal, but I tried very hard to keep it to a minimum when I met your dad."

There was silence while I digested what she'd said about siren offspring. "You must have thought your mom lied about that when I turned out to be a dud."

She chuckled, "I was pretty angry with her for a long time. But how incredible is it now to know that you were never a dud? And you have only just begun to learn what you are capable of."

"Try not to have too high of expectations, mom," I said wryly. "We've already spent too much time down that road. I can tell you right now that I don't have powers over water."

"I know, sunshine. I'm just thankful that you've finally had your rebirth."

I loved the idea of having a relationship free from siren deception, but how could I ever know if the attraction a man was feeling for me was genuine? I thought of what had happened with Antoni. I had thought maybe he was attracted to me before I became a siren, but how could I know for sure?

As a mermaid, I understood the desire to find the strongest and best mate. But as a girl who had been raised human all her life, I rebelled against the thought of luring a man with wiles that human women didn't have. At least I now understood the intense desire to be with Antoni, and thankfully had a tool to control it - fresh water.

"What about the sea here? Micah explained to me that it's brackish. Don't you think its weird that I finally had my change in water that has barely any salt in it?"

"Yes, I do find that odd. I've always been curious to swim in the Baltic because it's so unique, and now we're here. Strange how things work out."

"Let's go, Mom. Today. It'll be our first swim together. Take me to the ship? You have to go before Monday right, to prep the site? I could help you." I don't know why I was bracing myself for an argument. I should have known her face would light up like a solar flare.

"I can't think of anything I'd like to do more. Today is Saturday, the team won't be expecting me at work." Then her crystal eyes swept over me with a look of motherly concern. "How's your head? Did you sleep well?"

"I slept like the dead. My head is a little tender but it's already so much better than yesterday. I feel awesome, and really full." I rubbed my belly.

She laughed. "All right then. Let's go for a swim!"

As we made our way down to the beach together, I couldn't help but think of my future and what my mother might expect from me because of the change. After all, mermaids only left the ocean to find a mate and have a child, so didn't that mean that most of their lives were lived at sea? Away from humanity? I felt the shadow of a life-changing decision begin to fall over me and I pushed it out of my mind. I had enough on my plate; I'd deal with that later.

20

Mom secured a vehicle from Martinius' staff. He had been generous enough to extend the use of company vehicles to us while we were here.

I kept thinking about what I could do to prepare for the journey, after all it was a 48 kilometre swim. I had been less than a kilometre off shore when the laser tipped. The thought of going so far out into the deep made me nervous and excited. But I wouldn't be alone, and Mom always said that she was the most powerful thing in the ocean, so there was nothing to be afraid of.

"Do you think we should bring lots of water with us?" I asked, "for when we get back?"

She nodded. "It's always a good idea. I doubt it will be a problem, but there is no down side," she said, so we brought several litres with us and threw them in the back of the Jeep.

Mom told the staff we were going to Gdańsk for the day. Going to the beach wasn't a good excuse because no rational human would want to go swimming today. The aftermath of the storm was evident on the beaches and the sky was jammed with grey clouds. A chilly wind tugged at our hair as we got into the truck.

As we turned out of the estate, I said, "Go this way, Mom," and directed her north along the coast. "There is a secluded beach in between two rock outcroppings that I found yesterday when I came out of the water. We can park there and enter the water without being seen."

As we drove, I was reminded of the discomfort in my neck from yesterday. I rolled my head side to side but was happy to feel that there was no pain left at all. "My neck was so sore yesterday, and I had a burning sensation where my gills came out."

Mom nodded. "Your gills had never been used before. It makes sense they might burn for a little while. They'll be fine this time."

She parked the Jeep along a dirt road that ran parallel to the water. We chugged some water and stashed our clothes and towels in a sheltered area between two rocks. Then we ran naked and giggling into the sea, diving in headfirst.

The sweeping change down my body was instant and there was no pain anywhere, not like the first time. The temperature went from frigid to perfectly comfortable in a moment.

The marine floor dropped away from us rapidly as we swam out into the vast, open sea. Mom slowed and turned to look at me, taking in her mermaid daughter for the first time. Her eyes widened. "You're silver!" she exclaimed with surprise. "Wow, you're incredible. I don't know if you seem so beautiful because you're my daughter and I never thought this day would come, or if you really are just that gorgeous."

"Thanks, Mom." I looked down at myself. "I didn't expect silver either, well I didn't expect to be a siren at all, so... everything is a surprise," I said, twisting my tail in the water to watch it move.

"It's not like I've met a ton of mermaids in my lifetime," Mom said as she watched my scales glimmering in the light, "but I've never seen a mercurial one before. They've always been coloured, even sometimes with pinks and oranges or with distinct markings, like tropical fish."

"Does that mean I'm boring? Like vanilla ice cream?" I asked, laughing. I didn't care if I was as dull as a tuna, I was just so thankful to be a siren.

She laughed with the orchestra in her throat. "Nah," she winked at me. "You're classic, rather than trendy. It suits you." She peered closer. "Look at this." She pointed to a barely visible marking that ran down along either side of my hips. The back of my tail was a pearly white colour, while on the front my scales were bright silver. The transition was subtle but now that she had pointed it out it was unmistakeable. "Stunning," she said, admiring my markings.

She looked at my hands and the webbings in between, and my skin, which looked just like hers did underwater. "You'll have to be careful though," she said as she took in my overall appearance.

"Why?" I asked.

"You're the most visible colour you could possibly be. Light colours show up better in the water than darker ones, and you're bright and reflective. Just be aware that when you're swimming you need to be extra cautious. Steer clear of boats and people."

I promised I would and we continued to swim on. I admired my mother through my new eyes, seeing her more clearly than I ever had. I had seen her in mermaid form many times before during our night swims, but it was always dark and we were always in the shallows so I never really got a good view of her in her full glory.

She was remarkable. I stayed a little behind so I could watch her. Her long black hair flowed freely. She kept her arms by her side, not bothering to use her webbed hands. Her skin was pale and iridescent in the light, and the skin at her waist transitioned smoothly into scales. Her tail went from an incredible teal colour at her waist to a dark emerald green at the tips of her long, elegant fins. Her tail was much longer and fuller than mine. I supposed that made sense, she swam a lot and I figured that size equalled strength.

She saw that I was watching her. "Everything ok?" she asked. Her voice was a hundred violins coming from everywhere at once.

"Never better," I replied with my own strings. Mine was a thinner orchestra, but music all the same. "I forgot to ask you," I said as we swam, "why did my eyes hurt so much after I changed?"

She laughed, the melody ascending and harmonizing. "You have two sets of eyelids."

I pulled up short. "Excuse me? I have what now?"

She had shot forward when I stopped. She zipped back to me so quickly it was startling.

"Come on." She took my hand and we went to the surface.

We broke through the gentle waves and I took the opportunity to look around. The shore was a distant line of brown and green.

"So, what is this about two sets of eyelids?"

She came closer. "Yes, look. You've got these," she blinked with her regular eyelids, "and then you've got these." Quick as a flash I saw a transparent lid blink across her eye from the inner corner to the outer and then back again, while her outer lid didn't move at all.

"Sweet mother of crap!" I jerked back, startled.

The under-lid was completely transparent. When it was closed, you wouldn't even know it was there.

"It protects your eyes while you're swimming, especially at high speed. Also during storms, if you have to deal with intense waves and rain."

I put my fingertips into the corners of my own eyes. I held my eyelid still and felt the blinking of my transparent under-lid on its own. That explained why the rain hadn't bothered me yesterday. "Amazing!" I sang.

She laughed. "Yes, you have siren eyes now and everything that goes along with them. In the same way the salt made your gills burn, your eyes are taking in light and dealing with water in a way they've never had to before. Just the fact that your under-lids had to separate themselves from your eyelids for the first time would account for the pain. I don't know if you've had the under-lid all along, or if it grew in when the rest of you changed."

"Incredible," I said, blinking. It was hard to move the under-lid separately from my eyelid at first, but it got easier. My vision changed a lot when the under-lid was across my eye, everything was sharp and clear, sort of like a human wearing a diving mask only a thousand times better.

Mom dove again and I chased her and tried to keep up. The bubbles from her tail tickled my face and down my body. We played like a couple of dolphins. I hadn't felt such a sense of freedom or joy before, or such a unity with the world around me. I belonged here.

The world under the water was vast and beautiful and went off in every direction as far as my mermaid eyes could see. There was life everywhere. Schools of fish could be seen at every distance. I could also see garbage scattered along the floor. Every once in a while I'd see something that shouldn't be there – part of an antique truck, an anchor, an old tire, a rubber boot. It was amazing the amount of crap that had been dumped into the sea.

We swam for what must have been quite a while but I had no sense of time. We went through occasional clouds of plain-looking fish, and then passed a school of porpoises, and then a mother humpback whale with a calf. I was distracted by all of them and fought the urge to go and see if I could interact with these creatures.

All thoughts of playing with the ocean's residents vanished when we started to go deeper. Soon we were descending very quickly. I felt the pressure change around me, and my body adjusting in various ways. My ears made a succession of tiny squeaks as they worked to relieve the compression.

The landscape below us changed dramatically and became almost like a mountainscape that we were flying over like birds. There were ravines and huge crevices, boulders and spindle shaped rocks reaching up from the ocean floor. I realized that the marine floor was really just like land, with its varied terrain and distinct landmarks. A mermaid could actually get to know the sea in this way; the territory below her would become familiar in the same way the landscape around Saltford had become well known to me.

"I understand better now how you can always find a wreck once you've been there," I said to Mom as I watched the terrain going by underneath us.

"It seemed like magic to you before, did it?"

"Yes. But it's not magic, its just knowing your environment."

"That's right." I could hear the smile in her voice as she swam ahead of me. "It's as easy to navigate the ocean as it is to navigate the land once you get to know it. There's just a lot more of it."

A shape materialized ahead of us in the gloom.

"And, there she is," Mom said. She turned her face back towards mine and I had another shock as I saw that her pupils had dilated noticeably. The bright blue of her iris was gone and her pupil had enlarged beyond the size of her iris. The whites of her eyes were visible but the effect was still startling. I wondered just how big our pupils could get. I guessed my eyes looked like that too.

We were a long way down. Micah had said *The Sybellen* was at 90 feet. There was still sunlight down here, and plenty of life.

We slowed as we approached *The Sybellen*, stopping a short distance away and taking her in. I don't know why I was startled at her size; in my imagination she hadn't been so big, but she dwarfed us. The images that Micah had shown me had not done her justice. Gooseflesh prickled across my arms as she loomed out of the darkness and up from her bed of sand like a ghost from the distant past.

"Wow. I have never seen anything like it," I said. And truly, nothing I had ever experienced could rival this moment.

"Sometimes, I forget," Mom said. "I have seen so many wrecks that I forget that they really are a link to the past and always have a story to tell. Human divers never get to experience a wreck the way we can, let alone the worlds under the sea," she said. I followed her as we drew closer.

The Sybellen was sat upright on the ocean floor, as though she'd just drifted down slowly from the surface and had come to rest peacefully. The front two masts were still upright but the rear mast had snapped off and was nowhere to be seen. Ropes draped haphazardly across the ship, coated with algae. The wreck had portholes all along both sides and a bowsprit that shot out in front like the nose of a swordfish. A railing with shapely spindles lined the deck. The balustrade was broken in places and though algae grew on every surface, the spindles could be easily made out.

"Mom." I pointed at something white and half-buried in the sand not far from the wreck. It was a human skull.

"Yes," she said. "Wrecks are often tombs. You'll have to get used to seeing things like that I'm afraid, although less so in saltier water with fast moving currents."

A gaping hole where a hatch had once covered a ladder disappeared down into the hold. A doorway in the fore of the ship opened into the belly as well. The hollows yawned darkly, like a giant's frightening mouth. I had a lot more appreciation for the bravery my mother had to have in her job, mermaid or not.

"Listen." Mom's voice filled the water around me. She looked at me with her big black eyes. "I don't want you going inside with me. It's dangerous in there, even for a mermaid. I'll go in and take a look around. You can watch from the portholes, ok?"

"Dangerous how?" I asked, squelching my disappointment.

"Wrecks are fragile, things can shift and fall without warning, even here where there's very little salt. I've seen men become trapped in the blink of an eye."

"Have you ever been trapped or hurt?" I asked, now a little worried.

"Not seriously, no. But I don't want you to take the risk right now, ok?"

"Ok," I agreed. I was curious about what it was like inside but I understood.

I watched as she approached the square hole in the deck, the one with the ladder. She didn't touch anything, she didn't use any of the ship around her for leverage and she just let herself drift slowly down into the hold with barely noticeable movements of her body. The last bit of her long tail finally disappeared into the hold.

I swam down to the side of the ship and peered in through a porthole. The inside of the ship was a mess of barrels and chests, cannons, stairways, and beams both upright and sideways. Whatever had happened to this ship, it looked like it had been shaken like a snow globe.

I could see my mother easily as she swam through the gloom. She still didn't touch anything. She scanned everything around her, probably taking inventory in her head.

"It's not often you get to see a ship as old as this one in such good shape. It's like it was frozen in time," she said.

I thought it looked like a bomb had gone off but this was the first wreck I'd ever seen, so I took her word for it. "What is all that stuff?"

"According to the manifest, it's a lot of different things, much of which will be decayed beyond recognition, even in the Baltic. Spices, textiles, wine and spirits, ledgers and books," she paused and looked at me. "Coinsssssssss and Goooooold," she said, hissing on 'coins' and drawing out 'gold', waggling her eyebrows.

I got goosebumps at the spooky look on her face with its big black pupils and the resonance in her voice. She'd put the violins into a minor key, making her sound haunting. But I couldn't help but laugh at her clowning around. She didn't give a crap about gold. Everyone else did – that was what everyone was always after.

Suddenly, I remembered something. I couldn't believe we'd forgotten. "Mom!" I said with urgency.

She stopped floating to look at me. "What? What's wrong?"

"The figurehead!"

"Oh yes, I forgot about it. Let's go take a look." She swam towards a square gun port and gingerly floated through it.

As we approached the figurehead from the rear, I could see that it was a woman's figure after all. That made sense. The ship was named *The Sybellen*, after Mattis' beloved wife. It was probably a sculpture of her.

Soon I realized I was mistaken. It was not a woman but a mermaid. Of course it was. The mermaid was the symbol of the Novak family. I should have known. It was probably still Sybellen; only she'd been gifted with a mermaid tail by the sculptor.

We drew in close and examined her. She was covered in algae, so even though it was obvious what she was, her details were obscured.

For the first time, I watched my mother do something to disturb the wreck. She didn't touch it; she just took water in through her gills and expelled it through her mouth in a steady jet stream strong enough to remove the algae, but without damaging the sculpture.

For the first time since we'd entered the sea, the cold began to seep into my bones. I watched with a growing horror as the visage of the figurehead was revealed.

I was looking into the face of my own mother.

21

W e floated there in stunned silence – both of us in shock. I looked from my mother to the figurehead and there was no mistaking it, they were identical, even down to the tiny cowlick at her left temple where the hair flowed back from her forehead. The face of the sculpture was a mask of serenity, the lips closed and turned up slightly. I'd seen my mother with the same smile many times. My stomach filled with dread.

"But, this ship is 150 years old!" I cried, finally.

Mom didn't say anything. She drifted there, taking in her own wooden reflection.

"How is this possible?" I asked. And then, "Mom!" when she didn't answer.

"I don't know, Targa," she answered, slowly and quietly. She looked thoughtful, but I could see anger growing in her eyes. With her pupils dilated the way they were, it was an expression that struck fear into my heart.

When she finally moved again it was to put her hands on either side of the figurehead, feeling around for the crack between it and the ship.

"What are you doing?" I said, alarmed.

"I'm going to destroy it, of course." She sounded surprised that I should ask.

"No! Mom, you can't do that! You don't know how many people know about it. Maybe there are images of it floating around that you haven't seen yet for some reason. If it's all of a sudden missing, then they'll start investigating." I put my hands on her arms, knowing that I would not be able to stop her if she was determined to rip the figurehead away from the ship. "Let's think for a moment, please," I begged. "If you destroy it now, then you could be putting us in a worse predicament."

She hesitated, pulling her hands away. Then she seemed to get an idea. "Ok, lets go," she said, and took off at a speed I could barely keep up with.

The swim back from the wreck was tense. We were both disturbed by what we had discovered, and even more troubled that Martinius had directed my mom to it.

"Martinus asked you specifically to look at the figurehead. Why?" I asked as we swam, trying to keep the fear in my voice to a minimum. Our musical voices were far more expressive than a normal human voice.

"I don't know, Targa," she answered, without turning back. "But we're going to find out."

"How are you going to do that without giving us away?" I asked, straining to keep up to her. My tail had begun to ache with the effort.

"I suspect he already knows our secret, don't you?" she threw over her shoulder, and the stress in her voice was palpable. She was pissed. "I think this was his way of telling us that he knows. Other- wise, why would the figurehead not be on the manifest? No one else on the team even knows it exists. Why would he call me into his personal library, all alone without Simon, the project lead, and then tell me specifically to check it out?"

I didn't know what to say or think. She was right. It didn't look good. A horrible thought occurred to me, "Do you think he lured you here? Using the job as bait? Maybe we shouldn't go back?" I gasped, both in fear and exhaustion because I was working so damn hard to keep up with her. "Can you slow down, please?" I panted. It was a strange feeling to have my gills struggling for oxygen instead of my lungs.

She slowed just a little. I eyed her gills and realized that she wasn't panting at all. I had a sick suspicion that she was traveling at less than half her top speed. I had a lot of growing up to do, as a siren.

"I don't know what to think, but we are going back. I'm not afraid of him." She had a hard sound that gave me chills which remained as we pulled on our clothing at the beach and jumped into the Jeep. We peeled away, sending a spray of gravel shooting out behind us.

My mother brought the truck to a halt in front of the manor, shutting off the engine and getting out in nearly the same motion. She left the door open behind her. I scrambled to undo my seatbelt and follow her. She sprinted up the front steps and through the huge front doors; one of them opened with a bang.

The valet had been crossing the foyer and he clutched at his heart in a dramatic manner. I would have laughed if things hadn't felt so serious. He watched wide-eyed as we barrelled past him and sprinted up the stairs two at a time. We must have been quite a sight, my mother with her eyes flashing angrily and both of us with our hair still wet and tangled from our swim.

"Mom," I hissed, "what are you going to say?" I twirled my hair into a rope, trying to put it into some kind of order.

"I'm going to find out what's going on," she said, calmly. Her tone did not match the pace at which she was taking the stairs.

"Just, don't do anything crazy. Please," I pleaded, stumbling after her. She headed straight for Martinius' office on the second floor.

She didn't stop at the closed door; she barrelled right on through. I followed her into the room, an apology ready on my lips. The doors slammed open, startling two of the cleaning staff who were dusting and watering plants. Martinius wasn't there.

"Where is Martinius?" my mother asked, bluntly.

The maids looked at each other. One of them said, "I believe *Mr. Novak* is in his library, ma'am. Everything okay?"

Mom turned on her heel and left, storming past me.

"Sorry about that," I said to the ladies. I followed my mother up to the fourth floor through the narrow staircase. We arrived at the same room where I'd overheard her and Martinius talking.

"Mom, maybe you should..." I started. She barrelled through this door, too. I sighed. "Knock."

I looked around, finally able to satisfy my curiosity. The room was a small, cozy library. The fire was lit, casting a warm glow over the red carpet and brown overstuffed leather chairs angled toward the fireplace. A long sofa faced the fire, an antique coffee table in front of it. The legs of the table were sculpted wooden mermaids.

Why had we not suspected that mermaids were not just an icon for the Novak family? How much did he know? Even my own father never knew that my mother was a siren.

The ceilings of the room were sharply vaulted and the room had a dormer window. Ruby curtains framed the window and the seat below it was upholstered in scarlet and gold velvet. Bookcases lined the low walls, rows upon rows of antique books filling every nook. A ship encased in a green glass bottle with a short, fat neck and closed with a crumbling cork sat on a bookcase. I recognized it as *The Sybellen*.

What startled me the most was Antoni. He was gazing into the fire with a hand on the mantelpiece. He looked up when Mom and I came barrelling into the room.

Antoni's eyes flicked from her to me and widened. He thought we were there about what had happened between us that morning. The colour drained from his face. He opened his mouth and I gave him the subtlest headshake, no. He snapped his mouth shut.

Martinius was seated in one of the chairs in front of the fireplace, a closed file folder on his lap. He also looked up abruptly, but he wasn't surprised like Antoni was. He'd been expecting us.

"We've seen," Mom paused and flicked a look towards Antoni. "Do you mind?" She invited him to leave with an open palm.

Antoni and Martinius shared a look. Martinius nodded. Antoni walked towards the door, and me. I looked him full in the eyes and held his hazel gaze. His scent thrilled my blood as he passed, then the door clicked quietly shut behind him.

"We've seen your figurehead," my mother said. I detected a faint violin. "What game are you playing?"

"Have a seat," Martinius replied calmly, gesturing to the sofa. He closed the folder on his lap and tucked it between the cushion and the arm of the chair.

"I don't want to have a seat. I want you to tell me what the hell is going on."

"Please," he said. "I can see that you're angry. I did not mean to upset you."

Mom perched pertly on the edge of one of the chairs and I sat on the sofa. The leather squeaked and I stifled a nervous giggle.

"Talk," Mom ordered, as though she was the one in charge. And it certainly seemed that she was. It no longer mattered that Martinius was her client.

"My grandfather, Jan," he began, "used to tell me stories every night before I went to bed. My favourite were the pirate stories, the tales of murder and mayhem on the high seas-"

"Cut to the chase, Martinius," she interrupted, her teeth bared.

"Mom," I said, quietly. I wanted to hear what he had to say. There was nothing threatening in his demeanour so far.

He continued, graciously allowing my mother's rudeness to pass. "But my grandfather's favourite stories were about *The Sybellen*. He'd make up some wonderful adventure tale and put *The Sybellen* at the heart of it. He made Mattis out to be a privateer and the crew his fighting men. Sybellen, of course, was a mermaid, a magical creature that Mattis had rescued from the clutches of a kraken." Martinius got up, went to one of the library shelves and pulled out an old leather book. He came back and sat down, setting the book on the arm of his chair and steepling his fingers on top of it. From what I could see, the book didn't have a title and it looked antique.

"As a child, I knew it was all fairy tales but when I got older, I stumbled across some family records. Aleksandra, Mattis' mother, had kept a diary. She was concerned when Mattis returned from the West Indies with a mysterious woman and intent to marry her. In those days, the family all lived together in the same house. So you see, Aleksandra was able to observe her son's new wife, Sybellen, very closely."

It occurred to me that the book under his fingertips was most likely the diary. Curiosity fired up in me like it had a ripcord attached. I wondered if he'd let us read it, then I wilted when I realized it would be in Polish.

"Of course," he continued, "they were madly in love and that was what Aleksandra wished most for her son. But it bothered her that Sybellen appeared to have no family, no heritage, no personal documents, and she disliked very much to talk about herself. She was extraordinarily beautiful, or so the diary says. With long, wild black hair, bright blue eyes, and pale skin. Not unlike you two young ladies," he said pointedly. "Sybellen was known for being abrupt and distant with everyone but Mattis and her children. Eventually, even with those she loved most, she began to grow detached. Aleksandra writes that she spent an inordinate amount of time down at the sea, especially after she'd had her twin boys."

I stole a glance at my mother. She was nearly as expressionless as the wooden figurehead.

"Jan had always told me that Sybellen had sailed with Mattis on that final journey, but the truth according to the diary, was that Sybellen went missing the night before they were meant to depart. Mattis was beside himself, but he didn't go to the authorities or send a search party to scour the shorelines or countryside. No. He quickly gathered the minimum number of men required to sail *The Sybellen*, and took the ship to sea in search of his beloved wife. He left that very night, and Aleksandra writes that there was a fearful storm. He also took one of the twins with him, Emun Jr, and the diary reports that Mattis believed that he would find Sybellen faster if he took one of their boys. Rather a strange choice for a father, don't you think?" he raised his eyebrows at us and paused for a moment.

Still my mother didn't react.

He continued, "Aleksandra writes that Emun Jr was very attached to his mother. Perhaps Mattis thought that the attachment would be enough to lure Sybellen to the ship. It didn't make much sense to Aleksandra, and it didn't make sense to me when I first read it either. But now that I've met you..." He paused, perhaps waiting for us to fill in some gaps. "Well," he went on, "the ship and all of those on board were never seen or heard from again."

The flames were crackling cheerfully in the fireplace, completely unaware of the tension in the room.

Martinius continued, "The real story behind how *The Sybellen* went missing had to stay a secret because there was insurance money at stake. Aleksandra doesn't give a lot of detail about that situation, but she alludes to her husband meeting in secret with the sailors that had been contracted to sail but not been on the ship when it left that night. No doubt, he struck their names from the crew list so that the insurance company wouldn't be the wiser, and he promised to compensate them well from the insurance pay-out in exchange for their silence. If the insurance company had known that Mattis took the ship out of port on a stormy night to search for his missing wife, they might never have paid."

My mother spoke for the first time since he began the story. "Novak Shipping is guilty of insurance fraud?" I gaped at her thinly veiled threat. Intimidating Martinius was not going to improve our situation.

He paused, then said, "My dear, the statute of limitations has long since expired on the matter. The insurance company doesn't even exist any more. I believe they bankrupted in the 1930's, not long after the stock market crash."

My mother didn't respond, her face was back to being an expressionless mask.

He plucked the folder from between the cushions and opened it. He pulled out two yellowed documents that had each been slipped into a plastic cover to protect them. The first page was covered in pencil sketches of the figurehead, showing it from several different angles as well as whole images of the mermaid and close-ups of her face.

He handed the pages to my mother. They hovered in the air between them for a moment before she reached out and took them.

"These are drawings that the sculptor made for Mattis to approve while the ship was still being built."

We stared at the pencil sketches. My mom may as well have sat and posed for the artist. Mom flipped over to the second document. It was more of the same, only done in colour. The figurehead must have been painted at one time, either that or the sculptor changed his mind and kept it as bare wood. There was no colour on the actual figurehead anymore. Whether that was the effect of the sea and time, I didn't know. The eyes looking out at us from the page were a bright supernatural blue, the hair blue-black and the skin pale.

"How many people have seen these?" asked my mother quietly.

"These documents have always been kept in my private collection, not in the Novak archives. My wife and son both saw them, but as you know they've since passed. I'm sure many Novak employees from the past have also seen them but it has been many years since these sketches have seen the light of day. I had always intended to have it framed and put on display, but I never got around to it."

My mother visibly stiffened but Martinius was already opening the folder once more and removing another document. This one was not antique looking, it was a printout of a news article and it had a photograph with a caption.

"I'm sure you can imagine my surprise when during my search for the best salvage team in the world, I came across this." He handed her the printout.

The headline said: *Bluejacket Underwater Recovery & Salvage Team Salvages 'Un-Divable' Wreck To Return Priceless Heirloom.*

I recognized the photograph. It was taken less than a year ago. Simon was shaking the hand of a lady in a big hat, displaying all of his teeth in a wide grin. Tyler, Eric, and Micah were all in the shot as well. And of course, standing beside Simon with a bored look on her face, was my mother. The caption on the photograph stated: *Lady Margaret Stowe is thrilled to have her mother's priceless brooch back after freak accident claims her luxury catamaran.*

I remembered that contract. It wasn't a freak accident; it was an alcoholic captain who'd fallen asleep on the job.

"And then," Martinius continued, "I went to the Bluejacket website and looked at the team roster. There you were again, looking back at me clear as day through Sybellen's eyes."

He pulled out another printout and I recognized this one, too. Martinius had taken it directly from the Bluejacket website. It was my mom in her uniform, standing for a professional headshot. No smile, just a perfunctory pose to get the job done.

"Sybellen," Martinius said quietly but with such emotion that we both looked up. My heart squeezed painfully in response to the expression on his face. There were no tears, but his face was full of wonder and his eyes were shining. He looked heart-broken and full of joy at the same time.

His voice cracked with emotion. "You've come home."

22

I couldn't breathe. Something was very wrong. How could my mother be the long-lost Sybellen? It wasn't possible. She was Mira MacAuley - my mother and the deceased Nathan MacAuley's beloved wife. I had no siblings, I was my mother's first and only child. She'd told me so.

"You don't understand," my mother's voice broke through my swirl of thoughts. She spoke far more gently than I had ever heard her speak to anyone outside our family. "I'm not Sybellen."

"Please, don't deny it," Martinius said, leaning back against his chair and holding out his palms. "How can you look at those images and tell me that's not you?"

"Because it's true. I am not your long lost however many greats-grandmother. It's impossible," she said, gently.

Martinius looked at her as though he could not believe that she was denying who and what she was in the face of all of the evidence. I wondered if she was going to call him crazy next and make the poor old guy question his own sanity. I understood the need to protect our identities but I wasn't sure how she was going to explain it all away. Here we were standing on two legs but our hair was wet and we'd clearly just seen the figurehead for ourselves and we hadn't taken a boat from the fleet out to do it. There was no hiding from Martinius, it was clear that he knew what we were.

He had begun to splutter in protest but my mom went on. "We can live a very, very long time, that's true. But I'm still young for a siren."

I looked at her with surprise. So there it was. She'd admitted it. I looked at Martinius. He'd slumped in relief when she'd admitted the truth but he still looked confused.

"I'm nowhere near as old as your ship. My daughter is 17 and she is my first and only child. I left the ocean to find my husband when I was only 19."

Martinius did not look convinced.

"Look," she continued, "I'm admitting that I am what you think I am. And Sybellen was too, I have no doubt about that, but Sybellen is more than likely an ancestor of mine. My own mother died when I was very young, I was lucky to have survived on my own. She didn't tell me much about my lineage. Mermaids don't keep family records and I never knew anyone else from my line."

His expression was wilting and I thought maybe he was beginning to doubt himself. He took the pages from my mother's hands.

"But... these," he said, holding them up. "You are she. She is you."

Mom shook her head. "I'm sorry. Look at my daughter. We look a lot alike. We pass our genes down to our daughters. It is likely that I am related to Sybellen, but I don't know her. I wouldn't have come to Gdańsk in the first place if I had recognized the name. Do you think I would have endangered my daughter by bringing her to a place where people might know what she is?"

I thought from his expression that maybe he was beginning to believe her now, but he didn't want to. "It's true, Martinius," I added. "I know my mother. She wouldn't lie about this."

Mom gave me a grateful look and then said, "I'm very sorry," with real sympathy. Her kindness impressed me. When it was necessary, she did have it in her. She surprised me even more when she added, "Think how lucky it is that you got this far. You can say that it's very likely that Sybellen was indeed a siren. You've found your ship, and it's perfectly preserved and positioned for a successful salvage, which almost never happens. And you're the only man I've ever met who knows that we exist." Then with an edge in her voice, "And I hope you realize how important it is that it stays that way."

"Does Antoni know?" I blurted.

Martinius shook his head and I let out a breath I didn't realize I'd been keeping in. "No," he said. "No one does. Do you think they'd let me keep control of my company if I started raving that mermaids were real? It's on our family crest for Pete's sake. They'd think I'd gone stark raving mad." He chuckled dryly.

"Good," said my mother. "Do we have your word then that you won't tell a soul?"

"Of course," he said, affronted. "I have no interest in ruining my reputation and losing my business, as much fun as it would be to spook everyone. There is a clause in my Presidential contract that stipulates that if reason and I part company then so will Novak Shipping." He grew thoughtful. "Do you think that you could find her for me? Sybellen. I'll pay you whatever you want."

My mother was shaking her head before he was even finished. "You don't know what you're asking, Martinius. It would be impossible. There is over 330 million cubic miles of ocean out there and we're nomadic by nature. She could be anywhere. She could also be salt-flush by now."

"Salt-flush?" Martinius asked.

"If a siren spends enough time in salt water she'll slowly change over time. She becomes a primal creature with very little memory of where she's been or who she's known. Even if I found her, the odds of which are almost zero, she might not even remember Mattis. And I'm not about to try and force-feed a salt-flush siren with fresh water. I'd be taking my life in my hands."

"I see," he said, resigned.

We sat in silence for a time. The fire crackled peacefully.

"Well, I am grateful to have come this far. You can't imagine the efforts the Novak family has put into finding *The Sybellen*," said Martinius as he got to his feet, moving stiffly. We stood up as well. "It is remarkable that one of the stories that Jan told me when I was little actually turned out to be true. Sybellen truly was or is a mermaid, if she's still alive. How much I wish he was around today so I could ask him if he'd always known or if he'd just made it up to delight the ears of his young grandson." He then raised his bushy eyebrows at my mother. "You'll stay and finish out the project, I hope?"

"Please," my mother scoffed, "those boys are lost without me."

Martinius barked a laugh. "I'm sure they are. There's no salvage team on earth that could compete with you two."

There was no reason to tell Martinius that up until yesterday, we thought I was human. I was useless when it came to salvage work.

"Listen," my mother said. "We have another sensitive issue, one that I'll need to address before Monday and in secret."

"What's that?" Martinius asked, steepling his fingers. The emotion had been tucked away. The businessman was back.

"My team can't see that figurehead. I've removed the algae from it and my obvious resemblance to it is a danger to my daughter and I. May I have your permission to remove it from the ship? Very carefully, of course."

Maybe Martinius bought the sincerity of her request, but I knew Mom. She was only asking as a courtesy. Come Monday morning, with or without his permission, the wreck would no longer have a figurehead. She would do whatever was necessary to protect us. I held my breath and watched his face as he mulled this over.

"I had intended to remove only the cargo that was worth recovering. I had wanted *The Sybellen* herself to be left alone. But I understand your dilemma." He went quiet again, thinking it over. Finally, "I can have a preservation box released to you for the figurehead. If you can guarantee neither the figurehead nor the ship will be damaged upon separation, then you have my permission to retrieve it. Although, even for the two of you I can imagine it will be a difficult job. How do you propose to bring it back to shore?"

"Let me worry about that. You have a case for the box? We can't afford to have anyone inspect it," my mother replied. "Can we arrange to deliver it to you personally under cover of night? And where will you plan to keep it?"

"This is my personal library, no one comes in here without my invitation, except for you... today," he added, and his mouth twitched with humour. "Are you satisfied to store it here? We can cover it and lock it. Once you leave, it eventually won't be such a sensitive issue. Do you agree?"

She nodded. My mother was stretching herself a lot for him. She would rather destroy the figurehead altogether and erase any connection between *The Sybellen* and us. The agreement meant that we had to trust Martinius with our secret. The only reason she was bothering to negotiate was because he had no motive to expose us. Like he'd said, control of his company would be at stake.

My mother held out her hand. "To our understanding, and your word as a gentleman."

"We have an accord." Then he shook my hand too.

23

Martinius had his staff load a watertight box into the back of a truck for us. It was enclosed in a black crate with his company name stamped across it. Mom explained that he'd told the staff that it was for the dive the following week and since everyone knew that a salvage project was about to start, no one so much as blinked at it.

After dark, we drove the truck down to the empty beach and went back into the ocean for the second time that day. It was the first time I had gone for a night swim as a mermaid.

This time it was all business. We got to the wreck as quickly as we could. I was amazed at how efficiently our eyes handled the dark. The wreck was almost as visible to me now as it had been during the day.

Now that Martinius knew what we were doing, I had imagined some kind of delicate process where my mom used a tool to pry the figurehead loose in a more respectful way. I was wrong about that.

She first blew the remaining algae away from the whole thing with her powerful little stream of water, so it wasn't so slippery. Then, she had no problems prying it away from the ship with her bare hands. The waterlogged wood groaned and squeaked as the nails came loose. The sculpture came away in one whole piece, leaving a flat empty space behind it.

I looked at the bare wood. "Do you think the lack of algae on the empty space might tip off the guys?" It was clear as day that the figurehead had recently been removed.

"Don't think so," Mom said. "The figurehead isn't on the list, and human divers have so little mobility and time when they do these dives that they don't waste time exploring areas of the ship that aren't of interest to the task. "I wouldn't worry, but I'll keep an eye."

My mother carried the figurehead the entire way back to shore all by herself. So far, I had been no help at all. It took us a lot longer to get back to shore than it had to get out to the ship because the figurehead slowed her down considerably – not because she found it heavy, but because its bulky design wasn't aqua-dynamic in the least.

When we reached shore and traded our fins for legs, we left the figurehead submerged in water and went to the truck. We opened the crate and carried the empty box down to the beach where we submerged it to fill it with seawater. We floated the figurehead into the box, ensuring that it never emerged from the water.

Before we sealed up the box we just stood there, looking at the figurehead.

"Is it just a coincidence that she looked so much like you, do you think?" I looked back and forth between the two identical faces.

Mom eyed up her wooden likeness thoughtfully. "No, its not likely a coincidence. I'm almost positive Sybellen is related to us somehow. I've met enough mermaids to know that they're as varied in colour and shape as humans are. Maybe more."

"I wonder if she's still alive, and if she is, whether she remembers her past."

Mom shrugged as we sealed the box with the figurehead and water inside. "I doubt we'll ever find out. A shame, really. I'm curious about her but not enough to spend a lifetime in a futile search." She double checked the locks and added, "We have to leave it sitting in the seawater until Martinius decides what to do with it."

"Why?" I asked, as we floated the box towards the beach, one of us on either side.

"It's an archival thing," she said. "It's been sitting in seawater for so long that if we let it dry out without transitioning it slowly, it will rot at light speed. Not that I'd care, but this is what Martinius asked for," she said as she snapped the lid shut.

"How thoughtful of you." I raised an eyebrow at her. "Do you perhaps have a soft spot for the old fellow?"

She gave a half-smile and snorted but didn't answer.

Between the two of us, we carried what must have been several hundred pounds of figurehead, water, and box, and loaded it back onto the truck. Piece of cake.

It was sometime after four in the morning when we returned to the estate. The hallways were deserted. We put the box onto a waiting trolley and used the service elevator to take it up to the fourth floor.

Martinius was eagerly awaiting his delivery. He looked tired but his eyes were gleaming with excitement as he opened the door for us. We pushed it into his library and parked it in the spot he'd cleared for it. He pulled away the collapsible sides of the crate to look at the figurehead. He put a hand against the glass like he wished he could touch it.

He said some words in Polish to himself. It sounded like he was speaking to a lover. "I am still not entirely sure whether to believe you. You cannot deny that the resemblance is remarkable."

"It is," she agreed.

"Thank you for this," he said. "I wasn't going to take this piece from the ship but I'd be lying if I didn't say that I'm happy to have the excuse to do so."

We wished him a good night and went back to our suite. With that done, we both collapsed into bed.

Mom slept in until noon the next day but I was up and out of bed early. I was too excited by this big change in my life to spend it sleeping. I pulled on a pair of shorts and a t-shirt and went down to find some food. They always set out a buffet breakfast in one of the large rooms on the ground floor. They kept it hot until eleven and then cleared it away.

The breakfast room was empty of people and the food was untouched; I was the first one here. I loaded up a plate with a heap that would have embarrassed a lumberjack: Scrambled eggs, pancakes, sausages, scalloped potatoes, steamed asparagus and spinach swimming in butter. My mouth was salivating furiously. I put some steamed salmon on my plate as well.

While I was enjoying the tender fish, a memory surfaced. As soon as I was old enough to be aware of the irony of my mother eating fish, I'd asked her about it. "Doesn't it make you a cannibal?" She'd laughed and explained that it was no different from humans eating land animals. Mermaids don't have to eat fish to survive in the wild, but many of them do. The salt draws out their predatory nature.

I was patting my mouth with my napkin when Antoni walked by the open door. He must have spotted me in the corner of his eye because he reappeared and came in. "I was looking all over for you yesterday. Where did you go?"

Did his question sound nosy to me now because I had something to hide? I grabbed my glass of water and opened my throat, draining the glass in one gulp. Goodness knew, I was going to need it. He raised his eyebrows.

"I spent the day with my mom. How are your ribs?" I asked, trying to sound cool and detached. I piled my dirty dishes together and took them to the bins that the staff left out for that reason.

Antoni stepped closer. His scent drifted over me. I swayed unsteadily. "I'm fine. Can we talk?" he asked, reaching to put a hand on my shoulder.

"I don't think that's necessary." I ducked under his arm and left the breakfast room.

"I need to know what you remember, what happened to us in the water," he said as he followed me into the hall.

So that's what he was after. "What do you think happened?" I said, stalling for time as my mind went scrambling for an answer. Why hadn't I thought further about this? I should have known he wouldn't let it rest.

"Don't play games with me, Targa," he sighed. "Why won't you just tell me what happened?" The pleading sound in his voice gave me pause. I turned to face him. His eyes explored my face, seeking some kind of truth. He needed peace and I couldn't give it to him, not by telling him what really happened.

I closed my eyes and called the dormant violins in my chest to life. "You passed out," I said, opening my eyes and looking straight into his. The music poured out of my throat and washed over him. His face went still, listening. "I swam to you using my lifejacket as a paddle board. I dragged you to shore and went running for help. The boys in the boathouse found you."

He slowly repeated everything I had said, word for word, as though they were sinking into his mind and becoming his new reality. Goosebumps ran down my back. He believed everything; I could see the authenticity of his belief etched on his face. Once the violins came out they seemed to want to stay out. I pushed them away with effort, cleared my throat and said in my normal voice, "Now, have some peace about it Antoni."

He seemed to snap out of the reverie at the sound of my human voice but he no longer looked confused. "Thank you for saving my life," he said, solemnly.

I nodded and smiled, but inside I felt bitter. I had just used my siren wiles for the first time, on purpose, to deceive a man. A faint wave of nausea rolled over me, along with the sensation that I needed to scrub myself clean. I turned to walk away, resolving never to use my voice to deceive anyone ever again.

He followed me. "Thank you for explaining Targa, but that's not all. Can we talk about what happened after please? It's important."

I turned to face him, but kept my distance. "Ok, go ahead."

That pulled him up short. "Here?"

"Why not here?" I took another step back and crossed my arms. I realized that any gesture I made that was meant to protect him from my siren wiles would appear as defensive. I dropped my arms.

"You know why not here." He came closer and lowered his voice. "Just for a few minutes. Did I hurt you so badly that you don't even want to speak to me now? Your mom's work is just getting started; you'll be here for a while yet. Do you really want to avoid me all summer?"

My brain was fuzzing out again. I took in the hazel eyes, the soft mouth, and the sound of his voice. I was losing focus in spite of the water I'd just guzzled. I stepped backwards realizing with annoyance that once again, my body language and what I was about to say were going to contradict one another. "You didn't hurt me, Antoni," I said. "I just won't be responsible for you getting fired."

He took a step closer. "And I appreciate that, but it's going to cause even more suspicion if we suddenly stop hanging out. What conclusion do you think everyone will come to?"

His scent washed over me again. My heart was speeding up. My skin began to tingle. Electricity zinged through every nerve. Now I was the one who was grinding my teeth. "Will you stop that please?"

"Stop what?" He looked genuinely confused.

"Standing so close to me. I can't think straight."

He had the audacity to grin. My temper flared. He had no idea how hard this was for me. The squeak of a trolley wheel came from around the corner. I grabbed his wrist and pulled him through the nearest door, praying the room was empty. It was. It was an office of cubicles abandoned for the weekend.

"Stand there please. And for the love of Pete, stop moving around." I stepped away from him and my thoughts cleared a little.

"You are a very strange woman." He grinned, "I like it."

"Don't flirt with me, Antoni. You'll only make this harder."

"I want you, Targa," he said suddenly, using my own words against me. His eyes darkened and I recognized desire. I had seen it a million times before in the faces of men when they looked at my mother.

I let out a frustrated groan. "You're playing with fire, Antoni. You think you're in control here? You're not. You don't want to lose your job? Then stay away from me. Tell Martinius I irritate you. Ask him to assign someone else. Or better yet, tell him that I'm happier to be left on my own. I don't need a babysitter." This was certainly true. Now that I was a mermaid I wanted to be in the ocean, not drinking coffee along a canal.

"I can't stop thinking about you." He stepped closer.

"Don't," I warned.

"Don't what? This?" In two strides of his long legs he was on me. My brain checked out like I'd been shot up with morphine. We staggered backward together until my back hit the wall with a dull thud. His hands slid around my waist and his mouth covered mine. His fragrance surrounded me like a cloud. The siren in me thrilled to his touch and the tingle in my skin was back. A faint note of musk emanated from me.

He lifted me off the ground and pressed me against the wall. His tongue found mine as the kiss became hard and deep. One broad hand slid up the leg of my shorts and cupped my bottom, fingers splaying towards my centre. No one had ever touched me so intimately before. I gasped against his mouth, curling my leg around his waist. His other hand found the skin of my back and snaked around me, his fingers curling over my ribs from behind and grazing the bottom of my breast. An animalistic sound came from deep in his throat, vibrating between us. For a half second I thought someone else was in the room, the sound was so unlike him.

His mouth moved from mine, across my jaw to the skin under my ear where he inhaled. "What have you done to me?" he groaned. "Your smell, your taste. You've bewitched me."

"I've bewitched you," I repeated in a daze, my eyes closed. Somewhere down deep something sparked. My eyes snapped open. "Bewitched," I said again. I gritted my teeth and pushed at him, siren and human having a serious cage-match inside me. I squirmed and he put me down. I ducked out of the circle of his arms, moving away from his scent. "Yes, I've bewitched you Antoni." I heard a violin and swallowed hard, trying to shove it back down my throat.

"What?" he said, turning towards me, hands reaching. His eyes were barely hazel anymore, they were a rich limpid brown, his pupils fully dilated even with the morning light streaming in the windows. He looked drugged.

"This isn't real," I said fiercely, satisfied to hear that the music was gone.

"What are you talking about?" He looked confused. Didn't this guy ever get mad? I felt like the key was to get him angry.

"I tricked you," I said. Hating myself, I continued, "I was seducing you. I just..." my mind skittered, searching for an excuse. "I just wanted to see if I could get you to snap out of your professional facade for once." I moved back as he stepped towards me. "It was a dare from my friends. I guess I can tell them that I won."

"You're lying," he said. "You're lying to protect me." He stepped forward. "You don't need to do that. What I said before, about my job. I can handle it. We'll be smart."

That didn't sound like the real Antoni. He was bargaining, and he was advancing when I'd clearly told him to retreat.

"I'm not lying." I stepped back again but my voice was steady.

"Whatever I feel, I know you feel it too. It's real. We have magic, Targa." But he didn't take another step.

I had to go in for the kill now or I was going to lose my resolve. I wanted him, but I didn't want him like this – with siren tricks. "No, we're not magic, Antoni. I don't feel anything for you. I seduced you on a dare because I'm a stupid teenager and I'm sorry. I'm so sorry I did that. It's my turn to apologize to you now. I was foolish."

The dark desire drained from his iris'. He searched my face, hazel eyes imploring. He didn't look angry. He just looked sad. But I still couldn't tell if he believed me or not.

"Have it your way, Targa," he said softly, and then turned and pushed out through the swinging door, leaving me alone.

I let my breath out in a frustrated groan and kicked an office chair. It rolled across the carpet on squeaky wheels and then tipped over. This sucked. I could have any guy I wanted, but how would I ever know if he genuinely wanted me too?

24

After the day in the office with Antoni I got into a steady routine which centred around avoidance. During the day while my mother was diving with the team, I would leave the manor early and go down to the ocean. I would stash my clothes among the rocks at the secluded beach and then shed my human life just like I shed my legs and spend the morning exploring the Baltic. I knew where *The Sybellen* was and was always sure to stay far away from her and the dive team, my mother's cautions still ringing in my ear.

Mom and I discussed the figurehead at length, wondering whether Sybellen might still be alive, and where she might have gone after she had disappeared. For the first several days after we discovered the figurehead, I thought about the sculpture a lot, but as the summer days fell into routine, I began to forget.

There was a marvellous world under the water waiting to be discovered, at the speeds and depths that I could swim and the visibility that I had, nothing was hidden to me. I always stayed far from the shipping lanes, which were easy to detect by the scent of diesel in the water, and I never stayed where there was a vessel in sight.

I played with schools of dolphins and orcas. I made friends with a humpback cow and calf who frolicked with me like they were puppies. I joined a school of hundreds of thousands of flying fish and spent an entire morning leaping out of the water with them, seeing how high I could fly.

Whenever I found a sea creature in distress I would help them as best I could. I was shocked at how much garbage there was in the water. How could people use this beautiful place as their own personal dump? I borrowed a huge fishing net from the Novak boathouse and spent days doing nothing but dragging for garbage.

One day, while I was examining a strange graveyard of whale skeletons laying scattered across the ocean floor, the light suddenly dimmed. I thought maybe I'd lost track of time, as that could easily happen while underwater, so I surfaced to see if it was evening. As I ascended, I noticed that the light was greener than usual. Nearing the surface, I realized I was coming up under a thick layer of slimy green mush that was floating on the water.

My gills struggled and pulled, not able to find oxygen in the water. I felt as though I might suffocate. I descended again to where the water was clear and then swam along the ocean floor until the green light turned yellow, and then surfaced.

As far as my eye could see there was nothing but floating green mush. This must be the algae bloom that Antoni had been talking about. I was distressed to see how large the bloom was, and steered clear of the area from then on.

Even though some of what I discovered about the ocean was concerning, I felt carefree whenever I was in the water. It became a meditation for me. My worries melted away; thoughts of Antoni dissolved like powder. I was never once concerned for my safety. I had a communion with the creatures of the sea, even the predatory ones. I felt protective of them, like it was my job to be a guardian.

"Mom," I asked one evening as we were enjoying a cup of tea before bed. "What's salt-flush? You know, what you told Martinius about? You made it sound like something more than just the normal siren-cycle of salt and fresh water flushes."

"It is, it's very different. Salt-flush is not a state that any mermaid would ever pursue on purpose. I can only tell you the theory of it," she explained. "Sometimes, if a mermaid becomes over-saturated with salt, her system goes through another change. Usually, it'll happen to a siren who has experienced the urge to come to land and find a mate, but she's so far out in the ocean when the urge hits that she doesn't make it to fresh water in time. The salt takes her over and she becomes very much like any other creature in the ocean. She operates purely on instinct, and loses all of her human-like intelligence. If she's gone that far..." She shook her head. "There is usually no coming back."

I had some small idea of what salt-flush might feel like. What little salt there was in the Baltic seemed to wash away the concerns of my human life, but all the problems and stresses came rushing back to me as soon as I stepped on land. My siren consciousness would fade away and the human one would take centre stage. Sometimes, it would hit me with such force that it took my breath away.

In the mornings, I never went too far out because I wanted the staff to see my face over lunch so that people knew I was around. But I dodged Antoni with the craftiness of an undercover agent. I knew he was wondering where I was because everyday someone on staff would tell me he was looking for me. I'd say thank you and then ignore the message. I knew I couldn't avoid him forever, especially when it was his job to make sure I was looked after, but I would push it for as long as I could.

In the afternoons, I would explore further out. I found dozens of shipwrecks. Most of them were vessels that weren't that old, really just junk. I explored them anyway. I came to know the designs of different kinds of boats. Fishing vessels, schooners, and ferries, viking ships, even aircraft. I was amazed at how many wrecks there were on the ocean floor. I even saw a wreck that had settled on top of an older wreck.

I found myself researching at night, looking for the stories behind these disasters. Estimates put the number as high as three million wrecks on the ocean floor, and there were all kinds of reasons - fires, collisions, negligent seamanship, engine failure, storms, ice, insurance fraud, instrument failure, hydrogen sulphide bubbles, underwater volcanoes, running aground, naval battles. The list went on and on.

I was constantly fascinated when I was in the ocean and I desperately wished that I could share the time with my mother. I lay in bed with my phone in my hand, fingers hovering over the digital keyboard. I wanted tell my friends what had happened, what I was going through. Underneath the excitement around my big change was a loneliness and melancholy that I couldn't share it with anyone.

Texts from my friends were less frequent than I thought they'd be, but that suited me fine. I was totally out of reach most of the time anyway. I heard from Saxony that she loved Italy and that she'd bonded rather nicely with the younger boy, Isaia. She'd also met a couple of cute Italian men who were pretty much complete opposites of one another, and she wasn't sure which one she liked better.

Georjayna said that Ireland was turning out to be not what she expected, but that Jasher had finally shown his human side, so that was good. Akiko was noticeably absent from our group texts but she had warned us that might happen.

My phone chimed late one night, waking me just after I fell asleep. I rolled over and peered at the screen.

Saxony: *Have you guys heard from Akiko lately?*

Georjayna: *Nope, not since she first arrived in Kyoto. You?*

Me: *No, me either. Should we be worried?*

Saxony: *Well, she did say that she was going to be remote so maybe she has no connection.*

Me: *I'm sure that's it. It's not like her not to touch base.*

Saxony: *Yes it is. It's totally like her.*

Georjayna: *Well, there you go. She'll write when she wants to. Akiko, when you see this - we hope you're having fun, let us know that you're alive sometime, k?*

I shut down my phone, rolled over and went back to sleep almost instantly. If there was one friend that I never worried about it was Akiko. She was teeny and quiet but she was the smartest, most resourceful person I knew. I trusted that she'd write when she could.

Some evenings, if I wasn't tired and staying in our suite and doing research on what I'd discovered earlier that day, I would go out to sea again with Mom.

She showed me how she would set *The Sybellen* up so that the team would have a successful dive the next day. We did just enough to prep the site that the team wouldn't notice that anything had been disturbed, but enough to make artifacts visible to a human eye and place them out of danger. By the time we were through, artifacts were placed like cherries ripe for the picking.

We would move a piece of timber that looked like it was in a precarious position and might shift in a bad way. We untangled crates and barrels that were wrapped up in rope that might take a human diver hours to figure out. We gently uncovered artifacts on the ocean floor, blowing the sand back to reveal just enough that the men could easily spot them. With those that would be dangerous for a human diver to unearth, we would excavate and move them to a place that gave a diver easy access. Mom showed me how to use my tail and webbed hands to mimic the ocean currents and partially settle the sand over the item in a natural way. We were always careful to leave algae or barnacles on everything.

We'd be back at the manor in the wee hours of the morning and tucked into our beds like good little humans. Every two or three days, Mom would go out to the site without me because I'd finally crash with exhaustion from all the exercise. I would sleep from eight or nine in the evening until noon or one the next day. My sleep was dreamless and deep. I would bounce out of bed ready for more adventure.

I ate enough to fuel three men. I easily drank a dozen litres of water a day. I hid a lot of what I consumed, eating in private and at off-hours whenever I could, but the staff were still astonished at my appetite.

My body grew sleek, powerful and flexible. I learned how to use my assets. Through my gills, I could detect oxygen rich water, saltier water, and contaminated water. My tail wasn't just a powerful propulsion system, it could also detect currents and fine temperature changes as well as mineral content which would alert me to something metallic or artificial in the water, or a natural mineral deposit in the seabed. I sensed deposits in the ocean floor that mining, gas, and oil companies would have killed to discover.

With their protective cover, my eyes saw better underwater than they did above water. Even murky water, while a challenge, still proved relatively easy to navigate, although I didn't enjoy swimming in gloom very much. It was the vast expanses of clear, clean, life-filled water that thrilled me the most. My body quickly went from soft to strong and I felt indestructible.

I passed several weeks this way while skirting Antoni successfully. The men were bringing up items from the manifest and checking things off their list every day. Mom reported that the Novak team members who had free time had begun to come along on the dives just to watch the Bluejackets work, and they were amazed.

I ventured into the dining room one day at dinnertime to see that Simon, Martinius, my mom and a few other divers were having a meal together. Mom sat at the end of the group, always on the outskirts. She slid the empty chair next to her back from the table and patted it. I filled a plate from the buffet and joined them. They were talking and laughing and seemed relaxed.

Simon held up a glass of beer and the rest lifted their glasses too, I lifted my glass of water as he toasted, "To the Bluejacket luck, long may it continue."

"Luck?" said Eric, a little more red-faced than usual. "Skill's more like it. There's no such thing as luck in salvage. To us, the best in the world, and to our bonuses!" They all drank. I glanced at Simon but he was too happy to care that Eric had hijacked his toast. Martinius raised an eyebrow at Eric's vulgar mention of money in the presence of their contractor, but didn't say anything.

"Truly, you have a remarkable team," said Martinius to Simon. "What do you credit for your success?" Martinius was a consummate actor; there was no hint of sarcasm in his question.

I watched Mom out of the corner of my eye as I shovelled mashed potatoes into my mouth. She was a blank canvas.

"We hire only masters. Our divers are extremely experienced, they have thousands of dives between them, maybe even tens of thousands," answered Simon. He leaned in closer to Martinius. "She doesn't like it when I single her out, but Mira is by far the most gifted diver I have ever found. I know you've read an article or two but they cannot possibly do her justice. She pretends she hates it, but no one who is that good could ever hate diving. Watching her work is almost eerie," he said, barely over a whisper.

"Is that so?" Martinius answered as though this was truly a revelation. Martinius snuck a glance towards my mother. She caught his eye and hid a small smile behind her napkin. I stifled a laugh at their subtle exchange and then tucked in to my roast beef and gravy.

Sometimes, I would go down to the beach and meet the team as they came in with the day's salvage. I'd always have wet hair so, of course, I told them I had been out for a swim. They'd shake their heads at me and tell me I was just like my mother.

I would help them unload the haul and Micah showed me how to label and tag the artifacts. A lot of what they brought up had to stay submerged in seawater until it had gone through a process to prepare it for exposure to the air. The Novak team would take the items they'd recovered that day and ship them to their preservation lab to clean and catalogue.

I had been congratulating myself for the excellent job I had been doing of dodging emotional and confusion-riddled interactions with Antoni when, a little over three weeks after our last interaction, he finally cornered me.

25

I knew I couldn't dodge him forever but I wished it had been on a different day. It was a day that I'd gone trawling for garbage. I was dragging the net, which was full of trash, towards the 1960's dump truck, which I'd borrowed from the Novak's garage. I always had it back in less than an hour so people hardly even knew it had gone missing, not that I would have been in trouble for it, I was allowed to take it. I just wanted to draw as little attention to myself as possible. I had become very good at being a ghost.

As I hauled a huge net full of garbage across the sand, I recognized the Jeep that Antoni drove as it pulled up to park on my abandoned beach. I swallowed and took note of which way the wind was blowing, I needed to keep my thoughts and emotions as clear as possible. I braced myself for whatever it was that he'd come to say.

At least I was clothed and finishing up, I had been in mermaid form less than fifteen minutes before. Since my rebirth, I had undergone some physical changes that made even my human appearance a bit different than it had been before. My hair had darkened from dark brown to blue-black, just like my mother's, and had grown at an astonishing rate. My eyes had taken on a supernatural teal colour, not unlike my mother's. Hers were more blue than green, while mine were more green than blue. My skin had become even more pale and took on an opaque and slightly iridescent cast. It was subtle, but I knew that some people had noticed because I was getting a lot more stares than I used to. Freckles, veins, and scars had smoothed over and my skin became more reflective. I suddenly felt extremely conscious of all of these changes and tried to squash the panic fluttering in my breast as Antoni turned the engine off. Would he notice the differences?

I had a kerchief tucked into the back pocket of my shorts and I whipped it out. I raked my hair back into a low haphazard bun and tied the kerchief over my locks like a fifties housewife.

My clothes were damp from my wet body and I had large circles of moisture at my crotch and armpits. I was not a pretty sight and I told myself that, with Antoni, that was a good thing. I picked up the net of trash again, pulling it up out of the water and onto the sand.

Antoni got out of the truck, shut the door, and ambled across the sand. He wore a pair of aviator sunglasses which, along with his recently clipped hair, made him look like a fighter pilot. He was wearing a white Novak company polo that had an embroidered mermaid crest over his heart, red shorts and navy deck shoes.

I'd come to learn that European guys liked to dress this way, unlike the boys back home who liked to wear ripped t-shirts and their pants half falling down. Why did Antoni always have to look so sharp, so together? He made me feel like even more of a beach bum. As he approached, my heart did a little flip and I realized just how much I had missed him.

"What on earth..." He took his sunglasses off, his eyes widening. "I thought I'd find you reading a book and lolling on a beach towel not dragging what looks like about four thousand kilos of trash across the sand in a fishing net. Seriously, what are you doing?" His eyes moved from my trash haul to me and they skimmed my body from kerchief to bare feet. "You look incredible by the way. What is this, your daily workout? You know we have a gym, right?"

I'd stopped pulling the garbage and tried to make like its weight was too much for me. "Are you going to stand there gawking or are you going to help me?"

He hooked his sunglasses into the top of his polo and grabbed a corner of the net. Together we dragged it up into the bed of the truck. It was nearly overflowing.

"Targa, have you lost your mind? How did you even do all this by yourself?" He gestured at the mess.

"There's a lot of crap in the ocean. Or hadn't you noticed?"

For the first time since I'd met him, he looked really stung. "Of course I've noticed. It offends me too. In fact, I organize a volunteer crew every summer to do a clean up. But what are you going to do? Clean the entire Polish shoreline all by yourself?" He gestured down the length of beach.

It was good that he'd put it that way. At least he thought that I was hiking along the shoreline and picking trash up off the beach instead of dragging the net along miles of ocean.

The trash tended to gather in eddies. I used my sensitive tail to detect where the currents on the top of the water met, creating large, slow moving whirlpools which collected floating refuse.

"If I have to. I have to take the truck back. The dump closes at three. Thanks for your help." I headed around to the driver's side. I hoped he wouldn't kick up a fuss at me driving without an international licence. At least they drove on the right hand side of the road here so it was easy for me.

He followed me around to the driver's side. "Targa," he said, and the sincerity in his voice gave me pause. I had a feeling that my lack of a license wasn't on his mind. "I know you've been avoiding me, but will you please just let me talk to you for a minute?"

I took off my glasses and rubbed at the tender spot on the bridge of my nose. I looked him in the eyes, expectantly, "So talk." My human self knew that I was being unnecessarily rude, but my siren self didn't care, even if my heart was straining through my ribcage towards him. Sirens didn't get their mates by being polite. Manners had gone from a necessity of life to something that took too much energy.

As soon as I'd looked at him, he stopped and something in his face changed. "You... look different," he said, slowly.

I sighed, but didn't say anything. He hadn't asked a question, and I didn't feel like making up some dumb excuse.

"How are you even paler than when you first arrived? Haven't you been spending every flipping day outside?" His eyes scanned down my legs. "You haven't been in your suite, that's for sure."

I chose to redirect. "Did you come here to talk about my skin tone?"

"No, I didn't." He sighed. "I came to say, first of all, that it's not necessary for you to avoid me like I have some contagious disease. And second of all..." he paused, looking as though he was searching for words. "This is really dumb. I get it, you played a prank on me to show off to your friends. You apologized. Can we just put it behind us now and be friends? I miss hanging out with my Canadian buddy."

Now he sounded more like the Antoni I knew, the platonic one that I'd spent the first week with. I wished that I could go back to my old feelings, the new ones were so complicated. I took a breath, feeling myself softening, my defences coming down just a little. I was infinitely grateful that the wind was blowing his scent away from me.

"You're not mad? What I did wasn't nice," I said.

He shrugged. "I'm not mad. I was a teenager once too. We've all done stupid shit." I suppressed a laugh. It was the first time I'd ever heard him say 'shit' and it sounded funny in his accent.

He raised his eyebrows. "Friends?"

"Friends," I agreed. "But, you know the job is more than half over. I'll be going home soon anyway."

"Yes, the salvage is going at an unprecedented rate. I was hoping you wouldn't bring that up," he sighed. "Look Targa, I do feel something for you, something amazing that I've never felt for anyone before. And I'm trying not to imagine how I'll feel when you go home. If what you said was true..." he trailed off.

So, he still wasn't convinced. I couldn't tell if I was happy or sad about that. Everything was muddled.

"If what you said was true then I'm happy just to have met you. You are one of a kind and I can only hope that there will be a woman in my future who makes my heart feel like it does when I'm around you."

This sweet monologue was so humble, so vulnerable and so honest that it made me feel like a complete shit. How could I think that the desire he had shown me wasn't real after a speech like that? He cared about me enough to let me go because that was what he thought I wanted.

I wanted to tackle him into the sand and cover him with kisses. I wanted to tell him that he made my heart explode out of my chest. He made violins come out of my throat for crying out loud. I wanted to scream with frustration.

Instead, I lied to him again. "I hope that woman is in your future too." Something wilted inside of me like a blossom charred by the sun. What was I supposed to take away from this? Was I even doing the right thing?

He stepped forward to give me a hug and I turned away from him and opened the truck door. "Now, help me get rid of this heinous load of crap, please." I got in and shut the door.

I could see him in my periphery, through the open driver's side window. I couldn't turn my head and look at him, this was already hard enough. I turned towards the passenger's side and grabbed a bottle of water. A hot tear slipped down my cheek and I angrily brushed it away. I opened the water bottle and chugged it.

"Sure, Targa," he said, quietly. "I'll follow you so you don't have to come all the way back here and drop me off."

I nodded and he disappeared.

As he followed me the few miles to the dump, I couldn't stop the flow of hot tears. I wasn't sobbing; my eyes just wouldn't stop watering. This was new. Was this the way mermaids wept?

When we got there I had to make a show of splashing my face with bottled water to make it damp so it covered my tears.

As we unloaded the trash together, I could feel Antoni watching me but I still couldn't look at him, and I kept my sunglasses on.

I didn't feel strong enough to keep denying what I wanted most. *Only a few more weeks to go.* But the emotion that came with that thought was not relief but heartbreak.

26

After the day on the beach, Antoni was back to his old self. By which I mean he was perfectly behaved and professional. I stopped avoiding him, and there were no more seduction attempts from either side. I made sure that I kept my physical distance whenever we spent time together, which wasn't as much as before because I still wanted to be in the ocean as much I could, and it was hard to be around him.

I was running out of time. The job was winding down and we were scheduled to leave in a little over a week.

Towards the end of the job, I'd stopped going out to *The Sybellen* with my mom at night. She said there wasn't much left to do and she was happy to do it on her own. She told me to enjoy my time in the Baltic before we headed home, and to build up my strength as much as I could, so I'd been swimming all day everyday.

I collapsed on the couch in our suite with my usual cup of tea. It was after dinner and I was full and tired. It was one of those evenings where I felt the deep exhaustion from the last few days' activities and suspected that I'd be dead to the world for 16 hours or so. Mom was in a meeting to talk through a few things about the final schedule with the team.

My eyelids had begun to droop when the door to our suite slammed open and my mom came in. My eyes snapped open. "Mom!" My heart skittered.

She had a hard look on her face. She was upset about something. "Sorry, sunshine." She closed the door with more care than she'd opened it. "I didn't realize you were sleeping."

"Such manners." Interesting. Since we'd arrived in Poland, my mother's manners had improved markedly, while mine had degenerated. She'd been spending a lot of time in nearly salt-less water, a huge change from the Atlantic, while I'd gone from human to siren. I supposed it made some kind of strange sense. "What's wrong?" I pushed myself up straight and set my teacup on the coffee table. "Do you want some tea?"

"No thanks." She sat in the chair across from me. She put her fingers to her temples as though she had a headache. "It's Eric. What a piece of work."

"What did he do now?" Eric had been making himself a thorn in everyone's side for weeks. He'd been surly and disagreeable, distracted and disorganized in meetings and rude to both the Novak employees and his own teammates.

At one point, when I had gone to the beach to help the team unload artifacts at the end of the day, I heard angry voices as I came over the bluff. It was Jeff and Eric, who were supposedly friends. Jeff was saying, "Get out of here, Eric. You need to cool down."

I could see them standing on the beach and facing off. Jeff gestured to some men who were bringing gear off *The Brygida*, the Novak vessel they took out to the site of *The Sybellen* everyday. There was a mix of Bluejacket and Novak employees among them.

"They've got nothing to do with your problems, so you either figure out a way to be civil, or you get on the first plane home. We don't need your garbage attitude. You're spoiling a good thing, mate." Jeff's voice was harsh but there was also sympathy in it, like he knew why Eric was behaving the way he was, he just didn't think it was right.

Eric had planted a hand on Jeff's chest and shoved. "What, are you giving orders now?"

"That's enough you two," said Simon as he emerged from *The Brygida's* cockpit. "This ain't preschool. Eric, we already talked about this. Go back to the estate, you're done for the day."

Eric had stormed off the beach, muttering to himself. He'd passed by me without even noticing that I was there. As soon as he'd left, the mood of the team completely changed, it was like sunshine after a storm. Soon, they were laughing and talking as we worked, me among them.

I imagined that Mom had been dealing with something similar, but normally she never let stuff like that get to her. "I thought you didn't really care about your colleagues, Mom? What's got you so riled up?"

"He's never been a bowl of peaches, but Eric has really cranked up his inner asshole lately. I've always had the label of being the prickliest person on the team and that's the way I'd like to keep it. But Eric's become a real bastard." She sighed and leaned back in the chair. "Simon negotiated performance bonuses with Martinius before he signed the contract, he always does that. Payment should be partially made based on how successful the dive is and we're always successful so it's good business to do it this way. The client is happy, too, since it means that if they don't get what they want, then it doesn't cost them so much," she explained.

"My guess is that you're the reason the guys get those bonuses every time," I commented. Her team would never know how much they had to be grateful to my mom for, and for her trouble she was either ostracized or hit on.

She gave me a tired smile. "Yes, I suppose I am." Her smile faded. "Since the dive has been going off like clockwork, Eric has been harassing Simon to renegotiate the terms of the contract."

"He can't do that," I said. "Even I know that."

"Exactly. He knows we wouldn't even if we could, so I don't know why he's got this insane idea. He pestered Simon about it to the point where Simon blew up at him on the deck of *The Brygida* one day.

Simon has been so happy to have gotten this job that it seemed like nothing could get him down but I guess Eric finally frayed his last nerve."

"Did he stop, then?" I asked, pulling the teabag out of my cup and setting on the saucer. "Eric, I mean."

"No, he got worse!" she said, throwing her hands up. "Tonight at dinner, he actually brought it up in front of Martinius. Can you believe that?"

"Again? What did he say?" I was horrified and embarrassed for Simon and the team. I was surprised by how bothered my mother was about it though; I'd never seen her ruffled by dissension at work before.

"Martinius was congratulating the team on some of the artifacts we'd managed to bring up," she started.

"Thanks to you," I interrupted. "What were they?" I imagined gold bars or a tiara encrusted with jewels.

"A set of hand-carved chair backs," she said, brightening. "Actually they are really cool."

"That is so not what I expected you to say, but go on."

"Anyway, Big-Mouth jumps in and says that since the haul has been even better than expected, that the contract should be amended to stipulate that a percentage will be paid based on the value of each artifact. Not only that, that there should be an additional bonus given if we recover every single item on the manifest because that never happens in diving, period."

I was horrified but also amazed. "*Are* you going to recover every single item on the manifest?" If anyone knew the answer to that it was my mom.

"Yes, we are. The team doesn't know it yet but I do. I've already located all the items and planned out how they're going to find everything and when. It's in the bag. All except for one thing, but it's not on the manifest, so it doesn't count."

"What's that?"

"The bell." She snagged my cup and took a sip.

"Oh right. Martinius said that at the dinner on the first night," I recalled.

"But really, what Eric suggested was not only completely ridiculous but insulting and in poor taste. I mean, poor Martinius," she said. "The guy doesn't deserve that."

"Wow, Mom," I said, genuinely impressed. "We might make a human out of you yet. I've never seen such empathy. And I don't think I've ever heard you condemn someone for 'poor taste' before."

She laughed. "Must be the lack of salt. The Baltic is leeching all the salt out of my system with every dive. Soon I'll be a big softie, just like you." She set my teacup on the table.

"I don't know about that. Sometimes it feels like I'm well on my way to becoming the prickly-pear that you used to be. I did mean to ask you about the whole salt thing, actually. I've never swam anywhere else, is it really different swimming in the Atlantic?" I drained the last of my tea.

"Yes, it's night and day," she said, easily.

"What do you mean?" My curiosity about swimming in saltier water was already piqued but I wanted to prepare myself better for what to expect.

A thoughtful look took over her face. "Do you remember when your dad and I took you to that ranch outside of Saltford one summer? The one that your dad's friend owned, what was his name..." She paused. "Grant."

I nodded. "One Tree Farms," I said, wondering where she was going with this. "They were into horse racing."

"Do you remember the little Shetland pony that you took a ride on?"

I laughed at the memory. "Yes, Shortcake. I was amazed that a pony could come in pink, she was a dream come true for a little girl."

The pony wasn't actually pink but she was as close as a horse could get. Her hide and mane were a strawberry blonde colour, and she was cute and tiny. I had gone crazy as soon as I'd seen her, begging my parents for a ride.

"Right," my mom continued, smiling. "And what was she like to ride?"

"She was a breeze. I was a bit nervous that she'd run away with me but the owner told me that she never misbehaves with little kids on her back. And she didn't, it was like she knew that it was my first time on horseback. She really took care of me."

"Yes, exactly. Now do you remember the one that your dad rode?" she asked.

"Oh," I said, and my eyebrows crept up my forehead as understanding dawned. "Esquire." I said, recalling the animal's name.

A vision of the huge bay stallion filled my mind's eye. He'd been a gorgeous creature. He was a glossy brown colour with black legs, mane, and tail, and three white socks up to the ankles. He'd been kept in his own paddock away from the other horses because he was as fiery and aggressive as stallions were known to be. He was a two-year old and being trained to compete.

The owners of One Tree were involved in a horse-racing event called steeplechase. It was a dangerous sport requiring the horses to leap huge fences with water troughs on the other side. Esquire had shown promise because he was powerful, a great jumper, fearless, and full of the grit that a champion needed. My dad's eyes had lit up at the sight of him. Grant agreed to let my dad take Esquire out for a ride while we all watched nervously from the fence.

I had perched up on the top of a fencepost holding onto my mom's neck. She steadied me with her arm around my hips as we watched dad mount the stallion. My father had been a good rider, he'd grown up on a farm just outside of Saltford and was comfortable around horses, although it had been years since he'd ridden.

We watched as he took Esquire around the training track a few times, first just at a trot and eventually at full speed. I watched wide-eyed as Esquire's hooves flew and clumps of dirt spewed out from underneath him, leaving chewed up track in his wake.

I'll never forget the pounding sound of the animal, the incredible surge of speed he gave down the home stretch, legs moving like pistons, driving his considerable weight forward. His nose stretched out front and his nostrils snorting and flaring.

When my dad had finally slowed him down, Esquire had reared and pawed the air as though he didn't ever want to stop running. His flanks were wet and his ribs heaved. I remembered being frightened that dad would get bucked off but instead he got the animal under control, with some effort, then cantered the beast up to the fence, keeping a safe enough distance from us. My father was not afraid; rather his face was alive with energy and joy. He was breathing hard, even though it wasn't he who'd done the running.

I had snuggled close to my mom as the animal had approached. The stallion had looked straight at me – no, through me. He looked as though he'd ridden straight up from hell and he'd come for my soul. I couldn't have put words to it then, I was far too young. But I felt the power and spirit of the animal so keenly that day, and had an intense respect for horses ever since.

"What are you saying?" I asked. "That the Baltic is Shortcake and the Atlantic is Esquire?" I wasn't sure if it was dread or excitement pooling in my belly, probably both.

"It's a poor metaphor," said my mom, "but basically, yes."

"No," I said, shaking my head as I recalled the look in the stallion's eyes. "I think it's the perfect metaphor. And on that note, I do believe I shall turn in. Thanks for the terrifying comparison."

She laughed. "Good night. Oh, by the way…" She looked over the chair back at me.

I paused with my hand on the door handle. "Yeah?"

"Martinius has planned a wind-up party for the Bluejackets and the Novak employees. It's next week."

"What's a wind-up party?"

"To celebrate the end of the project, and all the successes and such," she explained.

"Ah." I shouldn't have been surprised, after all his family had been searching for *The Sybellen* for a century and a half. It was something worth celebrating. "What kind of party will it be?" My mind was going through the clothing in my luggage and coming up empty.

"From what I've gathered it will be quite the affair." She looked up at the ceiling with a pained expression, and then recited word for word what she'd been told in one long outward breath. "Friends of Martinius and prominent members of the community have been invited, also dignitaries and politicians from other Scandinavian and European countries." Then she took a big breath in. "I memorized that, just cuz I knew you'd ask."

I laughed, but now I was concerned. "We didn't pack anything suitable for that. I mean, I sure didn't, did you?"

"Nope," she got up and stretched. "We're going to have to go shopping."

I groaned and planted my head on the door.

27

I chewed on the dress problem for a day or so. Antoni had already shown me the fashion district in Gdańsk so I knew where to go for clothing, but I no longer had a desire to spend time in the city. Most girls would love to hit the brand name stores on high street with a wad of cash but I'd rather pick trash out of a tangle of seaweed than try on taffeta.

"I know," my mom said with empathy, "now that you're a siren you can hardly think of anything you'd rather do less than go shopping. But, I've got some cash for you, an advance on your part of the performance bonus. So at least you can get something nice."

"Thanks Mom," I said, giving her a hug. It never occurred to me that I'd be paid for the small amount of help I had given. "I'm still dreading it. Do you think Martinius would mind if I asked his secretary to go shopping for me?" I joked.

"Why don't you just order something online, lovey?" Mom said. She was probably sick of listening to me complain.

I blinked in surprise. "You're a genius!" I kissed her cheek.

"I'm not just any old fish, I'm hip to the times."

"I think the fact that you just said 'hip to the times' means that you're not," I laughed. "But that is a golden idea. What are you going to do for a dress?"

"One of our meetings this week is at a lab in Gdańsk, I'll just pop into one of the shops while I'm there and pick something out. It'll take me thirty seconds."

I knew it would, too.

I got the Novak estate delivery address from Antoni and borrowed my mom's credit card and laptop. Within the hour, I had found a simple black baby doll dress that I thought was perfect. As I was trying to figure out the confusing European sizes, Mom came into my room.

"Let's see, what did you find?" She turned the screen towards herself. "You're kidding, right? That's what you're ordering?"

"What wrong with it?" I said, defensively.

"It'll make you look like you're twelve, that's what's wrong with it. Move over."

I squirmed over on the bed and made room for her. "Since when are you a fashion guru?" Mom had the most boring wardrobe on earth.

"Just because I don't like to dress up doesn't mean I don't know how to." She scrolled through the dresses on the bespoke site that I had found. "Now this..." she turned the screen back towards me, "...is more suitable for a siren, don't you think?"

It was a gown for a princess, not a beach bum like me. The irony that she'd chosen a mermaid style dress wasn't lost on me. It was a strapless, body-hugging gown with ruching up the back. It was described as a one of a kind, ombre design starting with aquamarine at the top and ending in navy blue at the bottom. The silk had been hand-painted using a salting technique to leave a stain suggestive of swirling water. It was made to hug the curves and the 'tail' part of the dress was cut on the bias to give it an elegant draping effect. It was perfect. So why was the thought of wearing it so terrifying?

"If you order anything but that I'll strangle you with your own bikini." Mom slid off my bed and left the room.

I stared at the dress. I couldn't imagine myself in it. I'd never worn anything remotely so beautiful. It was a once in a lifetime dress for a once in a lifetime party.

I punched in my information and hit 'submit'. It was done. After that, I forgot about the dress until it arrived two days later. There was a knock on our door in the morning and I opened it to find Antoni standing there with a large box in his hands.

"Your hairpiece has arrived," he said, grinning.

I whacked him on the shoulder, took the box and shut the door in his face.

"Do I get to see it on you?" his voice came through the door.

"Mom!" I yelled into the room. "Is there anyone you *didn't* tell about this dress?"

"No, honey," Mom called from her bedroom.

"Shameless!" I hollered back.

"Is that a no?" came Antoni's muffled voice.

"Go away," I said, and heard him chuckling as he walked down the hall.

I tore open the box, a little embarrassed at how excited I was about a dress. I guess there was still a human girl buried in me somewhere. I opened the tissue paper wrapping and the dress came spilling out into my hands like a waterfall. It was soft and had the cool, clingy sensation of pure silk.

Mom came out of her bathroom brushing her teeth. She pulled the toothbrush out to say, "So, try it on."

I took it into my room and stripped down to my underwear. After a second thought I took those off too. I gingerly unzipped the back of the dress and stepped into it. I pulled it up my body, languishing in the cool feel of it against my bare skin. I held the front up to my chest, then discovered that I wouldn't be able to reach behind myself and zip it up without it falling down.

I waddled out into the sitting area where my mother was waiting, and turned my back to her. She zipped it up for me, and it closed around my body without pinching or drooping. The cool silk hugged every curve. I seemed to have a lot more of those since I'd started swimming for hours every day.

I turned to show my mom. Her expression said everything. Gone were her teasing remarks. What I saw in her face was an awe that her little girl really had grown up.

"You're perfect," she said, softly. "Go look."

I went into the bathroom where the biggest mirror in the suite was hanging on the back of the door. I closed the door and looked at the figure standing there.

It was a disaster. I looked like a fraud. My hand went to my mouth. The girl in the mirror did the same. Her teal eyes were wide with horror. Her long black hair fell in tangled waves down her shoulders. Despite hours of sunlight her skin was ghostly. She looked like she was trying to be someone she wasn't. She was a little girl playing dress-up and everyone would know it the moment they saw her.

"Targa?" I heard my mom's voice. "What do you think? She poked her head into the bathroom and the image in the mirror went out of my view.

As soon as she saw me, her face changed from happy to concerned. "What's wrong? You don't like it?" She came into the bathroom and shut the door. The fraud in the mirror reappeared.

"I don't want to go to the party anymore, Mom. I can't wear this. I don't feel like me."

Mom stood behind me and pulled my hair away from my face and off my shoulders. She looked into my face in the mirror and I looked into hers. Hers was a face that belonged over a dress like this, not mine. We did look a lot alike, it was true, but she was older, more womanly. My face looked young, unfinished.

"Darling, look at your reflection and answer me this. Do you see a beautiful girl looking back at you?"

I looked. And yes, I knew that I had beauty. I nodded. The girl nodded along with me.

"Well, I don't," she said. "You know what I see?"

I shook my head.

"I see a creature so rare that humans don't even believe she exists. I see an invincible being who is only at the start of a life that will span multiple centuries." Her voice morphed into a quiet symphony of strings. Gooseflesh had come out on my skin, but she wasn't finished. The violins grew as she spoke. "I see a creature who will go places that humans can only dream of going. I see someone who is gifted with everything she needs to find a deep and satisfying love, with or without her siren abilities."

Her body had become luminescent, like a million microscopic lights were sweeping under her skin in waves. It reminded me of the bioluminescent algae that sometimes graced the shores of the ocean at night, churning onto the beach. Her eyes changed to an even more brilliant blue and became lit from within like the luminescence lived in the iris of her eyes. Her voice was soft but held a promise of power. It was like listening to a hundred-piece orchestra playing low, with suppressed ability. "I see someone who knows when to go after what she wants, and when to sacrifice. I see a living legend, a myth come to life. I see my daughter, a mermaid."

I stared at her in the mirror, transfixed. A few moments of silence passed. "No wonder men find you irresistible," I said, finally. "If it's that important to you, I'll wear the bloody dress."

She laughed, her music fading away now and her luminescent skin and eyes dimming to normal. She let go of my hair and kissed me on the cheek. "Wear the dress. Don't wear the dress. Do whatever makes you happy. You have time to exchange it if you want to. Just come to the party. It will be dull as paint without you there."

28

I didn't wear the dress. I tried it on half a dozen times and I liked wearing it in the privacy of my own room, but I knew I wouldn't be comfortable wearing it in public. It was too flashy, over-stated. I would look like I was begging for attention. As a siren, with so many ways to attract men already built in, the dress felt like serious overkill.

So, I returned it and chose a strappy, black knee length dress with a lace overlay. It was elegant and comfortable. It came with a lace wrap to drop over my shoulders or wear as a scarf. I also ordered a pair of black vintage pumps, and thank goodness they fit. I put my hair up into a French twist and donned a simple pair of pearl earrings. I had a black clutch into which I tucked my phone and some lip-gloss. I felt good. My outfit was formal enough to be appropriate for the occasion, but simple enough that I wouldn't feel self-conscious all night.

Mom chose an emerald green column dress made of crepe. It was billowy and concealed her body most of the time but as she moved, it revealed a hint of shape. She wore a tiny pair of emerald studs in her ears which my father had given her and a matching necklace and bracelet. With her hair up in a messy bun and not a stitch of makeup on, she was stunning.

We were transported along with the Bluejacket team to the city in the same black SUV's that had picked us up from the airport. The party was to be held at a hotel in Gdańsk but I didn't know what to expect. Aside from school dances and a couple of weddings, I had been to no formal events.

Once we pulled up to the hotel entrance, a valet was there to open the door. We stepped out onto a red carpet and looked up at the huge stone building we were about to enter. It wasn't a hotel. It was a castle.

"Holy shit," Mom muttered under her breath.

"Yeah." My neck creaked as I looked up in awe.

We entered the lobby, which was a large courtyard open to the sky; only the seating areas and front desk were covered with stone archways. A sign saying 'Novak Stoczniowców Braciz' and an arrow pointing through an arched double doorway showed us the way. We went down a long stone hallway lined with antique furniture, paintings of green countryside, and suits of armour. Muted classical music came from somewhere and as we approached two huge wooden doors we were welcomed by a man and a woman both in black tie who opened them for us.

On the other side of the doors, we came to a halt. A line-up of formally-dressed people, including some Bluejacket team members, were waiting to be welcomed one at a time by Novak executives. We joined the line-up and waited our turn. Mom ushered me ahead of her.

The Novak team greeted every guest; Martinius waited at the very end. Antoni was also there, nearer the front of the line. I assumed Antoni's placement was in accordance with his authority within the company. The fact that he was in the line-up in the first place was already impressive.

When I got to Antoni, he took my hand and bowed to kiss it. He was perfectly polite. Trust him to be the consummate professional.

"Welcome, I'm so happy you're here. Thank you for coming," he said to me squeezing my small, cool hand in his big warm one.

"Thanks, um, you too." I kicked myself inwardly for not having thought of what to say ahead of time. By the time I got to Martinius, after greeting a dozen more people in the welcoming committee, I had finally pulled my words together.

Martinius took my hand and looked me square in the eyes. "You know you'll always be welcome here, Targa. Come home anytime you wish." He squeezed my hand.

"Thank you Martinius, that's very kind. Congratulations on finally achieving your goal. I'm very happy for you," I said.

I noted with sadness that his hand trembled in mine and his head shook ever so slightly. It wasn't nerves. It was age. I had never noticed the tremor before and I wondered just what the project had cost him physically and mentally. He had never shown his stress but there must have been a lot at stake for him both professionally and personally.

"Thank you my dear. Without you and your mother, it never would have happened," he replied generously, patting my hand and then letting me go to greet my mother.

I was distracted from listening to their exchange when it hit me that he'd intentionally referred to his estate as my 'home'. It made me wonder if he still didn't fully believe that my mother wasn't Sybellen.

It warmed me all over to realize that by now, I did feel like this place was a second home. My heart ached when I thought about leaving. Would I ever come back? Would I ever see Antoni or Martinius again? Would I ever swim in the Baltic again?

I was about to ask my mother what Martinius had said to her when we entered the ballroom and I barely kept my jaw from hitting the floor. The room was palatial. People milled about in gowns and tuxedos, making conversation and sipping champagne. It was all very civilized and I felt completely out of place.

As I looked out at the sea of white and grey hair, I realized that I was by far the youngest person in the room. Everyone looked like nobility. I even saw a few tiaras nestled in grey curls and princely red sashes cutting diagonally across masculine chests.

Elaborate crystal chandeliers hung from the ceiling and matching sconces lit the perimeter of the room. Tapestries and paintings hung on the stone walls while massive timbers criss-crossed over our heads. Round tables had been distributed throughout half of the room and set with eight places each. I had never seen tables so beautifully set with silverware, china, crystal and handwritten name cards. The presentation reminded me of the first dinner we'd had with Martinius, only this was even more sumptuous. Large flower arrangements which must have cost a fortune graced the centre of each table.

I came back to myself and turned to put my hand on Mom's arm. "What did Martinius say to you?"

"He said thank you, and that he couldn't have done it without us," she replied. "You?"

"Much the same," I said. "Only he also said that I would be welcome home any time I liked." I emphasized the word 'home'.

"That was kind of him," Mom answered. I couldn't tell if she'd had the same thought that I had about his choice of words.

I spotted the orchestra and realized with surprise that the classical music that had been playing in the background was actually live. A white video screen hung on the wall behind the orchestra and a vintage looking microphone had been set up in front of the conductor. The conductor had his back to the room and was moving his arms artfully to lead the music, his frazzled grey hair bouncing joyously.

"Look." Mom pointed to a far corner of the ballroom. Through a line of slowly moving people, I could see tables, but I couldn't see what had attracted the crowd. It couldn't be food because there was a sit down dinner to be served tonight, not a buffet.

"What is it?"

"It's artifacts taken from *The Sybellen*. Shall we go see?" She took my hand.

"Absolutely!"

Mom snagged two champagne flutes from a waiter on the way

and handed one to me. "Just one," she said, giving me a smile. "To celebrate."

We clinked glasses and took a sip. The champagne was sweet and fizzy. I let bubbles form on my tongue before I swallowed it down.

We approached the display and got in line. Spread out along four long tables covered in navy cloth were a plethora of artifacts. Each one included a label with a description - bottles of wine, vodka and cognac still with the corks in place, a dozen different kinds of coins of all different shapes, sizes, and metals. Heirloom earrings, bone china and silverware, candlesticks, knives, and pieces of armour.

"This is one of the hand carved chair backs that I was telling you about before." Mom pointed to an oddly shaped wooden carving.

If I hadn't known what it was, I'm not sure I would have figured it out. There was no seat or legs, only a slab of carved wood with two posts that would have attached it to its seat.

"There was a set of eight of them. Do you see the faces?" She outlined the shape with her finger. The design was of two bearded heads put back to back so they were facing away from the centre of the chair. Their mouths were open in an angry snarl and their eyebrows were knit down into an expression of fury.

"Friendly," I said.

"Threatening, right? Martinius has a historian looking into the origin. Only a destination was listed in the manifest. My guess is that a military general, or someone similar, commissioned them. Maybe they were to be used at a negotiating table."

"Where were they going?" I admired the fine detailing of the men's beards. Their hair swirled around their heads like an eddy in the ocean.

"The manifest says the Port of Tallinn in Estonia. Often the ports these goods were delivered to was not their final destination. They were picked up by other delivery services and taken further inland."

"Would that have been the case for most of these artifacts?" I asked.

She nodded. "Many of them, yes. Once Novak Shipping delivered them to port, their job was done."

We listened to the questions and speculations of the people around us. The cargo of *The Sybellen* was drawing people together. English accents mingled with Canadian, American, and Polish accents as well as accents I didn't recognize. There were at least three languages being spoken and all of them held tones of reverence and fascination.

We passed rosaries, silver candlesnuffers and tapirs, a pair of scissors, a snuffbox, jewelled cufflinks, a collection of spice jars and shapely oil and vinegar bottles.

"Does everything look different now that it's out of the water, or do they look the same as when you first saw them?" I asked my mom.

"Everything you see here has been cleaned, so they look much better than they did when they were first recovered. The Novak team took time to choose which artifacts to put on display and cleaned those first. We recovered a lot more than what you see here."

An elderly man ahead of us in the line overheard her. He turned towards us and asked in a British accent, "Excuse me, but were you part of the dive team that discovered *The Sybellen*?" Others around us looked at my mother with interest.

"Discovered, no. Salvaged, yes," she replied.

His eyebrows shot up. "Begging your pardon but are there many women salvage divers on your team?"

"No. Just me."

A woman with white hair said, "You see, my darling, how times have changed? Nowadays women do everything that men do."

"Only better," I chimed in, and everyone within earshot laughed.

I wasn't sure if it was because they were from an older generation or the fact that they were Europeans that triggered her to vocalize the observation. In North America, and to my generation, it was old news that women could do the same jobs as men.

"Are you going to be a diver too?" asked the woman.

"I wasn't planning on it until I came here," I said. Mom smiled at me.

"The magic of the treasure hunt has captured your imagination, has it?" said the man, kindly.

"Something like that," I replied, smiling.

I sipped the champagne as we chatted. Before long I felt warm and relaxed and no longer worried about not belonging. After a while I started to feel like everyone's granddaughter.

When word got out that my mom was one of the salvage divers, she quickly became a centre of interest. They wanted every detail about the dive, where the ship was, what shape it was in and how the salvage operation had been executed. All manner of questions came her way, one after the other.

Everyone at the party was connected to Martinius in some way, whether it was through family, business, or government. *The Sybellen* was a legend in this circle and many of them marvelled that she'd ever been found, against so many odds, let alone salvaged.

"Where was she found?" asked the British gentleman.

"What did you think when you saw her for the first time?" his wife added, a sapphire tiara glittering from atop her thinning grey curls.

My mom took a breath to answer when another lady asked, "Aren't you horribly afraid to be all those meters under the sea? I would think it to be frightfully dark and cold."

More well-intentioned people closed in and more questions came before she had time to answer. I felt Mom stiffen, her eyes darting from face to face. The people were just curious but my mother was starting to feel claustrophobic. She stumbled over her words in an effort to answer them but she had lost her composure.

I was desperately trying to think of a polite way to extricate my mother from the interrogation when a familiar scent washed over me. It erased all thought and made my knees weak. I felt his gentle hand at the small of my back and my eyes closed in involuntary pleasure at the warmth that swept over me.

"Ladies and gentlemen," Antoni said, without giving any hint that he was addressing the crowd purely to rescue my overwhelmed mother. "I'm pleased to inform you that there will be a presentation after dinner complete with video clips and animation to help you fully enjoy the salvage journey."

The crowd made comments to show how much they were looking

forward to the presentation and slowly dispersed. My mother took a deep breath and began to relax. She gave Antoni an appreciative smile, which was more than I had seen her give to any man aside from Martinius since we'd arrived here.

Antoni returned her smile then looked down at me. "You'd better save me a dance," he said, his hand still on my back.

"Of course she will," said my mother with an uncharacteristic stroke of gentility.

"Good," he said, and walked away.

"What did you say that for?" I shot her a steely look.

"Well, were you actually going to say no? He's a good man, Targa. They're few and far between. And relax, it's just a dance," she replied. "Let's find our seats."

I followed her with mixed emotions. She knew how confusing my feelings towards Antoni were, how just being near him made all my logic fail so utterly and the mating instinct kick in. So, why was she encouraging me to dance with him? It seemed unlike her to involve herself, even in so small a way. I wondered if the lack of salt in her body was to blame for this too.

Mom and I made our way to the seating map. We'd been placed at the table nearest to the head table, where Martinius would be sitting. We were seated with a blend of Bluejackets and Novak employees. I recognized the names of Simon and Eric; the other four names were Polish.

As everyone got settled and the room grew quiet, a dark-haired woman in a grey satin gown stepped up to the microphone. She waited until the orchestra finished before she began speaking. She spoke in Polish first and the depth of her voice surprised me. Once she was finished her speech she switched to English. She had a heavier accent than either Martinius or Antoni and so I struggled to understand a few words, but I so enjoyed the sound of her voice that I didn't care.

"Welcome friends, family, and colleagues," she said, looking completely at home in front of the mic. "My name is Hanna Krulikoski, Chief Financial Officer of Novak Stoczniowców Braciz. As many of you know," she continued, "In 1869 the Novak family and company experienced a heart-breaking personal and professional tragedy. The loss of Mattis Novak and his wife Sybellen nearly spelled the end for the company. *The Sybellen*, the company's prize ship, was lost at sea along with all the souls on board and the precious cargo. For over 150 years the Novak family has been searching for her and has never given up hope."

She gave a brief overview of the story and how the ship had been discovered before introducing Martinius. "I am so pleased and honoured," she crossed her gloved hands over her heart, "to be the one to welcome you to the celebration of her recovery and to ask our friend, colleague, and leader to the microphone, Martinius Joseph Novak."

The ballroom filled with applause and everyone stood up as Martinius made his way to the front. I looked around at all the warm faces and found myself thinking that neither my mother nor I would ever have a room full of people who were as fond of us as these people were of Martinius.

He too spoke in his native tongue first before he moved to English. He thanked everyone warmly for coming and teased someone named Otto of showing up only for the vodka. The crowd laughed when a balding man with a red face stood up and held aloft a small crystal goblet with a clear liquid in it.

"Many people believed we were foolish to continue searching year after year for the wreck of *The Sybellen*. We've been ridiculed mercilessly over the years for throwing good money after bad, and for our obsession. But you..." He swept both gloved hands out wide to the crowd and then brought them together with a loud clap, clasping them in a sincere gesture of gratitude. It would have looked funny on anyone else but perfectly suited an elderly European gentleman like Martinius. "You understood that without obsession, a task like this is only a dream. You are here because you never wavered in your support, you never stopped believing that she'd one day be found."

As he was speaking, four young men in black tie appeared behind him. It seemed that they were pushing something heavy, as they were bent at the waist. The sound of plastic wheels rolling across the hard-wood floor found its way to my ears. I craned my neck to see what was being presented; my imagination conjuring up an elaborately decorated cake.

As the big black box was rolled into view, I felt the blood drain from my face and a wave of dizziness swept over me. My vision fuzzed out at the sides and I gripped the table, hoping that I didn't faint. I recognized the box instantly. It was the one my mother and I had put the figurehead in.

29

M y blood turned to ice in my veins. "Mom!" I whispered, and patted her thigh under the table. She'd seen the box too and her whole body went stiff. She grabbed my hand under the table and squeezed it.

"What is he doing?" she said under her breath. "We had an agreement."

"This celebration is our thank you for your enduring faith in our quest. It is a thank you for the hard work of all those involved. And it is a celebration to mark the return home of our long-lost Sybellen," Martinius continued.

The black box had come to rest beside Martinius and the men hovered nearby. A spotlight had been lit and was shining down, ready to light up the carved face that would shatter our safety. Each of the men had taken hold of one of the corners of the box and was waiting for the go ahead from Martinius, to let the sides drop away.

"We're leaving. Now," my mom hissed under her breath. "Calmly. No need to panic. We'll be gone before anyone makes the connection."

I wasn't convinced that there was no need to panic. I took a deep breath to calm my nerves. As though we had the idea at the exact same time, my mother and I grabbed our water glasses and drained them. We pushed our chairs back quietly, keeping our movements smooth and unhurried. I was grateful that all attention was on Martinius. My heart pounded and the rush of adrenalin made my legs shake. The champagne/water blend in my stomach soured and I thought I might be sick. We moved slowly towards the door.

We had trusted Martinius; we'd believed him when he'd promised to keep the figurehead a secret. The enchanted evening had turned into a nightmare.

Martinius continued, "Please join me in welcoming her home again. I give you..." the men let the sides of the black wooden crate drop away from the glass box inside, "...*The Sybellen*." Martinius began to clap and the crowd joined in and stood up. People craned their necks to see the contents and a gush of appreciative sounds filled the air.

I was afraid to look, as though seeing the face would seal our fate. Mom grabbed my hand and I looked up to see her with an expression of genuine surprise. I followed her gaze. Inside the box was not the figurehead but a large bronze bell.

Mom and I shared an incredulous look and she burst out laughing, sounding almost giddy. I let out the breath I didn't even realize I had been holding. The realization that he hadn't betrayed us flooded my whole body with relief. We were safe. I held a hand over my heart in an effort to steady the pounding and then joined in the applause.

We hadn't gotten very far. We moved back to our seats and sat down along with the rest of the guests at our table as the applause died away. I glanced around, relieved to see that no one had even noticed that we'd been about to abandon ship.

As my heart calmed, I looked at the bronze artifact which my mom had told me had never been found. The bell had a crack in it but looked otherwise whole. There was an inscription along the base, which I couldn't read from this distance but I knew it would be inscribed with the date *The Sybellen* had been built.

Everyone was chatting about the beautiful bell. A few people from tables that were further away got up from their chairs and approached to have a better look. People were kneeling down beside the bell and taking photographs with it.

"How did you not know that they found the bell?" I whispered to my mother over the general murmur in the room.

She shook her head, baffled. "I had no idea." She leaned towards Simon, on her other side, and asked him about it.

He nodded and said, "We found it less than three hundred metres from the wreck. You weren't there because it was a Saturday."

She whacked him across the arm and he made a show of cowering against her mock fury. "And you didn't tell me? How could you not tell me?"

He held his hands wide. "I thought you knew. I thought for sure one of the guys had told you."

She turned back to me and rolled her eyes. "No one tells me anything."

Eric had watched the exchange with a smug look. He'd enjoyed keeping a secret from the team superstar. It was a testament to how poor my mother's relationships with her colleagues were that not a single one had bothered to tell her about the bell, not even Micah.

It was good that nothing her colleagues did could hurt my mom's feelings, but I was offended enough for both of us. I shot Eric a hard look but he didn't have the decency to look ashamed. He looked back at me as if to say, *what are you going to do about it*?

As the din died down and everyone settled into their seats again, I looked at Martinius to see if maybe he would look in our direction. Had he known that the rolling out of the identical preservation box would put us into a panic? Did he realize that my mother didn't know about the bell?

As though she knew what I was thinking she leaned over and said quietly, "Don't blame him, he doesn't know that my colleagues hate me. I'm sure he thought I knew about it. Its one thing they've found without my help for once. Let them have it."

She said it without any self pity whatsoever but in that moment my heart broke for my mother. Once again I was reminded of the sacrifice that she had been making for me and just how miserable her work life was. My lower lip trembled and I took a sip of champagne to cover it. Now that I was a mermaid too what excuse did I have to continue to let her suffer?

As the first course of dinner, a gourmet salad, was laid out in front of us, I looked down at it and frowned. I no longer had an appetite.

Mom noticed that I was pushing radicchio around on my plate and asked, "What's wrong, Targa? I cannot believe that you aren't as starved as I am."

I forced a smile and speared a few leaves, putting them in my mouth and chewing. They tasted as bitter as I felt. If I didn't at least pretend to enjoy the meal my mother would know that something was up and I didn't want to spoil this night for her.

So, I chewed and swallowed, chewed and swallowed, until the bitter feeling began to subside. Dinner was six courses plus coffee. I was stuffed by the fourth and felt sleepy by the time the video presentation came on during dessert.

The video was well made, and included interviews of people from Novak as well as the Bluejacket team. Animation showed the condition of the wreck and demonstrated how artifacts were removed from the site safely. Even the animated version of the ship had no figurehead. Martinius had been true to his word.

My mother didn't have any speaking presence in the video but I saw her in the background in some of the clips. In one, she was working on the deck of *The Brygida* in her diving gear and in another she bobbed in the water next to the ship and looked up as she spoke with Simon, kneeling on the deck next to her and giving instruction. Or maybe he was taking instruction from her, I couldn't be sure.

She never acknowledged the camera and never smiled. I could tell she was miserable and even saw her pulling at the neck of her diving gear uncomfortably while she worked. She looked like someone who hated her job. No, worse than that, she looked like someone who hated her life.

I looked over at her in the dim light and wondered what she thought about how she looked. She caught my eye and I'm sure she knew what I was thinking. She gave the tiniest shrug in response and took a swallow of coffee. She looked bored throughout the whole presentation.

After the video ended, the orchestra started up again and the sconces illuminated the room. In no time a few older couples were waltzing prettily across the dance floor. What was it with this generation? They all knew how to ballroom dance. My generation knew how to gyrate, not how to float across the floor like kings and queens. I felt like I'd gone back in time. I realized that I hadn't taken any pictures so I took my phone out of my clutch and snapped some photos of the dancers, the orchestra and the room.

I texted a few of the images to our group, letting them know where we were and that we were celebrating the close of the project. I sent a caption along with one of the photos of the people waltzing.

My mom's wind-up party is like a fairy-tale.

I put my phone to vibrate and it buzzed less than an hour later.

Saxony: *Holy crap, Targa. Why wasn't I invited?*

Georjayna: *What are you wearing? Send a pic of you and your mom.*

I asked Simon to take a photo of my mom and I standing in front of the ship's bell and he obliged. My mom hated posing for photos but she tolerated it for me. She even smiled. I texted it to the group.

Georjayna: *Aaaaaaawwwwwww! You guys look amazing.*

Saxony: *Bella ragazza!*

My phone went quiet for a while, but about ten minutes later it vibrated again.

Akiko: *Hi guys. Nice pix, Targa.*

Saxony: *Who is this?!*

Georjayna: *SHE LIVES*

Akiko: *Very funny.*

Me: *Everything ok? We've been wondering when we'd hear from you.*

Akiko: *All ok. Gotta run. Sorry, I only have a few seconds.*

Saxony: *Wait!*

Me: *What are you doing, intelligence work for a secret agency in Japan or something?*

But she was already gone. Whatever stories she was going to tell us when we got back had better be good.

Mom and I were soon both yawning and she leaned over and asked me when I wanted to leave. There was a prepaid cab service available to deliver people to their homes and hotels as needed and it had now started up.

I was about to answer that I was ready to go when Mom's gaze focused on something or someone behind me.

I turned and looked up into Antoni's face. He held out his hand. "How about that dance?"

I swallowed my yawn. "Sure." I put my hand in his and stood up.

"Try not to look so excited," he laughed as he led me to the dance floor. "I promise to let you go home to bed after this. Seriously, what are you, eighty?"

As soon as he put his hand on my waist and pulled me close I cursed my mother. His scent surrounded me and my thoughts no longer came in words or communicable ideas, only amorphous feelings and desires. I gripped his hand tightly and inhaled, revelling in the feeling of his palm against my back. It felt so natural there. I closed my eyes and moved closer to him. I lay my head on his chest and heard his beating heart, slow and steady. Heat radiated from him and enveloped me. I felt dizzy with longing and closed my eyes.

"Be careful, people are watching," he said so that only I could hear, but not unkindly. He stepped back from me to re-establish a respectable dancing distance for this company.

My eyes snapped open and I stood up straight. I fought for control. I envisioned the fingers of my mind fumbling to keep hold of a slippery, twisting thing; a wet eel otherwise known as rational thought.

As we danced along the outer edge of the dance floor I stopped us when we were close to my table. "I'm so sorry Antoni, I can't." I reached up and kissed his cheek just to show anyone who might be watching that we weren't having an argument. The last thing I wanted was to create drama for him. But it took effort to tear myself away; I wanted so much to leave my lips against his warm skin.

For just a moment, as I turned to walk away from him, I saw the confusion and disappointment on his face. I'd hurt him, again. My heart ached but I couldn't stay in his arms. I was bound to get him in trouble. I made my way to our table where my mom was already standing and holding out my wrap.

"You ok?" she asked, quietly.

I nodded tightly. "Let's go."

She put an arm around me and we slipped along the side of the ballroom towards the exit. I felt Antoni's eyes following us to the door.

30

Our gear had been loaded and all that remained, with less than twenty minutes to take off, was to board the plane. It was a clear day for flying; hot, sunny, and cloudless. Most of the Novak team had turned up to see us off. There were a lot of handshakes, a few resounding backslaps among the men, even the odd brotherly embrace.

Mom shook hands with people in a perfunctory manner. It was interesting to see the dynamics working between her and the almost entirely male Novak team. They would shake hands with her and then linger by her awkwardly until they realized that she really was done saying goodbye to them, and then they'd move on looking a bit sheepish.

Martinius was there of course, thanking everyone graciously. He lingered with me and my mom for a long time. When there was a break in the men swirling around us, he said, "I have a gift for you," He pulled an envelope from his breast pocket and handed it to me. "I had an excerpt from Aleksandra Novak's diary translated for you. The section to do with Sybellen and the wreck."

I gasped and took the thick envelope, stunned at his thoughtfulness. "Wow, Martinius," I said, opening the envelope and peeking in. "Thank you. How did you know that I was wishing I could read it?"

He smiled. "I would if I were you. You'll be sure to let Antoni know when you've arrived back in Canada safely?"

I looked at him in surprise, wondering how much he knew about Antoni and I. "Of course I will."

He nodded, his hand gripping his cane tightly. We watched my mother as she said goodbye to a few other people.

"Promise an old man that you and your mother will come back one day," his eyes on my mother's back.

"I don't know if I can make that promise, Martinius," I answered. "But I can tell you that I would like that very much." I meant every word.

I fought against stealing a look at Antoni every half minute as he moved through the crowd talking and laughing, shaking hands and wishing people luck.

I was distracted when I saw a dark-haired, broad shouldered man from the Novak team approach my mother. He was sort of a rough looking character with a week's worth of black beard and hair that curled around his ears. He was deeply tanned and weather worn, but fit and strong. I couldn't recall seeing him at the party so my guess was that he was a crewman from one of the Novak vessels. Those guys worked outside all day long and had very tough jobs, according to Antoni. I wondered how he and my mom came to know each other.

I watched him approach her and she gave him a warm smile which immediately made me suspicious. I watched them talk, their heads bent low towards each other. Then, shock of all shocks, they hugged. Mom hadn't hugged anyone, even Martinius. Who was this guy? I had been so preoccupied with my own life this summer that I had failed to ask my mother about what was going on in hers. I felt ashamed of how selfish I'd been. As they broke apart and finished their goodbye I moved through the crowd towards her, my curiosity getting the best of me.

I lost my train of thought completely when Antoni's scent hit me.

Half a second later he took my hand and pulled me around to face him. "Hi," he said, smiling down at me but not standing too close.

I gently pulled my hand away. "Hi," I said as I tucked my loose hair behind my ears and crossed my arms over my chest.

"So, I guess it's really happening. You're leaving," he murmured.

I nodded. "We always knew I would."

"Yeah, but somehow..." He looked past me, blinking in the sun. He shook his head and a wry smile touched his mouth. "I don't know, I thought maybe..."

"What? That I would give up my life, my school, my friends, my family, my language and my country and move to Poland to be with you?" I regretted it even as it was pouring out of my mouth. Was that the siren bluntness or just my own bitterness talking? My mood soured. It wasn't fair. There was too much weighing on me. I was supposed to be thinking about finishing high school and choosing a university, not trying to figure out if I was about to make a huge mistake and walk away from the love of my life. I wanted to disappear into the ocean where all this stuff didn't matter and life was simple.

He blinked in surprise. "Well, no. More like..." He paused and his eyes passed over my face. "...I'd give up mine."

He'd winded me. That was not what I had been expecting. I wanted to slap him and hug him. I'd never let him give up everything he had here to come and be with me, that would be insanity. But my heart melted at the thought anyway.

We had both frozen, looking into each other's faces, until I couldn't look at him anymore and dropped my gaze to the centre of his chest.

"I'm sorry," he said.

I blinked in surprise. "For what?"

"For whatever I did that offended you."

"No, Antoni. You didn't do anything." I was mortified that he was apologizing when he'd always been so perfect with me. "You just don't understand..."

"Yeah, yeah," he interrupted, "it's not me it's you." He said it with a smile but I could also detect his pain.

"It's true," I said, lamely.

"Right," he said, disbelieving.

I didn't know where to go from there, how could I explain to him how I felt without telling him what I was? So, I extended my hand to him the same way I'd seen my mom do, perfunctorily. "Good luck to you. I wish you all the best and I hope that you get what you want in life. Really I do, Antoni." I dropped my eyes again. I couldn't look at his face.

My hand was stuck out in space all by itself for an uncomfortable moment. Finally, he took it but he didn't shake it, he just held it. "Send me a text when you get home, Targa. Please?" He was always so kind. No matter how abrupt I was with him he never failed to be kind. And then... it wasn't even a whisper, he just mouthed the words, "I love you." I was sure that he hadn't meant me to hear them. But with my siren ears I heard his mouth form the words out of the air, loud and clear. I swallowed hard.

Then he was gone; lost in the crowd.

With his scent and presence gone I let out a long breath. I shoved thoughts of Antoni into the back of my mind to deal with later and resumed searching for my mom. The crowd was dispersing and the Bluejackets were boarding the jet. She was on the step leading up to the doorway and looking back at me with concern. She beckoned me to hurry up. She mouthed 'You ok?' I nodded.

I fell into line behind Eric, who was in a less surly mood than usual. He chatted with Simon and the two of them chuckled. Weird, they had barely gotten along all summer. Why were they all chummy now? I tuned in to them. There was something forceful in Eric's voice, something just a little bit desperate.

"Just imagine..." he was saying as we entered the plane in single file and started throwing bags under seats and into overhead bins. "A billion dollars. It's just sitting there, all lonely and waiting to be rescued."

Simon laughed and said to Jeff, "Am I the only one who finds it ironic that the guy who is supposed to keep us out of danger is trying to convince us to go straight into it?" He shook his head. "It's a fool's errand." He slapped Eric on the back. "I think you've had a little too much of that Polish wodka this summer, Eric."

Eric faked a laugh along with them as they settled themselves into their seats.

Repeating Simon's sentiment in my head, was *I* the only one who could tell that Eric was just acting?

We were on the same jet as the one we'd arrived on, and Mom had also chosen the same seats. I looked around and saw that everyone had gone back to their original seats, too. We were still a few rows behind Jeff and Eric. I made my way back to Mom and I noticed that Micah had his head cocked towards Eric as though he was listening. A frown creased his brow.

I took the seat beside my mom, "Did you hear what Eric was saying?" I sat and moved the safety buckle out from under my bum.

"Yeah, I heard," my mom said.

"What's he talking about?"

She shook her head. "Damned if I know." She yawned. "Seems like he's always on about some kind of foolishness these days."

I studied my mom more closely and noticed the line between her brows and the tightness around her mouth. "You alright, Mom? Can I get you anything?"

"I'll survive, lovey," she replied. "Thanks for asking. I've got lots of water, earplugs, an eyeshade and a pillow. Unless you have a horse tranquilizer, I'm good to go. How are you?"

"Good. Ready to go home. I guess."

"Don't want to leave?"

"I don't know." And I really didn't. I was both sad and relieved.

"I know what you mean." She looked out the window at the distant line of blue. "I like the Baltic. It's peaceful."

"Yeah. Me too." I looked around to make sure no one was listening in and then leaned in. "Martinius gave me an amazing gift."

"Oh really?" She said, softening her tone to match mine.

I pulled the envelope he'd given me from inside my jacket and handed it to her.

"What's this?" She took the pages out and unfolded them. She scanned the first paragraph. When she realized what it was she looked at me in shock. "The diary? He had it translated?"

"Just the part about Sybellen. Amazing, right?"

"Seriously." She shook her head and folded it up. "I'd love to read it when you're finished."

I stood and tucked the envelope back into my carry-on, planning to read it later in the flight.

There was no talk during take off, everyone was focused out the window and enjoying the view as Poland fell away beneath us. I held Mom's hand as I felt her anxiety climb along with the plane. She's indestructible and fearless, but stick her in a plane and she became a nervous wreck. "Try to sleep, Mom," I said.

She nodded and gave me a tired smile. She pulled the sleeping mask over her face and shifted to make herself comfortable. I listened as her breathing deepened. I hoped for her sake that she stayed asleep the entire flight home.

Another five minutes and I started not to feel well either. Concrete filled my limbs and chest, like there was a force that was trying to pull me down through the floor of the plane. My arms were made of iron and my head wanted to flop forward onto my chest. I felt my neck creak and groan under the compression.

So, now I knew. Flying did have an affect on my changed biology. I had a whole new level of appreciation for her hatred of flying. My eyelids drooped and a wave of nausea overtook me. I felt a headache creeping across my temples. I gave in to the heaviness, took a pillow and curled up in my seat using my mom's warm body to rest against. Within moments I slipped into a dense black cloud of unconsciousness that locked out the world.

"It's never going to happen, now just let it go already!"

A sharp voice startled me awake. I groggily opened my eyes and looked around, wondering if I'd dreamt it. I looked at my mom but she was still out. She had earplugs in.

Micah noticed that I'd been shocked out of my nap. "It was just Simon," he said. "Go back to sleep."

Curiosity fought drowsiness. My mouth felt like someone had

been carpeting it while I slept. I took a big drink of water and felt slightly better. "What's going on?" I tucked my water bottle back into the seat pocket in front of me.

Micah shook his head, his face a mask of disapproval. He shifted in his seat and leaned toward me conspiratorially. He'd clearly been wanting to talk to someone about whatever was going on. "It's Eric. He's got this crazy idea in his head and he's been pestering Simon with it nonstop. I don't get it. He used to be so..." He took off his ball cap and scratched his head. "...rational. He was the guy we could all rely on to make smart decisions. You know, give the go ahead on the jobs that would net out in our favour. He was great at it. No one had better instincts than Eric. Aside from your mom of course, but she's a different story." He shook his head. "Now? He's turned into a huge risk-taker. Not a good quality for the analyst to have."

"What does he want Simon to do?" So far, my curiosity was winning out over the desire to lay flat on the floor under my seat.

"There's this legendary wreck in the North Atlantic," he explained. "It would be crazy expensive and dangerous to try and recover anything from it. Eric knows that better than anybody, but he's turned into some kind of cowboy."

"What's the wreck?" Whatever it was, it wouldn't be out of reach for my mom or I. As far as I knew, nothing in the ocean was off-limits for a mermaid.

Micah's face lost its derision and he looked like the goofy guy that I liked. "Oh, it's awesome. I mean, I get it, I'm a wrecker. The Republic is famous in salvage circles. It makes everybody salivate."

"The Republic? That's what it's called? What happened to her?" I took another swig of water, begging the cobwebs to clear.

"Everyone knows about the Titanic, right?"

I nodded. "Sure, everyone and their dog."

"Yeah, but it seems like only the dive community knows about The Republic. See, three years before The Titanic went down the White Star Line had another unsinkable ship. The RMS Republic. But in January of 1909, early one very foggy morning, The Republic was T-boned by another ship called The Florida, who had been lost in the fog and sailed 30 miles off course. Boom!" Micah hammered his fist into his palm, making me jump.

"Why wasn't it as big a story as the Titanic?" I asked, fascinated in spite of my pounding head and lead filled legs.

"Well, it might have been at the time, it was all over the news because The Republic was a palatial ship too, carrying a lot of very wealthy people and valuable cargo. But it didn't capture the public's imagination the way the Titanic did, because the loss of life wasn't nearly as bad. Once the Titanic hit the news..." He blew on his finger-tips and dispersed the air out with his fingers, illustrating quite well that the story had gone up in smoke. "Nobody wanted to hear anything about anything else. It was all Titanic, all the time. So The Republic faded into history. Just like *The Sybellen* did."

"Where did she go down?" I wondered if my mom had ever been to the wreck site.

"In the North Atlantic, same as The Titanic," he said. "The Republic was just going the other direction, back to Europe."

"So, no one knows where she is and Eric wants to find her?" Even I knew that was a ridiculous proposition.

But Micah was shaking his head. "No, we know exactly where she is. She was found in 1981. She's less than 50 miles south of Nantucket. The wreck is sitting in about 270 feet of shark infested water in one of the busiest shipping lanes in the world." He shook his head, doffed his ball cap again and scratched his head. It was a gesture that had become classically Micah.

"What was she carrying?" I was fighting the heaviness hard now, I didn't want to miss a thing but my drooping eyelids disagreed.

"You name it, navy payroll and supplies, family heirlooms, disaster relief money that was headed to Italy. They'd had an earth-quake or a hurricane or something. Rumours have it that she was even carrying gold bars for the Tsar of Russia. They estimate the cargo to be worth over a billion dollars today. That's what makes it such a legend. It's the richest wreck known to man." He leaned back in his seat, signalling that his storytelling was nearing its end.

He yawned, "We don't have the salvage rights anyway, that's why I don't understand Eric. Maybe he forgot that everyone else lost the right back in 2013. Ain't nobody else can make a claim for her now."

"Who got the salvage rights?" My own voice sounded slower and deeper than normal, like a record winding down.

"Martin Bayerle, that old pirate." He chuckled. "Another legend in the salvage community. He's the one who found her, and good on him. Mark my words, there'll be a movie made about that guy one day."

I had no idea who that was. "You think he'll be able to do it?"

He laughed, "I'm sure he'll try. He's in for a devil of a time though. Wrecks in the North Atlantic with all that salt and those currents..." He shook his head. "She'll be a pile of rubble and as fragile as tissue paper by now. Not to mention zero visibility and she's a monster that goes on forever. He could spend millions and years on her and still come up with nothing more than a handful of White Star teacups."

He tipped his head back and pulled his cap down over his face. He chuckled again to himself and then grew quiet. I wanted to pester him for more information, but my eyelids closed of their own accord. I gave in to the heaviness and slipped again under the black satin covers of sleep.

This time I did dream – of a palatial ocean liner sailing through thick supernatural looking fog and heading straight towards her invisible death.

31

B y the time we arrived home I felt like a rung out old dishrag. I swayed with exhaustion behind Mom as she unlocked the door to our trailer. We fell in the door and I fought the desire to curl up on the floor and sleep right there.

"Bed," Mom said, the word whooshing out on a sigh.

"Uh huh." This siren jet lag business was a crock. Before crawling into bed I sent Antoni the world's shortest text.

Home.

I didn't wait for a reply, I shut my phone off and crawled under the covers. My last thought was to kiss ever seeing Antoni again goodbye because I was never getting on another plane for as long as I lived.

Of course, I felt differently when I woke up. I opened my eyes and my first thought was of Antoni. My stomach twisted into a knot of misery and my heart ached. A hot tear escaped and left a trail from my eye into my hairline. I picked up my phone and saw that he'd written back.

Good. Glad you're home safe.

Thankfully, my exhaustion was gone. I looked at the clock and it took a moment for me to do the math. It was two in the afternoon. We had gone to sleep at three in the morning. So, I'd had almost twelve hours of sleep. No wonder I had to pee something terrible.

I brushed the wet tear track off my face and threw the covers back. I heard the front door slam and felt the trailer shake. Mom was already up. I heard her footsteps near as I pulled a pair of jeans up over my bare legs. I had been too lazy to even put on pjs and had fallen into bed in my underwear. She tapped on my door and poked her head in.

"You're up!" she said, her face alight. She looked like a different person from last night. Her skin was plump and bright and her eyes were clear. Her hair was damp.

"You look fresh as a daisy. Did you go for a swim?" I had a stab of regret that I'd been asleep and missed out.

"Yup."

"Feeling better?" I asked, pulling my hair up into a ponytail.

"Yup again. Two days of rest will do that," she smiled.

"Two days?" I froze, my hands over my head.

"Yes, m'lady. It's Thursday." She looked just the slightest bit smug. We had gotten home on Tuesday.

"Are you kidding me?"

"Nope. You've been out cold for about..." she looked at the clock on the nightstand near my bed, "...33 hours."

"What?" I was stunned. "How long did you sleep?"

"About 18 hours I think. Come have some brekky," she said over her shoulder as she left my room.

I went to the washroom first and then found her in our little kitchen. She already had vegetables chopped and had opened carton of eggs in preparation to make omelettes.

"33 hours," I said, shaking my head. "And I didn't even wet the bed."

Mom laughed. "Our bodies use water in a different way than humans, you could sleep for a year and you wouldn't wet yourself."

"Good to know," I laughed. "How is it that you're so much better at this mermaid stuff than I am?"

"I don't think I'm better, honey." She lit the stove and put a generous pat of butter into a frying pan. "I think I'm just older and stronger. You've only been a siren for a little over a month now. And I have another theory, too. But it's just a theory."

"What is that?" I asked as I twisted open our stovetop espresso maker and scooped coffee grounds into the reservoir.

"I had my very first change at Little Manitou Lake where my mother had taken me on vacation. I was so young that I don't remember my life before being able to change but I do have vague memories of that vacation. So, while you were snoring the trailer down I had a thought and did a bit of research about that lake."

"Ha!" I gave a sarcastic laugh.

She chuckled. "I know, I know. The world-wide web is not my favourite place to spend time." She finished cracking eggs into a bowl and started whisking them.

"There's the understatement of the century." Mom would rather wear her cursed diving gear than sit in front of a laptop.

"Do you want to know what I learned, or not? Ungrateful little cricket," she pointed the eggy whisk at me, drooling slime.

I turned away from the stove and opened my arms in a gesture of gentility. "Please, Dr. MacAuley. Do go on."

She poured the eggs into the frying pan and scraped the bowl out with a spatula. "Do you know what the salinity of Little Manitou Lake is?"

"No clue, why don't you enlighten me." I twisted the espresso maker closed and set it over the flame.

"18%," she said, and looked at me with meaning.

My eyebrows shot up. "A salt water lake?"

"Yes, and it's pretty unique even by global standards. The Baltic, by contrast is only 1%."

Understanding dawned. "Holy shit."

"Yes, exactly. Don't swear." She said these two things in an identical tone and I laughed because I knew that she was doing that thing. She liked to deadpan phrases she'd overheard mothers saying to their kids and inject them into our conversations at opportune moments.

She finished making our dozen-egg omelette while I poured the coffee. We pulled chairs up to the island and ate while she explained her theory.

"I was born in Thunder Bay. We could have easily found a beach close by to enjoy for a holiday, but that's not what we did. We had no money for vacations in the Caribbean but she wanted the best for me so she took me to the closest, saltiest water she could find. Little Manitou is a day's drive from Thunder Bay. It's in Saskatchewan, which is not a place that people put on the top of their vacation list. Maybe my mother knew that the saltier the water a mermaid has her first change in, the stronger that mermaid will be."

"You could also just be stronger because you're older and you've been swimming your whole life." I didn't like where her hypothesis was taking us.

"It's possible, but I can also tell you that I met a siren named Aris who was born in Iran. I met her in the British Virgin Islands before I came north and met your dad. I was really only a teenager myself. She was..." she paused, searching for words. Finally she just shook her head. "She was really something. It's rare enough to run into another mermaid, there are so few of us. We swam with each other for a whole week. I watched her pull up a huge anchor that was half buried in the ocean floor, like she was picking up a pebble off the beach."

"You couldn't do that?"

"Noooooooooooo," she said, astonished at my estimation of her power. "I'm flattered that you think I could, but there is no way I could do what I saw her do. I remembered thinking at the time that she was either stronger because she was older, or her parents had genuine love."

"How does that tie to Iran?" I asked, shovelling the last of my omelette into my mouth. I was feeling back to normal now, like the plane ride hadn't even happened.

"Well, she never told me exactly where she was born, but you know what's in Iran? Lake Urmia. It's a lake with a salinity that can be as high as 28%. Maybe her first change happened in that lake. And maybe she was born at a time when the salinity was higher than the

18% that I had my first change in. Maybe her parents had genuine love and she was born in super salty water."

"You think maybe the brackish water I was born in cancelled out the advantage your genuine love with dad gave me?"

She shrugged, looking at me from over her coffee cup.

"It's an interesting theory Mom, but it's got a lot of holes. You don't know where in Iran she was born or what kind of life she led before you met her." If I was honest, I didn't like that her theory suggested I was inferior. After all, it was impossible for a mermaid to be born in freshwater at all. So if I was born in water with only 1% salinity, wouldn't that make me a bottom-feeder on the siren scale?

She sighed. "Yeah, I know. It just got me thinking about you being born in the Baltic and if that means something for you. Especially since you had to take water into your lungs and drown in order to change. As far as I know, it has never happened that way for any other mermaid. As if its not stressful enough for a mermaid to have a child and then take her daughter away from her father and into the ocean, if she had to drown her daughter to incite the change..." she shook her head. "Well, lets just say the world would have a lot less mermaids. Maybe none at all."

I mused over her theory as we finished our coffee. If she was right, could spending more time in saltier water make me stronger? Or was I stuck with what I got because of where I was born?

There was a knock at the door. A male voice yelled, "Courier!" and could be heard easily through the thin walls of our trailer.

I went to the door and opened it. A short man in a delivery uniform was mopping sweat off his forehead. He was standing to one side of the crack in the steps and looking down at it as though it was a ravine he could easily fall into and die. The sun and heat of the day came in through the open door and I understood why he was mopping his face.

"We haven't lost a soul down there yet," I said.

He wheezed out a soundless laugh as he tucked his kerchief into his back pocket. "I'm looking for..." he looked down at the clipboard, "...a Targa MacAuley."

"That's me," I said. Mom appeared behind me.

The courier handed me the clipboard and told me where to sign. His eyes darted from my face to my mother's, back and forth rapidly like a pinball. "Twins?"

I looked at my mom in surprise. No one had ever mistaken us for twins before. I knew my features had changed a bit since I'd become a siren but had they changed that much? Even though our colouring was nearly identical now, we still had our own distinct bone structure.

"Mother, daughter," Mom said, holding the door open.

"Ah." He tucked his pen into his front pocket and handed me the package. He turned and went down the steps with exaggerated care and back towards his waiting delivery van. We went inside and closed the door.

"It's from Poland," Mom said looking over my shoulder at the stamps. "Did we forget something in our apartment?"

"Can't think what if we did," I frowned. I grabbed a pair of scissors from the drawer and sliced it open with the point of one blade. Under the shipping paper, the box was white and had an elegant logo in the shape of a 'B' that looked familiar. Where had I seen that logo before? An envelope taped to the box had my name typed on the outside of it. I opened that first.

The card said, *Some things just belong together.* And it was signed, *Antoni.* My heart trip-hopped underneath my ribs.

I lifted the lid and pulled away the tissue paper to reveal the mermaid dress. I gasped and picked it up. As the cool silk slipped between my fingers, my heart ached for want of Antoni; his face, his smile, his presence. "How did he know?" I said, and then I saw the look on my mom's face. "He wouldn't have known if you hadn't told him."

She gave a small smile and shrugged. "I was going to get it for you, but when he asked me for an idea for a gift it seemed perfect to come from him. After all, it was made in Poland and it will remind you of him. He ordered it after you sent it back and it hadn't arrived by the time we left, so he had to have it shipped."

I held the dress close to my heart and the bitter reality that I probably would never see him again began to sink in. He'd move on with his life and I'd move on with mine. He'd meet a girl, fall in love, get married, have kids, and probably take over Novak Shipping. And me? What did my future hold? Whatever way I looked at it, it was a future without Antoni.

32

"Have you had a chance to read the diary yet?" Mom asked as we cleaned up the kitchen together. Our kitchen was tight but over the years we'd figured out how to navigate around each other in our small home.

"No, I meant to read it on the plane but that went out the window when my body turned to lead. I'll read it this week for sure."

She laughed. "Are you going to go see your friends this week?"

"No, none of them are home yet. To be honest, I have missed them but I'm nervous about seeing them," I replied, rinsing the espresso maker.

"Because you're a creature of myth, now?"

"Yes. It was easy to keep it a secret that my mother is a siren, but somehow it seems a lot bigger now that I'm a siren, too. They know me, do you think they'll notice that I'm different?" Except for Antoni, people in Poland didn't really say anything about the changes to my hair, skin, and eyes. But my friends knew me far better. They were bound to ask me why I looked different. I wasn't sure what I was going to tell them, yet.

"Well I don't think you'll have to worry that they'll figure it out on their own. Mermaids are fairy-tale creatures; it won't even occur to them. But yes, I do think they'll notice that you're a bit different from how you were when you saw them last. Does it really matter though?" She went and sat down on one of the couches and picked a book up off the coffee table.

"What do you mean? Of course it matters," I said, unconsciously opening my hand outwards for emphasis and forgetting that it was covered in dish soap. Foam flew across the cupboards and floor. I sighed and bent to wipe the mess up.

"No, not really, they'll move on with their lives and soon you'll be just a fond memory for them. Speaking of which, when did you want to set out for the open ocean for good? We should probably talk about how best to make our exit without freaking people out."

I popped my head up from behind the kitchen cupboards I'd been cleaning and stared at her. She had the coffee table book about shipwrecks open on her lap and her half finished coffee in her hand while she was flipping through the pages with her other hand. When I didn't answer right away she looked over her shoulder at me.

"Honey? Why are you looking at me like I just grew another head?"

"You want to leave? Just like that?" I stood up.

"Well no, not just like that. I'd have to put some things in order first, sell the trailer, resign. Put up the front of moving house so we don't have a search party coming after us. Prepare an account for you so that down the road when you want to find a mate there'll be a bit money available to you." She chuckled, "It would be pretty awkward coming out of the water and not having any clothes or money."

I felt the blood drain from my face.

Her cavalier tone vanished. "Targa, you're scaring me. You look like a wax figure. What's wrong?"

I went to the living room and sat down on the chair across from her, my back erect. My hands were suddenly ice-cold. "Mom, I can't just leave. I don't want to leave everything, my friends, my school. It's my last year of high school this year."

She blinked at me for a moment. Then she closed the picture book on her lap, took her leg off the armrest and set the book on the coffee table with exaggerated care. She folded her hands in her lap and took in a deep breath. "What," she said slowly, with emphasis.

"I can't believe you want me to just up and leave everything. What about my future? What about university?" My face suddenly felt as hot as my hands felt cold. I went from thinking I might pass out to feeling like I had a fever.

"University? Your future?" Her voice was incredulous. "You're a mermaid. Your future is out there," she pointed in the direction of the ocean. "Not here in some falling down trailer, working nine to five or being a housewife. You think you're going to be happy with life on two legs? What did you think, that you could just go for a swim a few times a week and then come home to your house and your bank account and cocktail parties with your friends?"

"Well..." I began. "Yes, actually. Something like that."

She jerked back as though I'd slapped her. Then she got up and started pacing our small living room. "Oh, this is wrong. This is so wrong." She put her fingertips to her temples as though she was getting a headache. "Do other siren mothers have this much trouble?"

Then she began to talk like I wasn't in the room. "Year in and year out of praying and hoping, and then finally giving up hope that you'd ever change; the mourning, the tears, the disappointment. Then losing Nathan, more grief, more heartbreak. Then another decade of alarm clocks and bills and paying taxes and enduring the looks and remarks of those men." She let all the venom out on the word 'men' so there was no mistaking how she really felt about her colleagues. "Their derision and their jealousy and their back-stabbing."

As she spoke, I heard the sound of her voice but it might as well have been the sound of our home crumbling down around my ears. Shame oozed from every cell in my body the way it always did when I thought about her life. She had sacrificed everything for me. I knew that she hated it here, hated the mundane human life that she'd been forced to live. She'd done it all for me. Guilt filled every vein in my body but it fought with the righteous anger and surprise that she'd assumed I would just give up my whole human life because I was now a mermaid, too.

She wasn't finished. "Years of burning the candle at both ends, wearing that infernal diving equipment and picking their trash up off the ocean floor, having to endure their incompetence and greed. And now a miracle, and she doesn't want to leave." She turned to me and the despair on her face gutted me. "Why? How can you possibly want to stay here?" She gestured with her arms wide, "Where did I go wrong?"

"Mom..." I began, but then she sat down beside me and took my hands in earnest.

"Targa, honey, you don't belong here. I know that it's all you've ever known but there is such a better life waiting for you out there. You might be fine here at first but eventually you'll feel trapped, suffocated, and you'll hate all the stupid hoops you have to jump through to live a human life. All the useless, frustrating tasks you have to bear. You'll battle depression and the desire to run away will never leave you. You won't have peace. Your human relationships will suffer because you'll feel like no one understands you and never will. You'll get tired of having to fend off men and their attentions will be relentless. Your friends' problems will seem more and more mundane and you'll appear disinterested and bored to them when you finally get tired of pretending that you care about their relationship dramas, or which dress to wear to the next birthday party, or going to the next buy one get one sale."

As I listened to her plead with me I realized that I thought I'd fully understood what she suffered by her choice to stay and raise me but I really hadn't. Memories of friends that we used to have in our lives who had gradually stopped coming around surfaced in my mind. The face of a kind and funny woman with blond hair fuzzed in and then out of my memory. When my dad had been alive our lives had been filled with the caring faces of friends and neighbours. After he'd gone those people had gradually faded out of our lives and now I understood why.

"And through it all," she went on, "the call of the ocean will only grow louder until one day it will be completely irresistible and you'll walk into the salt water and leave everyone behind to panic about what's happened to you. You might even be so deprived of salt by that point that you'll stay in too long and go salt-flush. And if that happens you'll be unreachable to me. Don't you understand the risk? For both of us?"

"Mom," I began, taking a deep breath. So much depended on what I said to her now. But I didn't know where we could go from here. "I understand better now what you've been through and I'll be forever grateful for what you've sacrificed," I opened my mouth to continue but I found that I just couldn't say what I had intended to say.

I wanted to tell her that I'd be ok, that she could go now. Her job was done and I didn't want her to suffer anymore. I wanted to tell her that I loved her too much to have her stay with me but nothing would come out of my mouth. I couldn't actually say it because the truth was that I didn't feel ready to let her go. I needed her. Who else in the whole world would understand who I was, how I thought and what I needed?

My mind jumped unbidden to Antoni and I scoffed internally at my own foolishness. Antoni was out of reach for me in so many ways. I could never tell him what I was, he'd never understand me, and he was half a world away.

What came out instead was, "I'm not you, Mom. Maybe it has to do with having my first change in brackish water but I like my human life, I love my friends and I want the chance to go to university and see what I can make of myself."

She put her hands over her face and her elbows on her knees. "This can't be happening. I can't be hearing this."

"Mom." I put a hand on her shoulder but she didn't respond to my touch. I didn't know what else to say. *Stalemate.*

Then I realized that what she feared for me was even more likely to happen to her. I had always seen her as infinitely powerful but I couldn't lie to myself about that anymore either, she wasn't infallible. One day, I was going to wake up and she'd be gone, finally unable to deny the call. And what would happen if she went salt-flush? At least if she left now of her own volition then maybe we had a chance of finding each other again.

"Mom..." my hands were trembling, my heart hollow. "You should go." I forced myself to say the words but my mouth was full of ashes, my stomach bitter. I was filled with dread that she'd actually leave me. I manufactured the biggest lie I had ever told. "I'll be ok."

She didn't lift her head, she just raised one hand with her index finger extended, telling me to stop talking. She sat like that for a moment and I couldn't bring myself to say anything else. I held my breath.

Then without a word, she got up and left the house, the screen door slammed behind her.

33

I got up and went after her. I wrenched the door open. "Mom, where are you going?" Even though she was already down the street I didn't have to yell, I knew she'd hear me.

"Where do you think? To the ocean," she said, without looking back and without yelling. I heard her loud and clear.

"For good?" I asked next, but I'd grown hoarse and it came out as a whisper. She disappeared around the corner. I stood there on our porch for a long time, not sure what to do. I clenched and unclenched my hands, feeling my heart pound. Should I go after her? What else could I say? I paced on our driveway, watching the road and thinking that maybe she'd come back. When she didn't, I grew so agitated that I knew that the ocean was where I needed to go, too. I needed to forget, if only for a little while. I went into the house and chugged as much freshwater as I could hold. It sloshed in my belly and threatened to come up. I gave it a bit of time to absorb before I left the house.

Before my re-birth, I would never have run down to the ocean from our trailer. We lived close, Mom had made sure of that but it wasn't a short walk. As a siren I didn't even think twice about it. I sprinted nearly full out for half an hour, watching the sparkling blue expand in front of me, calling as clearly as church bells on Sunday.

I half hoped I would catch up to my mom but another part of me thought it would be best to let her have some time alone. I didn't allow myself to believe that she'd gone for good. She wouldn't go and not even say goodbye.

I knew exactly where to go. Mom had shown me many years ago her favourite stretch of private beach. 'Private' was accurate, but 'beach' was more than generous. It was private exactly because it wasn't really a beach. It was a mess of toothed rocks and slimy, moss covered boulders. No human would want to spend a day there let alone swim there, not with the sandy beaches that were just a few miles up the shoreline.

I stashed my clothes in the jagged rocks, keeping my eyes open for a pile of clothing left behind by my mother but not seeing anything. I picked my way to the edge and slipped into the water. In a blink I was decked out in my mermaid regalia and heading out into the wild blue ocean. My anger evaporated and my cares dissolved away like cotton candy. This is what I needed. I couldn't bear up under all the guilt and confusion, the look of disappointment on my mother's face and the ache in my heart for Antoni, all at the same time. The salt water was where I could find solace.

This was my first foray into saltier water. I wasn't afraid of going out into the North Atlantic on my own, not exactly. But it was fair to admit that I was nervous and curious. Would I lose myself even more than I did when I was in the Baltic? Would I feel the pull of the salt so strongly that I wouldn't want to go back to shore? What if I really was a weaker sort of mermaid and unable to fight off the effects the salt would have on me?

The thoughts that peppered my brain began to fall away one by one as I swam deeper into the briny deep. I imagined them floating to the bottom of the ocean and dissolving into the sand. The water cradled me, its salty fingers soothing my skin and scales. It tugged gently at my hair and swirled in tiny eddies between the webs of my fingers. I let out a relieved laugh and exploded out of the water into a forward flip.

In the corner of my eye, I caught sight of a small fishing vessel while I was above the waves. My stomach turned inside out and when I splashed back into the water I giggled at the rush of adrenalin that made my limbs and my tail feel weak. It was not a good idea to go jumping out of the water when I hadn't checked to see whether I was alone or not.

I sped up and went deeper. The world down here was vastly different from the dimmer waters of the Baltic. It was clear and bright and brimming with life. If I had thought the Baltic was a busy place it was nothing compared to the North Atlantic.

I slowed as a new sensation came over me. The salt seeping into my system was making my skin and scales tingle as it saturated me. I let myself drift, paying attention to this new feeling. I pulled water into my gills, and pushed it out again. It seemed that with every inhale, the tingling inched deeper until finally, my entire body was thrumming. I thought back to how my mom had described the difference between the Baltic and the Atlantic. The image of a racing stallion, its pounding hoofs driving it forward flashed through my mind. *Thanks for the terrifying comparison*, I had said to my mom. But it wasn't terrifying, it was beautiful and powerful. I could really feel that now. I swam on, remaining aware of how different my body felt.

Schools of fish were everywhere as far as my eyes could see, which seemed like miles. The sun sent shafts of light down into the water and swirling clouds of krill danced under the surface. Towards the bottom, northern seahorses courted one another in an elegant dance. Their mottled yellow and brown bodies spinning and tail-curling. I was enchanted, becoming lost in the colourful seascape around me and how alive I felt. I found a pod of porpoises and joined their energetic play. I spotted a humpback whale far below me and I dove deep to catch up to her. I swam by her intelligent eye and looked back at her as her gaze followed me. She sang out, filling the ocean with her whistling song. I sang back at her with my own violins and swam below her, facing up and stroking her soft white underside.

My limbs and torso began to feel harder, stronger, more primed with power. Yet my tail felt softer, fuller and more robust. I let the whale swim on as I slowed, tuning in to my body as it seemed to be changing again. I looked down at myself, but I didn't see any differences. Was it just me or was my heart slowing down even more? *Thud.* Several seconds passed. *Thud.* Gooseflesh raised on my skin. I was changing and it was happening fast. I spread my hands before me, feeling a new relationship to the water through the webbing between my fingers, and in my palms. The water pushed at me from all sides, like it was asking me to interact with it. I reached my palms out and pushed back.

I shot backwards, my hair sweeping around my face. I gasped, looking at my hands. What on earth had just happened? The whale called in the distance, its song curled around me. It was joined by a succession of chirping and squeaking sounds echoing all around. The sounds had urgency, no not urgency... excitement. I picked up the presence of a powerful current far to my left as it whooshed through the ocean, moving fast. *Targa.* Startled I looked around. Had I really just heard my name? *Targa,* said the whooshing whisper. Its frothy voice was louder this time, seemingly right beside my ear.

Atargatis.

I couldn't have heard that right. "Hello?" My siren voice leapt to life, filling the water around me in a way it never had before. With my 'hello', my heart gave a single quake unlike any it had given since my birth. The water rippled outward from me in a mighty pulse, it bounced off fish swimming in my vicinity and the marine floor below me. It fed itself back to me, telling me exactly what was around me. I could have counted the fish, and described the shape of each species in detail based on the information that came back in the echo. There was a wreck not far away, judging from its shape it was a modern fishing vessel. I knew how far away I was from everything for miles around me - further than I could even see. The visual I had with this pulse made my eyes seem blind by comparison.

I put both my hands to my mouth, my eyes stretching open with amazement. I gave another pulse, but this time my voice stayed silent and it came from my heart alone. The echo that came back told me how far each animal I had detected earlier had moved since the last pulse, and how my position to the marine terrain had changed in the elapsed time. "I have sonar?!" I said out loud to no one. I drifted in awe, unable to move in my utter astonishment. I lost track of time as I stayed like that, processing.

I pulled my hands away, looking at my palms again, turning my hands over. They looked the same. Why did I feel so different? I held my fingertips up in front of my face and pushed at the water again. Five little jetstreams shot from the ends of my fingers. The little streams came together and formed a barrel of shooting water. It looked just like a current. I gasped again, and then gave a startled laugh. My laughter filled the ocean, and the whale sang back its own laugh. The chattering sound of laughing sea-life swept over me. Their joyful song filled me with an inexplicable happiness.

I put both hands out ahead of me and sent two currents out from my palms, I waved my arms up and down creating two serpentine streams. Amazed, I spread my fingers wide and separated them, making ten independent currents. I could feel the water molecules and how they answered to me. I focused, narrowing my eyes with the effort. I increased the movement of the molecules in the water, using only my thoughts to do it. The water boiled, bubbling as it shot out from my hands. Then I dialled back the other way, slowing the molecules down. The water became thick and slushy, semi-frozen. I pushed it even colder, and I heard a cracking sound as an iceberg formed in a long cone-shape before my eyes. I stopped and took a deep breath, feeling the shock at what I could do. I watched the little iceberg float upward, hearing the cracking sounds it made as it melted.

Getting an idea, I sent out a pulse with my heart again, tuning in to the world around me. I felt the presence of the wreck and swam straight for it.

The information the sonar gave me was right. This wreck was recent. A fishing trawl, maybe sixty years old, its outline still distinct. I eyed the mess, taking in the pieces and imagining how it would have gone together when it was new.

I held out my hands and the streams shot from my fingertips. I sent them towards the boat, extensions of my own limbs. The currents swirled, separated, and swarmed around the wreck. The ten individual streams broke into multiples, becoming many tentacles. The many arms became an extension of my thoughts, doing my bidding. Slowly, the currents buoyed up pieces of broken wreck - a piece of the stern here, a section of railing there, a bunch of boards. The streams worked together to lift and hold the pieces back into place, like a huge puzzle. I laughed as I watched the boat resurrect before my eyes, the currents of water and my thoughts holding it all in place. I released the current and the boat collapsed again, its pieces drifting down and settling on the sea floor.

My smile disappeared when I caught a whiff of diesel in the water and gagged.

34

Where had that come from? I hadn't detected any boats earlier, not actual floating ones. The scent had disappeared so I searched around in the water until I picked it up again. When it went through my gills, the reaction was immediate - I felt suffocated and my stomach lurched. I immediately moved to uncontaminated water to rinse out my gills.

I caught scent of something else too... something metallic, something that tasted like old copper pennies. I stopped and listened. There was no sound of an engine in the water. Aside from the sounds of sea life, all was quiet.

No, wait. There. Very faintly - water lapping against the metal hull of a boat. I heard the sound of something plopping into the ocean. I froze and listened. There it was again - something hit the water and made a small splashing noise.

I sent a pulse with my heart and the echo came back telling me there was a vessel at the outermost edges of my sonar. I also detected strange shapes in the water below the vessel, best described as torpedoes. I sent another pulse. The torpedoes were drifting down to the seabed at random. Was someone dropping bombs into the water? My heart gave a heavy frightened thud.

With this last pulse, I became aware of how it drained me. My eyelids drifted a little, and I stifled the urge to yawn. Maybe it was best not to use my sonar so often.

I descended to the ocean floor to make sure I wouldn't be seen, and swam towards the torpedo shapes. The marine floor undulated in an alternating seascape of sand, columns of seaweed, and rocky terrain covered in coral. Schools of fish, including small sharks, darted through the sunbeams shining down. I tuned in to the unnatural sounds of the boat and moved towards it. I slowed, my mother's words about how visible I was in the water reminding me to be cautious.

Following the choking scent of diesel, the tapping of water against a hull, and the frequent splashing, it didn't take long before the vessel became visible to my eyes. I could now see the underside of the vessel floating above its modern anchor.

Splash. Again the sound of something being thrown or falling into the water. I saw a white torpedo as it drifted down to the seabed. Curious, I swam closer. I was caught up short by a stronger whiff of the metallic taste and I realized what it was. Blood.

I was close enough now to see that the white shapes weren't torpedoes. Little clouds of blood drifted around each form. As I drew near I could now see hundreds of these white and grey bodies littering the ocean floor. My skin prickled with horror as I swam to the nearest one.

It was a small shark. Its dorsal fin and both pectoral fins had been sliced off at the base and the corpse tossed back into the ocean. My horror turned to outrage when I realized that it wasn't a corpse. It was still alive. This one was female and she looked at me out of a terrified, rolling eye. She couldn't swim, couldn't move. She struggled for breath. She was going to suffocate if she couldn't swim forward to keep the water moving across her gills. Blood drifted up from her wounds, filling my nostrils with the scent and bringing more sharks and carnivorous creatures from miles around.

I laid a hand on her side, feeling her agony and confusion. As I lifted my eyes and saw the hundreds, maybe thousands of finless bodies dotting the seabed, an indescribable fury filled me. My flesh crawled and my mouth filled with acid. My eyes felt hot with unshed tears and my fists clenched so tightly that the webbing between my fingers protested.

Suddenly, the engine of the boat rumbled to life and a new burst of diesel fumes filled the water. Whoever they were, they were going to drive away and leave this massacre behind, taking the fins that belonged to these creatures with them.

Not on my watch.

35

I shot straight towards the boat. For the first time in my life, I was ready to kill. Whoever these evil bastards were they were about to breathe their last. I envisioned tearing heads from necks with my bare hands.

As I shot towards the surface, intending to fly out of the waves like an avenging angel and land on the deck ready to mete out justice, a net was thrown over the side directly over my head. I swam straight into it at high speed. The thick rope pressed hard into my head and face and encircled me. My neck creaked in pain and instinct told me to thrash. I whipped my tail back and forth, the sea frothing around me. Like an animal caught in quicksand all I knew was the desperation to free myself, but for all my efforts I only became more tangled. Gone was the feeling of power I had only just discovered, I felt as helpless as a child.

Through the water my siren ears picked up male voices from the boat speaking in tones of surprise but I couldn't make out what they were saying.

I pulled a big draught of water through my gills and greedily stored up the oxygen it gave me. Then I willed my tail back into legs and prayed that they hadn't gotten a good look at what was thrashing in their net, that the churning bubbles had hid me.

My mother had seared into my mind that my identity had to be protected, unless I wanted to spend the rest of my days in an aquarium, a laboratory, or floating in formaldehyde.

I held the breath that I had taken and waited to be retrieved from the water. *Oh mother, what have I done? I need you now.*

I felt the vibration more than heard the sound of a winch running as the net dragged closer to the boat. The engine died and the only sound was now the whir of the winch.

The net tightened around me, pulling me through the water towards the surface. I felt my weight as the net lifted me out of the water and up over the deck of the boat. I took a deep gulp of air with my human lungs.

With every breath of the open air my mermaid instinct dissolved. The outrage about the sharks was still there, but my mind was also racing to find a way to protect myself, free myself. What story could I give? That I'd been snorkelling completely naked and miles from shore? That I'd stowed away on their boat, hid myself in some corner and then gone for a swim when they'd parked? Everything I came up with sounded ridiculous.

Why had I never thought to bring a weapon with me when I went out swimming? Because I'd never once felt in danger of the ocean's creatures. It hadn't ever crossed my mind that I might have to defend myself from people. I was the one who had powers over them, not they over me. Until now. All the power I had been playing with seemed useless.

I sank to the bottom of the net as it dangled low over the deck. My limbs stretched painfully at awkward angles. My back creaked. I couldn't see well through my tangle of hair and the netting that obscured my vision. The net was swinging and someone put a hand on it to steady it. Then I felt it lowered to the deck slowly and my body came to rest on the floor of the boat. The smell of blood was overwhelming.

I pulled my limbs toward me, disentangling them from the net and covering myself as well as I could, just the way a human girl would. I took deep breaths to calm my racing heart. I still couldn't see anything other than the wet and bloody deck of the boat and the net cutting across my vision.

"What have we here?" said an incredulous male voice. "I thought I'd seen everything. Never in all my life did I expect to catch a mermaid in my net."

Please be saying that as a metaphor.

"She's naked!" said another male voice, this voice was full of phlegm. The sound of wheezing and coughing blended with nervous laughter.

That last statement revealed something in my favour. If they'd seen my fins then they'd know what I was and being naked shouldn't come as a surprise. Or was he just a guy who liked to state the obvious?

I struggled to clear my vision but in the tangle of netting I couldn't reach up to brush my hair away from my eyes. I was not ashamed of being seen naked, that modesty had died in the Baltic when I did, but the cold air against my skin and the scraping of the net made me feel vulnerable. I fought against the fear that was threatening to overwhelm me.

"What the hell?" said a new voice, approaching from the boat's cockpit. Why did that voice sound so familiar?

The net was opened and pulled away from me. The sun glared down at me from the cloudless sky. I felt more exposed and more afraid than I had ever felt in my entire life. I was finally able to brush my wet hair away from my face and squint up.

"Targa?"

I didn't know whether to be relieved or more afraid as he stepped into view and I was able to look him in the eye. It was Eric.

36

"Grab me those shorts and that shirt, will you Donovan?" Eric said, holding out his hand towards them. "I know this girl."

As far as I could tell there were only three men on the boat. It was a fishing vessel with a closed cockpit at the bow, but it was too small for more people to be hiding somewhere. My mind skittered around for ideas of what to do next. For a moment my eyes lay purchase on a strange looking gun leaning up against a red plastic box near the cockpit. A speargun?

"You know her?" Donovan replied as he handed Eric a lump of clothing which Eric passed to me.

"Yeah, help her up out of that mess. I'll be right back." Eric went to the cockpit.

The other two men lifted away the net and one of them used the winch to lift it so it hung over the water at the back of the boat.

I had expected jeers and comments but Donovan and the wheezing man actually turned their backs while I pulled the clothes on. The shorts were men's red swim trunks and the shirt was a dingy, ripped tank top with stains on it. The smell of body odour hit me and I made an involuntary face of disgust. It was bad enough I had to accept help from these monsters, but I also had to wear their reeking clothing next to my skin.

Eric came back with a pair of old deck shoes in his hands. He put them down in front of me saying, "Better put these on, this deck is slippery."

I ignored the shoes and glared at him. "The deck is slippery because it's covered with blood." I gestured to the bins full of freshly amputated shark fins. "What the hell are you doing, Eric?" There were surely hundreds of pounds of fins in the bins that these men had stolen already.

I knew that shark-fin soup was a specialty in many Asian countries and sold for a disgusting amount of money. I also knew that it was illegal in these waters, and further to that, it was completely immoral. Not only did I plan to shame them until they felt like the pieces of crap that they were, this was also a tactic to direct the attention away from myself and what I was doing so far out to sea, naked and all alone.

Eric looked surprised, and then angry. "What do you mean what the hell am I doing? What the hell are you doing? You're miles from shore!" So much for the distraction tactic. "Where are your clothes? Does your mom know you're out here? How the hell did you even get out here?" He scanned the ocean surface. "Where is your boat? What are you, an Olympic swimmer? I know you like the water, but jeebus."

"You're going to have a lot bigger problems than catching a skinny dipper in your net. Don't you know that shark finning is illegal?"

He glared at me. "Yes, I know it is. Don't you rain your little girl judgement down on me. You have no idea the trouble I'm in." He actually waved a finger in my face. His voice became more threatening. "You're not going to tell a soul about this if you know what's good for you."

"Like hell I'm not. You leave hundreds of sharks to die on the ocean floor to line your pockets and you think I'm just going to let you sail off into the sunset? You're a butcher and a criminal." I took a step closer to him, vaguely aware that the boat had started to turn.

"You and your buddies..." I took another step and shoved my nose into his face. We were eyeball to eyeball, "...are finished."

He jerked back when he heard the multidimensional sound in my voice. I hadn't meant to use the violins but I was so emotional that they'd come out of their own accord. The look of fear that crossed his face was very satisfying. I noticed that the shadows on his face were moving as the boat turned under us.

"Uh... Eric," said the wheezing man, "We've got a problem."

Eric and I turned our heads towards him. Both he and Donovan were peering over the side of the boat into the water. We went to the railing and looked over the side.

Fish and sharks, thousands of them, were swimming around the boat in a perfect circle. Then I noticed there were turtles, squid, and dolphins in the crowd of fish as well and more were coming by the second, they could be seen swimming towards us from the surrounding waters. It explained why the boat had started to spin. The fish were creating a whirlpool.

I saw a flash of black hair and pale skin amongst the thickening crowd of sea-life. My heart jumped and then hammered hard, almost painfully, in my chest. My mother was here. The two other men must have seen something strange because they turned their heads toward each other in shock.

"Did you see that?" said the wheezer to Donovan. The whites were showing around his eyes, his irises were small blue circles of fear. He looked back into the water, bending over the railing of the boat to get a better look.

Suddenly, my mother leapt up from the water, grabbed him by the back of the neck and pulled him into the ocean with her. The sea closed around them and the surface went calm again. Eric and Donovan went stumbling back from the railing edge, yelling curses.

I waited, heart pounding, my eyes darting around for a glimpse of my mother or the wheezing man. They had disappeared completely into the thick mass of circling creatures.

I put a foot up on the railing to leap in when a hand grabbed my upper arm and pulled me back. "Where do you think you're going?"

Eric said as he yanked me back. I sprawled in the boat and we both toppled over. I landed on Eric's chest and he exhaled sharply. We went sliding across the slippery deck.

We scrambled to our feet, skidding in the slurry. "What's going on? That thing..." Eric yelled, "...that thing looked like a M..." He looked like he wanted to say it but couldn't get it out.

My mother shot out of the water a second time. She came flying over the railing and into the boat, landing on human feet in a crouch.

Eric and Donovan both screamed in terror. She slowly stood upright and with a sinister hissing rattle, a sound I had never heard from anything aside from maybe a rattlesnake, she faced the men.

She looked as I had never seen her look. Her skin reflected the sunlight as though it was still covered in scales. Her irises had grown in size and had changed from her beautiful bright blue into a golden colour and the pupil was a vertical black slash, not unlike a shark's eye. Inch long razor-sharp white fangs had appeared in her open mouth. She lifted a hand and pointed it slowly at Eric. She now had talons instead of blunt fingernails, and her hands had retained their webbing.

A breeze blew across the boat, touching my skin and raising gooseflesh. For the first time in my life, I was afraid of my own mother.

37

"What the hell is that?" Donovan yelled, his voice cracking. He moved to cower behind Eric. Before I realized what was happening, Eric had a forearm across my neck in a vicelike grip and his fillet knife at my throat.

"So that's how you've been doing it this whole time, you freak," he hissed over my head at my mother. "I knew there was something off about you, but this..." he seemed to be at a loss for words.

The creature that was supposedly my mother didn't respond. She didn't look afraid. It was hard to tell whether she'd even understood Eric's words. Her mouth was open in a snarl, her white fangs just visible.

"Mom?" I said, fearfully. I was more afraid that I'd lost her than I was of Eric's knife. Was this what salt-flush looked like?

"Now you listen to me," Eric continued, his voice in a low growl. If it wasn't for the quivering of his forearm under my chin I wouldn't have known that he was afraid. "If you want your daughter to live you're going to dive for me. We're going straight to The Republic. Today. Right now. And you're going to bring up every ounce of gold you can find. We'll wait for you. Just. Like. This." He pushed the tip of the knife into my throat. I gasped and drew back from the point. "And when we're done, I'll let her go and you can both swim off into the sunset never to be seen or heard from again. Understand?"

She'd had her predatory gaze set on Eric's face during this speech. After he'd finished, I thought I saw the corner of her mouth go up. Could that be right? She was amused? Her face was so foreign, so devoid of human expression that it was impossible to say.

Her eyes twitched upward and focused on something behind Eric and I realized she was looking at Donovan. She turned her head towards him and cocked it, like a predator evaluating her prey. She drew in a long, slow breath. It looked like she was getting ready to make a huge blast of air to hit the men with but instead she breathed out a single word, "Juuuuuump." Her siren's voice filled the air with a smooth, unbroken sound. It came from everywhere around us. The metal of the boat vibrated underneath my feet with the power of it.

I felt the shift in Eric's body as he looked towards Donovan. I heard the sound of Donovan's knife hit the deck.

"No!" yelled Eric. "Stop it!" Eric turned us enough for me to see Donovan put his foot up on the railing.

"Mom, no!" I wanted these men stopped, but not like this. It was bad enough that one of them was more than likely dead.

Donovan hopped over the side as serenely as though he'd decided to take a nice, refreshing dip in the ocean. We heard the splash as he hit the water.

Eric was alone. He panted in my ear. I could feel shock coursing through him and his heart pounding far too rapidly than was healthy. I wondered if he'd have a heart attack. I would have if I were in his shoes.

The mother I didn't recognize turned her focus on Eric. Eric must have realized he couldn't fight the power of her voice and he dropped the knife away from my throat and shoved me towards her. I stumbled forward and slid on the deck, falling to my knees and then to my hip. Eric backed himself against the railing, his eyes darted side to side, towards the cockpit, back at us. He looked like a caged animal.

"No, Mom!" I reached towards her. "Please don't do this."

She looked down at me and for half a breath it felt like she didn't know me. But as I watched, her eyes slowly returned to the bright blue ones I knew and her fangs receded. Her face became the one I loved. It was only then that I realized she'd been perfectly lucid the whole time. I then recognized fear in her eyes. My mother, afraid? She reached down and helped me stand.

"I'm ok, Mom. There's got to be a better way," I said.

She focused on Eric. He cowered against the railing, his knife on the deck at his feet. His chest moved visibly as he breathed; hyperventilating. Sweat poured down the sides of his face and neck.

She pulled in another big breath but before she released anything, Eric gave a horrific yell of absolute panic. He leapt towards the cockpit, slipped on the slurry and slid across the deck. His hands reached for...

"Mom! Dive!" I reached to push her out of the way of the speargun. I slipped on the slurry again and fell at her feet. I heard the sound of the trigger, and the thud as the spear hit my mother. I screamed as she fell back over the railing. I tried to grasp her legs but she slipped through my fingers and disappeared into the crowd of fish with a splash. Blood bloomed in the water where she fell and its red cloud was swept along with the current.

I screamed again, unable to think, unable to form words. I barely registered that Eric was loading a second spear. I scrambled up and dove into the water before he could aim, landing awkwardly in the midst of the circling fish. I bent and ripped the shorts off, and took a breath through my gills. My legs transformed. Fins and scaly bodies bumped me from all sides.

"Mom," I yelled hoarsely. A tentacle slapped across my cheek. I could see nothing with all of these fish around me, closed in so near that I could hardly draw breath. My heart pounded with panic, and I tried to sweep the fish aside with my hands to clear a visual. An orca brushed alongside me and gave a whistling shriek. I heard myself hyperventilating, the water whooshed through my gills and drowned out my thoughts. I had to get to clear water. I wriggled my way towards the centre of the whirlpool, directly under the boat.

I broke through the mass of fish and into the quiet space in the centre. The tank top drifted around my body, tickling my skin and irritating me. I ripped it off in anger. My eyes darted around at the cage of marine flesh. I couldn't see my mother anywhere. How thick was this circle of sea-life? The strangeness of their behaviour barely registered. I had to find my mom.

The diesel engine above my head came to life. I looked up, anger roiling in my blood. The propeller began to turn. Eric was going to drive away. He didn't care what happened to his friends, to my mom, he didn't care about the sharks that he'd murdered, only that he get away with it.

Anger changed my panic into focus. "No you don't," I said through a clenched jaw. I tuned in to the powers I had so recently discovered. I reached my hands towards the boat, targeting the propeller. I pulled as much oxygen in through my gills as I could and sent a jet stream of air at the prop. At nothing more than a thought from me, a perfect bubble formed around the blades as they began to spin, removing all traction. The engine whined as the prop spun inside its sack of air. The boat drifted, its engine screaming with effort. Diesel fumes filled the water. Leaving the bubble of air around the prop, I swam straight towards the bottom. I reached the rocks at the sea floor and looked up.

Thoughts of my mother clawed at my mind, but I could not let Eric go. My connection to the ocean and the power I had been given drove me to focus on what Eric had done.

I looked at the circling fish, the whirlpool they'd created. Maybe I could use it, somehow. I pulled on the centre of the whirlpool, making the dimple deeper and deeper. The boat sank into the funnel. I swirled the water with my hands and my thoughts and it responded. I imagined Eric going crazy onboard, completely terrified and baffled at why his engine wasn't doing its job as he got sucked down into a whirlpool of sea creatures.

I lowered the boat as though it was in an elevator shaft. I let the fish carry me around. Bodies bumped against me, fins and tentacles nudged me, wrapped around me. I watched the boat sink past. Eric was inside the cockpit, but all I could make out were his arms, working at the controls furiously.

The desire to let the water crash down on top of the boat was immense, I wanted to see it smashed into pieces and Eric's body torn to shreds by sharks. But I had a bigger purpose than revenge, now. I was not acting for myself anymore, but for the ocean, and indirectly - for all of humankind.

The boat's hull made contact with the marine floor. It tipped onto its side. I dropped and landed on human feet in wet sand and seaweed.

The funnel became a gorge as the water rolled back. Sharp rocks, sand and seaweed were exposed to the sun as I moved the water outwards, pushing it back with my mind as easily as moving a curtain of gauzy fabric. The bodies of finless sharks tumbled over as they fell out of the whirlpool.

Worry for my mother screamed at the edges of my mind, threatening me with a breakdown. My legs quaked and I prayed that she would not be among the corpses that tumbled from the sea, or I would lose all control and everything would come crashing down.

The sun streamed into the huge hole. More and more shark corpses fell out of the water and rolled across the rocks, blood oozed onto the sand and coral. I stood on the sand, my arms out, pushing the water back. The more I pushed, the more bodies fell, and soon hundreds covered the ocean floor. The sea bed looked like a battlefield.

I stopped the water and held it there with my mind, like a hand on a silk curtain. I walked around the boat. Eric was inside the cockpit, clinging to the wheel and his speargun. The steep angle of the boat had him mashed up against the glass on the side of the cockpit. He was white as a sheet. His chest heaved and his eyes darted around madly.

"Put down the gun and come out," I said, in my siren voice. His face softened, he dropped the gun and grabbed the door frame. He pulled himself up and out of the cockpit, fighting for purchase. He leapt down from the boat, his feet landing on the rocks. His entire body was quaking so hard that I could see it.

"Look around you," I said. I faced Eric, my back to the wall of water, the swirling fish going by, watching us. "Look at what you have done." He looked around at the thousands of corpses scattered around us. Patches of red laced the ocean floor as blood oozed from the shark's wounds. The impact of what he had done began to show on his face. He put his shaking hands to the sides of his head, his face contorting. Tears spilled down his cheeks as his eyes took in the innocent slain.

I stood there naked, my hair stuck to my torso and back, my white body dripping.

"Who are you?" he choked out. He took a step but stumbled on the wet rocks and fell to his knees. He stayed there, looking up at me, his face warped by regret and pain.

"I am the sea." My siren voice came out in full force, its multi-dimension coming from everywhere, as though even the fish were speaking along with me. "I do not belong to you. I do not exist for you to plunder and rape as you wish. Your actions do not go unseen, and will not go unpunished." Tears poured from my eyes now, flowing as fully as they ever had, rivulets of water poured down my face and body.

He bent at the waist and began to weep through his hands as though his heart was breaking. "I'm sorry, I'm sorry," he moaned.

"Do you deserve to live?"

He looked at me through wet eyelashes, over hands covering his mouth. A deep moan in his throat was my only answer.

"Fight for us, Eric," I said. "Not against us. You are more than this, better than this. Turn your energy against those who plunder us. Champion us. Protect us. Remember that you need us, and we need you."

He bowed his head and nodded, giving a choked sob. He wrapped his arms around his chest, tears dripped from his chin. All of his pride and arrogance was gone, his shoulders slumped, heavy with shame. "I will," he sobbed.

"Promise us."

"I promise," was his whispered reply.

I let water from the column around us trickle back across the ocean floor towards the boat, pushing the bodies of sharks towards Eric. He got awkwardly to his feet and stepped backwards, half falling in his horror. Corpses bumped around his legs and he gave a strangled cry at the dead eyes rolling up at him, the blood swirling around his feet. His face was waxy with fear.

The water reached his waist. He splashed towards the boat as it creaked slowly upright. Eric began to swim, grey bodies crowding around him. He latched onto the side of the boat, his body lifted from the bloody chum as it began to float. He fell over the railing and onto the deck, his head appeared a moment later as he looked out at me.

"Remember us as the voice of the sea," I said, the water rising up to my chin and lifting me off the ocean floor. "Remember this as your calling to change, to be a better human."

His face went slack as I changed my voice to give him a command. "Wait until I tell you to go."

"I'll wait until you tell me to go," he repeated.

I melted back into the wall of water as I let the sea lift the boat up past me and back to the surface.

38

The moment the boat returned to the surface and released my hold over the water, the sea-life scattered. I blinked at their rapid departure and sudden change of behaviour back to normal fish.

"Mom!" I cried as the fish cleared away I spotted her pale skin and black hair. She was a small figure, far away, her back to me. A cloud of bloody water surrounded her. I swam to her side and rolled her to face me. Her eyes were closed. Blood flowed through a hole just under her collarbone. The spear had gone right through her.

"Mom?" The fear in my voice was heightened by my siren strings. *Please don't be dead. Please. Please.*

"Targa?" Her eyes drifted open. All of her predatory features were gone, no more fangs, no more penetrating eyes or sharp talons. She was just Mira, my mom. But she was so very still. She gave a pained smile. "I'm sorry, I failed you."

"No. No mom, you didn't." I looked at the wound, feeling strongly like I should cover it, touch it. I put one palm over the hole in her chest, and the other palm over the hole in her back. I closed my eyes, tuning in to the water and salt inside her. I felt the energy and healing power of the ocean flow into me.

"Targa? What's happening?" Her voice grew stronger.

I couldn't answer her, I was too locked into her wound, watching in my minds eye as the ripped edges of her flesh and fractured bone stitched together. I felt energy draining out of my limbs and into her. I opened my eyes, sleepily, and pulled back from her.

She stared at me, her eyes wide. Then she looked down at herself. Her wound was gone. "How..." she gaped. She rotated her arm, feeling no more pain. The realization of what I had become hit her. I watched the understanding dawn. She touched my face with her hand, her eyes full of awe.

I couldn't stop a face-splitting yawn from cracking my face in two. As my eyes opened, I spotted Donovan's body, drifting and turning not far from the surface. My mom followed my gaze.

"Do you think it's too late?" I asked.

She looked at me tenderly and said, "You're so much better than me. Compassionate, just like your father was. I don't give a crap about them. But if it makes you happy..."

My mother went after Donovan.

I summoned my strength and sent out a pulse from my heart. The shape of another human form came to me. The wheezing man had drifted nearly half a kilometre from the boat already, likely pushed away by my whirlpool. Something was wrong with his shape, it seemed incomplete.

Bile rose in my throat as I saw the body. Blood clouded the water around him and a gaping wound had been opened on his thigh in the semicircular shape of a shark's mouth. I hoped that the bite had happened after he'd already drowned. I swallowed hard, and a large shark appeared in my periphery. It circled the body. I turned and swam back to the boat.

Mom was already working on Donovan on the rear of the vessel. She gave me a questioning look as I surfaced and I shook my head. She gave a remorseless nod.

This vessel was designed to spill slurry off the rear into the water so there was no railing across the back. Mom had laid Donovan's body across the back and was working to revive him. Eric sat against the back of the cockpit, watching my mom. She must have given him instruction to stay put. His face was calm and watchful.

Donovan was unconscious and not breathing, his heart still. She'd already pulled the seawater out of his lungs by the time I returned. She compressed his chest with her hands, massaging the heart. I heard his ribs crack and I winced, but sympathy for him was notably absent from my mother's face. She worked on Donovan for a long time before I heard the thud of his heart. I wondered as I watched her how many times she had done this for a drowned person.

Donovan finally took a breath on his own. He coughed and groaned. Just as Donovan opened his eyes my mother spoke to him before he had a chance to panic. "Listen both of you," she said. Eric tuned in to her. "You'll turn yourselves in to the Coast Guard. You're going to show them what you've done and accept the consequences of your actions. You will not remember seeing mermaids today, and you'll never fin sharks again." Her voice filled the air with its power.

Eric repeated everything she said, but Donovan said nothing. His face was vacant of understanding.

"Donovan?" I said, looking at his face, the lack of awareness in his eyes.

"There is nothing we can do," said my mom. "We are too late. He's brain-damaged. Our voices are useless on him. I'm sorry, love. I tried." She slipped back into the water beside me.

I swallowed, looking at Donovan's profile from where I bobbed in the water. His eye blinked and he looked up at the sky, but his expression was not lucid. Would he ever recover? What would his life look like from this day forward?

"Let's go," mom said. I nodded, feeling exhaustion in every bone.

"You can go, Eric," I commanded, and he got to his feet. He helped Donovan stand, and the two moved awkwardly towards the cockpit. Donovan staggered drunkenly. The engine roared to life and Mom and I moved away from the boat as it drove away from us. The sun was now low in the sky.

We submerged, and put our arms around each other in an underwater hug. I felt my eyes releasing hot tears into the ocean. We swam together for home. We didn't talk. In the salt water, things seemed simple and un-extraordinary.

But as I stepped out of the water on my legs and breathed air into my lungs, just as gravity pulled down on my body, my mind felt weighed down with responsibility. I felt completely drained - mentally, physically, and emotionally.

We arrived home in silence, walking up from the beach to the house. I focused on putting one foot after the other, not giving voice to my thoughts or emotions. We walked up to our trailer and entered our house. I realized that the trailer did not feel like home anymore, it just felt like a shelter, a shell. My mom squeezed my shoulder as we closed the trailer door behind us, and that simple caring touch soothed me.

I put a block in my mind and went through the motions of preparing dinner and then getting ready for bed. We still didn't talk. It was rare for us not to have a conversation over a meal, but both of us were exhausted and at a loss for what to say. We both knew that our argument from earlier was irrelevant now. After what had happened today, everything was upside down.

That night, mom and I both slept in her bed. We hadn't done that since my dad had died. We didn't talk about it, I just crawled in with her and she wasn't surprised when I did.

39

I was swimming in bright teal water, the ocean floor was rich with vividly coloured coral and beautiful tropical fish. Little white sharks flanked me on all sides and stayed with me as I swam, mimicking my every move. We circled and danced in the water, their cool bodies nestling in close to mine and then spreading out and swimming away only to return to me again. A group of manatees joined us and spiralled slowly around me, the movement of the water spinning my hair into a rope. Sea snakes and eels spiralled around the manatees creating a magical choreography of the kind only seen in animated movies.

I opened my eyes and looked straight into Mom's face. I felt a stab of disappointment. It had been such a nice dream that I wanted to go back to sleep.

Mom was just looking at me, watching as I'd slept. She smiled. "Good morning sunshine. Sleep well? You looked so peaceful."

I nodded and rubbed my eyes. "I was having a nice dream. How long have you been awake?"

"Awhile. Thinking a lot about what happened yesterday."

"Yeah." I let out a long, slow breath and rolled onto my back.

"Turns out my mother was right all along," she said quietly, and I turned my head to look at her. Her eyes were shining. "The love your father and I had..." her voice quavered in a rare show of emotion. She swallowed. "It produced an elemental." A tear slipped down her cheek. "All these years I thought she was either lying or mistaken. All these years, I have been so bitterly disappointed." She brushed a strand of hair away from my face and smiled. "But she was right after all."

I nodded. I thought of my father, Nathan, and my heart ached for him in a way it hadn't in years. He would never know the gifts that their love had given to me, and he wouldn't, even if he was still alive today. I took my mom's hand and squeezed. "You don't even know the half of it, mom." I pushed myself upright against the headboard.

"What do you mean?"

I told her about everything that had happened to me the day before: my sonar, my ability to control water. I explained to her what happened after she'd been shot. What I did with Eric and his boat, about the swirling sea-life and the massive hole I'd created in the ocean. The field of dead sharks that shocked Eric into tears. She listened, her eyes growing round.

"All of my theorizing about you was so wrong. Being born in brackish water didn't make you weak at all. It meant that the moment you stepped into saltier water and saturated your system, all of your powers manifested fully. Just like sunshine opening a rose." She shook her head. "Look what authentic love can do."

"And what about what happened to you?"

"Me?" She looked genuinely surprised. "Nothing happened to me."

"What are you talking about? You looked like something out of a horror movie! Is that what salt-flush looks like, because if it is then you're going on a no-sodium diet."

She laughed. "No, honey. That wasn't salt-flush, that was just really, really pissed off."

"Remind me never to get on your bad side. What was with the scary..." I pointed to my dog-teeth, "...and the slitty..." I pointed to my eyes, drawing my lips back in a snarl and rolling my eyes. "You were terrifying!"

She shoved at my shoulder playfully. "A lot of good it did us. You are the one who saved us, and without the fangs and talons. I'm so proud of you."

"Thanks, Mom." My heart suddenly felt so full I thought it might burst.

She took a sharp breath like she was about to say something, but then stopped.

"What?"

"No, nothing." She shook her head. "Never mind."

"Don't do that. Just spit it out."

"Well..." She was playing with the ties on the front of her sleep shirt, looking a bit embarrassed. It looked strange on her. "Does what happened yesterday, change how you feel... about... anything?"

I was quiet. It did, I could admit the truth to myself. My stomach gave a squeeze of anxiety as I realized that it had changed everything. "Yeah," I answered softly.

Kudos to my mom for not jumping up and down on the bed and shouting 'hallelujah'. Her eyes were shining with excitement but she also knew me well enough to know that just because everything had changed for me didn't mean things were any easier. I still had people I cared about here.

"I'm still not sure how ready I am to leave everything I've ever known behind and start a new life. But I also know that I can't just ignore the power I've been given," I said.

"Well, I thought the day would never come." She tucked a stray lock of hair behind my ear. "We don't have to figure it all out right this instant. It's just a relief to hear you're open to it."

Just then there was a knock at the front door. We shared a look of surprise.

"Are you expecting somebody?" I got up and combed fingers through my hair to get out the worst of the bedhead.

"No. Are you?" She pulled her robe over her pyjamas.

I shook my head and followed her to the front door. She unlocked and opened the inside door and there on the other side of the screen door was Antoni.

40

"A ntoni!" Mom and I exclaimed at the same time.

"Hello again," he said. "I hope I didn't wake you?" He gestured at our pyjamas.

"No, no. Come on in." Mom opened the screen door for him and he stepped into our entrance. "What are you doing here? How did you find us?"

He was wearing a Novak polo, the same one he'd worn the day he'd caught me garbage collecting on the beach. He was also carrying a briefcase. As soon as he stepped in the door and I caught his scent, desire for him washed over me. I took a few steps back as he came into the house and the screen door closed behind him.

He took off his sunglasses and tucked them into his pocket. "Simon was kind enough to tell me where to find you. I was trying to call and text you, Targa," he looked at me. "But you didn't seem to be available."

I grimaced. I was probably in the ocean when he'd called, I hadn't even plugged my phone in before I fell into bed the night before. "Sorry, I forgot to plug it in."

"That's ok. I'm here now and I need to speak with you." He looked from me to my mom. I turned to go to my room to put on some clothes when he added, "Both of you."

I turned back. "Okay. I'm just going to get dressed, I'll be quick." I suddenly remembered the dress and added, "Thank you for the dress, Antoni," I said, sincerely. "It was... an amazing gift. Truly."

"My pleasure." He was looking me warmly in the eyes but he wasn't smiling. It struck me that there was something amiss about him. Was my thank you simply too feeble an appreciation for the kind gesture?

I walked up and gave him a hug. I felt his surprise at first and then he wrapped his arms around me and we melted together. I basked in the warmth and comfort of his touch. I breathed in his scent but was pleased to notice that rational thought had not vacated my brain the way it usually did. The want was there, but it wasn't overtaking me, making me lose control.

He gave a small cough and I remembered that my mom was still there in the room with us. Her presence didn't embarrass me, but I was sure it embarrassed him. I released him and turned towards my room.

Mom looked down at herself like she forgot what she was wearing. "Well, if she's going to be all proper and get dressed then I guess I should too. Will you excuse us for a moment?"

He nodded. "Shall I make us some coffee?" He gestured to the espresso maker sitting on the stove.

"Good idea," she answered as we walked down the hall. Then added over her shoulder, "Coffee canister is in the fridge."

We gave each other looks of confusion as we each reached our bedroom doors, which were across the hall from one another. "What's going on?" she mouthed to me.

"I have no idea," I mouthed back.

She shut her bedroom door behind her and I did the same.

I scrambled to find a clean pair of underwear, I hadn't done any laundry since we'd got home. Finally, I found a clean pair of shorts and a short sleeved terrycloth hoodie. I raked a brush through my hair and gave my cheeks a pinch. It worked for girls in Jane Austen stories, why not me? Then I cursed myself for being stupid. I wasn't supposed to attract him, I was supposed to repel him, wasn't I? Somehow I had forgotten the reasoning behind it all. I sighed, feeling ridiculous.

I went back to the kitchen and took a seat at the island. I watched Antoni pour espresso into our mismatched coffee cups. Mom joined us moments later wearing a pair of jeans and a Bluejacket t-shirt.

"I can imagine your surprise at seeing me here, especially since you left us only a few days ago," Antoni started as he handed the espresso around.

Just then, my mom's cell phone rang. She looked at the screen and said, "Hang on a sec, will you?"

"Apparently, I should have taken her number instead," Antoni murmured. He took a sip of his coffee and cocked an eyebrow. I smiled, sheepishly. Between my mom and I, it was usually me who was always glued to my cell phone.

"Hello," Mom answered. "Oh, hey Simon." She mouthed an apology to Antoni over the mouthpiece.

He shook his head and mouthed back, "Don't worry."

I realized how much my mom's manners had improved since the trip to Gdańsk. She wouldn't have bothered apologizing to anyone for having to take a phone call before we'd left for Poland. I wondered how many swims in the Atlantic it was going to take before she was my brassy mother again.

"Oh, really?" My mom was saying, and she caught my eye. I was positive the call was about Eric. "Wow, that's a shock," she said, but her acting was horrible. She didn't sound shocked at all. "Ok, well I understand." She paused. Then, "I'm not going to pretend that, no." She moved into the living room to finish her phone call.

"How have you been?" Antoni said softly, so as not to disturb my mom.

"I've been good. How about you?" I cupped my hands around my warm mug. It wasn't like I could give him a rundown of everything that had happened to me over the last few days.

He cleared his throat, and I thought he appeared to be a bit nervous, which was unlike him. "Honestly Targa, I've been better." He had a way of completely disarming me when he was honest and vulnerable like that. I was thinking about how to respond when my mom said goodbye and hung up her cell.

"Everything okay?" I asked.

She nodded. "Simon has fired Eric for poaching. He was just calling to let me know not to expect him back at work. He's livid. He's calling the whole team one by one today."

Antoni's eyebrows shot up. "I can't say I'm surprised he's been dismissed if you'll pardon me venturing a personal opinion," he said. "But I would never have guessed it would be for that."

"Yeah, you think you know someone..." Mom said. "But more surprising is that Eric told Simon he's going to apply to join the Sea Shepherd once he finishes his sentence."

Antoni dropped his chin in shock. "Aren't they a vigilante organization who fight poaching?"

"They are," confirmed my mom.

Antoni shook his head, "That's one hell of a one-eighty on Eric's part. I can't keep up."

"Pretty weird," I said, biting my cheeks to hide my smile. "So, what's so important that it brought you all the way across the Atlantic to our doorstep?"

He gestured to the chair beside me and said to my mom, "You might want to sit down."

She did, draping her arm over the back of my chair.

Antoni continued, "I have some unfortunate news." He folded his hands together in his lap. "The evening after you left, Martinius had a stroke. To be more precise he suffered three strokes, all within a period of 9 hours."

"What?" A large, cold rock materialized in my stomach. "Will he recover?"

"No, actually. I'm very sorry to say that he passed away after the third stroke. Obviously, it was rather unexpected," he said, quietly.

I took a sharp breath. Only now did I noticed the dark smudges under Antoni's eyes, and he looked a touch gaunt. He was grieving. No wonder he'd said that he'd been better.

Mom was always quick to recover from shock, "I'm sorry to hear that Antoni, he was a good man," she said, simply.

"That he was," he agreed. "The funeral will be in two weeks. Of course, it would be wonderful to have you there but there are no expectations on you to do so. I just wanted to make sure you knew."

"Did you come all this way to tell us this in person?" Mom asked, sounding doubtful. He could easily have called.

He nodded, "I did, but that's not all. Before he died, Martinius was under enormous pressure to name an heir. As you know, he had placed a number of people from among the Novak executives as his successors, but he had never been fully happy with that. After he had the first stroke, which was a minor one, we thought he'd pull through, but it gave us all quite a scare. He lost some mobility in his right hand, but he still had the ability to speak. So, he called his lawyers and changed his will." He scratched at his jaw. He had more stubble there than normal.

"It caused quite a disruption in the company, I can tell you," he continued. "His wishes almost went unfulfilled. There were those who argued that the stroke had clouded his judgement. The Novak executives had a specialist run Martinius through a battery of tests in order to confirm that he was in possession of all of his mental faculties. He passed the tests with flying colours and the executives no longer had the right to say he was unfit."

My hands had grown cold. The thought of Martinius having to prove his sanity after a stroke and in order to fight for his wishes made me feel sick. I hoped it sounded worse than it actually was.

"How awful," Mom said. And then she gasped, and covered her mouth with one hand as though she'd had a sudden realization. "Oh gosh. It's you! He's named you his heir?"

I looked from Mom to Antoni, my eyes feeling like if they went any wider they'd pop out of my head.

"No," said Antoni. "Actually, it's Targa."

41

The silence was deafening. The clock above our kitchen window sounded like a hammer on metal as it counted by the seconds. The ticking sound fuzzed out and the edges of my vision blurred. I gripped the counter with both hands. Mom's hand touched my back, and it helped to ground me.

"What do you mean, it's me?"

Antoni held out his hands. "I don't understand it myself but I do know that Martinius was of sound mind when he made the change. I was there. I know him, probably better than anyone else in his life right now. He said you are family and that it couldn't go to anyone else as you are the youngest living Novak." His eyes bored into mine as he said these last three words, and they echoed around in my skull.

Youngest living Novak.

Mom and I shared a look. I knew what she was thinking. Martinius never believed her when she told him she wasn't Sybellen. Deep in his heart he believed she was his long lost family member, which in turn made me his family too. Maybe he thought that she'd just forgotten because as she'd explained, years in salt water can do that to a mermaid mind. Or maybe he just thought she was outright lying. We also had never said we *weren't* related to Sybellen. Hadn't

Mom admitted that it was possible or even probable that Sybellen was an ancestor? Whatever it was, it had been enough for Martinius.

"Are you?" Antoni's voice brought me back. He was looking between us from one face to the other.

"Are we what?" my mother countered, but she was fully aware of what he was asking. She was stalling for time. We had to assume that Antoni knew nothing of our real nature or our connection to Martinius. It would only lead to more questions and could get us into a real tangle.

"Family. Are you part of the Novak family? And if you are, why didn't you tell me?" Antoni had a minor note of accusation in his voice - hurt by the thought that I had kept it a secret from him.

"We're not," my mother insisted. "It's a mistake, Antoni. Martinius and I did have a talk about it. Martinius was convinced that we are distant relatives of the Novak family, but I'm sorry to disappoint you. It's just not true."

"Did this discussion happen when you barged into his library that day?" Antoni asked, this time keeping all accusation out of his tone. If he had any personal feelings about the way we'd stormed in on his former employer, he didn't show them.

"It was," Mom admitted. She didn't say anything else and several seconds of silence passed before Antoni prompted her for more information.

"Why would he think it to be true then? He wouldn't do so without reason."

Mom and I looked at each other. How did we explain this without telling him about the drawings of the figurehead?

"He thought that there was a strong resemblance between us and the way his grandfather had always described Sybellen to him. Pale skin, black hair, blue eyes," she offered. It was lame, but I couldn't think of anything better.

"I see," Antoni looked unsatisfied. "There wasn't any more to it than that? A family tree or a distant relative with the right name? Anything like that?"

Mom shook her head, no.

"You have to go back and have the will changed again," I said. "Put it back the way it was and leave the Novak executives in charge."

But he was already shaking his head. "You don't understand, that's impossible. The will has been legalized and signed. There is nothing to be done." He opened the briefcase and removed a stack of paper. "In fact all that is left is for the two of you to sign."

"Why me, didn't he leave it to Targa?" Mom asked.

"You're involved too," explained Antoni. "He's left you all of *The Sybellen*'s artifacts, the wreck site, the Novak salvage operations such as they are, and a few other tidbits, the bulk of which is artwork. Much of it is priceless, mind you."

He put a selection of documents in front of my mom and one in front of me. "Also, this is a bit complicated, but since Targa is a minor she can't fully take control of her inheritance until she turns 18. That leaves you in charge for now." He took two pens from his briefcase and set one before each of us. The stacks in front of us looked simply enormous. I watched all of this numbly.

"What if we refuse to sign?" I asked, hollowly.

"Please don't do that," he folded his hands in front of him. "His entire estate would go to the government. It would likely be dissolved and all assets liquidated. Or it will be dismantled and portions of it sold to competitors. That would, frankly, be a disaster. It would be unthinkable for a company with a 168-year legacy to end in such a way, and poor Martinius would roll over in his grave. I'm sure that you don't want to dishonour his memory."

Mom and I looked at each other with dismay. I saw that my mother didn't have a clue what to do. "We don't know how to run a company nor do we have the desire," she said, then turned to me and added, "I'm assuming you don't want to run a shipping empire, honey?"

I almost sputtered a laugh but the situation was too serious. I just shook my head.

"You don't need to run it," replied Antoni. "Once in charge you can assign whomever you wish to run it for you. You can be as involved or not as you want."

"Can't we just sign ownership over to you?" I asked.

Antoni's mouth twitched. "I appreciate the thought but no, you can't. The will stipulates that ownership of the company cannot be transferred for a period of fifteen years, unless in the event of death or serious illness." He focused on me, "I'm certain that Martinius was hoping that you'll eventually have a family and will continue the Novak line so that the company will remain in the hands of his descendants well into the future."

"But we're not even Novaks!" I said.

Antoni shrugged, "Martinius was convinced that you are. Perhaps you should have your family tree researched? Maybe there is a link that you're not aware of."

"Not you too," I said.

Clearly, Antoni trusted his employer implicitly, even over our protestations. "He was certain," he said, "and Martinius doesn't... didn't draw conclusions lightly. He was lucid and sharp when he made this decision. Do you think he would trust the fate of his company to just anyone?"

"Can we just put you in charge?" Mom asked.

Antoni took a deep steadying breath. "Ladies, look. I understand this is life-changing news, and perhaps I didn't deliver it in the most gentile way, but clearly Martinius trusted and believed in the two of you, family or not. My advice is to sign the documents because right now the fate of the company is in the hands of those that he has not deemed worthy. Once you've signed, then seek the advice of a lawyer, several lawyers if you wish. I know you may not fully understand the implications yet but this is a huge blessing, trust me. Now please," he put his hands together in a gesture of prayer. "Make Martinius a happy man, may he rest in peace. It was a nerve-wracking experience carrying unsigned documents of this importance over the ocean with me, please put me out of my misery. The company will run like clock-work without you until you've had a chance to digest everything. There is no rush to do anything, but there is a rush to have you step up and claim your inheritance."

He picked up the pens and set them down again with emphasis.

Mom and I looked at each other. Then we each picked up the pen in front of us.

I took a deep breath, scanned the document on the top and spotted the little yellow sticky tab pointing to the empty line. There were many more arrows poking out from between the sheets of paper in the stack.

I put pen to paper and began to sign my name.

42

"What time is your plane?" I asked Antoni as we strolled along the beach. This time it was a proper beach, not the usual jagged mess of rocks and seaweed. This one was beautiful, with miles of golden sand.

"I told Ivan we'd leave by two thirty." He checked his watch. "Should head back to the airfield after lunch."

We strolled in silence, the wind blowing against us gently. I caught his scent several times and it warmed me all over, but I no longer felt hammered by it. I was pleased by this change, guessing that it had to do with me coming into my powers. Someone really needed to write a scientific journal on mermaid biology, or better yet, elemental biology.

A few families enjoyed the beach along with us - throwing a frisbee around, having a picnic. The occasional jogger ran through the spray in bare feet.

"Nice country you have here," he said.

"I guess this is your first visit to Canada?"

He nodded. "Yes, it's a shame I can't make a holiday out of it but I really have to get back. I have a meeting with the executives tomorrow and I've been asked to report on the status of the will and present all the signed documents to the lawyers for review. I have never seen the company in such an uproar."

We stopped and faced the ocean, burying our toes in the sand. The surf washed over our feet and my body thrilled to sense the presence of salt.

"What are you going to tell them?"

"The truth, I suppose. That you did sign, albeit reluctantly."

"And the part about not being related to Martinius? Will you tell them that, too?"

"I've been thinking on that. I think it would be best to leave that quiet for now, after all there is always a chance that you are mistaken. Your lack of family records doesn't assist you in proving that you're not related, so..." he trailed off. And then, "Let me ask you this, Targa..."

"Might you be better off asking my mom if it's about my family?" I interrupted him.

"I did ask her," he replied. "Now I need to ask you."

"Okay."

"Can you say beyond a shadow of a doubt, with 100% surety that you're NOT related to Martinius?" he asked, squinting over at me in the sunlight. He'd left his sunglasses off even though it was bright out.

I was quiet. My instinct was to keep denying it but that wouldn't be the truth. I was also hesitant because it was important that my answer matched my mom's. What would she have said? I thought about the face on the figurehead, the curves and features of it so unmistakeably matching hers. Sybellen had without a doubt been a siren. How many mermaids were there in the world? "Truthfully? No," I answered, finally.

His eyebrows shot up. "See, there you have it. In the mouth of two witnesses let everything be established."

"I guess my mom said the same?"

"She did, but she was still adamant that the two of you should not inherit the company."

"And she's right. What do we know about running a company of any kind? Let alone one in Europe that functions in another language and in an industry we know nothing about." We started walking down the beach again.

"It's clear from Martinius' actions that it was more important to him that the company stay in the hands of a blood relative, even one with no business experience, than to be passed to an outsider. He always said to me 'hire for attitude, train for aptitude.' He believed everyone was trainable as long as they had the desire to learn."

I blanched and he added hastily, "I keep telling you not to worry about that anyway. Nothing has to change. Martinius is gone but we've been preparing for that eventuality for years. Mrs. Krulikoski will be stepping in as CEO for now."

I remembered the woman with the deep voice. "The CFO? From the party?"

"That's the one." He put his hands in the pockets of his shorts, kicking up tiny clumps of sand with his bare toes as we walked.

"Do you think she'll do a good job?" I had thought she seemed capable but what did I know?

"She will. She's been in the company for years and knows it inside and out. I'd be happy to report back to you regularly if you'd like to be kept informed?"

"I don't know what good that would do," I said.

"Wouldn't you rather know than not?"

"I suppose so," I replied doubtfully. I felt like I was walking on a moving sidewalk. Soon I'd find myself at an unintended destination in spite of my best efforts.

I'm not sure why I did what I did next. Maybe it was the control I finally had of myself around him that made me trust myself again. Maybe it was the sudden change in my life that I knew would eventually bring me back to Poland and The Baltic Sea. Maybe it was letting go of denying myself what I had wanted all summer.

A collection of boulders sat in the sand at the edge of the surf and instead of walking around them I stepped up onto one and faced Antoni. We were eye to eye. He blinked at me. I took a breath. "I have a question for you, and I need an honest answer."

"Always, Targa. I hope you know that." He stepped in front of me.

"At the airfield, in Poland, I heard you," I said, looking at him, unabashedly.

"Heard me..." he said, cocking his head slightly.

"When you said you loved me."

The smallest smile played about his lips. "Did you now?"

"Are you denying it?" My heart began to pound, but it was steady and slow.

"Absolutely not." He set his jaw like he was ready to take one on the chin.

We were less than a foot from one another, not touching. The space between us was nothing and everything.

"What I need to know was when. When did you know that you loved me?" My voice was soft but my heart fiercely prepared for the worst. If he answered that it had been after my re-birth as a siren, I'd know that his love wasn't authentic.

"That's what you need to know so badly?"

I nodded. "More than anything."

"All right," he said, smiling. "As much as anyone can put their finger on the moment they realize they love someone, I would have to say it was the day we visited Malbork Castle together. The day you snapped a photo of me when you thought I wasn't looking."

My jaw dropped and I threw my head back and laughed, I couldn't help it. The old Targa would have been horrified to learn that he'd known that I'd taken a picture of him without his permission. The new Targa couldn't care less and was thrilled that his answer proved that he'd loved me before I got supercharged with seduction skills.

I put my fingers on his shoulders, drawing him closer. He took his hands out of his pockets and put his palms on my hips. I put my forehead to his. "I'm sorry, Antoni."

"What for?" His hands squeezed me, pulled my pelvis against his warm stomach.

"For lying. For hurting you. There was never a bet with my friends." I put my palms to the sides of his neck.

He pulled back and looked at me with a lopsided grin. "I know that, Targa. You're not the kind of girl to do something like that. You were just scared."

My gaze dropped to his lips. "I'm not scared anymore." I kissed his cheekbone, then his cheek, then the stubble next to his mouth.

He cleared his throat, his hands slid from my hips to my lower back and found the skin underneath my shirt. "No?" he whispered. I closed my eyes with pleasure at the feeling of skin on skin.

"No," I whispered back and my lips found his. The kiss began softly, gently, but as we melted together the barriers I had built up to keep him at a safe distance crumbled. The kiss deepened and his hands moved under my shirt to my ribcage, his fingers splayed across my ribs and curled around the corral of my heart.

Suddenly his arms were around me, picking me up off the rock, his body as sure and hard as the knowledge that I loved him too. My heart cried truth with every slow and powerful beat. The yielding of my entire body to him made my nerves sing. He had me completely. I clamped my legs around his waist, pulling him tighter as I wrapped my arms around his neck and kissed him with all the passion I had denied all summer. As his lips parted mine my body came alive in a way it hadn't before and I finally let it, drowning in the smell and taste of him. The kiss was not just a kiss, it was a promise, made as clearly as though it had been spoken.

The squealing laughter of a child somewhere down the beach penetrated our passion and we broke the kiss, both of us smiling and breathless. He planted a hundred little kisses across my cheeks, on my lips, and down my neck as I tilted my head back and laughed. I found the rock with my bare feet again and took his face in my hands, my eyes closed, drinking in the moment.

His hands cupped my ears gently, his thumbs softly brushing the curve of my cheeks. "Targa."

I smiled and opened my eyes, devouring his face like I was seeing it for the first time. "Antoni."

"Now what?" he whispered, stroking my hair.

"You have to get on a plane, I guess." I quivered a little inside at the thought of saying good-bye but the promise was there, too, comforting me.

"I do," he agreed. "And you and your mom have a lot to discuss. But, you know you can send for Ivan anytime you want. Whenever you're ready, whatever you decide."

I nodded and pulled him into a hug, savouring our last moments alone together. I stepped down off the rock and took his hand as we walked back the way we'd come.

We got to the parking lot as Mom arrived in her work truck to pick us up. We took Antoni for lunch at our favourite little Mexican place along the beach. Mom and I wanted to talk about the company and what to do next but Antoni suggested we leave it for now. He told us to sleep on things, take as long as we needed, and then get back to him when we were ready. I was amazed at his maturity, his calm acceptance that we couldn't be together just yet. It made me love him even more.

"I guess the odds of you returning to Poland sometime in the future are a little higher than they were when you left?" Antoni said to my mother while the three of us were heading back to the truck after our meal.

She knew nothing about our kiss, our promise. But I wondered if she could sense the change between Antoni and I. "You could say that," she answered.

I tried to imagine what she was thinking. How could her daughter swim off into the deep blue sea with her if we were responsible for a big shipping company? She was now the owner of the salvage portion of Novak so what did that mean for her? Would she prioritize honouring Martinius' wishes over her desire to go to sea? She'd been so happy to think that we could disentangle ourselves from our current life. I would guess that she felt like she'd just escaped from a trap only to get caught in a bigger one.

Looking at my mother and trying to find some crack of emotion that would tell me how she was feeling, I remembered the man at the airfield in Poland, the one she'd hugged goodbye. With everything that had happened, I had forgotten all about him. As soon as we had a private moment, I promised myself to ask her about him.

I knew that I wanted to be with Antoni, but now the question was: when would be the right time to go? After I'd finished my final year of high school? Now? My mom had said that once a siren had found her mate, nothing mattered but him. I felt like I'd found mine, but that didn't automatically mean I'd drop everything right this instant. I guess I broke the mermaid mould in this way, too. What if I wanted kids but couldn't have them until I'd spent a few years in the briny ocean to trigger my fertility? That was how it worked with other sirens according to my mom. How would I explain the need to disappear to Antoni without explaining what I was? *Should* I just go ahead and explain what I was to him? I loved the idea of him knowing everything about me, but what if that meant he didn't want me anymore? I'm not sure how I would feel about marrying a mermaid if I was him. Probably not very good. But then, if I didn't tell him, wasn't that basically lying? I swallowed all these worries and questions. I wasn't going to solve them all in one day.

My thoughts turned to my friends. I missed them and I needed to talk to someone other than my mom. I needed people who knew me and cared about me but could be objective. Of course, they only knew me as Targa the human, they didn't know Targa the mermaid. And they weren't any older or more experienced than I was, but they were smart and I knew they wanted me to be happy.

I thought back to the beginning of the summer and how different my life had been. In a span of less than three months I had become a mermaid, fallen in love, experienced life in Europe, became an elemental, and inherited a multibillion dollar multinational. Two months ago I hadn't a clue what I wanted to do with my life. Was this destiny in action? Some guiding force shaping the direction my life was supposed to take? How was I going to decide what should be the priority?

How I was going to explain only part of the story to my friends and leave the rest a secret? I wasn't sure, but I had to try.

EPILOGUE

Georjayna: *How are you guys? Are y'all home yet? It's been a long two weeks without you! I have so much to tell you! Like. Seriously.*

Akiko: *I'll be back soon. Are you all around this weekend? Sorry I've been so MIA. It's been...uh...where do I start...*

Saxony: *I'm here! Me too. Nuttiest. Summer. Ever. Targa? You around?*

Me: *I'm around. Can't wait to see you guys. I missed your faces. Summer was mind-blowing. Still can't believe everything that's happened. I def have news.*

Saxony: *Sleep over? Georjie, your mom still away?*

Georjayna: *Yup, come on over. Saturday afternoon, anytime. Just shoot me a text. I'll get snacks. Bring your bathing suits.*

Akiko: *Sounds good.*

Me: *I'll be there.*

I closed my phone and smiled. I rolled over onto my back in my bed. I grabbed the pages of the diary excerpt and took them out of the envelope. I'd been looking forward to this since I'd gotten home. I took a sip of water, unfolded the document and began to read.

———

THE WRECK OF SYBELLEN

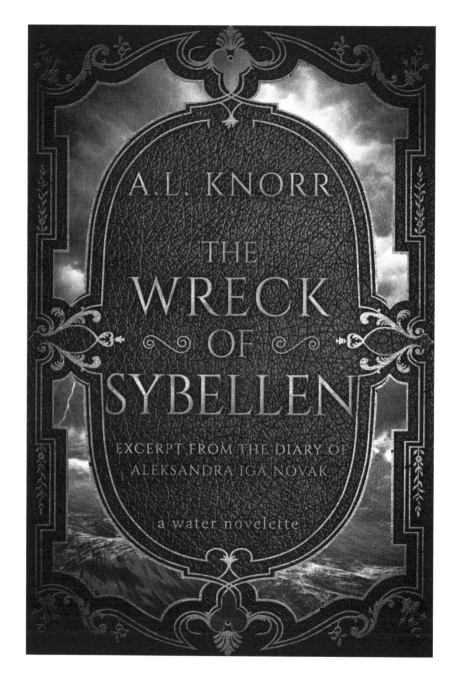

A.L. KNORR

THE
WRECK
OF
SYBELLEN

EXCERPT FROM THE DIARY OF
ALEKSANDRA IGA NOVAK

a water novelette

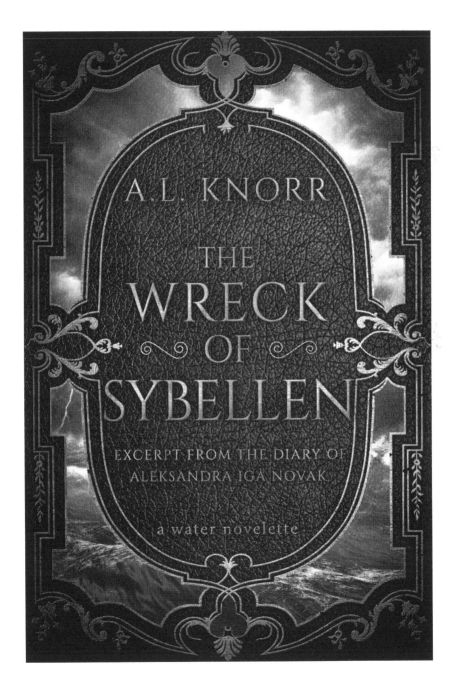

A.L. KNORR

THE
WRECK
OF
SYBELLEN

EXCERPT FROM THE DIARY OF
ALEKSANDRA IGA NOVAK

a water novelette

DEC 25, 1861

It is Christmas and my enterprising son has taken it upon himself to gift me with a beautiful leather book full of empty pages. It also came with a red satin ribbon with which to wrap it closed. I am not certain what to do with it as I am no artist or poet. What a laundry-woman can hope to render into these pages that may be worthy of viewing when she has long since passed, I lack the imagination to know. "Fill it with your thoughts, Mama," said Mattis when I asked him what his intention was by giving me such a pretty thing.

So as not to disappoint my son who patiently taught me to read and to write when he was young himself, I shall resolve to document a simple woman's hopes and thoughts. I have no delusions that a diary can ever remain private and so I shall write to you, dear reader, and imagine that you may be a distant descendant of mine or perhaps have come across this diary by happenstance a century after I have turned to dust.

By way of introduction, you may know me as Aleksandra Iga Novak. Wife to Emun Mattis Novak and mother to Mattis, whom I shall write more of in a moment. Iga for my mother, may God rest her soul, and Aleksandra as many a woman before me have been called in these parts. I shall not admit that for years I detested my name because it was so common, for I am a good Christian woman with much to be grateful for.

My husband and I have one child, and we have now arrived at my favourite subject. I had to stop myself from saying 'only one child' lest you think me greedy, but in the spirit of honesty I can admit to you, a stranger, that in my secret heart I had wished for a house bursting with children. But such things were not to be and I was told by good Doctor Woznick after a thorough inspection of my person that Mattis alone was a miracle. And so we have Mattis, our son. And what a son to have been given.

I can hardly understand that he has come from myself and Emun. Even as a boy he showed superior intellect and understanding (forgive me my boastful words. but I will be honest within these pages or write not at all). Perhaps all mothers feel such a way, but truly, even if I were an outsider looking in, I should be in awe of the young man Mattis. For at the tender age of seventeen he displayed a faculty for business unlike any in his family before him. He began his own newspaper before even finishing his studies and saved every penny he earned to pour into the shipping business he now runs.

I admit freely that his ambitions frightens me at times, for even now he is shouldering responsibilities that neither I nor Emun would ever dream to undertake. Mattis informs me with all sincerity that one day I shall be the lady of a great house and while I must bite my tongue to keep from laughing at such predictions, there is a corner of my heart that believes that if anyone can bring such a dream into reality, it is my son. I have watched him with pride and sometimes outright shock at the consistency with which he seems able to realize his ambitions.

When Mattis returned from his last shipping commission—a job that took him all the way to a place called the West Indies, where the spice trade is booming (it was the longest journey he had ever made and we missed him horribly)—he shocked both Emun and me by returning with a wife.

In Sybellen, my son could not have found a wife with stranger habits or a more secretive past. The girl is beautiful, to be sure, but has failed to provide a history for herself and seems hesitant to speak more than a few sentences to anyone but Mattis himself. I'm thankful that in the least she seems to be as eager for a baby as I am for a grandchild.

Mattis had not so much as written to warn us of her existence before he arrived with her by his side, but what could we do but welcome her into our home and our family? Sometimes the decisions that shape our lives are stolen away from us by our own loved ones. I imagine that had I a diary at the time of her arrival, my entry regarding her appearance in our lives would not have read so serenely. However, I have moved into acceptance and the four of us live relatively peaceably together in our small house by the sea. Perhaps, given our close quarters, I should be grateful for a daughter-in-law who rarely speaks instead of one who does not know how to be silent.

But this is the closing of our Christmas day and the light grows dim. Although Mattis tells me we are to no longer worry about wasting candles, old habits remain alive in me and I hesitate to light one. So for now, I shall say goodnight and Happy Christmas. I shall meet you here again when something is worth writing about.

I have my doubts as to what that might possibly be, for my life is as constant as the rain on a March day (look at that! Perhaps there is some small poet in me after all). Do not be surprised if this is my first and last entry. Perhaps the pages after this one shall be filled with scribbles of my grandchildren.

JAN 17, 1862

Well, my dear reader, I told you that I shall write when something of worth is to be saying and I can hardly think of a day that is more worthy of remembrance than this one. Perhaps only my wedding day and the birth of my son can rival the news I am about to share.

Today is Mattis' twenty-seventh birthday and while that is a happy occasion, it is not what makes this day worthy of dripping ink onto this empty page. Mattis and his wife Sybellen have reported that they are to have a child! When I look at the words written down on the page, I am dissatisfied they cannot portray the gladness in my heart.

Sybellen, whom I have not introduced to you in full detail yet (it may take me some time to work out how I am to properly describe her, since a more perplexing creature with a stranger name I have yet to meet) is the happiest that I have ever seen her and for the first time since she came so mysteriously into our lives, she has given me a proper hug and a kiss on each cheek. I almost fell over and Emun, whose eyebrows are growing bushier by the day, gave such an expression of surprise when she did that it confirmed for me that her lack of affection had not gone unnoticed by him either.

In my private thoughts, I hope that her condition means that she'll stop swimming in the ocean so much as she has. She's made a habit of rising early every morning and swimming for stretches of time that go beyond my comprehension. Even before the sun rises at times, I hear her leave through our front door and she does not return for several hours. What any person can hope to gain from so many hours in or by the sea is beyond me. I've given up asking Mattis to explain her habits, as it appears he thinks its good for her health and she can do no wrong besides.

One oddity I shall report is that I asked Mattis when Sybellen had seen Dr. Wozniak for I didn't remember her setting or attending the appointment. He shocked me by answering that she had not seen the Doctor at all. When I asked how she knew she was pregnant he replied (as though it was an everyday occurrence that a woman diagnose her own state) that she just knew. I have asked him to please ensure she has the Doctor confirm it for what a disappointment it would prove to be if she were mistaken. Mattis gave me the look that tells me I have overreached myself (oh how I've come to hate that look) and so I silenced myself.

For the time being I shall work to not be the meddling mother-in-law that I myself had to contend with, and shall content myself with happy thoughts of an addition to our little family.

I take much pleasure in thinking of what delicate little handmade thing I can concoct for my future grandchild, and Emun has already taken to calling the wee one a lad. Only time shall tell and as best we know (or as near as Sybellen can tell us at this time...would that I had the gift of prediction that my daughter-in-law has) that the time to meet the babe shall be this autumn.

AUG 30, 1862

Another day worthy of note has passed and I sit and write this some-time around midnight because I am far too energized to sleep. Dr. Woznick was here today to examine Sybellen and report on her progress. She is growing very large and I've been blessed with occasion to feel the movements through her belly.

Dr. Wozniak spent considerable time examining her with his hands and with a remarkable device he's acquired from France called a stethoscope, through which he was able to hear the heartbeats of two babies! So it seems that all is better than well because she is to have twins. This old heart of mine can hardly handle such a surprise for never before in either the Novak family or the Kalf (my maiden name) family have twins occurred.

Mattis was overjoyed to hear that they are to have not one but two babies, but Sybellen looked not surprised in the least. Perhaps she could tell but never said. She did however surprise us all by asking the Doctor if he was able to tell the sex of the children, as apparently this is one factor that was beyond her. To his credit Dr. Woznick told her he had his suspicions but that there was no exact science to learning a child's sex for certain while still in the womb so he wouldn't venture to say.

In a private moment just before our good doctor was to leave, I asked him if swimming in the ocean might be a poor practice for a pregnant woman. He surprised me that by saying if the water was warm enough that it might even do her some good (although he has colleagues that he knew would disagree with him).

These August days are hot and I must admit that even I have been tempted to frequent the shore a time or two to enjoy the delicious coolness that comes off the water. So I shall bite my tongue for the time being as it seems the doctor does not find it dangerous, but I'm in wonderment at her constancy and loyalty to her daily exercise. Most women I know take extra care and rest during these days of pregnancy, but not Sybellen.

Perhaps now I should put down on paper, since I find I have the energy to write, that Sybellen is a woman of the unexplained.

Mattis, since running his growing shipping service, has taken to being away for long stretches at a time. On his last journey (I forget if I have told you this, forgive an old woman her mind), he returned to us in the fall of 1861 already wed to the beautiful Sybellen. Upon meeting her, I remember thinking that I had never seen such a beautiful girl. Skin like porcelain, bright azure eyes and midnight black hair. However, it is not her beauty that truly sets Sybellen apart, but rather, her behaviours and passions. Or more precisely, her lack thereof.

From the very beginning, she has given us none of her story. Despite questioning about her place of origin, her family, her education and any of the normal items of interest one should like to know about the woman who marries into her family, she has remained silent. Sybellen has never once satisfied our curiosity about any aspect of herself. Indeed, she seems content to say as little as possible even in the fleeting moments she remains in the company of Emun and me.

I do not wish to give you the impression that she is unfriendly or rude, for when we do see her she is polite and respectful...there is even a warmth about her at times! But I get the sensation that her only wish is to be around Mattis This is heartbreaking for simple people such as ourselves who dreamt of an ever-expanding and close-knit family. The woman our son has chosen simply does not make this possible.

I have spoken to Mattis about these things when I have had the chance, but I hesitate to continue in this vein. He can become sharp with me and makes me feel like the nosy mother-in-law that I promised myself I would never be. The most I could glean from him is that they met on a small island in the West Indies when he had to make a delivery there and they knew at once that they were to be together always. They were a many months journey away from home at this time, which was the reason they were married away from home.

Mattis has described the people of the West Indies as warm, full of life, and dark skinned from the sun, but Sybellen is none of these things. But what does a barely educated elderly washer-woman to know about such things? I have never set foot outside my own village and cannot even imagine the worlds that my son sees while abroad. My (hopefully) now extensive vocabulary is a benefit of having such a worldly son, but my ambitions stop there. Indeed, at one time, I wouldn't have dreamed of filling empty pages with my own words.

SEPT 15, 1862

As the day draws nearer when I am to meet my two grandchildren, the summer seems ever more beautiful to my aging eyes. My daughter-in-law is by far the largest pregnant woman I have ever seen and Emun has wondered out loud more than once that the doctor might have been mistaken and that she is to have triplets. He jests, but our Sybellen does display a belly that could provide accommodation for three. Indeed, Sybellen is roughly the size of a house. Luckily, she is also the tallest woman for miles (Mattis thankfully surpassed his own father's height or he should feel unmanned by his wife) so she can bear such belly. The good doctor says to expect the babes at the end of the month which is only two weeks away and so preparations have already begun.

Sybellen has honoured me greatly by requesting that I attend her at the birth. She also accepted my suggestion to use the same midwife (Ana) who was of great help to me at the birth of Mattis. Dr. Wozniak humbly admitted that Ana is better educated than even he in matters of childbirth. I choose to see Sybellen's request as a sign of good faith in me and not as evidence that she knows not a soul in the village and certainly not any good midwife.

SEPT 16, 1862

You'll see from the dates that I wrote only yesterday. Such frequent entries are not a habit of mine but I'm so agog at the happenings from today that I simply must record them for fear that I'll wake up tomorrow and think that they were simply a daytime fantasy of mine.

Today is Sunday and as always, Emun and I attended mass. Sybellen never attends with us unless Mattis is home, and he's currently still away, so we left Sybellen to the privacy of her morning.

When we were returning from service we noticed as we approached the yard that our front door was ajar. We looked around for Sybellen but she was nowhere to be found. Just as we were inspecting the contents of the house to be sure there was no stranger inside or some accident (my heart has rarely pounded so hard as when sneaking into my own dark home afeared of what might be inside), we saw that the bathing tub had been set up near the fireplace and was half full of steaming water. The house had taken on the odor of seaweed.

Upon leaving the house with this strange scene, we came upon an even stranger one: Sybellen walking up the long path from the ocean carrying our yoke with two of our largest water buckets full and affixed to the chains. She was walking up the steep path and under this formidable burden (with her belly protruding out in front of her like the prow of a ship) seemingly without any effort at all. Emun nearly tripped over himself in his rush down the path to aid her. As he approached, she had the decency to look sheepish--though I'm convinced she was not regretful of her foolish behaviour, but simply embarrassed at having been caught in it.

As I watched breathlessly from the top of the path with sharp words on my tongue for the risk she had taken in her condition, she set the water buckets down and allowed Emun to take them from her. Nearly half of the water sloshed out due to the slope of the earth. I was relieved to see her meet with her senses again, but my shock was to be far from over.

My darling husband is not as young as he used to be and as I watched his noble effort, I could see clearly that he quivered and bowed under the weight of such a burden. The buckets merely shook and spilled more of their contents into the sandy soil.

I was shocked speechless to see that Sybellen also witnessed his strain and immediately begged him to put the yoke down. He did so, but it it was not because she asked, but rather that his legs and back were not hale enough. Sybellen's face expressed such concern to see him bow under the yoke and for a moment all my anger vanished and my heart swelled with love for her.

Before Emun could catch his breath, she shouldered the burden once more and strolled up the remaining way as though she were carrying no more than a knitted shawl across her shoulders. She greeted me with a nod and a 'Mama' as I stood there with my mouth agape (I was not delicate for I can tell you I have not had such a shock in my life before) and entered the cottage to dump the buckets into the large iron pot over our fire to heat.

Emun and I were too surprised at her to speak and it wasn't until later this evening that I asked her why she chose to fix herself such a bath. Surely the well water would have been suitable? Surely she could have waited until Mattis was home and given him the task? She answered that the seawater eased the aching in her hips and kept her strong. Furthermore, she needn't bother Mattis for such help when she was capable of doing it easily on her own.

For the hundredth time, I found my imagination full with wonderings of what a strange people my daughter-in-law must have come from.

If that wasn't such a shock for me, imagine my surprise when my own darling Emun elected to take a bath in the tepid seawater once she was finished. I had merely to look at him to earn the retort, 'Well, if she's able to accomplish such a task while pregnant due to seawater baths then who am I to call it foolishness? Perhaps some of my own youthful vigour can be recovered in this tub of ocean swill, too'.

OCT 3, 1862

Yesterday, our twins were born. They came early in the morning with barely enough time for Ana to arrive. I have never seen such an easy birth. Before I get to in the details, I must make mention that Mattis has not returned home yet although he was due several weeks past. These shipping excursions are never precise since so much depends on the weather (delays can be caused as much by storms as by lack of wind or poor wind direction), but I know that he will be making every effort to come home knowing that his firstborn children were to arrive at the end of September.

We do try not to worry when Mattis is delayed. It happens often as there are always storms happening in the North Sea and the Baltic. Mattis is as good a Captain as any and does whatever possible to be home. I am not convinced Sybellen sees this, as she becomes so melancholic when he is away. The poor girl, who barely strings two words together most days, complains about Mattis being late more than any other subject I've heard uttered since I've known her.

This morning I woke up to the sound of the front door. In our small house no one can leave without announcing it to the rest of the inhabitants. I glanced over the edge of the loft and saw Sybellen's large shape go outside, presumably to relieve herself. It occurred to me to check on her that morning for whatever reason and a good thing I did.

Emun awoke as I was getting out of bed and I told him that Sybellen had gone outside and I was going to check in on her. Without being asked, he suggested that he alert Ana. I told him not to worry, for there had been no specific warning signs as of yet.

I was wrong about that as I discovered when I made my way towards the door. Before I could put on my shoes, my bare foot detected something wet on the floor. There was a trail of moisture that could only mean that Sybellen had either spilled a glass of water from her bedroom to the door or her water had broken. So, I told Emun to get Ana after all and he was out of bed faster than a man his age has any right to move.

I became concerned when Sybellen was not between the house and the water closet, and I was heading back to Emun when I saw her walking down the path to the ocean. I tell you, such a jarring feeling shot through my stomach when I saw her wandering away from the house. Emun came outside, mashing his hat on his head, when he saw her too. We looked at one another in shock and went calling after her. Sybellen stopped and turned to look back at us. She was in labour, that much I could tell, but her face was so void of expression that I couldn't possibly interpret what she was thinking or what her intentions were. I could venture to guess that she might have been somewhat disappointed that we'd discovered her? Whatever her expression I had no time to dwell on it. We drew her back to the house and settled her in her bed while Emun went to get Ana.

I have not attended many births--only two others. I do not include my own since experiencing childbirth oneself and serving another in childbirth are so different they could be completely unrelated. One birth I attended was the neighbour Paula's, who laboured for a full day and gave birth successfully to a daughter. The other was my older sister, Adelajda, who died after a long and painful ordeal. I was only a young girl myself at that time and easily impressed. Naturally, I have not liked to think of it as it put the fear into me that childbirth is a cruel and dangerous thing. What I've learned now after attending a third birth is that no two women are alike and that childbirth is not always a long and arduous process (unlike my own).

By the time Ana and Emun arrived, the first child was already crowning. I would like to report that I kept Sybellen calm and steady during the ordeal, but it would be more fair and accurate to say that it was she who calmed me. Sometimes, my daughter-in-law is truly a marvellous creature.

Sybellen tackled the birth like she had done it a dozen times before. She did not complain or cry out, she simply focused on the task and did what needed to be done. While I watched this miracle in with incredulity, I wondered if it was her size and strength that gave her a clear advantage at birthing. Either way, I hadn't much time to contemplate before the first son came squalling into the world.

Ana tied a thread round his fat little wrist, lest we forget which twin came out first and should forever be called the eldest, and in short order his brother came out after him. We'd barely had a chance to clean them and Sybellen was asking after their sex. We reported with joy that she'd given birth to two healthy baby boys. The first and eldest by a full minute came with a shock of black hair and pale skin just like hers. And the younger, darker son came with no hair at all. She opened her arms for her boys and we settled them in. They both immediately gave suck and then the three of them dozed as Ana and I cleaned up and reported to Emun the news.

When she woke, and for the first time since I'd met her, Sybellen cried over the sleeping babies. She did it soundlessly, but there seemed to be no end to the tears running down her cheeks. I dismiss it as my foolishness and perhaps prejudice, but I had the uncomfortable feeling that she was mourning, rather than weeping for joy. It is nearly impossible to tell what Sybellen is feeling, which is why I'll not mention again the strange sadness that laced her expression. Instead, I shall attribute it to the absence of Mattis and go no further with my speculations.

Sybellen surprised us further by requesting that we name the boys. I asked her whether she had any preferences and she said she had none herself, but that Mattis had been scribbling down his favourites. She directed me to the list that Mattis had tucked into his desk and I was able to see a dozen or so names that he had selected for either sex. Assuming that the names at the top were his most favoured, Emun and I christened the eldest Emun Jan Novak. Emun went misty eyed to see his son's first choice and I will admit I felt my throat constrict myself at the gesture. Next, we selected the second name on the list for the younger brother, who will hereafter be known as Michal Ludwik Novak.

Of course, Emun and I are overjoyed and can hardly wait for Mattis to meet his sons. I am a grandmother and praise be to God for two healthy grandbabies.

OCT 12, 1862

I am pleased to report that Mattis arrived home last night, when his sons were 8 days old. His arrival did not come a moment too soon, for Sybellen was growing ever more melancholic. She has been an ever-increasing cause of worry for both Emun and me, so it is with great relief that I can write that Sybellen is the happiest I have seen her since she first found out she was with child.

To see my son with his two infant boys cradled in his arms at the same time has brought my heart close to bursting with love. I am resolved to forgive Sybellen her oddities for the happiness that she has given to my family. A woman who could birth such beautiful creatures should be thoroughly cherished.

OCT 4, 1863

It has been a year since I last wrote and indeed it was only the passing of my grandsons' first birthday that reminded me of my duty to report back to you from time to time. What a year it has been.

One child means constant doings and it seems two means three times that. Don't ask me to explain my calculations, for I know they are faulty but never have I been so in demand or kept so busy from morning until night. It seems that babies bring the gift of memory lapse with them as well, because I barely remember my life before Emun Junior (the elder) and Michal (the younger).

My grandsons are surely the most precocious ever born. And twins though they are, could any two boys be more unlike? Emun Jr. is like his mother in every way. His shock of black hair has only thickened since his birth. His skin is of the most porcelain colour, while his eyes are the colour of the sea on a bright sunny day. He is quiet and thoughtful, taking everything in around him with such a serious expression. Not all children are carefree for it seems Emun Jr has taken the weight of the world (or at least the weight of his own mother's melancholy) upon himself even at the tender age of 1. While I feel such a deep love for him, I do not understand his contemplative heaviness. It is very difficult to make him laugh, although when it is accomplished it surely is the most gladding sound in the whole world. He is very attached to his mother, not wanting to be away from her side for a moment.

Michal is in every way like his father. His skin is darker, his hair a chestnut brown and his ruddy cheeks project good health and appetite. His big brown eyes pierce my heart the way his father's did when he was a lad. Michal is full of life and curiosity, he laughs at everything and chatters constantly, loving the sound of his own voice. Sometimes I feel that I have been given the opportunity to go back in time and experience my own son as a babe again, so much the same they appear.

He is not afraid to go far from Sybellen even though he's only just learned to walk. He's explored every corner of the house and the yard already and I can see that there will be a time to come when he is running us all around and straight into our grey hairs (not that I've any left of colour, mind you).

Our home is full (Mattis says too full) once more of the sounds of little children and every day they do something new to fill me with wonder. It is only now that I've had a moment to write when they are both asleep and I am nearly asleep myself that I remember what this house sounds like when all is silent.

FEB 8, 1864

I am willing to admit it now. Mattis has been saying it for nearly a year and I've been fighting him on it at every turn, but he is right. Our house is far too small for our family. It seems we are constantly under one another. There is never a moment of privacy or peace with the goings on of the boys and the comings and goings of men inquiring after Mattis for this and that, even though he has an office near the harbour. I found a full house a pleasure while the boys could only crawl. But they have now long been running (not just walking), and my house feels like a circus.

While Mattis is on commission, it makes sense for Sybellen and the boys to stay with us and we've managed thus far. But for the times when Mattis is home, I swear I can hear the very boards of our home creaking with the strain.

So when Mattis said again just last week that he'd be looking at buying a new house, I finally let the comment pass without protest. I know when I am beaten. Emun suggested tearing down our house and rebuilding and I nearly threw a frying pan at him. This house is not to be torn down, not ever. And with my feelings made clear, Emun and Mattis went to market for a house.

I do not know the details around my son's fortune, I only know it has been growing steadily. I realized it fully when we went down to the harbour to christen the latest ship for his fleet. Mattis had told me he had commissioned another ship over a year ago, but I'd forgotten all about it and certainly did not realize he had such a grand ship in mind. When I saw it I came to understand just how successful my son has become.

We attended the christening of the ship, which was of course named after Sybellen. Mattis proudly showed us above and below decks as the ship sat in the harbour with the crowd around her and music playing on the wharf. I have never been aboard such a beautiful vessel--indeed I've hardly been aboard so much as a rowboat--, but I do know a fine ship when I see one. For the sake of posterity, I must tell you that I have never seen the like. She (for it seems that the men always refer to their vessels as female) was built at the shipping yard outside of Gdansk and was sitting in the water when I first saw her. I must say, she was simply glorious, all curves and crisp white sails that had yet to see a day's wind set into them. Even the ships wheel was remarkable and unique having been crafted after the ornate likeness of celtic knots. I assume Mattis may have seen such a design on his journey to Ireland.

Mattis proudly walked us through the Captain's quarters, which is large enough to accommodate 4 and which he had elegantly equipped with its own water closet and bathtub. The kitchen galley makes my own kitchen look like a closet, but I suppose this ship needs it to keep as many as 70 men fed and watered. He showed us the men's sleeping quarters, the belly of the ship where the goods and fresh water are stored, and the gun decks equipped with 8 cannons (it made me very nervous to think of their purpose). I cannot repeat all of the parts of the ship I was shown, for it seems that sailors like to give a name to every slab of wood, but I was comforted to see 6 large rowboats lashed in place should the men need to vacate the ship.

The item that was the most breathtaking and artful was the

wooden sculpture that was fastened to the front of the ship under the bowsprit. Mattis says it is called the figurehead. It is a creature of folklore, a woman who is human above the waist and fish below. It is clear as day that the mermaid's image was carved in likeness of Sybellen, and what a likeness it is. There is no mistaking whose face graces the front of the vessel.

I have never seen Sybellen angry before, with Mattis or anyone else. She can be dour, but never have I seen a display of temper towards anyone or anything - until today. The figurehead was a surprise for her you see, and one that no one should be too shocked to learn of for the ship itself is named for her. Far from being honoured, she was furious and no one was more surprised and disappointed at this than Mattis.

I am grateful, at least, that in her rage she did not choose to have it out with Mattis in front of everyone on the docks, but withheld until she pulled him into the Captain's quarters for privacy. This happened during our tour and the rest of us went onto the deck to pretend that nothing was amiss. I heard the sounds of raised voices but couldn't make out what was being said. It was then that I noticed the strange timbre of my daughter-in-law's voice.

I do not begrudge Mattis the deep love he has for his wife--that is as it should be. I know I long ago stepped down as the first lady of my son's heart. I am simply uncertain of the appropriateness of the mythical creature on top of which Sybellen's face has been set. I'm well aware of men's tastes for a bonny bare-breasted lass to grace the front of their ship. I have even heard of other more fearsome creatures being used for ships of war, which is all in keeping. I only hope that there is not some hidden blasphemy in the sculpture that might offend God and bring bad luck down upon our heads.

They must have resolved their difference somehow since neither of them has mentioned the argument and the figurehead has stayed in place. When they emerged from the Captain's quarters both of them were flushed but seemed relatively at peace.

But I digress, I meant for this entry to inform you that we are now on the market for a new house and it ended up being entirely about the addition to the growing collection of Novak sailing vessels.

And now I have exhausted my hand and shall lay my quill to rest for another day when I have more news to report on our new home or otherwise.

JULY 14, 1864

Who am I to think that a grandmother should have some say in what is or is not safe for her grandsons? Mattis has gotten it into his head that the boys who are not yet even two, will be needing horses to ride. Simply because the house (nay, manor, for it so large a home I should be too embarrassed to describe it) that he has purchased for us has stables. Must they be filled? We've never been a horsing family and I see no reason to start now.

But at the fair today, Michal was simply taken by a white gelding and Mattis nearly bought it on the spot. If it weren't for our protests (mine and Sybellen's), I do believe he would have had the boy up in saddle and gallivanting down the road like a highwayman. For once, it seems my daughter-in-law and I reside on the same side of good sense, although I suspect her preferences had less to do with the belief that the boys are simply too young and more to do with her own taste. She's never seen the appeal of horses nor displayed an interest in any animals, save birds and fishes. Either way, I'll take her as my ally in this fight against insanity.

It is interesting to note that once again, Emun Jr mirrors his mother in his disinterest for horses. He saw the white beast at the same time as his brother but while Michal was all squeals of delight,

Emun Jr gave an expression of disdain as he sat cuddled in his mother's arms. You could have painted the two of them into a fine fresco, a madonna and child, and used precisely the same expression of sleepy calm.

Whatever their preferences, we have managed to dodge the danger of a raving stallion crashing round in our stables and threatening to kick off the heads of my grandsons, at least for the time being. I suspect I've won the battle but not the war. At least I have time to pray that the boys will have mastered the skill of feeding themselves and tying their own shoelaces before their hard-headed father sticks them on the back of a war horse.

AUG 12, 1864

The renovations on our house (I beg your pardon - castle) are well underway and I've rarely seen Emun and Mattis in such high spirits. I have little interest in the details other than to ensure that every day they're fed and watered properly for their labours. Its a big job they've undertaken to get the manor ready for living in. Mattis spends part of his days working with Emun and overseeing the carpenters they have hired and the other part at the shipping office. Between these activities I have hardly seen my son all summer.

He reluctantly contracted a captain for this past spring's commission, for which I am overjoyed. I hope that he chooses to do so more often in future, although he says that it costs the company much more to have someone else captain *The Sybellen* and has warned Sybellen and me to not get used to the idea. He also has some anxiety about trusting the prized ship to someone else, but I think he realizes that sooner or later, he will have to share the workload. I think in several years he will find himself in the office full-time rather than captaining and I can hardly wait for those days.

The manor is outside the village and perhaps a half hour's walk from our house, which in comparison looks more and more like a shack with a broken back. On one hand, I am excited to be moving into such a glorious residence and on the other I have anxiety on all fronts. What will the village think? That we've gotten above ourselves with all this wealth? After all, Emun was a carpenter and he came from a family of carpenters, generations of them. It is only Mattis whose changed the fortunes of the Novak family and has done so against all odds. I am unsure how I will feel with the seemingly endless rooms. How does one choose where to spend one's time?

Mattis has informed me that he intends to fill the manor with staff and to live like a proper noble family (even though we are not noble). He has set aside large rooms for each of us, which is how he reports nobility lives. It seems excessive to me that we should each have our own enormous space and massive bed, not to mention assistance in dressing every morning. I have secretly asked my husband if we can continue to share a room since I've no wish to offend my son, and my darling seemed relieved that I feel the same way he does.

Mattis says that I'll no longer have to do the cooking and the washing up and I can pursue other things. But what? I have no idea, for I have no hobbies to speak of aside from this diary and helping to raise my grandsons. Perhaps gardening? I could hardly tell you a rose from a daisy, but the gardens at the manor are extensive and I can only imagine all the work required to be kept beautiful. Mattis says he'll hire a gardener, too, but I have asked him for the charge of it to start with. I know something about growing herbs and vegetables at least, it is merely the ornamental gardening about which I am daft.

Sybellen seems disinterested in the manor and all the goings on there. I have asked her if she is looking forward to moving into the home, but she shrugs and says it just means more rooms to chase the boys through. Once again Sybellen and I find something upon which to agree.

She knows that Mattis has another commission coming up in the fall and this one he'll be captaining. Autumn is never the ideal time to be sailing, but it must be done as this one is for the government.

There is a marked drop in the lightness of her demeanour whenever his disembarking date draws nigh; you can see it surely as a set of perfectly weighted scales.

MARCH 4, 1866

It's been years since my last entry and were I not so busy and full with things to do I should feel ashamed of being neglectful. Mattis is gone on commission and I write because weather of the kind we've been having makes me restless when I know Mattis is out in it. I can only hope he is far from the effects of it, for tonight there is a most wretched of storm moving in from across the Baltic. On nights like this I wish we were not a sea-faring family but had elected for a life much further inland, perhaps farming.

We are safely tucked into our new home and nearly every room has a crackling fire or hot ceramic furnace and yet the place seems hollow when Mattis is away. Sybellen is nearly unbearable in her sadness and the boys (especially Emun Jr.) can feel their mother's discontent, which in turn makes them grumpy.

This is the most dangerous time of year for Mattis to be at sea. His hiring of a captain while the house renovations were underway seems a cruel tease now that he is gone again. I would happily trade this fine house filled with foreign furniture and artwork to have my son home during these days.

As I write this, there are branches tapping against the walls of the house and there is nothing to be seen out the window save blackness and driving rain. Sybellen sits in her room with the fire crackling in the fireplace and the boys playing on the carpet at her feet. She most often elects to sit on the window seat and look out at the sea, although what she can possibly see on a night like this is beyond me.

I write this evening from our own quarters. Emun sits snoring in front of the fireplace with a book upside down on his chest and his spectacles perched on the end of his nose. I cannot decide whether to wake him and tell him of the peculiar conversation I had with Sybellen just hours ago.

I had gone in to check on her since I had not seen her or the boys for several hours and the storm was getting worse. I knew she would be in a state of worry for Mattis and I was not wrong. I found her sitting with her feet pulled up under her (she has the strangest way of resting sometimes, certainly not how proper ladies were trained to sit, even poor ones like me) on the seat in her bay window.

My grandsons, who are now three and a half years old, were playing with a set of wooden blocks in front of the fire with our nanny, Karolina (a recent addition that I am unsure is worth the expense).

I sat with Sybellen a while before I had gotten up the nerve to ask her why she was so down at the mouth: Mattis is an expert seaman and would surely be managing the weather as well as anybody could. She said that was not it, exactly. Yes, of course she worries about Mattis when he sails long journeys especially in winter, but it was more the direction her life had taken that was weighing on her.

I was shocked to hear this and fought the urge to slap her ungrateful mouth in that moment until I realized that she was philosophizing, not complaining about her material goods and way of life. I asked her to explain what she meant, as it was hard to understand how a beautiful woman with two lovely sons and a loving and wealthy husband could give her cause for such unhappiness.

It was then that she looked me full in the face with such an expression of yearning that my breath caught in my throat. You must understand, dear reader, that Sybellen rarely looks anyone in the eye.

Most often she avoids conversation entirely, but when she deigns to engage, she keeps her eyes averted.

She said to me, "You see, Mama, I wished for a daughter," as plain as day. In her eyes, I could see that the woman was missing a part of her heart that sons, for whatever reason, could not fill. Such a confusion of emotions filled me then--anger that she could so take her beautiful boys for granted and sadness that her secret desire had gone unfulfilled (although this latter feeling was swiftly squashed, for what would keep her from having another child?).

I asked her then why she did not try again, but her eyes unlocked themselves from my face and went back to the sea. "You don't understand", she said, seeming to speak more to herself than to me, "I would have to go away for a long time to have another chance."

"Well, you're right," I answered, "I don't understand. What do you mean?" That was the wrong thing to say, because she dismissed herself and there it ended. I don't know if she would have opened up to me if I had been gentler with her, but her words seemed so devoid of sense that I lost patience and with it my chance to understand.

I never had a daughter either, and having lived in a houseful of men for most of my life perhaps means that I no longer understand my own sex--their complicated wants and desires. But I do not think it is that. I think it is simply that my daughter-in-law is of mysterious origin, and of a mysterious people, and perhaps she has strange customs of which I have never heard.

So many times I have wondered why my son chose such a woman. Why could he not have chosen a nice local girl with which to settle down? I go to sleep with a heavy heart tonight, but trust that, as always, things will look better in the morning.

APRIL 12, 1866

Mattis arrived home two weeks ago and told us tonight that he'll be leaving again in July. Sybellen left the table without a word and went to her rooms. My heart is too heavy to write more tonight, dear reader, but I felt I had to make the occasion so I did not forget. My one comfort has come to be found in the gardens, in which I have surprisingly found solace and pleasure. It is there that I go now, with a new shipment of bulbs from Utrecht.

OCT 4, 1866

My wonderful grandsons had their fourth birthday yesterday. Their father was notably absent. We had a simple celebration with sweet treats and games with a few local children and mothers. I daresay many of the villagers wanted to have the excuse to see the Novak manor for themselves, as some of those in attendance were ones I know to have made biting comments about us since we've come into good fortune. But I won't be ungenerous and say more about those, for I'm thankful that there are many in the village and surrounding area that have supported Mattis and his enterprise since the beginning and are sincere in their congratulations on his success.

Mattis is once again late to arrive and has missed his sons' birthday. It is never as joyous an occasion as it is when he is here. The boys have gone from missing their father to an expectation that he will be away from home more than he will be in it, which is a sad reality in our present time. The blessing of growth and financial success never comes without a heavy price, it seems.

The boys are growing in their own directions and the differences between them are ever growing too. Emun Jr. grows more like his mother everyday, while Michal, more like his father. They are both beautiful boys, but when I take them out into the village, we are constantly told that it is hard to believe they are brothers, they are so unlike. I have to agree with these tiresome comments, for if I had not been at their birth myself, I would scarcely believe it.

Sybellen has become a daily worry for me, as I have seen her lose weight and have noticed that she is often absent from the manor at the strangest hours. There are as many meals that she is not present at than meals that she is, but when she attends she eats like one starving. Her increased appetite and weight loss seem to suggest a life of too much activity, but I will be stuffed if I can figure out what she has been up to. When she is not absent or eating her weight in food (which goes right through her), she is sleeping for hours on end, leaving the care of the boys to me and Karolina. She comes and goes like a ghost and always with sadness of expression.

I have promised myself to watch her movements more closely and if necessary, bring her behaviour to the attention of the doctor. The woman is a source of endless curiosity and worry for me and it seems this has only increased of lately.

OCT 6, 1866

Mattis arrived home yesterday and not a minute too soon. Sybellen's depression has become very. I brought it to his attention tonight after dinner. He listened as I told him how things had been for her since he'd been gone so often and I do believe he heard me. He did not offer any solution, for indeed this quandary will require some careful thought on his part, but I felt assured that he took me at my word. Sybellen may not be happy with me for my interference, but I am beyond caring at this point, since she is affecting the mood of the whole manor--not the least of which are my grandsons. Mattis said he would speak with her and so we shall soon see what will come of it.

OCT 10, 1866

Begging your pardon but curse this meddling grandmother for a fool. Why did I ever open my mouth? It seems Mattis and Sybellen have discussed the problem of Mattis' absence at length and come to a disruptive decision without consulting myself or Emun.

I should have suspected something ridiculous when I saw Sybellen smile for the first time in months. My heart, which was at first light when I saw her countenance, quickly plummeted as matters were made clear over dinner. I can hardly believe the misjudgement that has resulted and I have resolved to stitch my own mouth shut with my crochet hook from now on.

Mattis has decided that he will be taking Sybellen and the boys with him on his next commission. They are set to disembark next April. He has already published the announcement to his company, as well as the date of departure in the trade journals. I feel right and truly betrayed.

Mattis chattered gaily over dinner, wondering why it had not occurred to him before and I volunteered that perhaps because a seafaring ship is no place for women and children. He retorted that was nonsense, since families travel across the sea all the time, even as far as North America across the Atlantic.

We had a lively row over this when I called him foolhardy and selfish. Sybellen watched all of this with perceptive eyes, but ventured no opinion at all, even when I asked her how she felt about taking her boys to sea with them. She simply said she was not afraid of the ocean. Mattis added that they hit so many ports for delivery purposes that the boys would hardly have to stay aboard for longer than a few weeks at a time.

I must admit that I left the dinner table in anger and before dessert was served because I could not bear to listen to any more. Even my own husband sided with them and said that if families did it all the time, then why should they not? They were to sail the most sturdy and sound vessel known to the Baltic, so why should the boys not experience life at sea and stay with their parents the way that boys should? I could have smacked him.

Now that I've had a few hours to cool down, I find I feel no less disappointment over the whole decision, but I am calm enough to recognize that my emotions are rooted more in the fear of how much I'll miss my grandsons when they're abroad than fear for their safety. I still do not think a sailing vessel, and a working one at that, filled with men and cargo and ropes and holds, is a good place for children.

I am acquainted with the layout of *The Sybellen* and can take some small comfort in knowing that they are to share the Captain's quarters, which are broad and comfortable. I also have several months to prepare for their departure, but I must be honest and lay bare my heavy heart. I am distraught at this decision, which was made without my consultation, and feel a loosening of my grip on hearth and home. Why must things always change? Would that I could keep my grandsons small and safe and with me always. And so you will see, too, that indeed I have become a sentimental old woman. I will not deny it. It seems to be the destiny of mothers, that the little ones we have held close to our hearts and watched grow are only being prepared to one day leave us behind.

AUG 1, 1867

I write only because I have not written in so long--I have not had the heart for it. My grandsons have been gone for 5 long months and, though the sun is warming the air with its heat and the birds are singing, I gain no joy from my favourite season. I only await the day that my grandchildren return and I can once again hear their laughter through the halls and rooms of this mansion.

Emun bears up under the absence of our family much better than I, although I know he misses them, too. He keeps busy doing nothing (or so it appears to me), meeting with his friends in the village or puttering in the yards.

They are scheduled to return this fall as Mattis generally does-- they plan to dock no later than early October and to spend the winter here. I can truthfully say that I have never looked forward to winter so much as I do now.

We had a letter from them which arrived end of June. They report good health and clear sailing and, at the time of writing, to be ahead of schedule. So that is of some small condolence. Emun Jr. has taken to sailing with the heart of a master sailor, writes his father. Michal, meanwhile, has been plagued by bouts of seasickness. Once again, my darling boys prove themselves opposites.

Sybellen is in her element, he reports. Nothing cures her discontent like sea air. They have decided that the whole affair has been such a success that he is likely to take Sybellen and the boys with him on a more regular basis, only over the summers. At this news my heart has sunk into my shoes. So Emun and I are truly to be forgotten then, for what value do grandparents give to their grandchildren? Clearly none. Emun tells me not to be silly, that this is the life Mattis has chosen and the reason we live so finely now, but I have come to resent this life and crave a simpler time.

I shall amuse myself with my gardening and sewing projects until their arrival. And though I was never much of a reader in my early years, I have taken to enjoying the occasional novel on rainy days. I have recently finished *Wives and Daughters* by English writer Elizabeth Gaskill and have set my sights on a book of poetry next by an American writer named Alfred Tennyson, both of which have been translated into Polish by a friend of mine in Gdansk. Thankfully, the endless supply of translated works is serving as a good distraction.

SEPT 30, 1867

I am happy to report my grandsons have returned. Indeed, they have been home for two weeks now, which is the earliest Mattis has ever returned from a commission in the fall. My heart is full to have my family home safe again.

How the boys have grown in the months they've been away! They have both stretched up and become weather worn, though I would have expected Emun Jr. to have a darker complexion. It seems even his mother has not changed a shade since she left too.

Michal and Mattis on the other hand are as brown as natives and their hair has lightened to a shade of yellow. Michal looks hale and hearty, but when I asked him how he enjoyed sailing he said not at all, that it makes his guts turn inside out. Emun Jr., however, lights up like a firework when I ask him about the sea. He says he wants to do what papa does when he grows up. He also said that he wants to marry a woman like Mama and I'd not the heart to disenchant him of the realities of that idea.

Sybellen arrived home as happy as I have ever seen her and, in spite of my wishes not to have my family away from me for so long, I am glad to see that it has benefited her and Mattis in the way that they had hoped. I just wished for myself that it had not been quite the raging success that it was.

I have asked what they plan to do about Michal's seasickness and Mattis has put off answering for now, as he says he has winter activities to focus before they have to decide about next summer's commission. He says his office is flooded with requests and he needs to hire additional staff to handle the demand, as well as to oversee the building of yet another ship. He is bouncy and lighthearted when his business is doing well and this in turn makes the whole house feel full of joy.

FEB 17, 1868

Heavens, it has been a hard winter. I do not remember such a biting cold in all my years and such a quantity of snow and lack of sunshine, for it seems every day finds dreary clouds drifting in from the icy sea to cover us over and hide the light from our pale faces.

Sybellen, who was so happy in the fall after returning from the summer commission, has fallen into such a depression the likes of which I have never before seen. Most baffling about it is that Mattis is home, so it cannot be his absence that is making her so melancholic. I have asked Mattis to request the Doctor to come see her, but his only remark is that he does not believe a doctor can help her.

I neglected to write in January that I ran into her in the hallway late one night when I got up to use the water closet. Her hair was wet and her nightdress was damp. I could not imagine why she would take to bathing at this hour, so I asked her what she was doing. She said, 'I'm going to bed, Mama,' and walked on before I could inquire further. This strange behaviour spooks me, I am not ashamed to admit. I am accustomed to some of her unusual habits, but this is extreme in its oddness, even for the likes of my daughter-in-law.

But today, an even stranger and more upsetting thing took place. Mattis was out at the stables with the boys and Emun and I was on my way out the door to return three novels to my friend when I realized I had forgotten one at my bedside table and went back to retrieve it. I had to pass by Sybellen's room and, as I did, I heard the sound of weeping. This, in itself, is a surprise, since I have seen Sybellen cry before and she has always cried silently. She must have been suffering horribly to make such a sound.

I knocked gently on the door and asked if I could enter. The sound of weeping stopped immediately, but she did not answer at once. I asked again if I could come in and she said that I would not be able to. Not knowing what she meant, I turned the knob only to find that the door was locked!

When I asked her why her door was locked, she said, in her infuriating way, that it was to keep her in. When I asked her to unlock it at once she said that she could not because she didn't have the key.

Goodness gracious! At this I was lost for words for a moment before asking who had locked her in? I could not have been more surprised at her answer than if she had walked straight through the door and shown to be a ghost. "Mattis," she answered.

My blood ran cold and I begged her to be lying. When she did not answer, I ran to get the skeleton key. I returned and unlocked the door and found her sitting on the floor in her nightdress still (this being mid afternoon) and with a handkerchief as wet as though she had dunked it in a pail of water. She was in such a state, it was as though both her boys and Mattis had suddenly gone up in smoke and all she held dear had been stolen from her in a breath.

When I asked her to explain, she simply told me not to be angry at Mattis, for he locked her in at her own request. I could not get out of her why she would ask him such a thing and, I am afraid, that I begin to fear for my daughter-in-law's sanity.

When we had a private moment, I confronted Mattis about it and he confirmed that she had asked him to lock her in, just for the day. He brushed off the strangeness of the request and my admonishment for agreeing to do such a thing. He told me to mind my own business and leave them to themselves. "She is very sad, Mama," was all he would say by way of explanation.

"Well clearly," I responded, "How happy can a wife be when her husband locks her in her bedroom?"

When I asked him if it had to do with not having a daughter, he seemed startled for a moment that I should know such a thing, and asked me how I knew. I told him that Sybellen had told me of her heart's desire a few years ago. He did not confirm one way or the other if it was the reason for her turn today, but rather gave me a hug and told me not to worry, that he would take care of her as best he could. He said that his love would cure her and his belief in that seemed resolute.

Never have I felt so unsettled, so confused, so worried about my family. And though I know it does no good to bemoan the past, I find myself wishing so much that Mattis had found a different kind of woman. Since wishing is a useless exercise then I shall lean to prayer.

APR 5, 1869

Mattis and Sybellen are preparing for another journey. I dread their departure as always, but it has been such a miserable winter for Sybellen particularly that I am nearly eager for the date to arrive. She has become unbearable. Nothing has improved since my last entry, although I do believe Mattis has left off locking the piteous creature in her bedroom. I am loathe to report that truly I believe things to have deteriorated in Sybellen's mind in only a few short months.

She is absent from the manor much of the time, always returning by way of the beach paths, so I can only guess that she has spent the day near the ocean, taking whatever comfort she finds there. I have begun to be quite worried when she is away for long stretches at a time, and since Mattis is on a short commission with The Gus, a smaller vessel than *The Sybellen*, he has not been here to witness her behaviour and the abandonment of her boys...for it appears to me that she has all but completely lost interest in them as well.

Michal seems to bear up well enough under my care and the care of Karolina and his tutors, but poor Emun Jr. continuously asks after his mother. And why should he not? They are not yet 8 years old. He is at a loss to understand the depression and state of apathy in which his mother finds herself.

Her appearance has changed notably as well, though I hesitate to recount the specifics because sometimes I am not sure I can believe my eyes. She no longer cares for her long black hair, servicing it and having coiffed by her lady's maid as she used to. Instead she lets it stay long and unrestrained giving her a wild appearance, which is only accentuated by the feverish look her blue eyes have taken on. The blue of her eyes has always been beautiful to look upon, but now seems to have taken a molten cast (for lack of a better word) and I have never seen eyes so brightly lit from within. Her skin has always been pale, no matter the hours she takes in the sun. I recall warning her to spend less time under the sun's glare in the early days, but she never heeded me and I recall thinking that she would be freckled and dark as a heathen before long, but I was wrong. Even now it retains its porcelain colour--only it, too, has also changed but in a way I am at a loss to describe accurately. It has a kind of iridescence to it that can only be seen in the light. I made a private study of her the last time I came upon her coming up from the beach paths in her usual way, with her hair damp and blowing in the wind and her clothing haphazard. I found myself in a sort of daze as I took in her appearance, as though I could not look away. It frightened me, as did the expression on her face - such a mournful brokenness. I have not spoken to her again of her desire for a daughter--I am afraid to broach the subject for fear it would send her further into whatever hell she finds herself in.

I took the liberty to call upon Dr. Wozniak for advice, but he says that female problems of emotion are not his speciality. He said he would write to a friend and colleague from America who may be able to provide some enlightenment but so far I have heard nothing.

As for the upcoming journey I was in discussions with Mattis before he disembarked on this latest commission—Mattis has agreed to keeping Michal here, since he suffers horrible seasickness whenever he steps foot on a boat. This is my one bright spot during these days, knowing that I can keep one grandson here with me.

I feared we would have great repercussions from Sybellen, as Mattis and I had discussed this in her absence, but Mattis advised me to leave off talking with her about it. Since then, it has never come up again neither from his lips nor hers. I find myself fearful that she may bring it up at some point before they leave, but the date is fast approaching and there has been no adjustment to the plan to allow Michal to stay.

And so I wait humbly for a good doctor to reply and enlighten us, for my family to disembark, and for peace to descend upon this household once more.

MAY 18, 1869

My world has come to an end and there will never be another moment of happiness so long as I shall live.

DEC 2, 1870

It has been well over a year since my last entry. I have not had the heart to write of the events that have befallen my family, for they have been too awful to bear and too awful for words. Since I cannot form the words myself, I shall leave it to this passage I found recently while reading a tragic play; We are destined 'to suffer the slings and arrows of outrageous fortune, or to take arms against a sea of troubles, and by opposing, end them.'

With whomever preaches of free will I take great exception, because I, in my life, have experienced very little of it. I did not choose to be born a woman; I did not choose to marry my Emun (my father arranged it); I did not choose the sex of my child or to stop at only one...that, too, was determined for me. I did not choose my country, my city, my face or hands or form, my intellect and talents or lack thereof. And whether I choose corn for my supper over peas, or a blue dress over a green one is so petty and inconsequential that it cannot possibly be named free will.

I did not choose my son's wife for him and I did not choose my grandsons: they came to us as a gift from God and now one has been taken back, along with my own son and many good men alongside. But I digress into sentimental musings to avoid putting down on paper the horrors of the past year, so I'll get to task now so you can understand.

In May of last year, May 17th to be precise, Mattis and Sybellen were preparing to embark on their summer commission, to take Emun Jr. with them and leave Michal at home. But I get ahead of myself. In order to understand the following events, I must tell you of what led up to them. I have written before of Sybellen's melancholy and strange behaviour. You may recall, I asked Dr. Wozniak for advise, and he wrote to his friend to appeal for insight. I received a letter from a Doctor Anders at St. Peter's Psychological Institution in Boston (a place so far away and strange to me that it seems like it must be another world!). Dr. Anders had very little helpful to say since he was not here to examine her, but he advised a tincture of herbs for her to help lift her spirits as well as plenty of rest and sunshine, and broth of vegetables. He also recommended that we take her to an institution in Gdansk for examination. Since the date of their departure was so near, I resolved to talk to Mattis about this option for Sybellen but only upon their return in the fall. I was hoping that the trip abroad would prove a cure for her and the sordid business might cure itself.

But on May 16th, two events came together to form our ruin. One was that a sudden spring storm blew in from across the sea. Storms are unusual for May, but they can happen. Throughout the day the winds were whipped up and the sky became a dark mass of boiling clouds. Also in the morning, Sybellen did not join us for breakfast. I went up to her rooms to see if she was alright, but she was not there, and neither did her bed show that she had slept. At first, I assumed that she had slept in Mattis' rooms and went to check there, but Sybellen was not to be found there either.

I went back to the breakfast room to ask Mattis when he saw her last and he answered that he had seen her the night before. They had said good night and parted to their own rooms. When I told him what I had discovered, that Sybellen had not slept in her own room, he became instantly fearful, much moreso than I am accustomed Mattis being even when things go amiss. He and Emun Sr. immediately set off to search the beach and the beach paths for her, as we all thought for certain she would be there. I waited with the boys for their return and watched the skies darken with a sense of foreboding--it seemed they were mirroring the days events.

Only Emun Sr returned from the search and he reported that Mattis was going to get a boat to search the water. This talk frightened me greatly and I feared the worst for Sybellen. Why did he think he needed a boat to find her? Could they not simply take several men and continue to search the beaches? Had her depression and her attraction to the ocean collided to bring tragedy? What was he imagining?

It wasn't until the afternoon, by which time the storm had whipped itself into a frenzy, that I learned what Mattis intended when he had told Emun he was going out to search the waters. I was sitting and reading with Emun Jr. and Michal when Mattis came into the room. He was wet through and dripping from the rain.

He said he was there to take the boys because surely Sybellen would come if she heard their voices. I did not understand what he meant--it made no sense to involve the children. "You cannot possibly understand, Mama," he pleaded with me at first. When I asked him to enlighten me he spoke sharply saying, "There isn't time--every moment more we risk to lose her forever." His wild-eyed expression frightened me even further.

The boys became frightened, too, to see their father in such a state and I tried to send him away to calm down. He would not listen, and tried to compel the boys to come with him, but I told the boys to stay put. The poor children were becoming more frightened and confused by the moment.

Mattis told them that their mother was missing and that he needed the help to find her. Once he had said that, there was no stopping Emun Jr., who jumped up and took his father's hand. I tried to reason with Mattis—tried to convince him that to take the boys out and, in fact, to go out at all on a night like this was surely dangerous. But he would not listen and left the house in a hurry with Emun Jr. Michal and I huddled together to wait.

Little did I know that that was the last time I was to see Mattis or Emun Jr.

Emun Sr. arrived home an hour later, also dripping and wet to the bone. He had been down at the docks having his own row with our son and he reported angrily to me that Mattis had taken *The Sybellen* and 29 men with him--barely enough to sail a ship of such size. I nearly fainted for the shock of it. Why had he taken *The Sybellen*? Emun could not explain and he said that Mattis had left with much haste, proclaiming that the sooner they left the more likely they would be to find her.

After that it was as though the storm knew that my son was challenging it and it had an appetite to swallow him whole. Never before and never since have I seen a storm on the Baltic such as the one that took the lives of those on *The Sybellen* that night. Oh the foolishness; the sickening waste.

Michal slept, as children seem blessed with the ability to maintain some kind of normalcy even in the midst of the strange, but neither Emun nor I went to bed that night. Early in the morning as the storm was finally cooling, Emun went to the harbour to wait. But *The Sybellen* did not return.

That day, I found a lump of heavy damp cloth at the door beside the kitchens and held it up to see that it was one of Sybellen's dresses--in fact, the one that I had last seen her wearing. What it was doing there I could not imagine until Emun later told me that they had found the sodden clothing in the rocks down at the beach. He considered it a sure sign that Sybellen had walked into the ocean to drown herself in her misery, although why she felt compelled to remove the clothing to accomplish her goal was a mystery. Surely it would only have helped to pull her under, Emun wondered aloud. 'Listen to us,' I replied angrily, 'what talk we have been brought to.'

'If that was the case and she wished to drown herself then surely her body would wash up on the beach? Why did Mattis have to take to the sea in a ship if she had drowned?', I implored him further. It did not make sense. Had my son taken leave of his senses, too? Had his grief and worry overcome logic?

The searching—for Sybellen or her namesake--went on for weeks afterward and Emun and I barely slept or ate. But we did not see even a shadow of *The Sybellen*. Even now, not so much as a broken board has washed up on the beach. There have been no bodies drifting in on the tides, at least not in our area and, day by day, our hope has faded into dust. We had hoped, for a time, for reports from other ships that came and went from our port but there has been no word.

After the tragedy, Emun dealt with the insurance agents. For a time, we believed that we would lose the claim, as there were some factors that were not consistent with the commission when the insurance was set up, but Emun worked quickly and said what he needed to say in order to save Novak shipping from destruction. I was so lost in my agony that I did not follow what he was doing, although I vaguely remember him trying to explain to me that he had to hold a secret meeting with all of the company sailors who were not on the vessel the night it left, in order to solidify Novak's position with the insurance, otherwise all would be lost.

The newspapers have had their fun with the story that Emun had to concoct for them in order to be consistent with the insurance claim. Emun has protected me from the reporters and the curious villagers and it seems that thankfully the story has been eclipsed by other news.

I believe I have intentionally closed my ears and eyes to the things pertaining to the company, as I felt I could barely manage to get out of bed let alone consider matters of business. I do not know how Emun managed.

Michal cried every night for a very long time and I would stay with him until he cried himself into sleep. I remember wondering if there would ever be a night again where I did not bank the fire and crawl into my bed to the sound of a little boy weeping in my head.

Watching him recover from losing his entire family in one moment, though, has made me realize that children are far heartier than we give them credit for. He did eventually cease the crying and was back to himself (or nearly) inside of a year. It has been Emun and myself who have aged and I would even go so far as to say that I have sincerely wished for death at times over the past year.

Were it not for Michal, I believe both Emun and I might have given up. Emun would not have bothered to fight for the insurance and he likely would have sold the company for what little value was left after *The Sybellen* was gone. I knew *The Sybellen* was the pride of Novak Shipping, but I had not realized how much worth was tied up in the vessel alone.

As it was, the company passed to Michal who is of course far too young to run it. Emun's two elder sisters, Marcella and Rena, both of whom live in Gdansk and have their own husbands and lives to live, have been a Godsend. Emun held a meeting with them and their families to decide what to do and the decision was unanimous. Novak Shipping must not be sold or dissolved or in any other way cut up for parts. They have changed their lives to pull together and never have I been prouder of my family. It appears that Novak Shipping is now being run (how successfully I cannot say) by a collection of grey hairs, two of whom are in corsets rather than trousers.

The worst of it all, though, is the lack of closure and finality. I still feel a fool's hope that one day I shall see Mattis and Emun Jr. walking up the beach path to the manor to report that, yes, they had been wrecked at sea but that they had washed up somewhere remote and had to make their way home.

As for Sybellen, I have and still do feel so much anger and resentment towards her--so much confusion and hurt. But I also feel an enormous sadness for a woman who was clearly misunderstood by all of us. I feel now that no one really knew her, even Mattis, for if he had, surely he would not have taken her from whatever home she had. Surely she would have been happier to stay wherever it was she had grown up, wherever there were people like her.

I wish a great many things were different but the simple truth is that nothing can be changed through wishing or regret, so I must try to put such thoughts aside, "...leaving those things which are behind and press on to the things which are ahead". This simple scripture remains a comfort to me.

I am not through the grief, nor do I think I ever shall be. All I can say is that, for now, I am able to go through each day for Michal, to focus on his future. I am not sure that I shall ever be able to laugh or smile again, or appreciate the beauty of the day around me. But I shall press on. I shall press on until God sees fit to take this old woman to be with her family again.

———

AUTHOR'S NOTE

Wow, you made it all the way through all that, and now you're reading this too! Thank you for coming along for the ride.

"How did you become an author?" seems to be one of the more frequent questions I hear these days and I would hazard a guess that all authors begin as bookworms. Reading was my preferred escape when I was young. I used to stuff a towel under the crack in my bedroom door to hide the light so my parents wouldn't tell me to put my book away and shut my lights off. I'm pretty sure they knew what I was doing... they seem to know everything. I spent a lot of time with Frank Baum, Walter Farley, Piers Anthony, and later with JK Rowling, Stephen King, and Kelley Armstrong. My advice today to anyone who wants to write - READ! Read a lot. Read often. Read from lots of different genres. Always be reading something.

The Sybellen is a product of my imagination. The *RMS Republic* is a real wreck, and *Martin Bayerle* is a real dude. Shark-finning is also unfortunately a very real problem and has culled the world's oceans of 95% of the shark population.

Born of Water started as a vignette in my imagination... what if a mermaid found a shipwreck, and as she blew away the algae on the figurehead to get a better look she came to realize that the face staring back at her was her own?

I have always been fascinated with shipwrecks, nautical history, marine biology, pirates, and all things to do with the oceans and seas. What better way to explore a shipwreck than as a mermaid? Like many fantasy stories, *Born of Water* came from answering hypotheticals. If mermaids were real, what would they be like? How would they live? How would they procreate? How would they be affected by weather, salinity, seasons? What would their abilities and features be like?

I didn't start out to write a series. But while I was tapping out *Born of Water*, the creative muse gifted me with an idea for faerie mythology and I realized that I now had the idea for a story I could call *Born of Earth*. The rest, as they say, is history. Readers loved these characters so much that I have continued to write them and as of 2020, there are 15 titles available to enjoy, which I hope you do.

All the best,

Abby

EXCERPT FROM BORN OF FIRE

CHAPTER ONE

I closed my eyes, leaned my head against the plane window, and let out a big sigh. We were airborne. It was the end of a week of hell and I couldn't be happier to leave my life behind.

"That sounded awfully serious coming from someone so young," said the lady beside me. "First time on a plane?"

I turned to look at my seat mate. The woman had super short grey hair and was peering at me from over her glasses. She had a book open on her lap. Her expression exuded maternal warmth.

"First time going trans-Atlantic. It's not the flight, though."

"No?"

"Careful, if you get me talking, I might not shut up." I turned back to the window, my warped reflection mirrored my movement. "I talk too much. Or so I'm told."

The lady was silent for a moment. "We've got a long flight ahead of us. Why are you headed to Venice?"

"I got an au pair position. Two little boys. I'll be there all summer."

"Well," she said, her eyebrows lifting. "That sounds like the perfect experience for someone your age."

"Yeah, I'm super excited about it."

"Then why so glum?"

I chewed my lip. Shame heated my cheeks and to my dismay, tears pricked behind my eyelids. What was it about a kind stranger that made me want to dump out all my problems?

"I screwed up."

"How very human of you."

"But, I hate being a stereotype," I blurted.

"You're a stereotype?"

I tugged on the end of my fiery red ponytail. "I'm a redhead."

"And?"

"And, I have a temper. I'm a redhead, with a temper. Do you think it's true? That red hair comes with a temper?"

"Well, they say stereotypes exist for a reason, that there's always a thread of truth in them. A hair, if you will." She waggled her eyebrows.

"Very punny."

"Thank you. But no, I think we've all got a temper somewhere under the surface. Maybe it's harder for some of us to control, but that just comes with practice. And breathing." She held up a manicured finger. "Breathing helps a lot." She closed her book and tucked it into the seat pocket in front of her. "What was this horrifying screw-up?"

I twisted my headphone cord around my thumb. "I have two brothers. R.J. and Jack. Normally, we get along pretty good. But Jack - the younger one - he was pushing my buttons all week. He broke the clasp on my luggage, dropped chocolate on the couch which I then sat in and stained my favourite jeans, and then he hid my passport and laughed while I tore my hair out looking for it for three days."

"How frustrating."

I nodded. "Seriously. So three nights ago, after dinner, Dad told Jack it was his turn to do the dishes, but he went to play video games instead. I didn't notice at first because I went to pack. But then I came into the kitchen and everything was still a disaster. My mom had gone to bed with a headache and Dad was in the garage with R.J. I lost it. I was already so fed up that I just blew up." I paused, and my heart pounded as I relived the moment.

"What did you do?"

"I barged into his room and..." I took a breath and put my hands to my cheeks. My face felt like it was burning up. My voice hitched. "I kicked his controller out of his hands and grabbed the back of his neck, pretty hard. I picked him up and shoved him toward the door, yelling at him to pull his weight." I stopped and closed my eyes against the awful memory of what came next.

The lady waited in silence.

"I didn't mean to..." I cleared my throat. "He slipped on some paper. His room is always such a disaster. He fell. I mean, we both fell. But he hit the doorjamb. The sound of it... the crack..." I shuddered.

"Was he okay?"

"He hit it with his face."

She grimaced.

"He bit through his bottom lip, chipped his front tooth, and got a black eye." I rubbed my face, trying to wipe away the memory. "There was a lot of blood. I thought I was going to be sick. Not from the blood, well maybe partly, but I just..."

"You felt horrible."

I nodded and looked out the window into the black nothing. "I still do. My parents hit the roof. They told me I had to cancel Venice."

"But, you're here. So what happened?"

I turned back to her kind face. "Jack. He can be a real brat, but he's also one of the most forgiving people I know. He knew I was sorry. I didn't eat for two days. Which is *really* unlike me. He got my parents to change their minds. He even owned up to terrorizing me earlier in the week."

"Sounds like a good kid."

"Yeah, he is. Better than me."

"I'm sure that's not true."

"How good can I be if I can't rein in my temper and I end up hurting people?"

"Well, Jack forgives you. Sounds like your parents do, too. Why not forgive yourself. Wipe the slate clean, and use this summer to figure yourself out? You're an au pair, now. What a perfect opportunity to practice patience and control, right?"

"Right." In theory.

"Put the past behind you. Learn from it, and move forward. We all make mistakes. Resolve to be better."

My stomach clenched at the memory of Jack's bloody face. I crossed my arms and blew out a breath. "I will."

———

Don't miss the next adventure in The Elemental Origins Series!

SALT & STONE

UNDER THE SEA LIE THE SECRETS OF HER PAST... AND A
DEADLY THREAT TO HER FUTURE.

Targa fears the truth will lose her the man she loves. As she returns to
Poland to reunite with Antoni, she wishes she could share her
mermaid secrets without betraying her kind. But when a magical
stone goes missing from her museum, the siren may have to choose
between protecting her loved ones and treason.

As Targa tracks the stolen gem, she discovers a sinister plot
centuries in the making. And the power the thieves seek could leave
both the land and the sea utterly devastated.

Can Targa protect the secrets of her people, or will her attempt at
a double life take everything she loves away?

Salt & Stone is an enchanting book in *The Siren's Curse* YA fantasy
series. If you like conflicted heroines, simmering romance, and
modern mermaids, you'll love USA Today Bestselling Author A.L.
Knorr's aquatic adventure.

ACKNOWLEDGMENTS

Thank you to my parents for giving me a head for dreaming, a heart for believing, and fingers for typing (looking at my hands when I was born, they thought I'd be a classical pianist. Surprise!) Thank you to my sweet brothers, the kindest and best men I know, and their families, for your support while all this was just a dream.

To my incredible circle of supportive friends, many of whom went on to become my Beta Readers. I couldn't do this without your encouragement.

A hearty thank you to my editors; Christine Gordon Manley and Shandi Peterson. Special mention to Nicola Aquino for her incredible skill at spotting inconsistencies.

Thank you to Virginio, Lora, Patrick, and Alex Zanella of Magras Italy for being my Italian family and being so supportive and generous.

ABOUT THE AUTHOR

USA Today Bestselling Author, A.L. Knorr is an award-winning Canadian fantasy writer. Readers love her vivid characters and mesmerizing stories of elemental transformation, adventure, friendship, and love.

Known for strong female protagonists, cuss-free, no on-page sex, and well-crafted plots that keep you turning pages late into the night, A.L. Knorr is a masterful storyteller.

Sign up to A.L Knorr's VIP Reader List for FREE fiction, exclusive content and to automatically be notified as soon as her next book is released: www.alknorrbooks.com

Made in the USA
Columbia, SC
15 June 2020